GOLDEN ADMIRAL

F. van Wyck Mason

HLS

HUTCHINSON LIBRARY SERVICES/
JARROLDS, LONDON

Hutchinson Library Services Ltd
3 Fitzroy Square, London W1

London Melbourne Sydney Auckland
Wellington Johannesburg Cape Town
and agencies throughout the world

First published 1954
HLS edition 1975

With the exception of actual historical personages identified as such, the characters are entirely the product of the author's imagination and have no relation to any person or event in real life

Printed in Great Britain by litho by The Anchor Press Ltd
bound by Wm Brendon & Son Ltd
both of Tiptree, Essex

ISBN 0 09 122980 4

For

"PETE" AND "LIZ" BLODGETT

May they always shoot ahead of the birds

AUTHOR'S FOREWORD

UNDOUBTEDLY certain readers may wonder why I have not employed strictly Elizabethan speech throughout. I have not done so for two reasons: first, because I felt it would be difficult for the average reader to become accustomed to the unusual words and constructions employed, and second, because spoken English of the sixteenth century probably varied considerably from that which was written. Our Elizabethan ancestors, incidentally, were the original phonetic spellers, both as to family names and in general. These, the first moderns—most historians are inclined to credit the reign of Elizabeth I as the beginning of Modern Times—composed a rugged, brutal, and intensely vital society. In their day the quality of mercy indeed was not strained.

In this tale I have attempted to correct certain deep-rooted misapprehensions concerning Queen Elizabeth I and the part she played in English history. I have also attempted to set to rights a good many illusions concerning how the Spanish Armada—otherwise *la Empresa de Inglaterra*—was met and fought.

The tonnage and armament of ships herein mentioned, their movements, the names of their captains and principal officers are as accurate as a prolonged research in the archives of the British Museum and the Widener Library at Harvard College can make them. So, also, are the names of the Indians and their tribes in the Virginian sequence of this story. The "Naturals'" costumes, customs, and food were fully and vividly described in the journal of one Thomas Hariot, entitled *A Brief and True Report of the New Found Land of Virginia*, published in 1588.

I have endeavoured to follow history to the letter without sacrificing story interest. Whether I have succeeded in this, the reader must decide for himself.

Only obviously fictional characters are not historical. The Coffyn family, however, was and is real, and Portledge Manor still stands. My interest in this family was great in that my mother is directly descended from the Coffyns of Devonshire by way of Newburyport and Nantucket.

All ships herein named actually existed, with the exception of those commanded by Henry Wyatt and Hubert Coffyn.

I wish to take this occasion to thank my secretaries Doris Pomphrey and Jane West Tidwell for their cheerful assistance in preparing this manuscript. I also owe a debt of gratitude to Miss Margaret Franklin, who spared me much tedious digging in the British Museum. As usual my thanks for great assistance go to Mr. Robert H. Haynes and his staff of the Widener Library of Harvard College at Cambridge, Massachusetts.

F. VAN WYCK MASON

Gunners' Hill,
Riderwood, Maryland.

CONTENTS

BOOK ONE

GLORIANA

BOOK TWO

"TO ANNOY THE KING OF SPAIN"

BOOK THREE

THE WEROWANCE

BOOK FOUR

LA EMPRESA

Book One

GLORIANA

CHAPTER I

BILBAO HARBOUR

ON THE morning of May the twenty-fourth, 1585, the busy, sunlit harbour of Bilbao in the realm of His Most Catholic Majesty, Philip the Second, King of Spain, appeared nowise different than it had on any of the *Barque Primrose's* previous voyages.

For Henry Wyatt, Master's Mate, it proved difficult to credit that this countryside lay in the grip of a devastating famine—the worst in many generations—extensive vineyards still climbed a series of hills rising beyond the yellow and brown walls encircling Bilbao, and, near the water's edge, fields and orchards appeared to be green and fruitful.

As of yore, festoons of brown and black nets and varicoloured sails hung drying upon racks erected above a series of narrow cobbled beaches upon which leather-featured fisherfolk hauled out their boats. Painted green, red or, more often, a brilliant blue, these little zabias, sloops and canters lay on their bilges like crocodiles sunning themselves on a sandspit.

While intent on sighting an elusive channel buoy Wyatt heard Master John Foster's guttural command of, "Head two further points to steerboard."

Her grey-brown canvas flapping uncertainly now that the sea breeze was being cut off by a promontory dominating the entrance, the *Primrose*, 150 tons, and twenty days out of London Pool, sailed only sluggishly into Bilbao Harbour and history.

Because of that which was about to happen, rich and populous towns would, within the twelvemonth, be reduced to smoking, ravaged ruins. On the mainland of South America, on islands off Africa, and in the Caribbean as well as in the Spanish homeland, Philip's pride would suffer a series of blows which would shatter the legend of Hispanic invincibility.

Of all this Henry Wyatt remained sublimely unaware while standing at Master Foster's side with attention fixed on various yellow-grey battlements crowning hills across the harbour. From these, as from the walls of a great castello guarding the harbour's entrance, the muzzles of many great guns stared down like sable, Cyclopean eyes upon a vast tangle of shipping below.

Foster shaded his single eye. "Ye'd have thought, Harry, that before now we'd have recognized a couple o' vessels from home."

" 'Tis indeed surprising," Wyatt agreed. "I mark not a single Cross of St. George flying at any masthead."

Thoughtfully Foster's balding round head inclined under its stocking cap of red worsted. "To my notion there's not half the shipping here we encountered on our last voyage. Still, mayhap it means the more trade for us and at better price. Eh, Master Goodman?"

That dumpy, moonfaced individual who, as Factor, represented Messrs. Morton and Barlow, merchants in the City of London, displayed gapped yellow teeth in a grin.

"Better prices to be sure! Starving folk are not given to haggling overlong once they clap eyes on such victuals as I carry below. Aye, I'll venture, Master Foster, that we'll show an uncommon handsome profit on this cargo."

Although this was Henry Wyatt's second visit to the port of Bilbao the grandiose architecture of this ancient town and the foreign flavour of its waterfront had lost none of their original appeal.

Absently he noted how net-like shadows created by the sun among the *Primrose's* shrouds travelled lazily back and forth across her none-too-cleanly quarterdeck, then studied the ever-graceful flight of great grey and white harbour gulls as they wheeled and screamed above the ship's colours—a faded red Cross of St. George painted upon a field of decidedly dirty white cloth.

Goodman waved a plump hand at the swooping birds. "And where will you anchor?"

The barque's master ran an experienced eye over the mass of shipping ahead, noted nothing untoward. "At our usual anchorage, hard by the House o' the Genoese."

Wyatt meanwhile had noted the presence of two massive Portuguese-built war carracks; like the floating castles they were intended to be, their gilded and gaudily painted hulls towered grandly above dozens of humble, round-bowed hulks, hoys and cromsters. Their presence suggested that a convoy from the Spanish Netherlands might recently have made port, fetching victuals to allay that devastating famine known to be raging through Viscaya and Asturias. Beyond them were anchored two galliots and a low, rakish-looking vessel which must have been captured from some Turkish corsair in the Mediterranean. Of small native coasters and fishermen there were quantities hailing from half a hundred tiny ports scattered along the Bay of Biscay.

The vessel, however, which commanded Wyatt's most serious consideration was a swift, silver-and-yellow-painted Royal galleass swinging to her anchors hard by the harbour's entrance. From her mizzen's lateen the familar red-and-yellow ensign of Castile and Aragon dangled lifelessly. The fading breeze even at this distance brought an indescribably nauseating stench created by those miserable galley slaves who until they died were doomed to remain fettered to her rowing benches.

Wyatt shivered. On the occasion of his first voyage to Spain he once had boarded such a craft to find himself sickened and appalled by the bestial, inhuman aspect of a multitude of whip-scarred, filthy and nearly naked starvelings. A slave's natural needs, he had learned, were relieved by merely sliding backwards on his bench. The resultant excretions fell upon ballast below, there to reek, breed flies and fester until, in rough and ready fashion, they would once a week be sluiced away into a sump.

Soon the mass of anchored shipping loomed close and Wyatt turned to Foster, his broad, copper-brown features betraying concern. "John, have you as yet spied an English banner other than ours?"

"Not yet. Never before have I put in here but I'd come across a home ship or two to bear me company."

"In that case would it not be the part of prudence to drop anchor on the outer fringe o' yonder shipping?"

Promptly the Factor waved pudgy hands in expostulation. "So long a pull out from the shore would reduce the number of bidders for my wares, therefore I pray you to occupy your accustomed berth off the House of the Genoese."

John Foster hesitated, perplexedly combed an untidy brown beard with stubby fingers and permitted his single, bloodshot grey eye—its mate had been lost years ago during a savage brush with Flemish pirates off Flushing—to range over the pointed array of riggings and topmasts looming ahead. Um. Come to dwell on it, it *was* passing strange that not one other English flag should be in evidence—especially since he felt sure that a vessel very similar to the *Dolphin*, caravel, of Dover lay moored close to the Aduana—or the King's Custom House.

Henry Wyatt was thinking aloud. "Can a war have broken out? No, we were not challenged and the Castello's ordnance remains unmanned."

The *Primrose's* Master suddenly ordered his vessel brought into the wind. "I'll anchor here."

Forestalling the Factor's protest, he added, "Have patience, friend Goodman, an all proves well, I'll tie up to the Foreigner's Wharf and quickly. I'm keen to clear out o' this and get for home."

Once the *Primrose's* sails commenced to slat and shiver her crew scrambled into the rigging, like so many ragged apes to clew up sprit-sail, topsails and the weatherbeaten main course even before the barque's clumsy anchor could go bubbling down through the soiled, yellow water.

Hardly had the English vessel rounded up to her cable than a scattering of bumboats suggestive of gigantic and eager waterbeetles started out from shore. None of them offered fish, fruit or any other eatable, only pottery, hardware or leatherwork.

Having superintended a final clewing up of the sails, Wyatt then ordered the *Primrose's* cockboat readied for a trip over to the Port Captain's office. While waiting for this to be accomplished he watched the sun reappear from behind a bank of lead-white clouds and flood the whole harbour with radiance which pursued a rainsquall across the red tile roofs of Bilbao city and up a series of bare hills until finally it sketched a brilliant rainbow above the ruins of an ancient Roman watchtower.

Shafts of sunlight also illumined briefly a huge gold cross atop the Cathedral's greenish dome and lent a false lustre to the façade of the Corregidor's palace.

Surely Katherine Ibbott's sensitive imagination would appreciate the picturesqueness of the Corregidor's ornate palace, the red-roofed jumble of shops and those great warehouses which loomed beyond the infinitely varied shipping. Aye, Pretty Kate, who played the dulcimer so sweetly and admired all the arts, undoubtedly would sigh over the intricate filigreed jewellery, the lovely pottery and articles of leather-ware for which this port was famous.

As for himself, Wyatt never had ceased to admire the fine morions, swords and breastplates manufactured here. On this visit he intended to buy a stout bilbo—one of those heavy-bladed, useful and yet very handsome swords named after this same city.

Fervently he hoped Master Goodman would prove correct in his estimate that those flitches of bacon, hogsheads of salted beef, cabbages and bundles of salted fish piled in the *Primrose's* hold would fetch enough crowns in his share to admit the purchase of a brooch—one of the wonderful ornaments of gold inlaid upon steel such as could only be fashioned by Moorish slaves. How well such an ornament would become Kate Ibbott's pale beauty.

What might Franklin Ibbott's eldest daughter be doing this same spring day? She never had held herself above working at her father's looms nor of putting in a long day over her spinning-wheel, but, as became her father's position as a franklin of St. Neots parish in Huntingdonshire, she would lift her short and fascinating nose at the notion of milking a cow or of performing so homely a task as mucking out the family's henhouses.

What position might Franklin Ibbott take when he returned to St. Neots? Could he, in all honesty, object to a son-in-law who, at twenty-two, had progressed enough to own a quarter interest in the *Primrose*? Of course if luck attended this voyage he might become an equal half owner with Master John Foster. He grimaced over the rail. If only Kate's shrew of a mother was not so undeviatingly set upon her marrying some gentleman better endowed with this world's goods.

He took courage in the knowledge that every year small fortunes were being amassed by enterprising young sea captains of no particular birth or fortune, such as the fabulous Sir Francis Drake. The Great Navigator had been only ten years older when he had sacked Nombre de Dios on the Tierra Firma of America and for the first time had tweaked the King of Spain's whiskers. Both father and son, John and Richard Hawkins, had wrung a golden competence from Spanish-American ports and commerce.

Wyatt for a hundredth time began to vizualize certain changes he would make aboard the *Primrose* should he become her Master and half owner—John Foster having long fixed his one eye upon a certain handsome cromster back in Margate. A pair of sakers mounted as chasers on the barque's bow and five feet added to each of the barque's two stubby masts should render the *Primrose* a much handier and defensible vessel, and all without appreciably diminishing her cargo-carrying ability.

Came that happy day when he became a Master Mariner why then Harry Wyatt would select his crew with considerable more care than had One-Eyed John.

He judged a barque of the *Primrose's* size, 120 tons burden, didn't require a crew of twenty-six, excluding officers. Very likely sixteen stout mariners and half a dozen grommets, or apprentice seamen, would prove sufficient to haul, draw and to handle the barque's guns, if need arose.

While lingering in the waist to superintend bracing of yards and disposal of other running gear, Wyatt could visualize the *Primrose* as she would appear anchored off Billingsgate in the Thames. She would lie deep-laden with East Indian spices, Spanish leather, cutlery and gold. Kate, of course, would view the arrival from the door to that modest first home he intended to establish for her on the Thames' south bank, somewhere near St. Olave's Church.

It went without saying that a substantial portion of his profits must be dedicated to the support of his father, Franklin Edmund Wyatt, a gentle and quite ineffectual student of chemistry and medicine.

Unfortunately, certain garrulous neighbours back in St. Neots were given to muttering that Edmund Wyatt very likely must be dabbling in alchemy, too. Arrant nonsense. However improvident, confused and visionary Edmund Wyatt might be, he was not so great a ninny as to squander his pitifully scant substance on attempts to make gold.

Wyatt glanced out over the water and frowned with the realization that, for no good reason, his had not proved to be a very fortunate family. Was it anybody's fault that his mother was afflicted by the falling sickness? Then there was the sad fate of Margaret, his only sister—he had lost three brothers through the smallpox. Poor creature, a kettle of scalding soup cascading over her face not only had transformed her visage into a grotesque mask of scars but also had injured her mind.

For some reason poor Meg's wits never had matured beyond the date of that accident in her ninth year. Certain it was that that unhappy girl would never marry, not with her gargoyle's face and feeble intellect.

Should this voyage prove even half as lucrative as both Master Foster and the blubber-bellied Factor anticipated, then his own profit should at least ensure the family's continued occupancy of a certain modest cottage privily situated on the outskirts of St. Neots.

"Of course," Wyatt reminded himself while immobilizing the rudder's whipstaff, "Pa or all three of them may have died, what with so much plague abroad."

Come to think on it he'd not laid eyes on St. Neots' single street and thatched and moss-grown roofs in near two years. He reckoned it would prove mighty pleasant to fish for trout or to doze again during the heat of the day beneath holly trees which flourished, darkly green and shining, among the ruins of a Benedictine priory.

Also he intended, covertly, of course, to cut a new bowstave from among certain tall yews shading the churchyard. Centuries earlier these trees had been planted amongst the headstones both to preserve the precious yews from destruction and to frighten away malevolent spirits.

A yapping clamour commenced to arise from a bevy of small boats pulling up under the *Primrose's* counter.

"*Pan! Por el amor de Dios, un poco de pan!* Bread! A little bread for the love of God!" croaked he at the helm of a leaky rowboat. His two scarecrow companions dropped their oars in order to raise imploring, claw-like hands so their craft bumped into a skiff manned by an old, white-bearded man and a young boy rendered big-eyed by hunger.

"Food, señores," whined the ancient, "give us food of any kind, in the name of the Holy Virgin. We are famished."

That he was speaking no less than the truth was evident, for a half-grown girl's wasted figure, like a bundle of rags, lay huddled and listless amid inches of dirty water on the skiff's bottom.

All the Spaniards peering up so hopefully appeared emaciated, their dark-skinned arms and legs—never sturdy at best—suggestive of withered tree limbs. They rolled their eyes and chattered like monkeys but the bearded and red-faced English crew lining the rail only spat into the water. To them, brought up amid hunger and uncertainty, such misery was neither moving nor a novelty. More small boats came pulling out from wharves fringing Bilbao Harbour.

"Avast ye scum! Keep away from my ship!" Foster bellowed. "Boatswain! Lay a rope's end to any rogue who dares try boarding." His order came late for already half a dozen incredibly ragged watermen had seized the forechains and began clambering onto the spritsail yard.

The Master turned, his one eye kindling. "Harry, rid my vessel o' this noisy rabble and in haste. Methinks 'tis I sight the Port Captain's barge yonder and I'm damned if he'll find my *Primrose* reeking o' this gallows' bait."

Wholeheartedly the boatswain and his younkers, ordinary seamen, employed belaying pins to smash loose the grip of skinny hands upon the barque's bulwarks. Screaming imprecations, the tatterdemalions were forced to fall back into their scarred and leaky boats.

Although pleased to have the *Primrose* so quickly cleared, Wyatt was struck by the stark desperation written in the eyes of one gaunt starveling—a muleteer by his garb. He was kneeling on the bottom of a crazy little skiff and clasping hands in supplication.

In a hoarse voice he called up: "Most illustrious nobleman, pray God Your Magnificence will never stand in such need. Only yesterday my *niña* died of the hunger. In all our house there remains not even a crust nor yet a drop of olive oil. Without even little food my small son cannot survive another sunrise."

Wyatt's hand sought a pouch at his belt. In it he usually reserved a water biscuit and a lump of cheese with which to relieve an over-long watch.

Master Goodman noticed the gesture. Instantly his not unkindly round red face tightened. "None of that, Master Wyatt! You'll fetch the whole mangy pack o' them aboard us."

"True enough." All the same Wyatt tossed his pouch into the muleteer's dreadfully eager grasp and was rewarded by a look of such ineffable gratitude that he was long in forgetting it.

CHAPTER II

EL CORREGIDOR DE VISCAYA

By the morning of May the twenty-sixth, 1585, not only Master Goodman but John Foster and his red-haired mate found themselves consumed by exasperation tinged with mounting uneasiness. What was up? Not only they, but the *Primrose's* entire crew had become aware that the Bilbao port authorities were entering upon a devious official gambit.

Were they bidding for greater than the usual bribes? It would appear so. Don Francisco de Escober, Corregidor of Viscaya, and his Port Captain had yet to sign a permit for the *Primrose* to traffic, although these dignitaries kept promising, pleasantly enough, to deliver that all-important document.

"A murrain on such long-nosed Papist foxes!" Goodman growled, flicking sweat from a bulbous, sun-blistered forehead. " 'Tis indeed true Spanish to boggle for sly money whilst their people perish o' famine."

During the past two days the weather had turned unseasonably hot, transforming Bilbao Harbour into a humid and airless cauldron in which the English crew swore, sweltered and stewed amid noisome stenches rising from the barque's bilges. Further, a cargo of cabbages, stowed in the afterhold, were commencing to make their unhappy condition known, while what little water remained in the barque's scuttle butt turned pale green and was disclosing new and unpleasant forms of life.

"Stuff never was no nectar," the Boatswain declared, spitting, "but now, b'God, this tastes like it's stood a sennight in some trooper's boots."

"For the life o' me I can't fathom this delay," Master Goodman mumbled through a mouthful of salt fish and fried cabbage. "We know well enough that the curs'd Dons indeed are starving, and they know that we've fetched a floating larder i' their midst, so *why* won't they traffic?"

The Factor looked deeply disturbed, and with reason; further spoilage of his supplies was imminent. Under this torrid heat even salted fish and beef steeped in brine had begun to assume the iridescent hues of approaching putrescence.

The consideration uppermost in John Foster's mind, however, was the precarious state of the *Primrose's* water supply. Something must be done about it—and in a hurry.

Impaling a bit of salt fish on the tip of his claspknife the Master popped the morsel into his mouth and his black-bearded jaws set rhythmically to work.

"Aye, Master Goodman, I twig this shilly-shally on Don Francisco's part no better than you, but, win, lose or draw, I must refill my water casks here tomorrow or sail for Guipúzcoa or some nearby port where the Papists may prove readier to traffic wi' you."

Henry Wyatt trained dark blue eyes upon the many batteries frowning down upon the harbour. "In that case, John, I'm thinking we'd best try a run-out tonight—for all that the channel's main difficult."

Foster employed a tar-stained forefinger to dislodge a troublesome bit of fish from between his few remaining teeth. "No call to remind me o' that. So, Walter Goodman, I'll grant the port authorities till sundown to fish, cut bait or get out o' the boat, as the fishermen say."

The Factor scowled, pursed fleshy lips. "You'd best find patience a while longer. I warn 'e, John, my masters will take it ill an your timidity robs them o' their profit."

A snort escaped the *Primrose's* Master and his single eye glared at Goodman over a beard a-bristle with annoyance. "And what o' your masters? God burst my butt! I've my ship to think of, to say naught o' those twenty-six rascals you see gaming and scratching their dirty carcasses amidships."

The anchor watch raised a hail. "Ahoy, the poop deck! Boat pulling out from the Customs House and steering straight for us."

Henry Wyatt put down the wooden trencher from which he had been eating, crossed to the port bulwarks and jumped onto a cask. By narrowing his eyes against the noonday glare he was able to discern a yellow-and-red-painted barge pulled by eight half-naked oarsmen advancing over the harbour's glassy surface. From its stern dangled an ensign bearing the quartered rampant lions and crenelated towers of Aragon and Castile.

Wyatt descended to the deck and commenced to do up the buttons of his jerkin. "'Tis some popinjay out of the Aduana. He'll be fetching us our Licence to Trade, no doubt."

Once the yellow-painted barge, her scarred and splintered thwarts betraying long use, drew nearer, Wyatt's error became apparent. In the sternsheets two brilliantly apparelled dignitaries lounged in company with quite a number of individuals dressed in the sober black and browns of merchants. Soon it became apparent that approaching was no mere flunkey from the Port Captain's office, but no less a personage than His Excellency, Francisco de Escober, Corregidor over the entire Signoria of Viscaya, escorted by a pair of his principal officers.

Wyatt recognized that erect and saturnine nobleman from having watched him head a Corpus Christi procession the year before.

"Have a care, señores," the Master's Mate overheard Don Francisco mutter, "much depends on the next hour's results."

Praise God for those tedious hours he had spent as clerk apprenticed to the Casa de Obrien y Andrada, member of the Company of Merchants trading to Spain and Portugal. It had been with this concern he had first found employment after quitting St. Neots, and so had had drubbed into him considerably more than the rudiments of spoken and written Spanish.

He had quitted the Casa de Obrien y Andrada when his immediate supervisor, a drunken renegade from Barcelona, had attempted to knife him over some fancied slight to a Portuguese trull of no particular charm or grace.

In self-defence he'd had to break the silly fellow's head, then sign aboard the first vessel to clear London Pool. Pure good fortune had directed him aboard John Foster's *Primrose*.

Even as the Master's Mate started towards the gangway a lively doubt presented itself. Why should so exalted a personage as the Corregidor of Viscaya deign to appear aboard a modest English merchantman? Especially following a delay of two days.

While the expanse of discoloured water separating barque and barge narrowed Wyatt ordered the crew to adjust their dress and, not without a certain foresight, sent several of the more unkempt below.

His Excellency Don Francisco de Escober, resplendent in green and yellow full hose, a crimson doublet complete with huge ruff of Valencian lace and a short Moresco cloak of azure velvet, stood peering up at this scruffy merchantman's poop. Seen against the dark outline of his craggy features, the Corregidor's grey pointed beard and moustachios appeared almost white above a ponderous and glittering gold chain the value of which alone easily might have purchased the *Primrose's* entire cargo.

Once the oarsmen, gaunt, ribby fellows all, had ceased to ply their sweeps and allowed their barge to come coasting smoothly up under the barque's counter a minor officer in a faded red-and-blue uniform stiffly requested permission to come aboard.

"Aye! Come aboard and welcome! 'Tis high time," Foster called down, then issued a volley of commands, caused his crew to lower a rope ladder by means of which the broadly smiling Corregidor, his aides and sombrely dressed companions presently ascended to the *Primrose's* deck.

To Master Goodman, who spoke the most fluent Spanish of anyone aboard, the five soberly clad individuals announced themselves as merchants of the town come to traffic for the barque's cargo. To a man they appeared sallow, anxious and hungry, although by no means as famished as those wretched creatures who first had greeted the *Primrose's* arrival.

Somehow, these stiff-backed, black-clad fellows to Henry Wyatt seemed less servile, less hail-fellow-well-met than those merchants who appeared aboard the barque on the occasion of her last voyage. The Corregidor's manner was curt and he devoted considerable attention to the barque's six rusty sakers.

"Welcome aboard," boomed John Foster, bowing low as a common fellow should in the presence of his betters. He even had scraped sauce stains from his frieze jacket and, in honour of these distinguished officials, from somewhere had produced a round hat of sky-blue leather. After all, Don Francisco de Escober was the King's principal lieutenant over the Signoria of Viscaya, a rich, seafaring province which included above one hundred towns, villages and minor ports.

A cask of sound English beer was hastily fetched up to the poop deck and its golden warmth proved quite acceptable for all that Foster's cheer was served in misshapen jacks of waxed leather which could hardly have improved its taste.

Official permission to trade, Don Francisco gravely explained to Master Foster through Walter Goodman, would be forthcoming the afternoon of this same day. Indeed, he himself had come to purchase a considerable supply of stock fish, salted beef and other comestibles for the benefit of his garrisons.

He exposed large, amber-tinted teeth in a bleak smile. "To be truthful, Señor Capitán, I confess that here in Bilbao our need is dire, and we are most eager for your cargo. For every hour that passes many of my *soldados* die of hunger, therefore I trust, señor," he turned to Goodman and actually patted that portly individual on the shoulder, "you will be so good as to decide your prices today and make delivery tomorrow?"

"Your Excellency is too kind." Master Goodman drew so deep a breath of satisfaction that his globular stomach strained at a wide, brass buckled belt then drooped over it whilst he quoted a succession of prices he would not have dared to ask an hour earlier.

No trace of hesitation marked the manner of either the Corregidor or of his companions in accepting Goodman's truly outrageous quotations. Wyatt, standing to one side from these thin-nosed and broad-shouldered merchants, experienced a tingle of elation. God's Glory! Rumble-bellied Walt Goodman already stood to win an extra thousand ducats for the half of his cargo.

The Master's Mate scarce could credit his hearing. Why, if this deal were consummated he himself stood to clear seventy-five English pounds. By the Great Harry! This would more than double the sum encompassed by even his most optimistic reckoning. Now, for certain, he'd buy a fine bilbo and necklace of filigreed goldwork to grace Kate Ibbott's slender throat.

In John Foster's frosty grey eye satisfaction gleamed while his deeply-lined brown visage relaxed for the first time since his anchor had found the bottom of Bilbao Harbour.

"Pray inquire of these gentlemen," he directed Goodman, "whether they'd care to linger for a sup of honest English corned beef and cabbage?"

Don Francisco and his dark-eyed companions conferred, then declared themselves ready to partake of the *Primrose's* hospitality.

"They must indeed be perishing o' hunger," Goodman murmured in an aside to Wyatt. "Otherwise no *caballero* of a Corregidor's rank would deign even to come aboard. Methinks we are like little pigs in clover so to speak."

"Maybe so—but still . . ." Ever since the Corregidor's arrival Wyatt's uneasiness had been increasing. Said he in an undertone. "Aye. Curs'd if I understand why the Corregidor himself should visit us. As a rule some greedy and unwashed Teniente from the Port Captain's office suffices to fetch out our Licence to Trade and His Excellency hasn't even brought it along."

A luscious joint of beef only recently put to pickle was produced, tender green and white cabbages were sliced and sent to pot along with a supply of young onions and a few precious carrots. More beer, foaming and amber-hued, splashed into jacks quickly emptied by the visting merchants. Those lean and black-clad individuals wandered freely about the deck, critically eyed the barque's rigging, then peered down upon such goods as were visible through hatches opened against the heat of the day.

Meanwhile, on the *Primrose's* tiny poop deck a trestle table was rigged up on a pair of tar casks. More kegs and bales were trundled up to seat the visitors. To deck the board a leaden saltcellar, some battered pewter salvers were produced and, in honour of this unprecedented occasion, a peppercorn mill.

Sweating hard, Wyatt himself arranged the improvisation of an ancient topsail for an awning; the spring sunshine now was really pitiless in its intensity. The spread sailcloth soon created a mellow, golden light to enrich the sparkle of gems set into earrings and medallions worn by the Corregidor and his officers.

Soon the repast, smoking hot and succulent of odour, awaited the guests, who, their previous haughtiness forgotten, needed no second invitation and fell-to with ill-concealed eagerness. It came therefore as a considerable surprise that when the meal was but half consumed the Corregidor should push aside his platter and address his host: "A thousand pardons, Señor Capitán, but in view of your magnificent hospitality I feel it is only right that I go ashore for some special wines and also to fetch you your Licence to Trade."

The Spaniard's vitreous, dark brown eyes flickered from one to another of his aides. "Don José and Don Alfredo will accompany me. You, Señor Guzmán, Don Pedro, Don Luis and the rest will remain to enjoy this delicious repast."

The last-mentioned Spaniards remained wreathed in smiles whilst those ordered to accompany the Corregidor acted as "sour as so many whores in church", as Browne, the Boatswain, later put it. Despite protests genuine enough on the part of the *Primrose's* Master and Factor, Don Francisco de Escober descended into his little galley and was rowed off across harbour water turning yellow-grey under a thickening bank of clouds.

"A pox on all such ungrateful foreign bastards!' grunted Foster. "Never would I have credited that such flat-bellied gentry would quit a well-stocked board."

While lingering beside the rail Henry Wyatt tugged at red fuzz sprouting along his squarish jaw. At length he cast Foster a quizzical glance. "Curs'd if there isn't something wonderous queer about all this."

Under a well-darned woollen shirt Foster's shoulders rose. "Aye, Harry. 'Tis passing strange. Why should de Escober leave some of his number aboard of us? Perchance he spoke truth about returning for our licence?"

"I'll believe that when swine grow wings." Wyatt shot a shrewd glance up at the remaining guests laughing as they quickly appropriated dishes abandoned by their fellows. "Suppose, John, that, quiet-like, I alert our men whilst you occupy the Dons. Anon we'll learn whether there's mischief afoot—for all that we wot of no reason for it."

Once it became evident that Don Luis and his companions were ready to consume anything and everything offered, John Foster ordered up jacks of the strongest ale aboard.

"Yours is indeed a very fine ship, Señor Capitán," belched Señor Guzmán while running a critical eye over the barque's rigging. "She will make a good fictualler for the *Flota de Viscaya.*"

Foster's one eye became fixed and he caught his breath to speak, but, even more quickly, his Factor demanded, "Pray inform us, noble sir, is that not the *Dolphin* of Dover yonder?"

"*Pero sí, amigo mío,*" Don Luis nodded in friendly fashion. "She—er—entered into His Majesty's service only last week. Beyond her lies the *Swan* from your troublesome port called Plymouth."

Master Goodman choked on a bit of beef causing his normally prominent eyes to pop still more. "But—but—Your Honour must be mistook," stammered Foster, reddening like an angry turkey-cock's wattles. "I know their Masters well. Never would they sell such well-found vessels, especially in these times."

"Dare you question my word, you low dog of a mariner?" Señor Guzmán's narrow head snapped back and he glared across the improvised table. "What our Royal master needs, he takes."

"Their crews," Foster breathed hard over his tankard. "What's become of 'em?"

"They are safe enough," Don Luis informed with a careless wave towards the shore. "In fact, at this moment they are enjoying the hospitality of the Castello. When it pleases His Majesty they will be returned to that miserable little fogbound island you inhabit."

From the corner of his eye John Foster followed Henry Wyatt's apparently aimless movements about the deck. He was exchanging a casual word now and then with certain of the *Primrose's* hairy and rough-clad crew, with the result that, during the next half-hour, pikes, axes and javelins surreptitiously became concealed among the deck gear. To Foster's anxious ear activity also must be taking place below-decks, if various faint bumping and scraping sounds portended anything.

At long last Master Foster heaved himself to his feet. "I crave your pardon, gentlemen, but I must impart certain instructions to my Mate."

Señor Guzmán also rose, saffron-tinted cheeks suddenly suffused. "Señor Capitán, we would take it very discourteous were you to abandon your invited guests. Therefore you will remain with us," he cast a quick look shorewards, "until His Excellency the Corregidor returns." The silvered tang of a dirk had become visible under his short, dark blue cloak.

"Eh? Dis-courteous?" sputtered Foster, then added under his breath: "Well, I-I'm damned—well damned! But have it your way, you spike-whiskered bastard." Sullenly he sank back on to his barrel.

To the stupidest Englishman aboard there remained no doubt that perfidy of some sort was in the air, probably akin to that treachery which must already have overwhelmed the *Swan* and the *Dolphin*. How generally had it been applied Wyatt was wondering. Had this embargo been enforced against all English vessels in the face of supposedly peaceful relations between the Crowns of Spain and England?

Goodman, too, appeared desperately uneasy and must be growing angry in his slow and unimaginative way.

"Hah!" snorted one of the guests. "At last His Excellency returns." The Corregidor's gaudy yellow barge had indeed put out from the Aduana, but no longer looked so noticeable because vagrant clouds once more were obscuring the sun.

His uneasiness mounting, Henry Wyatt lingered in the barque's waist, then in rising apprehension noted that a large pinnace was following the Corregidor's barge. Both of these craft seemed extremely well peopled by sombre-garbed merchants, but nowhere did the twinkle of steel betray itself.

The *Primrose's* grizzled Boatswain grunted: "Master Wyatt, be I daft or do 'e Dons display an uncommon interest in our cargo? 'E Papists must be more hungered than we'd thought."

"*Oiga!* Throw me a line," the Corregidor's brown-faced coxswain directed through cupped hands. Everyone could see grey-bearded Don Francisco de Escober managing his sword in preparation to boarding the merchantman.

"Avast there in the waist!" suddenly bellowed the *Primrose's* Master. "Allow only the Corregidor's barge to come alongside!"

"Be still, you surly dog of a heretic!" snapped Señor Guzmán. "As many of our merchants will come aboard as His Excellency directs."

The Corregidor meanwhile bowed from his position in the barge's stern and called up, politely enough: "Señor Capitán, I have with me your Licence to Trade. You shall conduct a fine business in Bilbao, one to be remembered."

Wyatt, his nerves tautening like a cable under increasing tension, glanced at John Foster, saw him uncommon angry, red-faced and perspiring heavily under the awning. His single grey eye fairly blazed as he shouted down: "Wyatt, inform His Excellency that only he and six others may board my ship at this time. Tell him we're not ready to deal wi' such a swarm o' merchants." Both Goodman and the Mate translated but, nonetheless, a swarm of *mercadores* commenced climbing over the bulwarks.

All smiles and cordiality, the Corregidor ascended once more to the *Primrose's* small and now overcrowded poop, his azure cloak stirring gently under a breeze beginning to blow down from that row of harsh and treeless brown mountains rising behind Bilbao.

"Your Honour has indeed brought my Licence to Trade?" John Foster demanded stoutly.

"One of my gentlemen aboard the pinnace has it," replied the Corregidor.

John Foster's compact and homely figure seemed to expand and his voice rang out. "Then, Your Honour, pray instruct him to pass it over the rail. I'll tolerate no such mob aboard my vessel."

Don Francisco de Escober appeared pained. "Mob, señor? You mistake them. These are but honest *mercadores* of the town who have come a long distance to traffic with you."

Wyatt, tight-lipped, could see those in the pinnace getting to their feet and craning necks at the *Primrose*. Certainly, mused the Master's Mate, these newcomers resembled no merchants he had ever before beheld in a Spanish port. Half of this hard-bitten company bore scars, all of them looked sinewy and resembled not at all the plump and well-fed *mercadores* encountered on previous expeditions.

The smile vanished from Don Francisco's bearded lips. "Señor Capitán, I insist that these honest merchants be permitted to come aboard."

Foster braced his feet apart, unflinchingly confronted his guest. "Your Excellency, I must remind you that this is an English vessel and that I am her Master; as such, I allow aboard of her only those whom I list. Your Honour and my previous guests only will be well——"

He got no further. Responding to some undetected signal the "merchants" in the pinnace and those remaining in the barge poured over the barque's low bulwarks, shouting:

"*Viva el Rey! Abajo los heréticos Ingleses!* Down with the English heretics." Steel dirks, poignards and rapiers appeared from beneath the long and sombre-hued cloaks of Don Francisco de Escober's "honest merchants".

Simultaneously the Spaniards seated about John Foster's table produced daggers and levelled them at the English Master's chest. He, however, snatched up a heavy copper soup ladle, leaped backwards and succeeded in beating aside the threatening points.

"We are betrayed!" he roared, and retreated until he could catch up a handspike. At once he employed his weapon in furious quarterstaff play that drove back his immediate adversaries. These, hampered by the narrow limits of the barque's poop deck, lunged and slashed at the Master's thick-bodied figure but only succeeded in disconcerting each other.

Raising a chorus of high-pitched shouts and epithets, more pseudo merchants thudded onto the deck and assailed the badly-outnumbered Englishmen.

At the first alarm Wyatt had snatched from a fold of sailcloth a clumsy, heavy-bladed sword bestowed upon him by John Foster on the occasion of his promotion to Master's Mate. Instinctively the tall young Mate ducked beneath a cut aimed at him by a yellow-bearded Spaniard and quite distinctly heard the vicious *tchunk!* caused by that gleaming blade's biting into the rail.

More yelling, steel-brandishing Viscayans scrambled up the barque's dull red sides and started to clear her decks, but they were swept back against the bulwarks by a knot of Englishmen who came charging down from the forecastle. Javelins flew and several tacks and petronels—heavy hand-guns—banged and started echoes reverberating among the warehouses of Bilbao.

All about the *Primrose* shipping roused itself, much as it had in the harbour of San Juan de Ulúa in Mexico on a certain infamous day during the autumn of 1568 when, through a piece of villainy as brazen as this, John Hawkins and Francis Drake, then but a fledgling sea captain, had barely escaped with their lives and no profits in a hitherto successful slaving expedition.

For that treacherous and merciless assault, also delivered in time of peace, Philip II had paid millions, so costly had been the vengeance exacted by Drake and his captains.

Surging forward, the outraged mate glimpsed the Factor, Walter Goodman, manfully standing his ground. His round belly undulated under the strength of his pike-thrusts; indeed, that stout little merchant and John Foster had formed an effective team up on the poop deck. Already they had disabled or slain a majority of Don Francisco's original companions. As for the Corregidor himself, he was flourishing a rapier by the foot of the mainmast and urging on his followers.

"Upon them! Subdue these heretic dogs!" he kept calling, his voice shrill with tension. "In the King's name I order you to seize this vessel!"

A pain like the bite of some gigantic wasp stung Wyatt's shoulder through his leather jerkin and, wheeling about, he glimpsed a tall, lemon-complexioned Spaniard preparing to spring in, his bilbo's point already dripping scarlet.

Wyatt applied his full strength and, more by sheer power than art, parried that twinkling blade when it licked at him with the speed of a snake's tongue. The two blades rasped and shivered against each other, then, his hurt shoulder smarting, Wyatt lunged at the other. To avoid his thrust the Spaniard skipped sidewise but in so doing momentarily presented an opening. Instantly Wyatt's clumsy blade sank deep into the fellow's black-clad shoulder at that point where it joined his neck. A hoarse screech escaped the other as, dropping his bilbo, he employed both hands in a futile attempt to check rhythmic spurts of bright blood escaping from a severed artery.

Another assailant rushed up just as Wyatt's former antagonist slipped on to his knees, his doublet drenched by a vivid scarlet cascade.

The shivering clash of weapons, the high-pitched foreign voices and the deep shouts of the embattled English crew all gained in volume—but no more firearms were fired—there was no time to reload.

When the Boatswain, his yellow-grey beard bright in the torrid sunlight, drove a broad axe's blade deep into the skull of a garishly apparelled Spanish officer a slow movement towards the barque's starboard rail became initiated.

"Ha! At them! At them!" Wyatt yelled. "Now's the time!"

The enemy's retrograde movement gained momentum until the Spanish line suddenly broke and such of them as were able scrambled over the bulwarks and dropped into their boats. Others, the badly wounded, traced their progress in blood about the *Primrose's* littered deck in search of even temporary shelter. Still others raised hands and shrieked for mercy—without success, more often than not, so infuriated had the English become.

The Corregidor's two boats pushed off, abandoning a handful of Spaniards still fighting about the barque's mainmast. When these grew aware of being deserted they commenced to run about the deck with the frantic aimlessness of so many rats dropped into a box stall occupied by a fox terrier.

"*Por piedad!* Have mercy!" begged the survivors; and either dropped their weapons onto the deck or flung themselves into the turgid waters of Bilbao Harbour.

Comparative silence prevailed aboard the *Primrose*, silence in which the victors dashed sweat from their eyes and glared about to decide their next move. To them it seemed typical that despairing shouts raised by Spaniards struggling and drowning alongside accomplished nothing in recalling those small boats in which they had arrived.

Reminded of that stabbing ache in his left shoulder and aware that streams of blood were drenching his sleeve, Wyatt was using a poignard to cut away its fabric when an especially imploring hail attracted his attention to the Corregidor's desperate plight.

Don Francisco was proving a very poor swimmer indeed, so Wyatt contemptuously tossed him a rope's end and directed a pair of mariners to hoist the Corregidor back aboard to augment a group of six or eight prisoners who stood holding high their hands and swallowing hard on their fear.

John Foster, sweating all over his bald head, breathing hard and purple of face, came clumping down from the poop, his single eye balefully aglow. "Diccon, Harding and the rest o' you younkers—pitch me this carrion overboard." He spat upon the nearest of several of the black-clad figures sprawled at his feet. From beneath these streams of blood meandered about the *Primrose's* tarry oak deck until they escaped through the bulwarks and dripped down the barque's side to tinge the harbour's water.

"Now, ye high-flung Castilian son of a gutter-bred bitch, I'll give ye yer just deserts and break yer treacherous neck with me own hands." He strode over to the Corregidor, standing, grey-faced, among the prisoners, seized the Spaniard by his throat and squeezed it so hard that several drops of harbour water fell from his sodden spade beard. Don Francisco's knees had commenced to buckle when Wyatt hurried up, his hurt arm supported by a sling improvised from some fallen Spaniard's belt. "Hold hard, John! Had you not best spare this old swine?"

"Why? He's tricked us nigh unto our undoing."

"Aye, but listen. D'you hear those trumpets in the Castello sounding an alarm?"

"Aye, yer right, Harry. We'd best look ahead." However, before releasing his grip on Don Francisco de Escober, John Foster expressed his contempt in an incredible insult. Deliberately, he pulled a handful of hair from the Corregidor's beard, then dealt that high functionary a couple of slaps which sounded loud as any tack's report.

"Try to seize my vessel and murder innocent seafarers o' a friendly nation, would ye?" Foster snarled. "Well, God send you'll hang for this in England, like the common pirate you are."

Partially dazed by the violence of Foster's cuffs, the Corregidor—he had lost his splendid golden chain—could only cling to the shrouds and gasp. He offered a most forlorn spectacle, what with water dripping from his sodden clothes and creating a puddle about his shoeless feet. A big hole showed in the toe of his left hose, Wyatt noticed.

CHAPTER III

KING PHILIP'S COMMISSION

GRIMLY, John Foster's single eye took note of morions and armour gleaming among the crenelations of nearby batteries, also the retrograde movement of cannon being hauled back for charging.

"Goodman!" he directed. "Call to the barge hovering yonder that I hold prisoner their Corregidor and seven o' his fellow rogues; an those forts offer the least hostility, I'll swing the parcel of 'em out o' hand."

Once the Factor had shouted Foster's threat and the yellow barge had started threshing back towards the Aduana, Foster grinned as he picked up his blue leather hat.

"By the Great Harry, Walter, I'll keep these dogs hostage till we're well out to sea, then I'll stretch their dirty necks. Browne," he flung at his Boatswain, "what's the sum of our losses?" With the aid of his teeth and an undamaged hand Browne was knotting a clout over a dripping gash across his left forearm.

"None so heavy, John, but I'll count noses." He tramped about the deck which the *Primrose's* crew were clearing by the simple expedient of dropping dead and dying Spaniards over the side.

Presently he called up to the poop deck. "Five others besides Harry Wyatt and myself ha' taken wounds. None of them heavy, but John Tristram's wife's a widow the now, for he's been well and truly sped."

"Aye, sped through the villainy o' this noble pirate." Foster spat full into the Corregidor's face.

"Señor Capitán, have mercy!" Don Francisco extended bound and trembling hands. "Do not slay me! *Por Dios*, I am no *pirata*, only humble *functionario* who tried to follow his orders."

Foster's ragged black beard bristled and twisted like the hair on an angry dog's neck. "Orders? Blast me! Whose orders? Don't deny 'twas only the promptings o' yer own greed!"

While wiping away the Englishman's spittle Don Francisco tried to resume his dignity. "On the honour of my mother, Señor Capitán, I did but obey the direct commands of my liege lord, His Most Catholic Majesty of Spain."

"D'ye mean to say the Spanish King *himself* ordered so dishonourable an act? Bah! Ye lie in yer teeth, ye greedy, murdering Judas."

The *Primrose's* crew scanned a long series of grey-yellow battlements teeming with activity. All of them recognized the distinctive creak and rumble of gun-carriages being run back over the parapets—that and a feverish rattling of drums. Wyatt deemed it wise, therefore, to repeat to the nearest Spanish warship, a tall galleon, Master Foster's intention of hanging Don Francisco de Escober and the other prisoners if so much as a single firelock were discharged.

"Ye're Corregidor over this Seignory," Foster was insisting, "so took the responsibility on yerself. Come, ye Papist dog, and admit it."

"Nay, Señor Capitán, on the Holy Cross I swear I speak only truth." As far as his bound hands would permit, the Corregidor fumbled into the bosom of his doublet and he fished out a scroll of sodden paper. Eagerly he thrust it forward. "Here, Señor Inglés, read for yourself and judge whether or no I have offered more than to obey His Majesty's commands."

Foster accepted the document, eyed it doubttully, then shook his head. He could not even read English. "Wyatt!" he bawled. "Come up here. I want you and Walter to give me what sense ye can make o' this claptrap."

Hampered by many hesitations and pauses, Henry Wyatt presently wrote down Master Goodman's translation, for the Factor was by far the more fluent in Spanish. What presently took shape proved to be one of the most shameless and cynical documents ever signed by a ruling monarch of Christendom.

In Barcelona. May 1585.

Licentiate de Escober, my Corregidor of my Signoria of Viscaya, I have caused a great fleet to be put in readiness in the haven of Lisbon and the river of Seville. There is required for the soldiers, armour, victual and munition that are to be employed in the same great store of shipping of all sorts against the time of service and to the end there may be choice made of the best upon knowledge of their burden and goodness; I therefore do require you that presently upon the arrival of this carrier, and with as much dissimulation as may be (that the matter may not be known until it be put into execution) you take order for the staying and arresting (with great foresight) of all the shipping that may be found upon the coast, and in the ports of the said Signoria, excepting none of Holland, Zeeland, Easterland, Germany, England and other provinces that are in rebellion against me, saving those of France which being little and of small burden and weak, are thought unfit to serve the turn. And the stay being thus made you shall have a special care that such merchandise as the said ships or hulks have brought, whether they be all or part unlade, may be taken out and that armour, munition, tackle, sails and victuals may be safely bestowed, as also that it may be well foreseen that none of the ships or men may escape away. Which things being thus executed, you shall advertise me by an express messenger of your proceeding therein: and send me a plain and distinct declaration of the number of ships that you shall have stayed in that coast and parts, whence everyone of them is, which belong to my rebels, what burthen and goods they are and what number of men is in every of them and what quantity they have of armour, ordnance, munition, tacklings and other necessaries to the end that on sight thereof, having made choice of such as shall be fit for the service, we may further direct you what you shall do. In the meantime you shall presently see this my commandment put into execution, and if there come thither any more ships you shall also cause them to be stayed and arrested after the same order, using therein such care and diligence as may answer the trust that I repose in you wherein you shall do me great service.

Felipe Rex.

When Wyatt had finished driving his quill across paper steadied beneath his injured arm the stillness of profound astonishment descended upon the *Primrose's* poop. During this silence sounds of furious activity taking place aboard the Royal war galley and other men-of-war became painfully evident.

Foster's one eye anxiously surveyed the nearest forts. "And just what, my friends, d'ye take to be this Royal Judas' meaning when he writes of 'outfitting a great fleet in Lisbon and in the river of Seville'? Against whom would such squadrons be readied?"

Walter Goodman argued that the impending onslaught could not be aimed against the French, in fact the letter itself so stated, nor yet against the Scots, clinging with such fierce loyalty to their Queen, still imprisoned in Tutbury Castle.

"An expedition 'gainst the Turks scarce would be mounted along the west coast of Spain," Wyatt pointed out. " 'Tis plain as a pikestaff, is it not, that his attack is intended 'gainst the Queen's realm?"

"Aye. England must be his object," Foster admitted, then, prompted by an ordering of sweeps aboard the great war galley, he added briskly: "Now let's to work. Harry, rig me a noose to our lateen yard and seven more from the main yard."

Once his commands had been executed Foster caused the Corregidor, easily recognizable because of his grey hair and long beard, to be lifted up onto the poop transom where a noose promptly became adjusted. In similar fashion the other prisoners were forced to stand, swaying precariously upon the barque's rail.

To even the dullest officer on the ramparts or aboard the warships it must have been abundantly clear that the first hostile move on their part would set all eight hostages to kicking out their lives. In terror the prisoners kept calling out, warning their compatriots against the least effort to hinder the *Primrose's* deliberate departure.

"Slip the cable," Foster flung at his Boatswain. "Harry! Order all sail made, an offshore breeze should pick up soon."

Suffering reaction from the fight and from the sharp pain gnawing at his shoulder, Wyatt commenced gently to tremble. "Aye, aye, John. Thank God, the tide's at full ebb and may carry us out faster than yonder carracks."

Of that big green-and-gold-painted galley now getting under way towards the harbour's mouth Wyatt made no mention. The sharp, brazen ram of this swift craft had commenced to shear the water into trailing white streamers so great was her speed.

Soon it became apparent that John Foster's threat to hang Don Francisco out of hand had achieved a deterring effect at least upon the commander of the Castello.

Foster, himself handling the rudder's whipstaff, looked up at his prisoner teetering, grey-faced, on the transom and growled, "I'll grant that ye seemed to act upon yer perjured King's orders so I promise ye'll not hang, provided yonder forts and warships leave us be, so pray to yer graven images that they don't so much as fire a petronel at me."

The *Primrose* commenced to pass by the great carracks but her progress was slow and all thanks to the tide; her patched canvas still flapped, limp and impotent.

From across the harbour sounded the percussion of a gong rhythmically struck to mark stroke for the Royal galley's oarsmen. Gunners were grouped about the galley's two bow chasers, figures in armour commenced to collect upon the enemy's huge fore and stern castles. Steadily she sped towards the harbour's mouth with spray flying and frothing about her twenty-five-foot sweeps—each was pulled by three slaves.

Both to forget his pain and to ease the tension of the moment Wyatt clumped over to a heap of captured weapons piled upon the main hatch and found that same gold-hilted bilbo which had dealt him his wound and had come so close to stretching him out forever. Although essentially designed for use, this bilbo was uncommon handsome, boasting a guard of pure red gold fashioned in the likeness of a griffin which held a sizeable emerald between its jaws.

A dry, creaking sound and a slight rustling of canvas caused all hands to stare into the rigging in time to watch the barque's dun-coloured topsail lift and fall, then lift again and finally fill. A low cheer arose, although for all that this incipient breeze was not yet strong enough to unfurl the barque's flag of St. George, a banner which displayed a Latin cross scarlet horizontal upon a field of white.

Anxiously, unwounded crew members trimmed the weather-stained mainsail then broke out the barque's spritsail while the injured anxiously whistled for the wind. Certes! They entertained no desire to join such of their countrymen as now might be languishing among rats and roaches in the Castello's dungeons.

Irregularly but ever stronger, an off-shore breeze commenced to blow, filled the barque's sails and set her slipping handily across the harbour. But now the great green-and-gold galley had swung half about and came churning straight towards the stubby English barque at such a rate that twin plumes of spray spurted far out from under her heavy bronze ram. Much like a farm dog running down a heifer, this long, low enemy sped forward, her banks of oars, three to each side, hesitating at the horizontal then dipping in perfect unison.

"God help us, lads, we're for it," groaned the Boatswain, and fell to cursing. "Yonder Papists cannot fail to cut us off."

"Aye, 'tis bitter hard," muttered the Factor, absently biting at a forefingernail. "They'll catch and hang us, sure enough, if Foster strings up the Corregidor."

A tide of despair arose within Wyatt. "And I fancied this voyage might gain me some small fortune!"

Once he was clapped into some Spanish dungeon—and God knew he couldn't bear confined places—what possibility remained that he, or any of the *Primrose's* company, might ever again see England? Worse still was the probability that, as heretics, they would suffer the rack, branding irons and fiery death of the Holy Office of the Inquisition! Every beat of yonder galley's oars diminished his chances of ever meeting demure Kate Ibbott beside the London road.

What fate then would befall futile old Edmund Wyatt, his mother and poor scarred and embittered Meg when their rent fell still further in arrears? The patience of even Sir Joseph Tapcote, as tolerant a landlord as ever lived, must have its bounds.

Louder, ever louder, sounded that ominous *click-swish-splash!* created by the galley's crimson-painted oar blades. Now details of her armament and complement became discernible and everyone aboard the merchantman could see black-and-red-clad gunners crowding about their two bow chasers—they looked to be demi-culverins—and the rich costumes of officers crowding her lofty poop.

Under an ever-freshing land wind the *Primrose* now began to heel over so far as to cause her hostages considerable difficulty in maintaining their precarious footing on the bulwarks. Although the barque was making good progress towards the entrance to Bilbao Harbour none could doubt but that inevitably she would be cut off.

Only the working of John Foster's broad, black-bearded jaw betrayed his anxiety when the galley continued to close in.

Finally he called to Don Francisco. "An ye value that vulture's neck o' yers, ye'd best warn yer officers yonder that unless their craft stops oars within the minute and falls astern ye'll start dancing the Devil's hornpipe."

Because his noose was tightened and Goodman had seized his belt ready to launch him into Eternity, Don Francisco de Escober screamed a series of orders across a hundred-yard gap now separating the two vessels.

If the Colonel in command did not instantly comply then he, and his whole staff, forthwith might expect death for having disobeyed a direct order from His Most Catholic Majesty's Corregidor.

"As ever, Your Excellency, your wish is my command," yelled back a tall, dark-faced officer splendid in a gold-and-black corselet and white-plumed morion. He raised his hand. Immediately the slave driver's timing gong fell silent, then all oars were raised dripping to the horizontal. Her great steering oar then was employed to bring the galley onto a parallel course. She coasted smoothly along for a few moments, then fell astern.

A knot which had formed at the pit of Henry Wyatt's stomach suddenly dissolved itself. He looked Goodman in the eye and grinned.

"Good," grunted the Factor. "But, methinks, my masters in London Town will prove damned ill-tempered to see their cargo back in the Thames spoiled and wi' never a penny o' profit to be shown on their ledgers."

CHAPTER IV

LONDON POOL

IT WAS upon an unusually fine June evening that the *Barque Primrose* returned to her moorings in the Thames, off the Royal Custom House and opposite to a row of solid, grey stone warehouses belonging to the Company of Merchants Trading to Spain and Portugal.

The river below London Bridge, Henry Wyatt remarked, appeared to be nowhere near as crowded with shipping as it had been two months earlier. Was this because too many English merchants had responded to King Philip the Second's plea for importation of wheat, stock, fish, beef and other comestibles to the relief of his starving realm?

Visible, however, were three of the Queen's great men-of-war, the *Bonaventure* of six hundred tons, the *Aid* of two hundred and fifty tons, and the *Christopher*, one of Drake's prizes, which was scarcely larger than the *Primrose*. In lazy semi-circles these anchored men-of-war swung under the impulse of a current tawny-grey at this time of year.

Seen by the warm, translucent sunlight of early June, the countryside visible beyond London appeared especially verdant and lush after the scorched, yellow brown coasts of Northern Spain. Behind the suburb of St. Catherine's and along Horsey Down on the river's south bank, hedgerow after hedgerow, gay with red and white blossoms, marched right down to the Thames' shiny and malodorous tidal flats.

London, teeming now with near 200,000 souls, had burst beyond the old city walls that ran in a long, flat ellipse stretching from Blackfriars to the Tower. New dwellings of all descriptions were springing up along a line of low hills which paralleled Thames Street—the capital's main artery—just as commercial structures were rising above the smelly and crowded but lusty stews that ended at the water's edge among busy wharves and docks.

Here and there a few green trees did manage to survive but they were not to be seen in any number until, far to the west, the vicinity of Leicester House, Charing Cross and Westminster was reached. All the same, Henry Wyatt decided that London seemed to have changed very little since that day when as a youth of nineteen he, with Peter Hopton, his yellow-polled scamp of a cousin, had entered it through the Barbican after having travelled down from St. Neots to try their fortune.

Had Peter Hopton reached Plymouth in time to join Sir Richard Grenville's expedition to the New World? If but half of what was related concerning North America proved to be so, why then Cousin Peter must long since have filled his wallet with those great pearls which certain travellers swore were washed up by every tide.

After saluting the port as was the custom by a discharge of the *Primrose's* sakers, Master John Foster, tight-lipped and quite conscious of the gravity of the tidings he bore, directed that his barque's port culverins be discharged at minute intervals, in the manner of alarm guns. This, the merchant Master reckoned, should fetch the port authorities aboard in a hurry.

The firing of alarm guns won Master Goodman's fullest approval; the arrival of such startling news might go far towards distracting the attention of his masters from his failure to produce crowns and escudos in exchange for the *Primrose's* cargo. Alas that the barque's voyage returning across the Bay of Biscay had been deadly slow and the weather so unseasonably hot that all the vegetables became a total and most malodorous loss; worse still, even the pickled meat had turned rancid and fit only to be sold to the Queen's Purveyor of Victuals for the Sea.

Boom-m-m! The first minute gun's report echoed along the river's banks and reverberated from the Tower's four turrets, then rumbled upstream all the way to Westminster Abbey. Not until the *Primrose's* third minute gun had been discharged did activity manifest itself in Her Majesty's Custom House nearby, also aboard those three scarlet-and-gold-painted war vessels of the Queen's Navy.

The afternoon being windless, smoke from London's thousands of chimneys climbed vertically, bluely veiling the spire of St. Paul's Church. Traitors and others suffering the Queen's displeasure in the Tower, had they tried, might have discerned the stubby little *Primrose*, lying to her anchor and about to disseminate her portentous tidings.

No less a personage than the Captain of the Port, a choleric, red-faced and white-haired gentleman, was rowed alongside demanding to know what was amiss. He swore mightily on hearing of the perfidy in Bilbao and many another Spanish port.

"Icod!" rasped his companion, a gentleman very elegant in doublet and French breeches of claret and silver. "So *that's* why we've fifty vessels so long overdue."

Furious were the oaths and imprecations sworn aboard nearby merchantmen once the near-incredible news of the Spanish King's embargo was bellowed from one vessel to the next. Soon the report reached shore and with the speed of St. Anthony's fire spread from Billingsgate to Smart's Key, over London Bridge and thence up Fish Street and into those dens of vice composing the Cold Harbour district. Cobs—porters lugging tankards of drinking water from Dowgate—soon spread the ill tidings to Queenhithe, Puddledock and up to Paul's Wharf.

Presently a soberly gowned delegation representing the Company of Merchants trading for Spain were rowed out and left their cockboat to rock beside that of the Port Captain. Sour indeed were the expressions of those well-fleshed merchants when in their turn they ascertained the reason for the *Primrose's* profitless return.

Narrowly the Port Captain eyed first John Foster and then his muscular, red-haired mate. "Come now, my good fellows, touching this matter of the Corregidor's commission, do you not embroider upon fact? 'Tis so scurrilous and unknightly a deed with which you charge His Majesty of Spain."

Foster grunted, spat over the rail. " 'Tis small wonder ye doubt such epic treachery, good sirs, yet I've proof. Harry, pray fetch it forth."

There was something ominous about the way the Port Captain's lean shoulders stiffened when he read a translation of the Corregidor's crinkled and water-stained commission.

"God's Wounds!" he growled. "Such knavery passes belief."

Sir Francis Knollys' thin mouth contracted in a smile of savage satisfaction. "Nay, my friend. The Spaniards' intent here is set forth plain as a pikestaff."

Knollys read on until he came to the end, then folded the letter with the greatest of care. "Master Foster, 'tis a fine and gallant thing the way you have won free, but better still ye've brought Drake, Hawkins, Walsingham and the rest the sure proof they've hungered for—that the rumour'd Enterprise of England is no old wives' tale such as my Lord Burghley and Señor de Mendoza would have Her Majesty believe."

"Aye," snapped Sir Peter Waltham, most senior of the merchants. "Here you've proof and to spare, but what of our lost cargoes—and, of course, what of those English mariners rotting in dungeons of the Holy Office?"

Sir Francis Knollys cast a glance at the *Bonaventure* and spoke succinctly. "Master Foster, do you and your Mate, Wyatt, prepare instantly to accompany me." With a bleak grin he added, "You, Master Goodman, I will leave behind that you may reveal to your employers the small facts of this perfidy which so unkindly has flattened their purses."

It was over to Her Majesty's great ship *Bonaventure*—by far the largest vessel in the river—that the Port Captain's barge was now propelled by eight sturdy if ill-smelling oarsmen. During the brief trip across the Pool, Rear-Admiral Sir Francis Knollys, a lean, horse-faced man with eyes as cold and grey as winter ice, levelled question upon question at the *Primrose's* two officers. With each answer Henry Wyatt sensed that this hard-bitten veteran's satisfaction was mounting.

"Now, by God's bright eyeballs," he slapped himself on the knee, "we have them on the hip at last, at last!"

Foster's red-haired mate would have given considerable to learn who those were Knollys referred to by "we". To become obtruded on the fringes of great affairs and famous men was proving stimulating; the young fellow remained far too awestruck even to open his mouth before Rear-Admiral Sir Francis Knollys, who occupied much the same exalted plane as redoubtable, if irascible, Martin Frobisher, those enterprising Hawkinses, John and William, Fenner, Sir William Winter, Sir Richard Grenville and the rest who, in the public esteem, stood barely a cut below that nonpareil, that rambunctious and peerless seaman, Sir Francis Drake. Not only was he the first Englishman to circumnavigate the globe, but the first to come home laden gunwale-deep with the spoils of Peru, the East Indies and certain colonies in the Pacific.

Back in the early fall of 1580 not less than 1½ millions pounds' worth of booty had been discharged from the *Golden Hind's* hold. Small wonder that throughout England, Holland and Protestant France, in manors and cottages alike, toasts were offered in all manner of liquors to the Golden Admiral.

Think of it! He, insignificant Henry Wyatt, hailing from Huntingdonshire, was about to confront that illustrious, almost legendary sea captain.

Beyond doubt the firing of those minute guns and the hurried arrival of the Port Captain's cockboat had evoked interest among the *Bonaventure's* complement. Quite a number of sunburnt, rough-clad fellows had lined the rail and were peering curiously, but silently, down upon the Port Captain's boat.

It had been Drake who had horrified and earned the enmity of many of the older nobility by insisting that any gentleman serving aboard his ships must "hale and draw with the mariners"; a revolutionary innovation. Heretofore no gently born officer would have deigned to soil his hands with the working of the ship in which he sailed. Indeed, in many cases these dainty fellows had perished through their stubborn refusal to lend mariners assistance in a moment of common peril.

Smartly the cockboat glided up under the *Bonaventure's* lofty counter and her rowers tossed oars after a fashion. Wyatt meanwhile stared upwards, delighted by brilliantly painted and gilded carving ornamenting the flagship's stern gallery and poop; for an English vessel it was elaborate, although scarcely to be compared to the decorations to be found on a similar Italian or Spanish vessel. These would have displayed a breath-taking riot of scrolls, fretwork and any quantity of religious figures.

"Yonder on the poop deck," Knollys stated suddenly and with something like awe in his tone, "stands that valiant gentleman to whom you must repeat your tale."

On the highest level of the poop was waiting a short, stocky figure brave in a light blue jarnet cloak and a canary-yellow doublet set off by yellow-red galligaskins—full, unpadded breeches—above silken hose of a similar hue. Yellow, too, was this famous figure's short, sharp-pointed beard, brief moustache and collar-length hair.

Even as the *Bonaventure*'s watch threw a line snaking down to the cockboat, he in the short blue cloak leaned over the red-painted rail, and so, for the first time, Henry Wyatt found himself looking into the face of him whose name was invariably coupled with a curse by every Portuguese and Spaniard.

Drake's small and well-modelled features were set in a face which was florid and rather round; his large, wide-set eyes were of a clear and very bright blue; Wyatt also noted how the great seaman's strong blond brows lifted sharply towards their outer ends, then dipped. By the warm June sunlight a large, pear-shaped pearl could be seen hanging from his left ear while a huge diamond blazed from the heavy golden chain he wore below a small and simple ruff.

Glancing down in some curiosity, Sir Francis Drake became surprised to find his attention attracted to a certain tall, chestnut-haired fellow staring so intently at him. Somehow, he felt as much attracted by the "plain English" air about this young man as by the frank directness of his regard and his short nose, powerful jaw and even, dark red brows. The width of this merchant mariner's shoulders, to Drake's experienced eye, also stood in his favour. Long celebrated for a certain indefinable ability to appraise, as well as to handle, men, the Queen's Admiral found himself puzzled; why should this particular young fellow out of several in the cockboat so arouse his consideration?

To his final hour, Henry Wyatt would never forget any detail of that scene which presently became enacted within the *Bonaventure's* spacious Captain's cabin. A series of heavily leaded windows opening upon the stern gallery had been flung open to admit both the sun and a land breeze blowing in from the Kentish countryside, all blue-green with spring and fragrant with the homely scent of clover, of many a lush meadow and flowering fruit tree.

That Sir Francis Drake was neither self-effacing nor retiring immediately became evident. He sat bolt upright in his tapestry-hung cabin on a massive armchair of oak, marvellously carved and upholstered in stamped scarlet leather. Wyatt reckoned it must once have been among the prized possessions of some Spanish or Portuguese viceroy.

To either side of this compact and ineffably vital figure stood a brilliantly attired aide and a young, fair-haired page boy. The handful of high officers present—they included Flag-Captain Thomas Fenner and Captains John Vaughan and George Fortescue—remained uncovered, quietly waiting for the Queen's Admiral to speak.

To Master Foster, red as any beet with embarrassment, this was astonishing. Aboard any other English man-of-war he had ever visited one could scarcely have heard a word, what with the gentry each attempting to outshout his companion.

Encased in pure yellow-red Italian silk, Francis Drake's sturdy but slightly bowed legs remained thrust straight out before him, with high, scarlet-painted heels resting upon a little tabouret. The thick, brown fingers of his left hand toyed with a handsomely enamelled medallion supported by a heavy gold chain set with innumerable tiny pearls and small rubies.

When everyone had found a place facing his throne-like chair Drake abruptly leaned forward, his short, well-pointed beard aggressively outthrust; challenging as a rapier's point.

"Master Foster, pray favour me with a direct and *unadorned*"—he emphasized the word—"account of your experiences in Bilbao Harbour. Omit nothing, add nothing."

The creaking of one of the *Bonaventure's* yards travelling lazily across their parrels could distinctly be heard amid an anticipatory silence. Well aware of the moment's terrific significance, Drake's hard-bitten Captains clustered about, their weather-beaten, disease-marked and battle-scarred features affording a grotesque contrast to the foppish richness of their raiment—a reflection of the Court's modes.

Once John Foster had commenced to speak, awkwardly and without imagination, Henry Wyatt's dark blue eyes commenced to travel that he might study and memorize the likeness of these great folk. At any time he guessed he now would recognize Captain Henry White of the *Sea Dragon* whose completely hairless head gleamed dully in the light of the stern ports. He wore simple gold rings in his ears by distinction to Flag-Captain Thomas Fenner, who affected huge topazes. Like the Admiral's younger brother, Captain Thomas Drake, brave in hose of yellow-and-green-striped Venetian silk, he was adorned by many finger rings and a huge ruff. This item was starched yellow according to a mode introduced by Mistress Dinghen, a Dutch woman who, for the stiff price of five pounds, would teach anyone how to make starch and the use of it.

His peacetime finery contrasted oddly with Captain James Erizo's leathery countenance, especially because the *White Lion's* Captain had parted with the tip of his left ear during action against the Turks off Lebanon.

These gorgeous gentlemen resembled each other only in two respects, Wyatt decided: in their abundant vitality and keen attention to every word of Master Foster's discourse.

When Rear-Admiral Knollys presented to the Queen's Admiral King Philip's private instructions to his Corregidor, Drake's wide mouth curved into a smile of savage satisfaction, revealing irregular but uncommonly sound and white teeth for that era. He jumped up, and the better to study the incriminating document spread it upon a ponderous refectory table which once had graced the Franciscan monastery in Venta Cruz.

"Come, gentlemen," he invited, "come and read for yourselves what Royal treachery our friend of Spain is contemplating." Whereupon those Captains who could read crowded about Drake's blue-and-silver figure like so many schoolboys peering at a forbidden book. Their brilliant doublets, cloaks and boots of yellow or crimson stamped Spanish leather created a rainbow-like effect in the cabin while they shifted around to obtain a better view of Francisco de Escober's wrinkled and water-stained commission. Various stale and strong perfumes worn by the gentlemen created, Wyatt decided, a curious blend of stinks.

"By the gullet of God!" rasped Captain Edward Winter. "Was ever a fouler piece of villainy conceived and carried out by a Christian monarch?"

"Never!" vehemently agreed the Port Captain. Captain Erizo looked steadily at Drake. "When do we commence reprisals, and where?"

Rear-Admiral Knollys laughed mirthlessly. "I'fackins, Sir Francis, 'twould appear this year we'll not be constrained to sail a voyage out to the Carib Sea for a thrust at the Papists?"

"Aye, we'll find rich and easy pickings off Ushant, Trafalgar Cape and i' the Bay of Biscay." Captain Winter licked his lips so hungrily that Wyatt could readily visualize that sable-bearded individual swarming over some high-sided carrack's rail.

A harsh laugh escaped Francis Drake. "Avast there, Ed! Before we start charging our ordnance someone must kindle some kind of fire in that cold and cautious fish Lord Burghley, or else win the Queen's favour from him."

"A pox on that timid dodderer!" snapped Knollys and employed his fingers thoughtfully to comb a heavy, dark brown beard trimmed into twin points. "God knows William Cecil at the last minute has stayed our hand against the Dons time and again, but when he reads *this*"—he tapped the Corregidor's commission—"will he dare to say us nay again?"

"Not openly. But I fear he'll bespeak half-measures." Drake's voice soared, filled the *Bonaventure's* hot and overcrowded cabin. "I've beaten this wretched, forsworn King in the Escorial before, time and again, and with but feeble ships and sickened crews. I've made this same Philip's haughty viceroys whine for mercy, I've sailed where I listed throughout his dominions, I've sacked his cities, taken or sunk his treasure ships and freed his slaves. Alone and all but unaided, I did it despite William Cecil and other snivelling lack-guts at Court."

The Golden Admiral glared about. "Do any of you doubt that I'm the Master Seaman of England? Of the age? Does anyone else wot what *I* know of navigation, of ship construction, of gunnery?"

No one spoke but Wyatt noted several flushed faces and sidelong glances.

"Aye! I'll shatter the might of Spain forever and a day, if"—like the skilled orator he was, Drake paused—"if the Queen's Majesty grants me permission to harry this Royal Judas *in his homeland* I'll beat Philip to the very ground."

In a characteristically abrupt gesture Drake turned to his aide. "Order my barge readied alongside within the half-hour and have a relay of lusty oarsmen aboard. 'Tis a long pull upstream to Hampton Court.

"Captain Fenner, pray ready yourself to accompany me upriver." The Admiral's gold collar glittered he swung so sharply about. "Captains Winter, Moone and you, Master Richard Hawkins, repair to the Port Captain's office with Captain Foster. There you will make every effort to ascertain exactly how many of our ships have cleared from all ports for Spanish and Portuguese ports within the past two months." Unexpectedly he winked a brilliant blue eye. "And—er—do not by any chance underestimate their number."

To Henry Wyatt's vast astonishment, he then added with a singularly winning smile: "Young Wyatt, I pray you to attend me immediately upriver. At Court I've learned that eye-witness information carries a deal of conviction."

The Captains commenced quitting Drake's sunlit cabin, bending their heads to avoid bumping its carved deck beams and gold-leaf-covered bosses. On a door fashioned of heavy oak, a coat-of-arms granted to the Golden Admiral had been tastefully reproduced in very vivid colours. A herald would have described it thus: "A shield sable, a fen wavy between two stars argent; its crest a globe terrestrial, a great-ship, or, under sail guided by a cable held in a hand emerging from a cloud argent."

Master John Foster had started for the companionway when Drake caught him by his sleeve of coarse brown-grey frieze. "Tell me, my good man, was it you who first suspected this Corregidor's true purpose in boarding you?"

"Lor' love ye no, Yer Excellency, 'twere my mate here, Harry Wyatt. He's young, but he's alive and owns a shrewd eye for trickery—as I first learned in the Levant yesteryear."

"So honest an answer," Drake boomed, "deserves as honest a reward. Richard!" Imperiously he beckoned his page-boy—the lad might have been all of twelve. "In yonder coffer you'll discover a silver goblet 'graved with my arms. Pray fetch this cup that I may present it to an honest, plain-spoken mariner."

CHAPTER V

AT HAMPTON COURT PALACE

ALTHOUGH he had witnessed something of the gaudy pomp and glittering circumstance attendant upon royal and religious occasions both in Spain and in Portugal, it somehow had never occurred to Henry Wyatt, any more than to most Englishmen, that, in this year of 1585, Henry the Eighth's and Anne Boleyn's homely, red-haired daughter existed amid splendour of a somewhat comparable nature.

Staring shorewards, while Sir Francis Drake's blue-and-silver-painted barge was steered for the massive water gate to Hampton Court Palace, it seemed as if a congregation of brilliant, giant butterflies had collected upon and were moving about various velvety lawns advancing down to the Thames' reedy banks. Numerous tame white swans paddled curiously towards the arriving small boat but a few wild ones among them sprang up from among the rushes and flapped off up the glassy stream.

On lawns beyond the Water Gallery lounged or strolled dozens of ladies and gentlemen attired in colours more vivid than any collection of tropical birds.

At regular intervals stalwart yeomen of the Royal Guard walked their posts with burnished halberds shouldered. These lusty fellows wore uniforms of green and white—the Tudor colours—and displayed on their broad chests a red Tudor rose adorned by Queen Elizabeth's personal cipher, ER, embroidered in pure gold thread that would never tarnish.

Smartly, guards on duty at the Water Gate presented halberds when Sir Francis Drake stepped ashore, a short, sturdy and dapper figure in blue, yellow and red. He was followed by his Flag-Captain, Thomas Fenner, resplendent in a doublet and trunks of plum and silver and wearing draped negligently over one shoulder a short cloak of bright yellow Moorish leather.

Henry Wyatt, garbed in a dark brown kersey shirt, leather jerkin, grey woollen galligaskins and stockings of unbleached linen, presented a drab contrast for all his muscular figure, coppery complexion and gleaming, dark red hair.

After passing under the Water Gate itself the trio re-emerged into sunlight and followed a Sergeant of the Guard along a path skirting the famous Lantern Arbour situated on a low rise. Bordering this broad and evenly gravelled path, which wound on between hedges of well-clipped yew, were a series of curious stone effigies known as "the King's Beasts". Antelopes, lions, greyhounds, dragons, bulls, hinds and leopards and representations of many other creatures stood on stone bases; for some reason each of them supported a weather-vane.

Her Majesty's Chamberlain, a venerable old gentleman wearing an immense white ruff, appeared bearing a long ebony rod topped by a hand skilfully carved out of ivory. He hurried forward, his costume of unrelieved black velvet at marked variance with the dazzling brilliance of the Queen's other courtiers.

To Drake's request for an immediate audience the Chamberlain spread apologetic hands and explained that Her Majesty at the moment was in her privy closet conferring with William, Lord Burghley, and that Councillor's bitterest rival, Sir Francis Walsingham. Under no consideration could she be disturbed.

"Am I indeed so unimportant?" Drake coloured and snapped fingers in vexation, but yet managed to assume a patient manner. "None the less, I beg you to convey my humble service to Her Gracious

Majesty and bespeak my urgency; indeed, my lord, I and my young companion here bear tidings of imminent and deadly import."

"I am—to—to *speak to the Queen*!" stammered Wyatt.

"Aye."

"But, noble sirs, I—I have neither the m-manners nor the s-speech, nor the g-garb to enter the Royal Presence."

"Cheer up, man," Fenner encouraged. "True, your garments are as dun as any jackdaw's, yet 'tis well said that Gloriana can discern a loyal heart beneath plain attire; besides, she dotes on what she calls 'mere English'."

Wyatt straightened, tried to control an unfamiliar tremor in his voice. "But—but, pray, how sh-shall I conduct m-myself?"

Drake laughed, clapped the merchant sailor on his shoulder. "Why, God bless you, all you have to do when you enter the Presence is to drop on to one knee and wait until Her Majesty bids you rise. Then take no fright but speak straight out and you will fare the better for it.

"Remember now, Master Wyatt," he fixed him with piercing blue eyes, "you must dwell on the sad havoc the King of Spain's treachery has wrought among our shipping and the losses of revenue to the Crown that must follow. It would be well," Drake bent so close that a pungent perfume he favoured was more noticeable than ever, "innocently, mind you, if you were to remind Her Majesty that these ships and supplies stolen from her are intended to feed and equip King Philip's *flotas* being raised against the security of her own realm and person."

A seemingly interminable half-hour elapsed during which Drake strode back and forth across an oak-panelled antechamber decorated by several of those colourful tapestries from Holland which had taken the Royal fancy. Hampton Court's well-polished oaken floors were softened not by the customary rushes but by a vast turkey-red carpet which effectively silenced the restless tread of Drake's high red heels.

By twos, threes and sometimes by the dozen, various courtiers passed through the antechamber; most of them bowed readily, almost obsequiously, to the Queen's Admiral then treated that great man's oddly assorted companions to unabashed stares.

Wyatt's perturbation diminished proportionately as his interest in these glittering, gaudy creatures mounted. Never had he fancied such extravagant costumes to exist. Men affected ruffs of a dozen exaggerated designs, the most elaborate of which Captain Winter explained, *sotto voce*, were called percardels and piccadillies—the latter designed by one Higgins, called the Master Tailor of London. All about were padded trunks of slashed and diapered satin, Morisco capes and gloves of perfumed leather, doublets of turquoise-blue Genoa velvet, and gowns—really cloaks—trimmed in miniver, wolf and marten.

The dazed young Master's Mate soon became dazzled and utterly astounded by the plethora of jewellery in evidence. Why, a gallant might be seen wearing as many as ten finger rings, two or three neck chains and enormous pearl earrings in addition to a gem-encrusted pomander and toothpick case. Diamonds, emeralds, sapphires and other precious stones flashed from the guards and petit point sheaths of the Italian rapiers and poignards that swung to every belt.

Quite as varied as the ruffs was the trimming of beards performed by the Court's tonsors. Some of these highly perfumed and painted courtiers favoured the Dutch mode, others fancied French or Spanish cuts while still others had caused their red or yellow dyed beards to be trimmed in the alley or forked style; a few gentlemen favoured the spade, the bravado or the bodkin trim.

As for the ladies, Wyatt scarce could credit his vision. Almost universally they affected masses of "borrowed" hair frizzed and dyed red and adorned with seed pearls, small emeralds or rubies in deference to the Queen's example.

Their lace ruffs, edging a *décolletage* which more often than not revealed the upper rims of their nipples, were marvels of delicacy and elaboration and sustained in position by under-proppers. These elegant creatures wore standing ruffs laboriously purled into points and folds; others among them preferred enormous wing ruffs and a few displayed two or three lace ruffs turned over, the one on top of the next. All the ladies wore gloves of bright yellow, blue or red, to the backs of which pearls and gems of all sorts had been stitched, while from their girdles dangled little gold-rimmed mirrors which continually winked and glittered.

It was their complexions that most amazed the *Primrose's* Mate. Old, middle-aged and even very young ladies had so enamelled their cheeks that they shone white and lifeless as gravestones. Further, they had painted round red spots on their cheeks like poppets; having plucked out their natural eyebrows—the Queen, it seemed had none—these, too, were painted on.

Noticing his companion's preoccupation, Winter commented: "You're of the opinion these *grandes dames* look thin and pale? Well, 'tis because Her Majesty, being sallow and gaunt, these silly creatures do eat ashes, fine gravel and tallow in order to achieve a similar bleak colour."

Drake turned to Flag-Captain Fenner, meanwhile playing absently with the pearl pendant from his ear. " 'Tis now abundant clear the King of Spain means to launch his attack within a matter of months. What say you?"

"Aye. The intent is beyond question—as proved by the commission."

"Well, Thomas, please God I'll be allowed to prevent this knavish assault."

"Aye. But how?"

"I've ways and——" He broke off in order to bow profoundly towards the Duke of Gloucester and anxiously await that great nobleman's response. When it came, Wyatt observed that the greeting was haughty and reserved—as were the salutations of most of the ancient nobiity.

"But we're so pitiful unready," growled Fenner. "If only Her Majesty and her Councillors lent an ear to your many cautionings."

"Aye, there's the rub. They have not and now 'tis late—*late*! If only Gloriana three years gone by had not, at the last hour, forbade my sailing against Spain itself we'd read naught of the 'Enterprise of England', as they call it, this day."

Fenner blinked. "Perhaps after Sir Francis Walsingham hears of this affair at Bilbao he will carry the day."

Out in the sunlight Yeomen of the Guard were being relieved to a blare of silver trumpets and the dry rattle of many drums. Soon the Court would disperse for supper, that second and last meal of their day.

At long last the Lord Chamberlain reappeared, bald head showing like a pink melon above his enormous ruff. He appeared to stoop under the weight of the heavy chain of office slung above his sable robes. "Her Majesty will now deign to receive you."

Drake smiled, readjusted the set of his short Flemish ruff and pushed back into position a stray lock of yellow hair before checking the pearl buttons securing his doublet.

Again the mariner's knees commenced to quiver. God above! He, simple Harry Wyatt of St. Neots, was about to *appear before the Queen*! *The Queen*—that remote semi-deity who reigned supreme over all England and directed the destinies of near five million subjects.

By the Great Harry! What would the villagers of St. Neots say when they learned that old Edmund Wyatt's son not only had seen but actually had been received by Her Majesty? How pridefully sweet Kate Ibbott's grey eyes would glisten!

"Come, come, Master Wyatt, you've no call to appear so terrified." Drake patted his forearm. "Her Majesty is very human, and, as a rule, the most kindly of ladies. Stand you straight now and walk unafraid as you would on the *Primrose's* poop deck."

" 'Tis all very well for Sir Francis Drake so to advise," the terror-stricken Master's Mate told himself but then found consolation in the recollection that the Golden Admiral once had been quite as poor, friendless and as undistinguished as himself.

Aye, come to think on it, Francis, the eldest of Edmund Drake's twelve children, was rumoured not even to have possessed shoes when first he shipped aboard a clumsy howker trading between Zeeland and the Medway. This son of a poor Protestant rector had come so far partially through the influence of his relative, John Hawkins, but chiefly on his own merits.

Outside a handsome walnut door to the Queen's privy closet a pair of gigantic Yeomen stiffened and presented crimson-tasselled halberds. The Chamberlain's fur-trimmed black gown fluttered sedately along a short corridor in which a fragrance of potpourri grew ever stronger.

"His Honour, Admiral Sir Francis Drake and Captain Thomas Fenner!" the Chamberlain announced in a low but penetrating voice. "Accompanying them is a seafaring person by the name of Wyatt."

Rays of late afternoon sunlight were pouring through tall mullioned windows with such rich intensity that they lent life to a series of tapestries lining the walls of a spacious, oak-panelled chamber and drew flashes from the collars and rings of two grey-bearded gentlemen who stood just within.

The sunbeams also wrought copper hues amid the elaborately puffed, frizzed and curled hair of her who was sitting, stiffly erect, upon a low-backed armchair.

Wyatt's most vivid impression was of small, but immensely vital and brilliant black eyes shining beside a slightly hooked nose. Elizabeth Tudor's features had been so whitened by cosmetics that they appeared to have been chiselled out of Carian marble, and so lent cruel emphasis to a great circle of rouge applied to either cheek. Next he became aware of innumerable deep wrinkles criss-crossing his monarch's features.

The *Primrose's* Mate roused from his bemusement in time to note that Drake and Fenner had already dropped onto one knee and so remained with heads slightly bent. Meanwhile they managed their rapiers in such a fashion that these stuck diagonally upwards from beneath their gaudy leather cloaks like the tails of pheasant-setting dogs on point.

When Wyatt followed suit his ponderous sea-boots creaked so noisily that the mariner's always ruddy features flushed a richer crimson and his embarrassment grew the greater because he had knelt upon his left knee—of course it should have been his right. When, hurriedly, he shifted his weight several courtiers lining the audience chamber's far wall snickered.

"Arise, gentlemen." The Queen's voice was harsh and anything but melodious, yet it was by no means unpleasant. "And what is this vast urgency, Sir Francis, which fetches you in greater than usual impatience into our presence?"

Drake's short blue figure advanced a few steps into the sunlight where his yellow hair and beard became touched with gold.

"A matter of the greatest moment to Your Majesty; I offer for your attention an affair so perfidious and of such immediate peril to your person and to this your realm that I would I had possessed wings to speed me here the sooner."

Quite deliberately, the Queen picked up a pomander of gilded silver and held it beneath pinched nostrils while studying, none too patiently, the sturdy figure before her.

"A pox on you, Sir Francis! Must you always come flying to us? Must you ever be a purveyor of alarums and tall tales of conspiracy and treachery? My Lord Burghley, do you wot of anyone more possessed of hatred for the Spaniards?"

"—Nor a worthier chastiser of them, Your Majesty," swiftly interjected Sir Francis Walsingham.

Elizabeth set down the pomander and settled back in her chair. "Out with your plaint, my dear Admiral. What *can* have frighted you this time? Do you wish again to sail against my cousin of Spain?" The Queen's tone was mocking, yet before Drake had spoken half a minute her amused expression vanished under that ghastly coat of enamel.

She leaned far forward and spoke in shrill accents. "Sirrah! Take care how you speak. If what you say is not truly so, then beware our wrath!"

Again Drake dropped on to one knee and, seizing the Queen's hand, kissed it humbly. "May I lodge forever in the Tower if I exaggerate one whit of King Philip's villainy. That Your Majesty may hear first-hand from one who witnessed all that chanced aboard the *Primrose*, I have fetched here her Master's Mate." Drake's bright blue eyes were blazing when he rose and fairly hauled Henry Wyatt forward.

"Come closer, young sir," the Queen directed pettishly. "Nay, do not kneel again but give us a plain-spoken account of exactly what chanced in Bilbao Harbour. And," she added, directing acid glances at Drake and Fenner, "make sure that your tale gains naught in the telling."

An unfamiliar tightness suddenly constricted Wyatt's throat and forced that tall, copper-complexioned young man to gulp several times before he could command his voice at all. At first, his head continued to swim at this terrifying proximity to his Queen and he spoke stammeringly. Not until he was describing the Corregidor's arrival and that hungry gentleman's inexplicable departure half-way through dinner did his voice deepen and steady itself. The Queen shifted onto the edge of her chair and her long bony fingers, loaded with rings, gradually tightened until they suggested glittering talons.

"How many were you aboard the *Primrose*?" Elizabeth broke in.

"Eight-and-twenty, Your Highness—I—I mean, Your Majesty!" Wyatt blushed to the roots of his dark red hair.

"—And the Dons?"

"Ninety-seven or so, we reckoned, Your Majesty."

The Queen drew a deep breath and stared thoughtfully across the room at Lord Burghley standing mute and obviously thunderstruck. On the other hand Sir Francis Walsingham was making no effort to conceal a satisfaction bordering upon elation.

"A very pretty bicker," Walsingham observed. "How many of the enemy were slain, my good fellow?"

"Above a dozen—and, surely, as many more lost their lives by drowning, my lord."

"And how many Englishmen fell?"

"Only poor John Tristram was sped, sir."

"Would it not appear that Your Majesty was uncommon well served in this matter?" Drake demanded. "It could not have turned out better had I been there myself. And now, Master Wyatt, pray relate how you fished that serpent-tongued dog Don Francisco de Escober out of the harbour."

Henry the Eighth's ageing daughter devoted full attention on the speaker, her little jet eyes intent, chin and hawk-like nose out-thrust.

At precisely the right moment and with no little flourish Drake produced King Philip's infamous commission. "Here, Your Majesty, is that very document Don Francisco offered in excuse for his treachery."

Through a gold-rimmed reading-glass she wore suspended from her girdle the Queen of England then read the whole document in deliberation and with great care. Her painted brows continually rose and fell until eventually she flung down the document, and commenced to curse her "dear Cousin Philip" as earnestly as any whore in Cold Harbour on being cheated of her fee. Certainly no Royal figure of the age had been half so thoroughly—and obscenely—reviled when Elizabeth at length was forced to pause to catch her breath.

"But this is monstrous!" she panted. "How dares that long-snouted Hapsburg swine, that lying, blue-jawed villain, to prize our ships and imprison our subjects—the very ships and men we sent to succour him in his hour of need?"

In a mounting fury Elizabeth of England seized a porcelain sand-caster designed to dry ink on official documents and flung it blindly across the room. It narrowly missed Henry Wyatt's head, crashed against the panelling, and rained fragments upon nearby gentlemen.

"By God's great glory! Philip shall pay dear for this treachery." Her whole bony figure quivered. "Aye, smile an you will, you two Francises." She glared first at Walsingham then at Drake, standing quietly to one side, his blue doublet and yellow-red hose showing up bright against the dark oak panelling.

"Mayhap we would have been wiser to heed you, and not my Lord Burghley. 'Twould appear the pair of you understand the true measure of that canting rogue in the Escorial. Why, oh why, have we been cozened by cautious strictures and stupid optimisms? Out upon you, William Cecil! Ever you have seduced us from that boldness which alone can preserve us from the Papist Powers."

Sir Francis Drake barely succeeded in suppressing a smile. None knew better than he that Elizabeth herself, not Burghley, at the last instant had recalled his fleet in 1581 on the very eve of sailing against Spain. Not since the reign of John Plantagenet had so vacillating, whim-ridden, and dangerously indecisive a monarch occupied the throne of England as this raddled, over-bejewelled old woman across the room.

Entirely typical of her character had been that obstinacy with which, even at this late date, Elizabeth continued to refuse to sign a death warrant for Mary of Scotland for all that her pretty, thrice-married cousin, beyond any question or doubt, had been linked with three assassination plots.

Surely, mused Drake, a stateswoman of even average intelligence must long ago have perceived that the continued existence of Mary

Stuart constituted a cause, a rally point for not only the powerful Catholic princes of the Continent but also for those great nobles in Scotland and in the North of England who yet clung to the Church of Rome.

Shrill as any peacock, the Queen raged until spittle flew from her encarmined lips, and at last she wheeled upon Sir Francis Drake.

"Damme, Sir Francis," she shrilled, "on the morrow you are to drum for crews; you will victual and otherwise supply our fleet, and we'll so encourage private ventures you will all not want for ordnance and men sufficient to deal this Hapsburg cheat such a blow betwixt wind and water that he will never forget it!"

"This blow, Your Majesty, I trust will be directed against King Philip *in his own realm*?" Drake suggested smoothly. Lord, how long had he not struggled and intrigued for just such permission?

"Aye!" wheezed the Queen. "You are to harry my Royal cousin's coasts, you will sink or seize his vessels and so plunder his ports that this priest-ridden Judas will squeal for mercy, pay indemnities and disgorge my ships, cargoes and men!"

Walsingham made a pretence of resettling his cartwheel ruff while flinging a quick look at Drake. Here, at long last, that Councillor was deciding, a real opportunity presented itself to regain the Queen's first favour and so wage war against the Spaniards. Long since he had been convinced that the princes of the Counter Reformation were planning an invasion, pitiless in execution and fatal to those religious and personal liberties so close to the hearts of all true-born English.

Indeed, it now appeared, thanks to this affair of the *Primrose*, that he and Drake soon could undertake certain plans, long in preparation, for an assault upon Philip's home ports. Sir Francis, whose ambitions and abilities were boundless, he felt would prove bold and unorthodox in his strategy. Although an upstart and considerable of a braggart, this tempestuous sea captain from Devon none the less admittedly was a prince among navigators.

His enemies, of course, had whispered that Sir Bernard Drake, a West Country gentleman, had once boxed this parvenu's ears for daring to adopt his coat of arms. Whether this were true or not, the Queen had granted her favourite Admiral a coat of arms indisputably his own, while administering at the same time a sly dig at pompous Sir Bernard. Clever courtiers at once had perceived that the ship appearing on Sir Francis' own crest displayed a wyvern or griffin caught upside down in its rigging. Oddly enough, a wyvern formed the principal device of Sir Bernard Drake's arms.

Walsingham's weary and deeply lined features relaxed into a reminiscent grin when he recalled Sir Bernard's helpless rage.

As became a Privy Councillor and principal secretary, Walsingham possessed a long memory. For years he had held the office together with Lord Burghley.

For instance, Walsingham could call clearly to mind the day upon which Captain Francis Drake had first appeared, bumptious and ill-dressed yet infinitely embarrassed, before the Throne. And now he was known as the Golden Admiral in Court circles and all through England for that matter. Why not? What other sea captain had produced even a fraction of such treasure for Her Majesty's privy purse?

Sir Francis Walsingham next shifted his attention to that not unhandsome and well-set-up young fellow standing at Drake's elbow. It crossed his mind that perhaps here was represented a new breed of Englishman which the realm of late had been producing in generous numbers. Standing at least a head taller than Admiral Drake, young Wyatt suggested deference to authority combined with innate self-respect; and a certain alertness of manner.

When at last Elizabeth ended her tirade, she settled back in her chair the better to survey this coarsely dressed figure standing rigid and completely bemused before her. She exposed the black stumps of her teeth in a rare smile and said, "How many Spaniards fell before your own particular thrust-and-cut?"

"Why-y, God love you, Ma'am, beyond the Corregidor's lieutenant, who pinked me i' the shoulder and whose bilbo I now wear, I slew two, perchance another. Amid that hurly-burly 'twas impossible to tell."

The Queen broke into cackling laughter. " 'Hurly-burly'? Yon's a good mere English. Mark you, gentlemen, Master Wyatt employs no mongrel French such as '*mêlée*'." A massive necklace of emeralds and diamonds glittered when the Queen turned to an equerry. "Edward! Our pocket."

Even Drake was startled, so rarely did Elizabeth Tudor call for her privy purse. Throughout the courts of Europe Her Majesty of England—and with reason—was rumoured to be closer with her pounds, shillings and pence than bark on a birch tree. "We will bestow upon this worthy young mariner five golden pounds—and of full weight, mark you, Edward—as encouragement to like deeds of prowess."

Wyatt's features flushed brick red and, dropping on to one knee, he looked up into the old woman's raddled features. "God bless Your Majesty! I—I scarce know how to——"

"—Since you do not know, do not attempt it." Elizabeth actually patted Wyatt's shoulder. "It would please us if you would seek service aboard one of our ships-of-war. Sir Francis, we charge you to find Master Wyatt a suitable station."

Confusion thickened Wyatt's tongue more than ever on remembering patient grey-eyed Kate Ibbott. "I crave Your Majesty's indulgence, but—but I—I long have been m—minded to command a vessel of my own."

Sir Francis and Captain Fenner started and Walsingham frowned: it had been long since that a subject had dared to cavil at the Queen's expressed wish.

"Pray forgive this seeming impertinence, Your Gracious Majesty," Drake begged, darting an angry sidewise glance at Wyatt. "This fellow is but a plain and honest mariner."

The Queen picked up her pomander, sniffed it. "Go to, Sir Francis—and you, young fellow, feel free to employ our gold towards the purchase of a vessel an you must. We warrant you'll use it to good purpose—and in our interest. And now, gentlemen," she collected the silent courtiers with a glance, "let us to the Council Chamber."

Elizabeth of England gathered voluminous skirts of golden brocade and, a little wearily, for her costume, farthingale and all, weighed nearly thirty pounds, stumped out of the Privy Cabinet followed by Walsingham, Burghley, Drake and Fenner. Henry Wyatt was left behind, tongue-tied and feeling uncommon churlish.

CHAPTER VI

AT THE SIGN OF THE RED KNIGHT

LIKE a gigantic warren, London's waterfront all the way from Queenhithe to Billingsgate became alive to the wildest of rumours, combined with a mounting sense of outrage over the treachery at Bilbao and in other Spanish harbours. Hardly a merchant, ship owner, chandler, victualler or sailmaker but had been affected to a ruinous, or to a lesser, degree by the Spanish King's incredible perfidy.

In streets, alleys and waterside courts such as the Puddle Dock and Cold Harbour ragged women, brazen trollops and gaunt, grimy children howled or maintained a numbed silence, being convinced that lovers, sons and fathers never again would be seen about Fish Street; precious few Protestants ever reappeared once they had been dragged down into the Holy Office's ample dungeons.

Ever louder arose the clamour for reprisal. Blood-chilling threats were to be heard on every quay and aboard those hundreds of little vessels which lay berthed or at anchor in the Thames all the way downstream from London Bridge to St. Katherines.

No positive report yet had circulated concerning the departure date of a punitive squadron but even the stupidest clod shoving his barrow along Thames Street felt that the passage of a month would see the redoubtable Golden Admiral leading a fleet out of Plymouth. By Saint Peter's toenails, *there* was the lad who really understood how to make the Spaniards squeal! Certain older mariners, however, were not so sanguine concerning the chances of an expedition launched against Spain herself.

" 'Tis one thing," growled a toothless old fellow lacking his left arm, "to run down and plunder well-nigh-defenceless vessels i' the Southern Ocean or to sack an unarmed city on the Main, but I wot well 'tis a different matter to challenge the Spanish King's ships i' their home waters and under the guns of the great castellos which guard Philip's ports."

Although the Red Knight was a tavern patronized by mariners and sea captains of the better sort the place remained, nonetheless, a dark and malodorous hutch in which oaths and imprecations flew like hailstones Henry Wyatt decided while elbowing his way into its tap-room. Why had he and Peter Hopton decided to rendezvous here whenever one or both happened to be in port? Soon he ascertained that a ship had made port from the Low Countries that afternoon bearing news of fresh oppressions and a persecution of Dutch Protestants by the Duke of Parma, King Philip's grimly able viceroy and Captain-General over that stubbornly rebellious dependency.

So low were this tap-room's smoke-blackened roof beams that several times Henry Wyatt was forced to duck his head ere he took place at a trestle table dripping with spilt beer. Once his eyes had adjusted themselves to the smoky gloom—the habit of tobacco smoking had been growing by leaps and bounds—he noted that although the majority of the Red Knight's patrons were quite as English as himself there also were present a number of Dutch and German mariners. Probably these had wandered over from the Steelyard where vessels from cities belonging to the Hanseatic League were wont to tie up. Red-faced serving wenches, perspiring freely under gowns of coarse wool, staggered about bearing trays of wooden piggins that overflowed ale, mead and honest English small beer.

All round the big chestnut-haired Master's Mate the usual fanciful tales were being recounted by mariners new returned from the Levant, from Mauritania on the west coast of Africa or from the frozen White Sea of Russia.

The magic word "America" attracted Wyatt's attention so, all the while protecting a well-filled noggin of ale, he made his way towards a long table set immediately before a window, the tiny panes of which had been so often repaired with lead that but little light could penetrate into the tap-room. Firmly he elbowed his way to a spot from which he could glimpse the tale teller, a regular giant of a man at the moment engaged in earnestly bussing a full-bosomed serving wench.

At first he scarce recognized this bronzed, yellow-bearded fellow as his first cousin, Peter Hopton, but when he did he raised such a shout of incredulous delight that several patrons over-set their tankards and others gripped their side arms.

"Is it indeed you, Cousin Peter?" he called, surging forward. "And how many riches have you fetched back from Mexico?"

"By Beelzebub's dong, 'tis Harry himself!" Peter spilled his blowsy, squealing doxy on to the floor, then came charging through the crowd like a bull through a clump of alders.

The two entered into that bear hug of deep affection which is peculiar to Anglo-Saxons, then pounded each other vigorously between the shoulders. The other patrons saw that while Wyatt and his cousin stood almost of a height Peter was by far the bigger and more powerful of the two.

"Avast, friends," boomed a gap-toothed fellow speaking with a Cornish accent, "we were a-hearing about Zur Richard Grenville's latest voyage." He pointed a dirty forefinger at Peter Hopton. "Speak, ain't it true that in America the sand there is of the purest gold and a body has only to scoop up all he's a mind to?"

Peter shook a shaggy yellow head. "Nay, friend, you mistook me. The land I've visited lies far to the north o' the gold and silver mines o' Mexico and Peru."

"Then there are diamonds?" persisted the Cornishman.

"No rubies or diamonds either, friend."

"But surely pearls?"

"Aye, to be sure there are some pearls," Wyatt's cousin conceded. "But the true richness lies in the land——"

"What land?"

"Why, on the Island o' Roanoke, so named by the Naturals who inhabit it."

"I haff heard in North are many fine furs?" broke in a big Dutch shipmaster. "Furs sell well anywhere."

"Aye, there are furs to be had in Virginia, Mynheer—masses of them, and with small trouble," the wanderer declared, "but hearken to me, fellows, the real wealth o' this great far land lies not in gold or jewels or spices or furs, but in the wondrous fertility o' its soil."

Wyatt eased himself into a position next to the wall where he could view not only his cousin's broad red countenance, but also the ring of rough, bearded faces crowding in; some looked incredulous, some greedy, some hopeful, but all were curious.

"This land of Virginia is vast and stretches endlessly, no one knows how far, towards the west," Peter explained over his black leather jack of ale. "The rivers, which are huge, at times swarm so thick wi' the most succulent of fish that they can be dipped up in a bucket. Fallow deer, elks, bisons and many similar creatures abound in the forests whilst waterfowl are so plentiful that their flight darkens the sky. Moreover very small effort is required to grow corn of all sorts."

He grinned while deliberately viewing his hot, decidedly smelly audience. "Deeming us gods or the spirits of their ancestors returned to earth, the Naturals of Virginia worshipped us, laboured for us, and e'en made us free gift o' all the victuals we could consume."

"What o' their women?" a hoarse voice demanded. "Be they comely and agreeable?"

"None more so, in their way. Their principal men deemed it an honour to offer their daughters to the commonest of us mariners—and as many as he could handle. *I know!*" Peter added, rousing a bawdy ripple of laughter.

"You'll take oath there ain't no gold in the country of Virginia?" the gap-toothed man demanded.

"None that we discovered."

"Silver?"

"Only a little, and that obtained by barter wi' tribes further to the southwards."

The serving girl Hopton had been kissing made bold to sidle up and slip her arm through his. Hopefully she lifted a wearied, once-pretty face. "In this America o' yours, Ducky, are there great cities like Lunnon where maybe a poor lass could find an 'ome and an 'usband?"

A guffaw attested the disappearance of Hopton's hand beneath the wench's petticoats.

"The Indians do indeed construct villages, Dolly, some o' them even surrounded by a rough palisado, but in all verity, you'll come across nothing like Cartagena, Nombre de Dios, or those great cities which Dons have built in San Domingo, Mexico and Peru."

"Faugh! A pox on such a poor land," grunted the gap-toothed man and, hawking loudly, turned away. "Given the say, I'll take me chances on the Spanish Main."

"But there's space out there, ain't there?" persisted a big, round-shouldered fellow wearing the singed leather apron of a blacksmith. "There's space out there for a fellow to breathe, to watch the sun rise and the trees blossom on his own land?"

Peter offered the smith a draught from his own tankard. "God love you, my friend, any industrious man jack presently in this sink hole o' London could, wi' small effort, win for his own holding a—a whole township or a hundred in this fine new land."

The smith shoved his way to the wanderer's side. "Ye mean, sir, that I, a poor landless dog, could become a—a *landholder* out in America?"

"I vow, friend smith, there is no reason why not. The richness o' this new soil surpasses imagination—and I am farm bred. Although Sir Walter Raleigh has not yet given it a name, 'tis deemed certain he will christen this colony 'Virginia' in honour of our Gracious Queen's virgin state."

It was remarkable that not a single snicker arose, for all that the dullest subject present was aware that this, indeed, was a courtesy title if ever there had been one. What if gossips did murmur concerning Essex, Leicester, Raleigh, Sidney and "little Lord Beaumont" among other illustrious gentlemen?

The atmosphere grew thicker, the sour reek of stale sweat soaked into wool grew stronger.

"You vow there's no gold in North America?" The gap-toothed man seemed unwilling to credit his hearing.

"None that we found, though the Naturals tell tall tales o' very rich mines to the westward of their kingdom."

No gold quotha? Saving the smith and that trull clinging so hopefully to Peter Hopton's arm the company lost interest and drifted away to replenish their beer pots.

Once they had departed Wyatt managed the Spanish lieutenant's handsome bilbo in order to permit his occupancy of a settle beside his cousin. "You are indeed just returned from beyond the seas?"

"Nay, 'tis been the best part of a year since we sighted Plymouth Hoe, but now, at last, I am on my way home to wed Master Tom Fuller's daughter—a duty I long should have fulfilled."

"She may be already wedded."

"Well, then there are the Marquand twins—they should be near sixteen now," laughed Wyatt, "and more sought after than untried virgins."

"And what makes you dream you'll entice such coy young doxies into a hayloft?"

"Their vanity. The silly little tits ape as best they may the gay dress o' the Court. Here," after casting a quick glance about Peter tapped a sizable leather wallet and said in an undertone, "I carry certain pearls such as will cause your eyes to start out like unto those upon a fiddler crab. Within this is enough to provide many a night's frolic and perchance add a few acres to my sire's holding." Suddenly serious, he directed a quick glance at his cousin. "How long since ye've visited St. Neots?"

A grimace altered Wyatt's expression. "Not since we departed together above two years agone." He gathered his legs under him, gazed steadily, fondly upon Peter Hopton. "Since then I've sailed to the Levant in the Dominions o' the Grand Seigneur o' the Turks—and twice to Spain——" He commenced an account of the affair at Bilbao but Peter interrupted on a distracting subject.

"I trust ye've had good tidings from sweet-voiced Kate Ibbott?"

A frown momentarily merged Wyatt's rather heavy red brows. "Alas, no, Peter, not within this year. And I've had never a line from my sire." He shrugged. " 'Tis not to be wondered at, though, since they've scarce known where to write."

"Harry."

Wyatt leaned further over the table but avoided a puddle of spilled ale. "Aye?"

"I'm minded to journey home to Huntingdonshire."

"And so am I, ere I dicker for a vessel o' mine own. 'Twould be a main fine thing to see the old people, especially, Coz, were you to journey along."

Peter paused long enough to turn his head and bellow for more ale and some slices of gammon before clapping his cousin on the back. "Aye, so 'twould. Rest easy, Harry. I'm your man. I reckon there'll be time enow to journey thither and back afore Sir Walter Raleigh collects a further expedition to this Island of Roanoke I spoke of just now. Being mariner yourself, you'll wot that such never sail even close to the appointed day."

"True enough," Wyatt agreed, employing the point of his case knife to spear a succulent slab of ham from its bed of onions. "I've no taste to travel afoot so tomorrow let us discover what manner of craft may be sailing for the Wash. Meantime, lend me your ear, I've a rare tale concerning certain occasions in Bilbao Harbour."

Peter's bright blue eyes flew wider open. " 'Fore God's love! *You* weren't aboard o' *Primrose*?"

Wyatt grinning, nodded. "Aye, that I was, Coz, and as John Foster's Mate. More, no longer ago than yesterafternoon I—I was received in private audience by Her Gracious Majesty the Queen!"

CHAPTER VII

THE ESTUARY

SUCCESSIVE billows of ghostly, silver-hued and salt-smelling fog continued to drift inland, further restricting a wayfarer's already limited field of vision. The sun, although riding high, created only a peculiar pale radiance which cast into dark and unreal relief such twisted willows and clumps of rushes as were visible from that wretched highway which led southwards from Sutton Bridge towards the village of Wisbech.

Two tall men sweating under heavy woollen boat cloaks plodded along and set down ponderous sea-boots regardless of miniature quagmires of mud and water. Between them a ewe-necked and pitifully gaunt sumpter horse stumped along beneath a heavy pack, its head held low and ears drooping dispiritedly earthwards.

Time and again, as the road wound onwards through that great fen which extends inland from the estuary of the Ouse River, reed-bordered tongues of water licked right up to the highway's edge. Out of the fog emanated subtle noises such as the gabble of wild geese feeding, the contented chuckle of some mallard drake drowsing nearby over a well-filled craw. The rank odour of mudbanks exposed by a falling tide and the reek of innumerable stagnant pools hung heavy in this chill and murky atmosphere.

The larger of the two travellers used his staff to whack the pack horse across its rump. "God grant this curs'd road don't fork," grunted Peter Hopton then flicked drops of moisture from a short yellow beard trimmed in the bodkin style. His deepset and bright blue eyes swung to the right and left.

"By the Great Harry, Peter," Wyatt replied, peering carefully into the shifting mist, "for all I can tell we might be the last mortals left on Earth."

Across a grimy tarpaulin protecting the pack horse's load Hopton nodded somewhat uneasily. " 'Tis a fey place, this fen. I'll grant it harbours many a hobgoblin and warlock."

"Aye, Peter, 'tis indeed grisly hereabouts and I'll rejoice once we tread high ground. Best look alive, such fog is a fast friend to highway robbers and masterless rogues."

Wyatt's fingers closed over the hilt of that bilbo taken aboard the *Primrose* and the heft of this useful weapon lent him an immeasurable sense of reassurance. Let Peter sport a showy Spanish rapier acquired God knew where or how. When matters came to the sticking point Harry Wyatt would simply twist the boat cloak about his left arm as a guard, then batter down any assailant armed with such a weapon.

His cousin, Wyatt noted by this unreal light, presented a broader, more powerful image of himself. Both of them betrayed certain Hopton characteristics such as round heads, wide brows and powerful, high cheekbones.

Since he last had parted from his cousin, someone's blade had nicked the bridge of Peter's short, thick nose and had left a dull red scar which traversed it diagonally.

As they tramped along a small pearl set into a slim gold ear-ring in Peter's right earlobe swayed rhythmically to his stride.

When, suddenly, Wyatt held up a hand, the weary pack horse halted immediately and dropped its head still lower amid swirling tendrils of fog. To Wyatt's dumb show of caution Peter listened, hand cupped to his head, well sheltered against the weather by a flat, narrow-brimmed leather cap. "Eh?" he whispered. "What's amiss?"

"Thought I heard voices," Wyatt explained at the same time easing his bilbo in its scabbard.

During a long moment the cousins remained quite motionless, listening hard while the chill, sour-smelling miasmas of the fen eddied about them. At length the mists parted sufficiently to disclose the gnarled black outline of a willow. Wythes had been lopped off it during so many years ago that, at its top, a huge, fist-like growth had been formed.

Wyatt grinned a trifle sheepishly while retrieving the pack animal's halter. "Must have been some geese. A murrain on this curs'd clammy fog! It bites through wool and leather as though they were lawn."

In silence the two resumed the journey their clumsy boots extracting squelching noises from the roadway's muddy surface.

"How think you ye'll find yer sire?" at length queried Peter.

Self-reproach embittered the red-haired traveller's tone. " 'Tis the Lord's mercy if he's not in the Almshouse—together with my poor mother. I should have penned them at least one letter long months ago—yet, plague take it, Peter, I've ever been a poor scribbler and they wot it well."

"And what of Meg?" Hopton demanded while hauling the pack horse across a boghole. "Is she still alive?"

"Aye, for all I know. 'Tis over Sister Meg I'm the most concerned. Ever since the poor lass's face was botched by scalding she's been meaner nor any vixen robbed of her cubs. 'Tis only of late I've come even to hazard what it must mean for a comely young girl to find her face, in an instant, transformed into a fearsome thing."

Peter nodded, shrugged a dark green cloak higher about his massive shoulders. "Poor Meg."

Wyatt tapped a heavy leather pouch securely attached to his belt. "What I carry here, thanks to Her Gracious Majesty's bounty, should buy poor Meg a brave new kirtle and set her to smiling again. Eh, Coz?"

The other had jerked their sumpter horse to a halt, freed his long, basket-hilted rapier as, in startling abruptness, a pair of figures materialized amid the shifting mists. Wyatt also heard the disconcerting sounds. In quitting its scabbard his bilbo's blade caused only a soft rushing noise.

When they saw the wayfarers and their animal one of the other apparitions jerked a heavy hand-axe out of his belt while the other menacingly raised a huge cudgel the head of which was bright with points of iron.

"Who are ye and whither are ye bound?" demanded the foremost, a towering individual.

"By whose leave dare you ask?" retorted Wyatt. "Stand where you are and account yourselves."

Both strangers lowered their weapons, attempted to smile. "We be but poor journeymen who've lost their way amid this accursed fen. Kind sirs we beg 'e gi'e a crust and permit us to find safety in yer company."

Even while Wyatt studied the two miserably clothed creatures looming so gaunt and pitiful amid the slowly undulating fog Peter observed good-naturedly: "Indeed, Coz, these fellows *do* seem to be in a hard case, both as to arms and to belly. Shall we allow 'em a bite and our company on the way?"

Wyatt made no immediate reply. Were there others like these lurking deeper amid the baffling mists? He stared in all directions yet all he could see were the tops of cat-tails and a series of dully shining puddles behind these two wiry strangers.

"Let's give them a half loaf and a lump of cheese then speed these worthy fellows on their way; this is a chancy road if you'll but recall what the constable at Sutton Bridge warned that the fens fair swarm with all manner of rogues and masterless men?"

"Please, kind sir, I swear we be none o' the like." The taller man approached, returning his broad-bladed hatchet to a wide leather belt as he came.

" 'Fore God, gentlemen," croaked the other, "we're no cut-throats or highway robbers, only a brace o' poor farmers ruined by enclosure on our way to seek employment in Huntingdon Town. We be nigh to falling wi' hunger, Dick and me."

A certain ring of earnestness in the speaker's voice swayed Wyatt. Too well he was aware that many a small farmer throughout Engand had been forced into vagabondage by the enclosing of what once had been common farming lands.

"Why then, you've leave to join us," Wyatt declared. "Nonetheless you'll keep ahead of us and, for your own good, raise no outcry nor make any sudden move."

"God bless ye, young gentleman"; both the rag-clad and shoeless fellows broke into gap-toothed smiles. " 'Tis many the long day since we've been so kindly spoke."

Once the promised bread and cheese had been produced the four men moved on in silence broken only by the squelching of feet and hoofs travelling an ever-miserable and deeply rutted road. Presently the highway reached slightly higher ground where willows, birches and alders laced themselves overhead and often marched right down to the roadside.

Wyatt felt his finger-tips tingle and tighten. Had he indeed detected voices speaking in an undertone somewhere in the fog? That and a soft, sucking noise such as a foot might cause when pulled free of mud. Still, the disturbance might have been caused by nothing more threatening than some hart and his doe.

"Walk steady, you two," Wyatt warned in a voice calculated to penetrate far into the dripping woods. "Let any move be made and there'll be two vagabonds dead on this quagmire of a road."

"Ain't we sworn to ye by all that's holy that we be poor but honest fellows," growled the shorter stranger—he with the cudgel. "Ye've naught to fear from us." He offered his reassurance in a voice fully as loud as Wyatt's. Did he perhaps slightly emphasize the word "naught"? At any rate, no more sounds emanated from the underbrush.

At the end of an hour's slow progress the wretched road at length commenced gradually to climb. Correspondingly the mists thinned so much that small pastures and clumps of trees became visible; even a cottage of grey stone, deserted and with its roof fallen in. The ruin stood among some young pine trees sprouting in what once must have been a grain field.

To all four travellers such a sight was painfully familiar. All over England one would discover hundreds of such tiny abandoned holdings the owners of which had been starved out or driven away on becoming enclosed by some powerful landlord during the short, bloody and unhappy reign of Philip and Mary.

All this misery was due to the fact that the price of woollen cloth for export to Germany and Scandinavia had risen to such dazzling heights that owners of rich grain fields had ceased to grow crops in order to graze sheep. The principal results of this shift from agriculture to sheep raising were to create a brand new moneyed class—and a veritable army of honest men and women dispossessed of their holdings and rendered desperate through want of employment.

As sunlight dissipated that silver-grey gloom blanketing the fens, Wyatt's spirits rose proportionally. How fine to realize that now his every stride brought him nearer to St. Neots, home—and Kate Ibbott. At the same time a doubt needled his peace of mind. Suppose Squire Franklin Ibbott had won his intent and so had betrothed his eldest daughter to someone more suitable, more substantial and of more equal station than a landless mariner? After all, Harry Wyatt hadn't possessed a shilling with which to bless himself and had remained unheard from these past two years.

What a vast fool he'd been not to write more frequently! Frowning, he swung along behind the two vagabonds who, in the rags fringing goatskin jerkins, tramped along, bent-shouldered and wonderfully shaggy of head. By full daylight they appeared even more forlorn than they had when partially masked by fog.

When at length the road grew drier, Peter pulled up the bat

animal. "Ye'll be safe and able to find your way now, my lads, so go yer way and may better fortunes follow ye."

" 'Tis passing strange ye'd be so kind to poor clapper-claws like us," grinned the larger man. "Here's my fist on it." He extended a gnarled and dirty hand.

Smiling, Wyatt grasped it and found his hand imprisoned in a trap-like grip. Peter, however, sprang sidewise and ducked under a sudden murderous sweep described by the other outlaw's bludgeon. Wyatt felt himself jerked violently forward to a hoarse grunt of triumph. At the same time his left hand grabbed at a parrying dagger he wore slung on that same side of his belt.

The pack horse again lowered its moth-eaten head and remained a quite disinterested witness to the silent but deadly struggle which ensued. Wyatt's assailant apparently had not yet encountered a new school of fighting recently imported from Italy—that of the swordplay complemented by use of a dagger. Once he had imprisoned Wyatt's sword arm the bigger vagabond already fancied himself the victor and it was not until the Master Mate's dagger had pierced his right forearm that he perceived his disastrous miscalculation.

Peter meanwhile had grappled with the smaller ruffian and, by main force, wrenched away his cudgel to bring it smacking down on the greasy cap of coarse brown wool. Emitting a grunting cough, the second robber tumbled inert on to the trampled mud. The whole affair had not required half a minute for enactment.

CHAPTER VIII

A MATTER OF JUSTICE

THAT tavern which stood at a crossroads in the depths of Ramsey Forest could offer no justifiable claim to distinction. Dwarfed by giant oaks all about, the Pied Bull's four gables of moss-greened thatch suggested a low bank rather than an hostelry. However, an encouragingly rich swirl of greasy-grey smoke was purling from a massive chimney of weathered brick. A haphazard collection of outbuildings such as sheds and privies stood scattered about. A barn was leaning crazily forwards towards a wide puddle lying directly before the inn's principal entrance. In it a trio of scrawny red-and-white cattle stood knee-deep, gazing in curiosity at the new arrivals

—also a number of muddied pigs and a dozen-odd grey and white geese.

Closer inspection of this hostelry added nothing to its charm. Many layers of mud raised by trampling hoofs had splashed its plaster and timbered walls and more panes were missing from its small leaded windows than remained.

"A truly fetching sink-hole," sourly commented Wyatt. "And 'twould seem there's no nearby village, either."

He fetched his particular bound and dispirited prisoner a shrewd lick in the stern.

"Get on with you! Pray God, Peter, we'll discover a constable to make gift o' this walking carrion."

A few patrons, wandering packmen, drovers and such filed out into the tavern yard still clutching beer piggins the better to view this oddly assorted group of newcomers. Sunlight, bright even for this early June evening, lent warmth to the scene.

Wyatt picked a course among the mud-holes towards the iron door. "We've fetched here a brace of gallows birds. Where lodges the nearest constable?"

A bent old man in a food-splashed smock leaning heavily on a hawthorn stick shuffled forward, surveyed these two brown-faced young men an instant, then knuckled his forelock.

"At yer service, young masters. So ye've taken these outlaws i' the fens no doubt?" He cackled. "Icod! 'Tis a lusty pair of rogues you've fetched in. They should dance long and spry on their gibbet."

"But what of the constable?"

"Alacks, ye'll discover no constable this side o' Warboys."

"A scarlet pox on ye, old gaffer!" snarled the prisoner called Dick; his reddish eyes narrowing. "I warrant ye'll split yer rotten old slats watching a pair o' poor clods swing 'cause their farms was enclosed and they couldn't come by honest employ nowheres."

Bitterly the two vagabonds glowered at the ever-increasing number of grubby children, inn servants and travellers.

Peter dealt the taller prisoner a cuff that nearly knocked him flat. "Stow yer snivelling. Tell these folk, rather, how you and yer hangdog mate tried to cozen and lay by the heels a pair o' honest seafarers fresh home from beyond the seas."

"Seafarers?" Immediately the crowd's interest mounted. "Ha' ye been to the Spanish King's islands i' the South Sea? Is't truth riches yonder are to be had for the mere picking o' them?"

"Did yer see any man-eating sea horses—or—or Cyclopses?"

A trifle wearily Wyatt commenced to scrape heavy, blue-black mud from his boots and allowed the pack horse to browse a tussock of grass.

"All in good time. Master Hopton, here, will, for a few jacks of ale, relate to you his truly wondrous adventures in America." He grinned. "I warrant they'll glut your credulity."

"Aye." Good-naturedly Peter haled forward the prisoners. "An you feed me well I'll tell you o' the pearls in Virginia—large as robins' eggs, they are."

The host, a scrawny, yellow-faced individual, advanced, jerking a succession of bows over raw red hands locked above his stained leather apron.

With the discernment of long experience the innkeeper ran an eye over these stalwart young fellows and, quite accurately, placed them as of neither mean nor yet of noble origin, but representative of that new mariner-merchant class which, of late years, had been achieving ever-increasing wealth and influence.

"Welcome, young masters," he whined. "Welcome to the best the Pied Bull can offer. I trust ye'll favour me wi' your custom?"

Wyatt pretended to deliberate. "Aye, we'll bide with you, provided you find a place in which to secure these pretty fellows against the constable's arrival."

The landlord turned, beckoned a large, loutish youth. "I've a lodgment from which not even a stoat could escape. Diccon, show these young gentlemen to my stone milkshed. I vow 'twill secure these clapper-claws well enough. You, Stephen," he called to a gangling, red-nosed lad, "saddle my dun mare, hasten over to Warboys and fetch Sir Andrew of Thurston. He'll see these rascals' necks well stretched."

Awkwardly because of tightly bound hands the taller outlaw sank onto his knees before Wyatt, eyes rolling in frantic despair. "Ye'd not truly turn us over to the hangman? 'Fore God! Two year agone I, Jim Turner, were an honest farmer working my own holding hard by Alkmundbury." He strained forward through the mire and cow dung. "For God's sake send over there and ye'll learn I speak true. Will ye? Will ye?"

The prisoner's gaunt and deeply lined features quivered, then, perhaps imagining compassion in Henry Wyatt's expression, he scrabbled still closer. "Kind sir, noble sir, ain't ye never been down on yer luck? Ha' you been kicked from manor to manor, from farm to farm, shop to shop, like some poor cur wi' the mange? Please, young masters, Dick an' me ain't true robbers—else we'd not have bungled our business the way we did."

His dirt-caked and hairy visage jerked in the access of his terror. "As ye'll hope for mercy some day, don't hand us over to 'e hangman."

Wyatt hesitated. In those fear-choked accents he seemed to recognize the speech of many a breathless fellow who had dropped over the *Primrose's* rail with the law fairly snapping at their heels. Later, so many of such hunted men had proved their worth. All the same, the sea right now lay far away. Had not this Jim Turner and his shaggy fellow treacherously, savagely attempted robbery and murder?

"Stow yer patter. Lucky fer you this is England where ye'll be accorded a fair trial," Peter reminded not without a certain grim humour, "and justice, rest easy on that, according to Her Gracious Majesty's laws."

The inn's menservants employed oaths, cudgels and hayforks with which to harry the wretched vagabonds into the milkhouse—a sturdy, windowless stone building equipped with a massive oaken door banded in iron.

"'Tis well you reached shelter before nightfall, my friends," commented a tough-appearing freighter from the far end of the inn's stable yard. There he was supervising the efforts of some apprentices to unload a line of heavily laden bat horses. His pack train must have travelled far for grey-blue clay was drying on the canvas hamper covers.

The apprentices, hungry-appearing youths clad in shapeless fustian jerkins and frayed breeches of frieze, eased the freighter panniers on to dry ground. Weary as they were, they still could rally at the tavern's serving wenches. Wyatt noticed that they kept cudgels and staves ready to hand.

"Aye, as our friend the chapman here declares, 'tis wise to find shelter such as mine afore dark," the red-nosed host assured his newest guests. "Strong bands of lawless men and old soldiers roam these fens; they'll slit your weasand as readily as they ease themselves."

"What's your merchandise?" Peter inquired of the chapman. "Have you aught by way of trinkets that would please a certain pair o' twins I wot of?"

"Young master, I'm yer man," the freighter declared, kicking mud from thigh-high boots. "In yonder panniers I've lengths of very fine wool cloth, some dyed blue, some scarlet, some Tyrian purple, and linens as airy as you'll come across this side o' Heaven. Just the thing for a Sunday kirtle or a wedding-gown. Whither are you bound, may I ask?"

"To St. Neots in Huntingdonshire."

"St. Neots?" The travelling merchant pursed thick lips while pushing a greasy black gabardine cap onto the back of his head. "St. Neots? Out upon it! I've heerd o' some such a place and not so long ago, either."

In the act of unstrapping the pack from the sumpter horse Wyatt queried: "And what might you have heard? Come, speak up, man."

"Why I can't for the life recall at the moment, but perchance a draught of beer will refresh my wits."

Effortlessly Peter Hopton heaved the heavy pack from the bat animal's back on to his shoulder and had started for the Pied Bull's entrance when into the courtyard rode a stalwart, grey-haired individual wearing a weather-bleached Lincoln-green doublet, red hose and heavy riding boots. He bestrode a coarse-bred but well-cared-for brown mare. The stranger's surcoat, Wyatt noticed, was of russet leather scalloped about its neck and sleeves and his silver-mounted steel spurs had an air of well-worn elegance.

By the presence of a pair of miniature crossed silver staves suspended from a heavy chain of the same metal, this wiry, hawk-faced gentleman Wyatt decided was no mere constable but undoubtedly the High Sheriff. In his wake rode a couple of archers wearing pointed steel caps, half breastplates and breeches and jerkins of leather.

In no great hurry he who proved to be Sir Andrew of Thurston, and who was indeed High Sheriff of Huntingdonshire, dismounted, flexed long legs a few times then, after removing his gauntlets, came striding over to where the tall young cousins stood before the Pied Bull's entrance.

As he drew near Wyatt became aware of uncommonly keen brown eyes that held a noticeably peculiar metallic gleam, a thin slash of a mouth, grey-streaked brown beard trimmed into aggressive twin points.

When Wyatt bowed and doffed his flat green hat, Peter awkwardly followed suit.

"Your business and station?" crisply demanded Andrew of Thurston.

"We are seafarers homewards bound after long absence," Peter explained easily. "I am a Boatswain Gunner but Harry, here, is a Master's Mate—and will be Master of his own craft eftsoons."

The Sheriff then demanded and received a terse account of the outlaws' attempted attack.

"Good—a plain and simple case of attempted robbery and murder. Where are these rogues now lodged?"

"The innkeeper holds them secure in a stone milkhouse."

"Good, good. Come morning I'll try them—I'm also Justice of the Peace," he added casually, "and then my men will string them tidily to yonder oak beyond the crossroads."

The Sheriff sighed, slapped dirt from dark blue French breeches. " 'Fore God, this has become a lawless county! Yesterday I caused Long William yonder to hang a band of outlaws who'd stolen and eaten one of Sir Robert Kinsman's prize ewes."

"How many was hanged, Yer Honour?" the innkeeper queried while flicking foam from the pint of beer he was offering as largesse to that very important personage.

"Thank you, Egbert—I'm all of a thirst." Once Sir Andrew had wiped thin lips he chuckled. "Why, we stretched an even dozen. I vow 'twas a sorry business, but moral, very moral. This sheep-lifting must cease.

"All the same, I don't fancy hanging boys and women, nor does Long William, generally. They blubber so it touches his tender heart. Don't it, Will?" He scratched bristly grey hair and at the same time winked at a sturdy, black-haired archer engaged in fetching off the Sheriff's saddle. A handsomely cased long-bow together with a quiver full of yard-long arrows remained slung to the archer's back.

"Please, Yer Honour, what's new about the witch trial over at Huntingdon Town?" demanded a blue-smocked farmer.

Sir Andrew looked grave. "Why, my good man, they've been found guilty. All three of them have been condemned to hang as a solemn warning to all who would sell their souls to Satan."

"If only I could see them executions!" sighed the serving wench sent to refill the tankards. "I dote on such. Lor' 'twill make a main fine show."

"This seems a matter of note," Wyatt remarked.

"Aye. This particular trial has been a nine-days' wonder in the countryside."

At the mention of witches those in the tap-room became self-conscious and talked louder than was necessary, as if reassuring themselves that none was present, or that they themselves might come under suspicion.

Peter slowly shook his big yellow head. "I like it not. Was there sure proof o' their witchcraft?"

"Rest easy, young man," the Sheriff advised, wiping his beard on the back of his hand. " 'Twas conclusively proved that this devil-worshipping crew certainly bewitched to their deaths poor Lady Addison and her two grand-daughters."

"God save us!" Wyatt said. "Why, they're neighbours of ours."

While Wyatt was shifting the heavy bilbo and its scabbard of stained leather into a more comfortable position Sir Andrew removed a brimless green cap and bent forward, elbows on table.

"Indeed? Then I'll relate what I know, which is considerable, since I was present at these witches' secular trial—together with Sir Henry Cromwell, Master Buckbarrow and Sir William Jackman." He looked hard at Peter. "That no fairer-minded gentlemen have ever drawn the breath of life no one will deny in my presence."

The Sheriff's audience became augmented by a group of carpenters travelling to construct yet another of those many fine new manor houses which were arising in this vicinity—thanks to Huntingdonshire's thriving wool-cloth trade with Scandinavia and the Hanseatic Ports in the Baltic.

Scullions, ostlers and maids also shuffled forward to cluster about Sir Andrew of Thurston as he sat stiff-backed in a wooden arm-chair set before the Pied Bull's huge fireplace. At the opposite end of the chimney-piece a fat and sweat-soaked cook tried to listen while plucking a plump goose.

Various ribby mongrels wandered about and sniffed the travellers' boots before slumping into discouraged attitudes along the wall; then they commenced to crimp fleas.

"This evil affair commenced," the Sheriff began, "nigh on a year ago. 'Twas then that Lady Addison, whose husband is a great land-holder in the county, commenced to be taken by strange fits. During them she accused her neighbour, a certain Mother Ann, of possessing a devilish familiar distinguished in the form of a dun chicken. Soon after the beginning of her seizures Lady Addison travelled to visit her daughter, a Mistress Henderson who dwells at Parton." He raised a brow at Wyatt. "You'll wot where this property lies?"

"Aye. Parton is a hamlet scarce two miles distant from St. Neots."

"Well, it was deposed and sworn that Lady Addison had not long been in the Henderson house than her grandchildren fell into similar fits, to the great distress of Mistress Henderson who could not restrain her tears."

A low murmur circulated the inn. Eyes intent upon the speaker's aquiline features variously expressed incredulity, awe and horror.

"Mistress Henderson therefore caused the old woman, Ann, whom she knew to be skilled in the matter of physic, to be sent for. Her husband being tenant to Sir John Addison this beldame therefore durst not refuse, but so soon as she was come to Mistress Henderson's the children grew much worse. The Lady Addison then took Mother

Ann aside and charged her deeply with witchcraft, which she stiffly denied, declaring that Mistress Henderson and Lady Addison did her great wrong so to blame her without cause."

One of the Sheriff's archers, tramping in from bedding down the horses, trod square upon some dog's tail. The creature's sudden shrill yelps caused all present to start as if the Foul Fiend himself had suddenly spoken from among the smoke-blackened beams above. Once the injured animal had been clouted into silence and the archer had lumbered over to a seat beside the chimney-piece, Andrew of Thurston's grave, even tones continued:

"Lady Addison answered that neither she nor her daughter accused Mother Ann, but that one of the children, by the name of Ellen, on falling into a fit had cried out that it was the old beldame who had caused all this. The little girl, 'twas sworn, gibbered, 'Even now, I hear something squeaking loud in my ears. It doth plague me so. Can you not hear it?' "

"The Lord preserve us!" muttered one of the carpenters, round-eyed. "This indeed is a most devilish business."

The Sheriff absently patted the head of a round-eyed toddler who had advanced quite unabashed by the fact that his only garment was a single and very ragged shift so torn that there could be no doubt as to his sex.

"Aye, that it is. Mother Ann having persisted in her denial, Lady Addison ordered her conveyed to a cabinet where one James Wynter, a Doctor of Divinity, would have examined her more closely, but Mother Ann refused to stay and ran out, whereupon the lady, perceiving that she could not prevail, pulled off Mother Ann's kerchief and, taking a pair of shears, clipped off a lock of her hair and gave it privily to Mistress Henderson, together with her hair lace, willing her to burn the same."

Henry Wyatt stirred uncomfortably on his backless bench. Curiously enough, Andrew of Thurston's discourse had begun to render him mightily uneasy. It was all very well, perhaps, for Germans, Frenchmen, Spaniards and other foreigners to burn, hang and torture wretches suspected of witchcraft, yet to him such persecution seemed somehow alien to England—for all that such had gone on for centuries.

"Hold your tongue, Harry," silently he advised himself. "There *may* be a small something in this matter of necromancy."

Only the clanking of a spit manipulated by a large dog trained to run on a treadmill broke the silence before Sir Andrew resumed.

He dropped his voice and stared hard at embers in the hearth.

"That same night Lady Addison was very strangely tormented by a cat which she proposed Mother Ann had sent to her. The witch creature offered to pluck off all the skin and flesh from her body. Such a tumult the Lady made in her bed and the weird sounds that she made in talking to the cat and to Mother Ann that she awakened her daughter, Mistress Henderson. After this the poor lady continued strangely sick and so continued until her death which occurred about six months ago."

Peter Hopton grunted, leaned forward, and fanned broad, short-fingered hands before the flames. "In what manner did this dire sickness manifest itself, Your Honour?"

"Pains struck the said lady and her grand-daughters sometimes in one part of the body, sometimes elsewhere; the grieved part always trembling as if in a palsy. Their senses, however, remained clear. Oft and again Lady Addison would repeat Mother Ann's declaration: 'Madam, I have never hurt you *as yet*!'

"Some time after Lady Addison's demise this Mother Ann fell very sick and, being penitent in her sickness, did confess her practice of witchcraft, although later the beldame swore 'twas only light-headedness which had persuaded her to confess, that she had never wished Lady Addison nor Mistress Henderson's daughter the least harm."

Complete silence now ruled the tap-room but the pungent reek of frying onions and a strong stench given off by an old hound assaulted Wyatt's nostrils.

"When the Reverend Doctor Gage, Minister of the Church at Parton, went to learn the truth of the matter he found the old woman, her husband and daughter talking of the business. Having asked whether she had not confessed, she now answered, 'I confessed, indeed, but it is not so.' This so angered Doctor Gage that the next morning he went to Sir William Jackman, J.P., and did demand him to send constables."

The Sheriff paused long enough to swallow a draught of ale from a tankard always kept a-brim by the red-nosed publican. "This was done and both Mother Ann and daughter were delivered into their charge, that they should go before the Bishop of Lincoln at Buckden. They therefore were both taken before the Bishop and further examined."

"And what chanced then, Yer Honour?" demanded a scullion, scarlet-faced in basting a suckling pig which, impaled on a spit, was beginning to turn temptingly brown and succulent.

" 'Twere a frightening thing," broke in one of the archers. "I were court guard when the old beldame was asked whether a dun chicken had ever sucked at her chin, and whether it was a natural chicken."

A soft groan circulated when the simple fellow continued, "She answered that the fowl had sucked twice and no more since Christmas Eve." The archer commenced to make the sign of the Cross as he had been taught in childhood, but now that such Popish signs were frowned upon, his big, tanned hand faltered and dropped.

"He sucked at her chin!" nervously exclaimed one of the carpenters. "Lor'! That weren't no natural fowl."

The archer, reaching inside his leather jerkin, scratched vigorously. "Nevertheless, the old creature insisted it were a natural chicken for when it sucked at her chin she scarce felt it and when she put it off the place bled. Ain't that so, Yer Honour?"

"Aye, Alwald. Furthermore, this Mother Ann deposed that all the trouble which had befallen Lady Addison's family was due to this dun chicken," concluded the Sheriff solemnly. "And right glad I am that, at high noon tomorrow, Long William here," he nodded towards his second follower, "will fit a noose about her ugly, wry neck. Such devilish arts are not to be endured."

"Will ties the daintiest hangman's knot ye'll find in all the East Ridings," averred the archer, Alwald.

"Pray continue concerning the trial," Peter prompted. Like everyone else, his gaze continually sought a string of garlic cloves suspended from the eaves. Garlic, everyone knew, was the best of all specifics against ghosts, werewolves, warlocks and witches. Tonight he meant to beg a bud or two the which to place in his boots.

"Mother Ann, together with her husband, was haled before the Bishop of Lincoln, Sir Henry Cromwell and Richard Joyce—all Justices of the Queen's Peace. At this examination the old hag declared she knew that her dun chicken had departed from the afflicted children because it had returned to her and now lay at the bottom of her belly, which made it so full she could scarce lace up her coat and it weighed so heavy that her horse fell down."

Horrified gasps escaped the audience.

"She avowed she owned three such chickens, known by the names of Pluck, Catch and White. She was then committed, with her husband and daughter, to the jail at Huntingdon to be held until the Assizes. Meanwhile, the fits continued very grievous with the Mistress Henderson's daughters for all that she was not present and no amount of entreaty could persuade the old beldame to raise her spell. Presently the unhappy children perished in struggling foamy fits."

Sir Andrew of Thurston sighed, looked very grave. "The very

next day Mother Ann, her husband and daughter, also evil characters, were indicted for having bewitched to their deaths Lady Addison and her two grandchildren, contrary to God's laws and a statute made in the fifth year of our Gracious Queen's reign. These things and many others having been sworn in testimony against them, the jury brought in a verdict of guilty and all three were condemned to be hanged by the neck until dead in Huntingdon Town market place tomorrow."

CHAPTER IX

TWO WITCHES AND A WARLOCK

BECAUSE, early in the morning, a detachment of pikemen passed on their way to Sutton Bridge there to take ship for the Medway, it was rumoured that My Lord the Earl of Leicester had begun to collect an army raised to fight Spanish oppression in the Netherlands. Loud cursing and the rattle raised by pikes dragged by their handles over a patch of cobblestones—such weapons were far too heavy to be carried on the shoulder for long—roused Sir Andrew of Thurston who was sharing a bed with Peter Hopton and Henry Wyatt.

After clearing his throat and spitting onto the floor, Sir Andrew shuffled down, blear-eyed and short of temper, to address the officer commanding. He proved to be rather an ugly young gentleman for all that he wore a jarnet—or travelling cloak—of green and gold over doublet and trunks of blue slashed in mustard yellow. Further this officer affected a very modish flat cap garnished by an enormous scarlet ostrich feather which at the moment drooped damply over his shoulder. With a patent waste of effort he, at the same time, spurred and reined a grey stallion back on its haunches. Unavoidably the gallant's mount reared and pawed the air in bewilderment. The effect was dramatic at least.

The young gentleman bowed over his pommel. "Good morrow, good sir. You are up early indeed."

Sir Andrew of Thurston, for all his harsh visage and curt manner, bowed in return. "Who could slumber wi' all the racket you and your men do raise?"

"Then I'm sorry for it," declared the ugly young officer. " 'Tis such a fair fine morning we broke camp early. Is there aught I can do to make amends?"

"Aye," Sir Andrew replied, and clearing his throat spat into a puddle. "An you need a couple of stout rogues to swell your muster then you may have such of me and welcome."

"My thanks and service to you." By now he must have noted the Sheriff's crossed silver staves. "Your gallows baits are sound of wind and limb?" The other spoke in a lisping voice. At Court it had become the mode to pretend a French, an Italian or a Spanish accent.

"I warrant they'll last long enow bravely to spill their guts in our Queen's service."

The company, some eighty in number, disposed themselves around the Pied Bull's stable yard and, after resting their ten-foot pikes against a low wall enclosing an orchard, commenced to produce bits and pieces of food from their pouches. A few tramped over to drink at the horse trough, others flung ribald invitations at the tavern's thick-ankled serving-girls who, still red-eyed and bedraggled after their night's dalliance with various patrons, came out to stare incuriously upon these hard-faced troopers.

Out from the milkshed Andrew of Thurston's archers hauled the two masterless men. Thirsty and long unfed, they were smeared with cow dung and speckled with bits of straw. Confident that their hour of doom was at hand, they struggled and cursed.

"Aye, go ahead and hang us i' the name o' justice," sobbed the smaller. "First ye rob us o' our rights on the common lands, next you enclose our holding—so 'tis only meet ye'll stretch our necks for merely trying to stay alive. To what a sorry pass England has come!"

The archer Alwald dealt his prisoner a resounding cuff. "Silence in the presence o' yer betters, you insolent, over-ripe gallows crow."

The officer kicked his mount over to gaze upon these grey-faced, filthy wretches. "Sergeant, do you examine these clapper-claws and tell me whether they indeed be sound of limb and teeth."

Much like a horse dealer at a fair, the Sergeant then employed a sheathed dagger to pry open the outlaws' mouths; next he jabbed their bellies unmercifully, seeking evidence of rupture and concluded by punching their backs lest they be afflicted with the stone.

"Be these dogs half so strong as they stink, they'll do, Sir Cedric," grunted the Sergeant.

Before long the pike company—this was no troop of fire—was kicked and cursed into formation and departed sullenly towards the fens and the Wash lying beyond. They dragged the recruits along by ropes secured about their necks.

This particular morning, Wyatt esteemed, was as glorious as any plain Englishman could ask; in fact it was almost as perfect as the two wayfarers had imagined while sweltering or freezing on some foreign shore. Even their pack animal felt inspired to raise its blunt head and gaze dully about. At times the poor beast even stretched its ewe neck in order to snatch a mouthful of green leaves from some low-hanging branch.

Probably because Huntingdon Town—the county seat where the witch hangings were to take place—was situated on the opposite side of St. Neots, that rough track Henry Wyatt and Peter Hopton followed proved to be deserted.

Now the fields were larger, interspaced here and there by spinneys of evergreens, little orchards and hedgerows all fragrant with primroses flowering under the gentle sun.

Wyatt threw back his head, inhaled deeply. "See, Peter? Yonder's the tip of our church spire." His smooth, copper-hued features relaxed into a wide smile. "God's Love! How many times has my poor backside ached of a Sunday under three hours of sermonizing." He grinned. "Would that Doctor Gage had heeded my grandsire's belief that precious few souls are salved after the first twenty minutes of preaching."

He snapped a little branch from a flowering hawthorn and tucked it into his cap then noisily sucked in deep breaths of fragrant fresh air. The sun was just peeping above the horizon at silvery mists yet lingering in various hollows and vales. On a nearby hilltop the yellow-brown sails on one of the several windmills in sight commenced lazily to revolve.

"Where but in England, Coz, can one behold blossoms so fair, trees so stately, earth so richly dark, or a tinkler so drunk as he who snores under yonder hedge?"

Peter licked fingers free of grease left by a breakfast of cold suckling pig.

"Barring the tinkler, I'll answer you that, Harry, and truly."

"Where then?"

"In America. Mark my words, Harry, yon lies a vastly rich and still untainted land. There the forests grow taller, the fields are more fruitful and the game! God's Glory, Coz, you should behold for yourself! None but a lazy dolt ever could go hungry there."

From beneath level red brows Henry treated his companion to an amused glance. "So? Then why did you take to seafaring? God wot you've ever been farmer at heart."

His hulking cousin shrugged. "Can the like of you or me hope ever to own a real property in Huntingdonshire? Besides, Father's cottage got a mite crowded when my tenth brother, or sister—I forget which, started mewing." Peter laughed easily. "One day Father fetched me in from our byre. 'Peter,' says he, 'I reckon yer man enough to go fend for yourself. Now off you go and here's a sixpence for luck and yer first meal. Remember,' says he, 'always touch yer headpiece to yer betters and serve God and our Queen well and truly. Remember that, my lad, and ye'll come to no bad end.' "

Absently Hopton ran an eye over a herd of red-and-white cattle loitering belly-deep among lily pads on the edge of a millpond.

"But why did you join me in seafaring? You were always set on farming."

"To be sure, Harry, to be sure. Gladly I would have 'prenticed myself to some yeoman farmer but, as you know well, farm lands hereabouts ha' been so reduced there's little place for a hired hand. So, hearing that Sir Richard Grenville was beating the drum for an expedition towards the coast of North America, I sailed as a younker along of him."

He beamed. " 'Fore God, Coz, that was indeed a chancy, blessed day!" He talked on, eagerly, as always he did when on the subject of Virginia. "Till ye've beheld this land I speak of ye can entertain not the least notion of how vast it must be. Why, I reckon you could lose a dozen Englands within the borders o' this Virginia."

Wyatt grinned tolerantly—why cavil? Let Peter be happy. He even lured him to speak further. "Then America must be even greater than the Kingdom of France?"

"Aye, mayhap two or three times larger. Man, man, you've no notion o' the great rivers there, o' the richness and vastness of the soil and forests. Certes, no honest clown need ever come, cap in hand, humbly to beg his landlord's permission to cut a few wythes or faggots. Neither would he be called to bend his knee before anyone saving God and the Queen's Majesty.

"D'you know what was in the air when we returned to Plymouth?" Peter considered his cousin with care.

"No. What?"

"That famed explorer, Sir Walter Raleigh, within the year plots and plans to plant a lasting colony in this new country which he calls Virginia."

Like a great overgrown boy Peter suddenly turned a cart-wheel among daisies nodding by the roadside and burst into a laugh of pure joy. "Know what? An I can come across some sturdy lass who'll make me a good wife and brood mare, why I'm minded to 'list in this venture of Sir Walter's. Whyn't you come too, Harry, you and your Kate?"

"Not I. Kate is too fond of her family and comforts. I know. Besides, I have set my purpose on becoming rich and famous, a merchant-mariner like unto John Hawkins, Martin Frobisher and Sir Francis Drake."

From the brow of a low hill the two paused, both to catch their wind and to gaze down upon the dew-brightened roofs of St. Neots. How poignantly familiar was the least detail of this scene! They could identify each and every one of those dwellings giving off spirals of bluish-white smoke. The hamlet lay clean-looking, peaceful and prosperous amid surrounding farm lands at the bottom of a natural bowl created by softly rounded and well-wooded hills.

The remains of a monastery, which had been plundered and burnt to the ground during the religious troubles nigh on seventy years ago, by now had become all but smothered beneath masses of dark green ivy—only the grey stonework of the bell-tower emerged from the foliages and afforded a haven for hundreds of rooks.

So far away to the westward as to resemble a toy arose another square, grey-white tower marking Sir John Addison's manor house. On a hillock between the travellers and the village stood a third landmark—the crumbling remains of a watch-tower constructed by the legions of the Emperor Septimus Severus.

Between this ruin and Sir John's manor lay that cottage in which Henry Wyatt had been born. For the moment Edmund Wyatt's humble home remained invisible since it lay concealed in a pleasant little vale.

As foreseen, that highway leading from St. Neots to Huntingdon Town already was dotted with carts piled high with produce, pedestrians and men driving cattle to the market.

"What with those executions, I reckon we'll find scarce a soul left in St. Neots," Peter predicted. "For sure my old sire will have gone—next to a bear-baiting he's ever doted on executions."

Wyatt made no comment. His eyes were fixed on that big, sharp-gabled and half-timbered house which sheltered Kate Ibbott. Her father, Franklin, although an esquire by birth, in his youth had elected to cast away his social position by entering trade. As a draper, he had prospered with the years. Because Franklin Ibbott, as was the custom, preferred to shelter the bulk of his stock in a spacious loft above his living apartments his, by consequence, was by far the largest structure in St. Neots.

Presently the *Primrose's* Mate was able to discern that pretty, ancient, but ill-kept cottage in which he and Meg had gambolled and tussled for so many years and sometimes had heeded their father's curious, but sometimes stimulating and scholarly discourses.

On the outskirts of St. Neots, by a pool where the villagers' stock was watered they encountered a half-grown boy who, with the noisy assistance of a long-haired cur, was driving a flock of black-faced sheep towards a wide meadow spangled with buttercups.

"Hi, there, Jeremy!" Wyatt hailed, delighted at this first glimpse of familiar features—be they as freckled and stupid as these.

The boy's jaw dropped clear down on to his threadbare smock. "You—you be Harry Wyatt, ben't you?"

"Of course, and there's no need to gape like a loony. Peter and I are fresh home from the sea and right glad to see you, Jem."

But the tow-headed youth continued to goggle, then backed off muttering something. He extended his right arm at full length and parted his index and second fingers into a Y, cried, "Lord save me!" and ran like a hare, leaving his shaggy dog to fetch the sheep along after him.

Peter lifted his leathern cap the better to scratch the yellow tangle of his hair. "And just what do you make o' that, Coz? Jeremy never was exactly bright, but he must have grown worse."

Wyatt shook his head. " 'Tis beyond me. Why should the little ninny fancy I'd turn the evil eye on him and so level the countersign?"

"We may have been reported lost and be fancied ghosts," came Peter's sensible solution. "Mariners for ever are being deemed dead and only to eventually return after being cast away or long enslaved by Turks."

Once among the outlying cottages of St. Neots, Wyatt pulled from his pack a new cloak of orange velvet edged with coney's fur and slipped over his head a slim silver chain bestowed upon him by Sir Francis Drake on the occasion of his departure.

Wyatt's broad, coppery features formed a smile of anticipation. Wait until these simple villagers learned that not only had he seen that demi-god in the public's eye, the fabulous Golden Admiral, but that he had appeared in privy audience before the Queen's Majesty and even had conversed with her! By God, that should make stiff-necked Colonel Christopher Phillips, the Watkinses and purse-proud Franklin Ibbott to consider old Edmund's son in a new light.

His eye roved to the sumpter animal. Icod! Mother should be well pleased with the gay shawl, scarf of pure silk and the pretty silver and turquoise brooch he was fetching her, whilst Father was bound to be pleased and find interest in a copy of Andrew Boorde's *Breviary of Health*, a volume on chirurgery he had discovered in a bookstall in the shadow of St. Paul's Church. As for Meg—well, wait till she beheld the yellow-and-blue camlet kirtle he was bringing.

Nothing in St. Neots seemed to have been altered. Joseph the webster's dog rushed out as usual, snarling, to bare its teeth and then slink aside, its bravado evaporating before Peter's abrupt flourish of his walking stave. As always, pigs and chickens were foraging about in the mire which invariably engulfed St. Neots' one and only street. A battered stone cross raised in the centre of the village square by some long-dead Norman knight in fulfilment of a vow looked as grey and lichen-stained as ever.

A woman they recognized as Mistress Holden appeared leading a small child by the hand. "Good morrow to you, Dame Holden!" Wyatt called jovially. "We're back from seafaring, Peter and I."

"Mercy on us!" In a flash the woman slipped her apron over the child's face, turned her back and looked the other way.

Old Job, the cobbler, when he recognized Wyatt's tall figure, jumped up from the bench outside his shop, spat out a mouthful of the oaken pegs with which he was re-soling a boot and slammed his door shut.

" 'Fore God, 'tis a rare warm welcome our neighbours grant us," Peter observed in growing bewilderment.

Wyatt said nothing, a suspicion, tiny but sharp as the point of a needle, was stinging his imagination. At the next open door, that of Simpkins, the baker, he marched inside and before that floury individual could escape grabbed him by the shoulder.

"What's amiss?" he demanded harshly. "I'm just returned from beyond the seas. Why does everyone turn away from me as though I were the Devil himself?"

This old fellow with flour-streaked beard a-quiver rolled terrified eyes. "The son and brother of witches may also be a servant of Satan."

Furious colour flooded Wyatt's broad cheeks and he shook Simpkins so hard that flour from his apron floated free.

"Witches? Have done with maunderings, old man, and answer me."

Gagging, the baker still flinched away, but summoned an appeasing smile. "Why, Harry, lad, ain't ye *heard*?"

"Heard what? You whey-faced loon, I told you I'm just returned from foreign lands. Speak out, damn you! Has this nonsense aught to do with my dame and sire?"

Simpkins managed a nod then cringed and cried out before the baleful glare in Wyatt's dark blue eyes when his first dreadful suspicion exploded upon his consciousness with the force of a bursting petard. *Mother Ann?* Ann was his mother's name; the hamlet of Parton lay scant miles away and so did the *manor of Sir John and Lady Addison!*

"God help ye, Harry, this is indeed an evil hour for yer return."

The baker twisted himself free of Wyatt's suddenly nerveless grip. "Your father and mother and sister are to be hanged in Huntingdon Town market-place this same day! D-don't harm me, Harry," he babbled. "I—I had naught to do wi' the m-matter. I s-swear it!"

A bludgeon descending on Wyatt's head could not have produced a more stunning effect, yet he hesitated only an instant. "At what hour is set the execution?"

"Can't say for sure, Harry," quavered Simpkins. "Some say 'tis to take place at ten—others say the hanging's set for high noon."

Wyatt ran out into the street, caught the pack animal's halter and dragged it up to the baker's front door. "Guard this beast with your life. Be there so much as one button missing when I return, I'll slit your weasand."

Peter Hopton had already gone pelting down the street in search of riding horses. Huntingdon, after all, lay but eight miles to the northward. Were the executions ordered at noon, then Harry and he might hope to arrive in time; but had they been set for ten then there remained no hope.

Only by the dint of threats and a few hard blows were the cousins able to obtain the loan of a pair of clumsy and big-footed farm horses.

CHAPTER X

IN HUNTINGDON TOWN MARKET PLACE

THANKS to its longer legs and better condition, Henry Wyatt's mount pounded into the environs of Huntingdon Town a good quarter of a mile ahead of Peter Hopton's nag. The rider drew his breath in great tearing gasps and became aware of muscles, long unaccustomed to horseback riding, that burned like fiery cords. Recklessly he lashed his foundering mount through huddles of sheep and cattle until, at length, the wretched beast tripped over a foraging sow and went down all of a heap. Despite frantic tugging at the bridle reins it remained stunned, quivering like a pole-axed ox.

The fact that so few people had remained behind to guard animals brought to market lent Wyatt a sickening conviction that the hour of execution must be at hand. When, in the distance, was raised a resounding shout, a thousand furies howled in his ears. How could otherwise decent neighbours conspire and so doom to death an old woman because of falling fits to which she had been subjected since childhood?

How could sober, God-fearing Englishmen have condemned poor scarred Meg and doddering and ineffectual Father? Admittedly, Edmund Wyatt off and on had dabbled in chemistry—but not with alchemy—which must have told strongly against him at the trial. Yet in all his life Father had never harmed so much as a mouse.

How *could* Lady Addison, ever a charitable and an upright figure in the community, have conjured up so fantastic a web of nightmares that their mere telling was about to encompass the death of three unfortunate but guiltless persons? Why? Had she been ill of some malady unknown to chirurgeons?

Breathless, with eyeballs straining, Wyatt raced on foot along Cobbett's Lane towards Market Square and the Shire Hall. Before the latter a permanent gibbet had stood for centuries, ever since Huntingdon Town had grown from a little village.

The lane he was following was cobbled and wound on between ancient dwellings which leaned forward as if to touch gables above the thoroughfare. In the near distance he heard a sudden blare of trumpets and the roll of drums rise above the babbling of an excited multitude.

"Dear God, let me arrive in time!" Half blinded by sweat, he heard Peter's heavy-footed mount overtaking him so turned and gasped: "Ride 'head! Stop them! There's little time!"

"No!" roared Peter. "Grab my stirrup!" Stumbling in near exhaustion the lathered plough horse lurched on, by weight alone battering a passage through an ever-increasing throng. Another great shout echoed among the houses and sent rooks to circling high above the roof-tops. Ignoring furious curses and blows aimed by outraged townsmen intent on enjoying the spectacle, the cousins charged past St. Bennett's Church and glimpsed the Shire Hall's grey façade and gilded weather-vanes looming ahead.

A fresh torture to Wyatt was his realization that had he and Peter followed the direct route from the Pied Bull to Huntingdon Town in company with the Sheriff and his men instead of going by way of St. Neots they must have reached this place in time to—to accomplish what?

Why, oh why had he not possessed the wit last night to ask the names of the condemned? True, Sir Andrew of Thurston several times had mentioned a 'Mother Ann', but there must easily be a hundred women of that name dwelling in Huntingdonshire.

By a frantic use of his fists Wyatt fought his way through the throng until he could dive under the haft of a pikeman's lance held horizontally to restrain the crowd. "Hold hard there!" rasped the pikeman. "Get back with ye."

Wyatt halted, but only because he had raised his eyes to the tall H-shaped oak and stone gibbet. Something like a red-hot blade seemed to pierce his heart. Dreadfully dark and limp against the brilliant June sky two attenuated figures were dangling, revolving slowly. He could only be certain that recently had perished a man and a woman. Whether the female already hanged might be his mother or poor Margaret, Wyatt had no time to learn for already Long William, wearing a black hood and cape, had begun urging his third victim up a short ladder.

"Shove her off, Will!" "Set 'e bloody witch to dancing!" "Hang her! Stretch her neck!" The crowd's clamour was raucous, infinitely merciless—never to be forgotten. "Burning's better for such spawn o' Satan."

It was Meg, dishevelled and gibbering in the extremity of her terror.

The sibilant *zweep!* caused by Wyatt's bilbo quitting its sheath and the ominous glitter of its blade warned the nearby onlookers to flinch aside and so expedited his rush towards the gallows. Peter, meantime, was using his rapier's hilt to stun a pikeman who attempted to prevent his advance into the open space dominated by the gibbet. Together the two men darted across the muck-splattered cobbles towards a knot of hard-faced officials eddying uncertainly about the hangman's ladder. "Stop! Hold hard, you damned perjured butchers!" Wyatt screamed.

He was an instant too late in reaching the ladder's foot. Long William had already shoved the last prisoner's frail, rag-clad figure off the ladder grotesquely to swing and writhe in space. The square for a third time resounded to howls of bestial satisfaction.

"Oyez! Oyez! Oyez! The Queen's justice hath been execu——" The High Constable of Huntingdonshire broke off his proclamation.

"Arrest and truss these lawless knaves!" he shouted.

A whole rank of pikemen and both of the Sheriff's archers sprang to obey but as quickly recoiled from the furious play of Wyatt's heavy bilbo.

"Cut Meg down," Wyatt implored. "Mayhap she still lives. I'll hold 'em off!"

" 'Fore God 'tis those mariners who were at the Pied Bull!" Sir Andrew burst out in astonishment. "Stand back! How dare you interfere with the Queen's justice?"

To the hawk-faced Sheriff Wyatt paid not the least heed, only hurled himself furiously at Long William and slashed hard. Howling, the executioner lurched sidewise and became lost to sight behind a stalwart, black-bearded pikeman who levelled his weapon and thrust viciously. Wyatt ducked under the pike's head, lunged, and felt his wrist jarred when his point was turned by the fellow's breastplate. Halberd blades flashed in from all directions, and, in a frenzy, Wyatt beat them aside as, back to back with Peter, he fought in outraged fury. Pikemen, archers and arquebusiers alike now left the crowd unrestrained. Promptly the townsfolk surged towards the gallows.

"They are too many," Wyatt told himself. Aye, many too many dancing pike points and clutching hands ringed him in. His precious Spanish bilbo was dashed from his hand, then someone's pikestaff dealt him such a woundy knock on the head that his eyes became drenched by countless fiery sparks such as one sees flashing from beneath a blacksmith's hammer.

Like the deck of the *Primrose* in a heavy gale, Huntingdon Town market place swayed under his feet and he sank backwards and in so doing glimpsed his sister's purplish, dreadfully contorted features high above him. In that instant he realized that Meg's tongue had forced itself out from between her teeth, that her eyes bulged out large as pigeon's eggs. Fortunately, his mother's streaming grey hair had fallen forward and so veiled her countenance though it could not disguise the fatal angle of her head to her shoulders. Of his father's corpse he received no impression because, at that instant, a second blow stunned him and sent strange dark tides rolling in to engulf his consciousness.

That so many events of critical importance in one man's life could transpire within a single dawn and sunset appeared to the prisoner incredible. Yet these events beyond a doubt *had* taken place. Yesterday morning he, Harry Wyatt, had been free, a hale young man possessed of a modest competence and, because of his appearance at Court and his introduction to Sir Francis Drake, contemplating a future in which all manner of fine things might transpire. He had been, and for that matter still was, deeply if awkwardly in love. Could Kate Ibbott have learned of his return? Assuredly. St. Neots was far too small.

Human suffering, he was discovering, no longer affected him as previously it had. Had he not seen humans shackled, branded and maimed—all in the name of the Queen's law? Had he not witnessed despairing and emaciated creatures such as the vagabonds, Dick and his companion, termed felons and marched off to perish fighting the Queen's battles with the alternative of swinging from a gibbet in some town similar to this?

Crouched upon a truss of rushes which must have remained in this same cell since time out of mind, Wyatt supported an aching head between his hands and tried not to vomit again. The floor and the walls of his cell already felt greasy, sickeningly clammy to the touch.

Once, when a small boy, he had, by accident, locked himself into a box-stall belonging to Colonel Phillips. Luckily the stallion usually stabled there had been put out to pasture, otherwise his clamour of childish terror would have frightened that great charger into trampling him flat.

As matters had chanced, grooms, laughing, had led the terrified lad out by an ear and no harm had come of the adventure. Nevertheless, Wyatt ever since had retained an inexplicable dread of confined places. Aboard ship he had experienced agonies when forced to occupy some unusually tiny cabin—no matter what the weather, he had often elected to sleep on deck among the younkers and grommets.

Now his bruised head ached intolerably, throbbed with a nauseating insistence. In his ears lingered the rasping accents of Sir Henry Cromwell, the unctuous purr of Franklin Richard Joyce, and the barking of Colonel Thomas Grant—all three Justices of the Peace. Before them he had been haled, charged with murdering an archer, one William Benton, alias Long Will the Hangman. Further, and as a more serious crime, he had attempted to impede the due and lawful execution of the Queen's justice and had offered bodily harm to the High Constable of Huntingdonshire and to Sir Andrew of Thurston.

Wyatt stared vacantly at that small patch of blue beyond the cell's one narrow window. Save for the presence of a bar of wrought iron the aperture looked wide enough to permit the passage of a man's body. While suffering the first paroxysms of despair he had tugged and wrenched blindly at that bar and in vain, for all that it had appeared so slender that surely it could be snapped or bent aside.

At his hearing, terminated scarce an hour ago, Justice of the Peace Sir Henry Cromwell had been dour as his grandson, Oliver, would prove a generation later.

So long as the rest of this devil-worshipping family had been disposed of, Sir Henry had argued, why not make a clean sweep of the whole infernal brood? The other two Justices, however, had considered Wyatt's case with less vindictiveness, for all that he must have presented a sorry spectacle standing there marked by blood and mire and with hands lashed tightly behind him. No one had found the kindness to wipe from his face blood that kept seeping down from a badly wounded scalp.

Colonel Grant had declared, "By St. Paul's toenails, Cromwell, I'll not readily hang a man who can fight as manfully as did this prisoner."

"Aye, manfully and to the death of my best archer," growled Andrew of Thurston. "Still, he's no warlock, say what you will."

"Is it within reason, Sir Henry, to hold this poor dog responsible for his assault?" Bushy brown brows had mounted. "Clearly, the fellow was distraught—as who would not be upon returning home to find his kith and kin freshly a-swing upon a gibbet?"

"Besides," the Sheriff had informed, albeit grudgingly, "if Master Wyatt lies not, he has served England well in that touchy matter of the *Primrose*. Nor do many subjects gain their reward from Her Majesty's own hand. No, let us not hang him."

"What then?" Colonel Grant had demanded while picking at a hairy nostril. "Shall we sentence him to list i' the Army?"

"This rogue displays too much spirit and would instantly desert," Sir Henry had objected. "But have it your way, Sir Andrew, and spare him the noose. Say rather that, in all mercy, that he suffer three years' imprisonment."

Because their day had been long and troublesome Sir Andrew's fellow Justices of the Peace had not proved disposed to bicker. So, Wyatt reflected heavily, tomorrow or next week therefore he must suffer branding before being committed to the dungeons of Norman Crosse Castle the which lay far from St. Neots—and poor Kate Ibbott. How bitterly she, a sensitive and warm-hearted young female, must have suffered during his family's prosecution!

"Three years a prisoner!" muttered Wyatt to himself. To be lost to God's sunlight for thirty-six months? A shiver descended the length of his back. Only a year ago in London Town he had beheld a batch of recently released felons; parchment-skinned and with near all their teeth gone, they had stumbled about St. Paul's Church begging of the gaudy, hard-hearted trulls and moneylenders there a crust. Their every bone had seemed visible beneath their noisome rags. Dully, Wyatt wondered what fate might have overtaken Peter Hopton? The last he could recall of that yellow-haired stalwart was a glimpse of him straddling a fallen figure and laying about like a paladin.

Did his cousin, too, lie in jail like himself, facing imprisonment or hanging? On the other hand Peter might have been slain or be even now writhing in agony from some heavy wound. That he might have fought his way free of that tumultuous market place was scarcely credible, and yet, and yet—fervently, Wyatt clung to the slender hope that, amidst such a press of excited human beings, an escape might have been possible.

His jailer he had discovered to be a dullard whose invariable response to any question, no matter how civilly advanced, was a kick and a curse.

By now Wyatt had ascertained that his cell contained no furniture beyond a three-legged stool, a cracked earthenware pot and that truss of mouldy rushes upon which he was squatting.

"I'll not remain here," he muttered. "I'll not suffer branding." Somehow, the determination lent him confidence, for all that he could not conjure up any means of escape.

CHAPTER XI

HANGMAN'S ROPE

Two days dragged by, endless-seeming days during which homely sounds from the street directly below his little window tantalized the prisoner with an infinity of familiar sounds—the creak of ungreased axles, the singsong of hawkers calling their wares, the clatter of horses' hooves and the breathless shouts of boys at some rough game.

After these last years at sea and its far horizons, the closeness of this tiny cell appeared as crushing as the pressure of the water when once he had dived too deep.

Although daily he tore fresh strips from his none-too-clean body jumper with which to bandage clumsily his wounded scalp the bleeding from it never quite ceased. He reasoned that this must be so because when he changed a dressing bits of scab necessarily came away with it.

Try as he would, he could not rid his memory of that ghastly impression of poor Meg's contorted features. How *could* folk supposedly reared in the gentle creed taught by Jesus Christ so torment and betray one another?

Wyatt suffered tortures from inaction—idleness for him was a punishment terrible in itself. He resolved when he escaped—as surely he would—to seek Sir John Addison and slowly strangle him so that he might hear: " 'Twas thus your lies caused my family to perish. Tell me, Sir John, how do you enjoy feeling your lungs burst? Do you know that your eyes have begun to spring from their sockets? That your tongue is sticking out? Now I'll really choke you."

On the afternoon of the third day of Wyatt's imprisonment no branding iron had yet been produced and nothing was said about his transfer to the dungeons of Norman Crosse Castle. Much like a bear confined in too small a pit the *Primrose's* Mate, for hours on end, took three strides up his cell, then three strides back. Whenever he became aware of voices in the low, arched passage beyond his door of rusty grillwork he halted, slumped at once on to the malodorous truss of rushes. It would never do to let his brutish jailer imagine him to be anything other than immersed in the stupor of hopelessness.

"Another damned hanging!" The jailer was grumbling. " 'Fore God, Jack, we grow near as busy as we were in Bloody Mary's day."

"Stow it. Ye'll get his clothes," a second voice reminded. "Who's to be stretched?"

Wyatt's heart contracted for fear that Peter's name might follow.

"Some snot-nosed 'prentice caught lifting a purse the day them witches was executed."

"What was in it?"

"Two shillings—and one and six's a hanging matter." Evidently liquored and breathing heavily they paused in the corridor opposite Henry Wyatt's cell.

"Cast yer peepers on this, Jack. This rope has swung near a hundred men. Think you 'twill serve again?"

The fellow called Jack put down an earthenware pitcher to run the cord through experienced hands. He nodded. "Aye, 'twill do for this 'prentice. He'll be easy on 't, being but a starveling youth scarce bearded. In tears the rascal vowed he stole only to eat."

"Ha! Much good that did him before Sir Henry, I warrant."

Wyatt, from the corner of an eye, watched Jack, a bent ugly fellow disfigured by a great lump on his jaw, drop the rope in order to retrieve his pitcher. "Come to my lodge, Tom, and we'll cool our gullets a while wi' this."

"Gramercy, friend Jack. I vow my weasand's drier nor any lime kiln."

Heavy, wooden-soled boots reverberated along the arched passage as the precious pair disappeared. The pitcher must have contained ale and to spare Wyatt decided when, presently, bursts of thick laughter came echoing down the passage. The hangman's rope, abandoned for the moment, remained loosely coiled like an attenuated brown serpent in the corridor.

Forcibly those coarse and greasy strands reminded Wyatt of Huntingdon Town square and of certain events three days back. Later, this length of rope inspired thoughts of rigging, of that ship which now, almost certainly, he would never own. Um. Such a line would be about the correct thickness for a halyard, or would it be more suitable as a sheet line to some mizzen's lateen sail? On the other hand, it could be used to even better advantage as an anchor line for a small boat. Anchor line—anchor line——?

Wyatt's sunken eyes flickered across to a heavy iron ring bolt let into the stonework just inside his cell's door. Praise the Lord—or possibly Sir Andrew of Thurston—the warders had neither manacled nor gyved him to such a ring. An idea presented itself and he felt seized with the eagerness of a famished soldier falling upon food when relieved after a long siege.

That rope! After listening breathlessly for footsteps Wyatt flung himself on to the stone floor and forced his arm between those close-set bars which constituted the cell door. In panting impatience he then pressed his body against the grillwork, squirmed, strained and scrabbled with his feet in order to extend his reach to its fullest. Damnation! Struggle as he would, the nearest loop of hemp remained some six inches beyond his quivering finger-tip.

Trying to ignore sickening stabs of pain caused by his hurt scalp when he pressed his head against the bars, Wyatt made a supreme effort but, tantalizingly, his fingers could only graze the ends of the rope's fibres. Granted half an inch more, he felt positive he could hook a fingernail into those precious strands of hemp. Aware of pain-induced tears running down his cheeks, Wyatt slumped panting on to the greasy stone flooring.

After a little while he sat up and, gazing miserably about, suddenly noticed his stool. He leapt across the cell and inspected its three rough hewn legs. Any of them should serve to prolong his reach.

After wrenching fruitlessly to loosen a leg from its socket, he waited until a bibulous chorus from down the corridor swelled especially loud and then, breathing a petition to the Almighty, he flung his stool crashing against the wall. He lingered in a torment of anxiety until he became convinced that no feet were charging along the corridor.

A little later the hangman's rope had vanished beneath the truss of rushes and, trembling as though seized by an ague, Wyatt examined the bar securing his window. Minute inspection revealed that, about its base, mortar had been chipped away probably by some long-dead and forgotten prisoner—but not nearly enough to free the iron. However, the unknown's effort had created a cup in which rainwater might have collected, off and on, for perhaps a century—water which had encouraged rust to form and eat at the iron.

Unbelievably calm all at once, Wyatt set to work. Twice he threaded the captured line first through the ring bolt and then around the window-bar. Next he contrived a woodsman's hitch not far from the bolt after having drawn those four lengths of stout hemp as tight as his failing strength permitted.

Through the centre of his hitch Wyatt next inserted a pair of stool legs, then commenced to revolve them, twisting the hangman's rope until the tension upon it caused knots to form. Presently the sweating, breathless prisoner was hard put to force over the pieces of wood operating his improvised windlass; also to prevent their breaking free and possibly fracturing his hands.

Wyatt's nearly empty stomach quaked, his shoulder muscles crackled and his breath escaped as does that of a wrestler struggling in the final throes of a bitter bout.

"I cannot. I lack sufficient strength." The awful realization was dawning when a vivid recollection of those three bodies dangling so limp and dripping from the gibbet's crossbar tapped an unsuspected reserve of power. Once more he concentrated his whole weight upon the levers with such effectiveness that the windlass gave suddenly and flung him headlong on to the cell's floor with the rope coiling about him like some serpent out of a South Seas jungle.

His effort had failed. The realization left him sobbing, sick and trembling. When at last he raised a swimming head it was to emit a hoarse croak of astonishment. The bright blue oblong formed by his little window no longer was bisected; the bar, torn loose by the terrific pressure he had devised, lay beside the wreckage of his stool.

Now that a path to freedom seemed opened Wyatt lost not an instant in bestirring himself. In an agony of suspense he hurried to conceal that providential rope beneath the rushes, together with the displaced bar, which he noted indeed had yielded at its lower and well-rusted end.

Long since he had come to the conclusion that the cell he occupied was probably situated fairly high above the street he knew to lie below. He would have to tarry before making his attempt, because this lovely June evening remained so bright that anyone swinging out of the jail's windows would be instantly detected.

He'd have to wait a good while, too, for darkness does not descend early during the late spring.

Wyatt's apprehensions increased when the jailer and his boon companion quit singing and presently came teetering along the corridor.

"By God's shining forelock," the jailer grunted, "some swine's stole me rope!" He belched, lingered, swaying outside Wyatt's cell.

That window remained dreadfully bright. *Would* he peer in and notice the missing bar? Wyatt's heart plummeted like a stone dropped down a well shaft.

"Wot d'ye expect?" snickered the thickset turnkey. "Wot's there in this bloody place but a parcel of thieves on either side o' the bars? I warrant 'twas Sam Jones, the new warder, has got it. Never trust a Welshman, Tom, they'll steal the very teeth out o' your jaws."

"But he ben't on duty today."

"He is. Curse you for a numskull lout!"

They lingered in the dim and smelly passage, bickering in such loud voices that, presently, various prisoners commenced to curse and shout, bidding them be still.

Indecision gripped Wyatt. What with all this clamour he could not continue to pretend sleep, else a jailer even as stupid as this would take note and become suspicious. Neither did he wish to attract undue attention; the outline of that little window still glowed against the sunset sky clear as a rectangle of stained glass.

Wyatt reared up on one elbow and mumbled, "Near an hour ago a small, darkish man came and carried away your rope saying he expected it might fetch a shilling i' the market place."

"Small and dark, eh?" belched the jailer. "Then 'twas Jones, as I've said all along. Come, friend, whilst I make yon thieving dog disgorge."

They tramped off down the corridor but not for another half hour did the sky darken sufficiently to permit Wyatt's knotting rope to ring. He employed barely sufficient line to tie a secure hitch because God only knew the distance from his window-sill to those hard cobbles he certainly would land upon.

A clock in the tower of St. George's Church had just boomed nine reverberating notes when, weakly, the prisoner leaned out of his window and commenced to lower out the rope. Despite his delay a faint luminosity lingered in the sky but it should be too feeble to reveal the end of his line. Breathing a prayer that his emergence might pass unheeded, Wyatt thrust his legs through the window—then his hips. His head swam when he found difficulty in squeezing his shoulders through so tiny an aperture. By dint of frantic exertions and at the cost of a long rip in his doublet he at last squirmed through, then clung fearfully to the swaying hangman's rope. The street lay infinitely far below, it seemed, but, fortunately, only very few lights gleamed here and there amid a dark tangle of roofs and chimneys.

Was he hearing excited voices in the cell he had just quitted? Not pausing to make sure, he lowered himself hand-over-hand—an easy matter for an experienced mariner—until, all at once, his legs were groping in vain for more rope. While summoning courage to risk a drop for an unguessable distance he learned that, sure enough, a hubbub was being raised above. When he glimpsed a light glimmering at his cell's window he released his hold, prayed that he might break no bones on landing.

As it was, Wyatt tumbled only six or seven feet on to some mud-coated cobbles and so suffered no worse damage than a shrewdly bruised knee which caused him to limp when he lumbered off through gathering darkness. Familiar with Huntingdon Town since boyhood, the fugitive pelted down a series of foul-smelling alleys then dodged behind a row of shops guarded by watchdogs which snarled defiance and lunged to the end of their chains.

The pain in his head was diminishing, Wyatt noticed, and he was running easily once he put foot to the St. Neots road. While gulping deep breaths of fragrant night air he noted that the eclipse of many stars indicated an overcast sky; besides, the familiar odour of rain was in the wind.

By alternately dog-trotting and striding along, he gained the outskirts of St. Neots about midnight. Dared he accost Simpkins, the baker, and demand his property or at the very least that small sack of gold which lay locked within a wooden coffer? A mastiff kennelled before the bakery came running out of its hutch, commenced a furious barking and decided him against such a move. A pox on the brute! If it kept up its clamour much longer the village was bound to rouse itself; then indeed he would be hard-pressed to reach the secure fastnesses of Robesden Forest where he intended to lurk until the immediate hue and cry should die down.

There remained but one single necessary act. Come what might, he must speak with Kate Ibbott.

CHAPTER XII

THE GLEN

How to waken Katherine Ibbott without at the same time arousing the draper's household became a prime consideration; if only he knew whether grey-eyed Kate were a light or a heavy sleeper. A tiny drop flicking Henry Wyatt's cheek warned that soon the rain would commence. From a pyramid looming in the draper's garden he selected a bean pole and with it commenced a gentle tapping against those tightly closed shutters securing Katherine Ibbott's bedroom. He knew the window well, having for years directed love-sick glances at its sturdy shutters.

The wind, rising, had commenced to stir trees behind him into restless activity when, to his infinite relief, sounded a soft scraping noise such as might be caused by bolts being drawn with care. By degrees the shutters swung out until, as he waited beneath boughs threshing under gusts of an increasing wind, he made out the pale outlines of Kate's face. As ever in his eyes she looked supremely lovely, crowned as she was with braids of pallid, white-gold hair the like of which he had yet to behold elsewhere.

"Harry?" she called down tensely. "Harry, is it indeed you?"

"Aye, Kate darling, 'tis I—but in sorry case."

"Nevertheless may God bless this moment, Harry." Her voice sounded low and rich like a passage played on one of those viols in Master Shakespeare's theatre on Carter's Lane in London.

To the fugitive it proved surprising that Kate should accept his untoward appearance so calmly. But then he realized that, undoubtedly, a score of St. Neots villagers must have witnessed the futile fight he and Peter had waged.

"Bide where you be, Harry," he heard her say, then the shutters swung slowly back into position. For the first time in many a bitter hour joy supplanted anguish in Wyatt's heart. Why had he half expected Kate either to ignore his tapping or to send him away under some fearful pretext? He still could scarcely credit the fact that the back door's lock had clucked softly, was opening.

"Harry, my sweet love! What agonies have I not suffered in my fears for you!" Ignoring alike his muddied and malodorous garments, wildly streaming hair and gore-streaked cheeks—that wretched scalp wound had recommenced its bleeding—she fairly flung herself into his arms.

"Ah—ah. Kate, my Kate!" was all he could say when he strained to him her body, lithe, soft and warm under a thin night rail.

"Oh!" The cool fragrance of her cheek under his lips was like the balm in Gilead.

"'Twas most shameful," she blazed, "how certain pious dolts of this countryside harried your poor folk to the gallows."

Her hands groping upward tenderly encompassed his rough, unshaven face. "And you, Harry. Are you—unhurt?"

"Aye, but only fresh broke out of Huntingdon Town jail. Already a pursuit is gathering, so, my poppet"—he employed an old term dear to them both—"our time together must be short."

"Short?" In the darkness Kate looked up in a quick, bird-like way. "Nay, my own love, this will prove no passing encounter. Two endless years have I hungered and waited for you, and a whole twelve-month has passed since last I had word from you. Oh *why*, you great dear fool, did you not tell me where you were?"

"I was none so sure mine ownself," he explained. "Nor of you."

"Why?" she demanded fiercely.

"Oh, Kate, my precious, where found you the obduracy to withstand your father's intent?"

Before making reply she pressed her lips sweetly, yet ardently, to his. "Am I not Edward Ibbott's own daughter? And therefore just as fixed in my purpose as he is in his."

"But—but, just now you seemed so little astonished to see me."

"I *knew* that nothing could prevent your coming for me." Tall, straight and ghost-like in her night shift Kate freed herself. "So convinced I was of this that I have hid and held ready food, money and a dagger which belonged to poor Rufus."

Rufus had been her older brother, a privateer slain a few years back during a brush with French pirates near La Rochelle.

When he commenced to protest she only kissed him and darted

back indoors as silently as the wraith she suggested. So he had no choice but to retreat through an increasing rain to the shelter of an apple tree planted to shade an oaken watering trough. From this he drank deeply and presently became aware of a consuming hunger. While waiting he made efforts to wash his face and hands and employed fingers to comb his greasy hair into some sort of order.

He stiffened on hearing the back door's hinges whine softly then relaxed because Kate's slight figure emerged. She was no longer garbed in white but wore a grey hooded cloak over a dark gown. He hurried forward to relieve her of a basket and the heavy bundle she supported.

"I'll carry the basket," she insisted. "It's not heavy at all. Come, Harry, the further from St. Neots dawn discovers us the better 'twill be."

"Discovers *us*!" he gasped. "God above! You aren't coming with me—a hunted felon?"

"Most certainly I am!" she insisted in a fierce undertone. "An you dream I intend to wear out my years in virgin loncliness about this pigsty of a St. Neots, then, Harry Wyatt, you're vast loony!"

Frantically Wyatt argued against such folly. Did she wot aught of the fatigues and dangers of travel? Did she not realize that he must travel like a vagabond, shunning the highways, sleeping under hedges and fleeing the sight of honest men? No. She must not desert this comfortable home and the security of her father's good name —and her own.

"You've been gently reared," he reminded her while icy rain commenced to trickle down his back. "So you must not come with me. When your father misses you he'll raise the entire countryside to a hue and cry. Kate, my darling, you can entertain no notion about the misery of plodding on and on through mud, of being rained upon for hours on end. You have yet to suffer the pangs of hunger or sickness."

Her fingernails dug into his forearm like talons. "Harry, an we don't quit this spot within a minute, I promise you a scream fit to wake all St. Neots and you'll be took. You dear, sweet dullard, *can't* you understand that I'll not be parted from you ever again?"

"Oh, Kate! My own sweet Kate." In trembling joy he grabbed her off the ground, kissed her, then caught up the bundle and quickly departed from Edward Ibbott's lightless garden.

How strangely familiar it was once more to steady Kate's feet over a narrow plank bridge spanning that brook in which as a boy he had angled for trout. A few strides more then Master Richard Amnet's plum orchard obliterated the pointed roofs of St. Neots.

Under a cold lashing rain they followed all morning various cow paths, forded muddy brooks or splashed across meadows verdant and spongy between copses and spinneys that dripped endlessly beneath a lowering sky. The route he had selected was by no means unfamiliar for, during boyhood, Wyatt had ranged most of the forests in the countryside with a yew bow and cloth-yard shafts in pursuit of certain red deer which properly belonged to the Earl of Huntingdon.

Even higher into a range of low, wooded hills he led. Kate's hood had fallen back so often, thanks to low sweeping branches, that now she allowed it to dangle between her shoulders, permitting her white-gold hair to become drenched and matted with leaves, bits of twig and bark. The basket she insisted on carrying had gradually become rain-sodden and consequently so heavy that she kept shifting her burden from one hand.

During one of their infrequent pauses Wyatt cut a length of branch in order that she might swing it over a shoulder and so relieve the ache in her arms. He noted that Kate's mouth was tight drawn now and her lips turned pale lavender while her hair had become reduced by the rain into lank strands which adhered heavily to her breast and back.

Midday found them among the crests of the Robesden hills with a chill rain still lashing down as if to castigate Edward Ibbott's daughter for having deserted her home for the love of a felon possessed of little save wits, heart and hands.

"H-Harry." Her voice sounded faint through the drifting rain. "I—I fear I must rest. I—I—my—well, in truth I have a tremendous blister on my heel. It—it hurts terribly."

"You should have spoken earlier," he chided. "The larger the blister, the longer to heal."

When he set down his bundle and knelt to examine her shoe, a light affair hopelessly unsuitable for this purpose, he locked his jaw. Blood was seeping through her stocking of light brown wool.

Kate looked almighty small and forlorn standing among the silver-grey boles of a beech grove with her gown of grey kersey sagging. The skirt of it was muddied a good foot upwards from its hem. "I'm sorry, Harry. Don't fret. I only need to rest a moment."

He rose, peered through the grey, steadily dripping woods. "We've not much further to go."

"Not much further to go where?" She attempted a smile.

"A hut I found in the old days when hunting Robesden Forest. You see yonder slope?"

"Aye, and 'tis steep, too." Involuntarily, Kate glanced over her shoulder and found that through silvery slants of rain she could see nearly all of the southern part of Huntingdonshire. Home lay back there. Home with a warm bed, tight roof and ample food.

Bone-weary and nigh to famished, Wyatt shivered. "You're near the end of your tether and no mistake about it. You'd best let me carry your basket," he insisted gruffly.

"No!" Her chin lifted so quickly that a raindrop fell from the tip of her short and slightly upturned nose. "When we quit St. Neots did I not vow that I'd bear my share of whatever burdens God sends our way? Besides, you're not to know what I have in here." She patted the big rush basket. "Until—until we reach your hut, which, God send, won't be tenanted by masterless men."

"It won't be. Look! Yonder's a good omen, I think." Far away to the north the sun had broken through and now was scattering patches of bright gold among billow-like dark green hills and valleys.

He wiped the wet from his brow with his sleeve and attempted to be convincing. "Nay, I'm sure the hut will prove empty. You see, 'tis situated too high among these hills to be of easy access. Besides, vagabonds are lazy and prefer to skulk along the roads."

Wyatt wondered briefly what fate might have befallen the two rogues he and Peter had captured. Had they escaped service in the Army? How curious were the ways of Fortune, for now, to all intents and purposes, he now was no better than they. Was he not fleeing the Queen's justice? Certainly there would be a price placed on his head; long-jawed Sir Henry Cromwell would see to that. Further, the coincidence of his escape from Huntingdon Town jail and Kate's nocturnal disappearance must long since have been perceived. Beyond a doubt Franklin Ibbott in addition would post rewards and organize a pursuit.

He presented, Wyatt guessed, a definitely unsavoury figure what with being dirty and long unshaven and wearing a bloodied clout about his head. His already ragged doublet and trunks had become further ripped by branches and torn by brambles while his green-and-black-striped hose displayed a dozen great rents, but, praise God, his boots had remained whole.

"My sweet"—he helped her to her feet—"we must get on." Firmly, he then added Kate's surprisingly heavy basket to his own bundle and was amazed that she could have carried it so far.

She smiled uncertainly while accepting a branch he had trimmed to serve as a staff. "You're not sorry I came with you, Harry? I—I fear I prove a sad hindrance."

He shook his bandage-crowned red head. "Hindrance? Never! Have you not kept up and bearing such a burden? In the old days you could never have managed it. Your endurance amazes me."

"Whilst you were abroad," she explained quietly, "I often walked by myself as far from St. Neots as I might in order that I might dream of you with none to intrude." Her full, rather wide mouth formed a fleeting smile while she replaced her hood. "At home Papa saw to it that I found little or no occasion to talk concerning you."

Although rain continued to sift down, the sky appeared to be brightening a trifle when they started on, following a narrow trail which threaded an upward course between wild mounds of time-worn boulders. They surprised a family of deer—timid red-brown creatures, which stared a long instant on the travellers before dashing off through a growth of birches which were not whiter than the flags they displayed.

Presently the track mounted so precipitously that soon they were panting and bathed in sweat.

"Wait here," Wyatt directed, then, without waiting to learn whether the girl obeyed, he climbed on alone. He returned, dripping and leaf-plastered but smiling almost before Kate realized that he had departed.

"Praise God, the hut still stands and the roof seems sound enough, but its door is gone."

The hut proved rude, indeed windowless, and even lacking a floor. The only attempts at furniture were a log bench and a crude table which stood at one end of the place. A bed of long-yellowed and dead spruce boughs paralleled the far wall. There was no chimney but, in the centre of the floor, a fireplace of blackened stones lay situated beneath a smokehole cut in the solid enough roof of turf. Rain had beat through this aperture and so had sketched a dark damp circle on the dirt floor, but otherwise the hard-packed ground seemed dry.

In abrupt apprehension Wyatt turned to regard his wet and forlorn companion peering dully about the mouldy-smelling gloom. He had to put a critical question.

"You—did you fetch along a flint and steel?"

"In the basket," Kate informed wearily. "You'll find tinder there, too."

CHAPTER XIII

ELYSIAN INTERLUDE

BY SUNDOWN the hut had undergone a considerable transformation. With the help of a birch broom improvised by Wyatt, dead leaves, acorn shells and the droppings of fieldmice and other small animals had been swept out. A small but warm fire snapped and hissed comfortably on the hearth, raising a column of acrid blue smoke to linger under the roof until it found its way out of the hole into clear spring sunshine now glancing in dazzling, golden slants through the tops of some magnificent tall beeches towering over this tiny clearing.

A deep couch of fresh and fragrant spruce tips appeared invitingly springy. There was only one, for, blushing furiously, Mistress Kate Ibbott had quickly put a period to her companion's deliberation over the sleeping arrangements.

"Since we've no blankets, my love," she pointed out with eyes fixed on the fire, "nor the likelihood of coming by some, had we not best lie together and so keep each other warm?"

"Of—c-course you—you're right," he stuttered, going scarlet as any rooster's wattles clear up to that clean cloth which Kate had bound about his dark red head. "But, s-sweeting, what w-would the—the Reverend Doctor Gage say to such notion?"

"Doctor Gage need never know," she returned serenely. "Besides, Harry, we're as much married now as ever we can be barring certain lines which we can speak before a minister at our first opportunity." Her laugh rang sweetly above the fire's snapping. "Modesty and this manner of life are impossible companions."

"Aye—t-true enough and b-bless you, dear heart, for your sense and understanding." He strode hastily out, muttering something about gathering fern shoots for their supper.

When he returned displaying a double fistful of those succulent woodland greens she already had arranged their entire supply of food on the table. "Now," she announced, brow prettily wrinkled, "you shall learn the sum of our supplies."

No wonder Kate's pannier had been so heavy! Exposed before his sunken eyes was a red-painted Dutch cheese, a flitch of bacon and three thick slices of gammon, a dozen dried fish together with two loaves of unleavened bread and, as a rare and expensive treat, an unbroken cone of sugar.

"Father will be furious when he finds this gone," she smiled. "How long think you we can survive on this?"

"With care and a deal of fasting, I'll venture we've enough here to last three, perhaps four days." An anxious frown crossed Wyatt's forehead and he went over to pass an arm about her waist. "And at least a week must pass ere the search for us is like to be abandoned."

Her grey eyes flew wide open. "Three or four days *only*?"

"No more." Yet he smiled encouragingly. "Of course, I can and will snare us rabbits, rob nesting pheasants and perchance tickle some trout in a certain stream I wot."

"Tickle trout! Are you mocking me?"

"Nay. Tickling fish is a tinkler's and poacher's art which I'll soon teach you. Had I only a bow, then surely we could dine on venison to our heart's content."

"La!" She laughed. "You'll transform Franklin Ibbott's silly daughter into a real Romany."

When he had gulped cheese and a slice of bread Wyatt lingered outside wearing a broad smile. He felt almighty set up to see smoke curl from the roof in so homely, so settled a fashion. Come to think on it, yonder stood the first home he and Kate were to share—out of how many? He paused and attempted to peer into the future, ignoring the leaking of a cracked iron pot he had discovered beside a spring on the far limit of their clearing.

After this rough shanty he visualized, first, the rough wattle-and-daub walls of a modest thatched cottage; next would come a larger dwelling of half timber and clean white plaster; finally he visualized one of those E-shaped manor houses of dressed stone such as nowadays were going up all over England.

Surely, someday, his endeavours beyond the seas would provide so suitable a setting for Kate and such children as might appear to attest the fullness and the perfection of their love.

Her pale tresses now plaited into a neat and gleaming crown, Kate appeared in the doorway. "Don't stand there like a ninny. Come, darling, our supper is ready."

He almost dropped the pot for, draped about her shoulders and emphasizing their gracious slope, Kate was wearing the blue and yellow scarf he had purchased for her in London Town!

"My—my pack! You rescued it?" He bounded forward and swept the yielding warmth of her into his arms, then, on glancing over her shoulder, experienced a great surge of delight. Among the eatables arranged on the table reposed that small wooden coffer in which he had secured the Queen's golden gift!

"Oh, Kate, Kate, is this magic? How did you——?"

"Once word got about St. Neots that you'd returned, my love," she explained, clinging to him with both arms and pressing her smooth cheek against his rough one, "I inquired about till I learned how you and Peter had entrusted a pack horse to the care of that stupid old oaf of a baker."

"And Simpkins let you have it?"

The bright line of her lips hardened. "Not without a struggle. But when I swore that we were betrothed and threatened to expose him to the constables he durst not refuse any longer."

As the sun in setting swung low over a line of rounded hills visible from the glen, he unlocked the coffer and let her handle those fourteen glittering, yellow-red coins which constituted his entire capital.

" 'Tis a pretty clink they make, eh, poppet?"

"Aye. And so, add these." She groped into the topmost petticoat beneath her simple gown of brown linsey-woolsey, and drew a small leather bag from its pocket. Laughing lightly, Kate poured into his hands a brief stream of gold and silver coins.

"There's no call to look so aghast," she reassured, studying him beneath wide, gently curving brows. "To be sure, I helped myself from Papa's strong-box. But I took far less than the dowry Father would have bestowed upon me had I wed Herbert Smollett of Parton, as he wished."

"But, but, all the same you took this sum lacking Franklin Ibbott's permission?"

Kate coloured and her small chin went up. "That I did. Had I waked Father in the midst of the night to ask him—what then would have happened?"

The realization that she had in fact rifled her father's strong-box was sobering; another and a heavy count against them should they be taken up! Now, more than ever, they must remain hidden at least a week.

"Come, Harry, let us learn the sum of our fortunes," she suggested brightly. "To understand the scope of our resources is but common sense."

That Kate during the past two years had learned more than to play sweetly on the viola—she ever had entertained a passion for music—became evident through the deft manner in which she sorted

French soleils, Portuguese escudos, Spanish and Italian ducats and coins quite unfamiliar to him. They slipped through her tapering fingers like sheep through a broken stile. He was still struggling to count those Spanish coins which constituted the bulk of their modest hoard when she announced, "Our capital, Love, by my reckoning, amounts to fifty pounds, sixteen shillings and threepence."

Grinning, he pretended to cock an ear the better to catch the anguished lamentations raised by Franklin Ibbott in the distance. All St. Neots knew the draper to be "uncommon near" and that he clung to his every groat with the persistence of an imp dragging a sinner to roast in the eternal fires.

"Alack that we could not fetch along the rest of your belongings," Kate remarked while packing the money in the little coffer. "Indeed, sir, you appeared uncommon well stocked with fine raiment."

"Oh, that? The most belonged to Peter Hopton. We shared a pack animal to fetch our goods up from the Wash. Tell me, did you hear aught concerning Peter's fate? I am most concerned."

He cast an uneasy glance at the doorway. Plague take it, the odd chance did remain that their fire might attract fellow outlaws.

"No, never a word," Kate replied. " 'Twas reported, though, by the crier that Peter Hopton slew three pikemen before escaping amidst the hurly-burly."

"Escaped!" he demanded, clutching her arm. "Are you certain?"

"No. But so it was rumoured."

"Pray God 'tis so. Had harm befallen Peter 'twould lie heavy on my conscience since the quarrel really was none of his."

"How so?" the girl demanded instantly. "Your mother, was she not also his aunt?"

Once they had consumed a meal of bread, broiled gammon and boiled fiddlehead ferns which, to their famished taste, seemed like a state banquet, they reclined on the spruce-tip couch with their backs against the log wall, staring into the embers on the open hearth.

Contentedly, and because of her almost complete exhaustion, Kate pillowed her head against his shoulder. "How wondrous peaceful it is here, Harry," she sighed. "And lovely, like the end of some brave and beauteous fairy tale."

Perhaps it was this tender contrast to those lonely and often harsh years at sea, to the horrors attendant upon his home-coming and to the terror of his imprisonment, that set Wyatt's frame to quivering, then to shaking, then more and more violently until Kate peered up in wide-eyed wonderment.

Wisely, she remained silent, only tugged that battered beloved head downwards until her lips could find his, cling, warm, vibrant and infinitely reassuring. Small incoherent sounds escaped the girl—similar sounds such as might have been heard in an Aurignacian cave when some primeval female welcomed home her mate from a long and perilous hunting expedition. She was too utterly fatigued and uncertain to seek words.

He turned, clung to her like a small and frightened lad until gradually the tremors diminished, dispelled by the delicious warmth and firm softness of the body with which she cushioned his aching, sinewy body.

"There, there, my heart's contentment," she whispered. "We've naught really to fear, now that we are together at last. Put your hand here on my breast, feel how my heart beats? 'Tis for you, only you."

To Wyatt, ever since his childhood, Kate's eyes had been; together with her incredibly fine pale hair, her chiefest loveliness. At the moment they appeared indescribably soft and luminous and pure.

The resinous perfumes of their couch enveloped them and the fire's roseate throbbing created an aura of enchantment so delicate that it might have escaped them had they not been exhausted. As it was, this release from reality became magical and the joining of their vigorous young bodies transported them into that rare Elysium into which only true lovers may enter. Diffidently at first they explored each other's mysteries, then blended without restraint.

Near dawn Wyatt's long service at sea—where a man sleeps soundly only at his peril—caused him to rouse up, wide awake in an instant. A rustling had sounded from among a clump of bushes opposite the doorway. His hand sought the hilt of that dagger Kate's brother Rufus had worn, but fell away when he recognized the acrid stench of a dog-fox. Sighing in relief, he settled back among the boughs only to rouse again on one elbow the better to stare in wondering amazement upon the ineffably graceful outlines of her who lay beside him, lost in a profound slumber.

Kate's face, pillowed on a muddied but dry petticoat, was relaxed in tender repose, the piquancy of her profile accentuated by the dark material; her head suggested a pool from which the tangled lustre of her tresses escaped like spilt water. During her slumbers that shift which was doing duty as a night rail had slipped far enough to bare to the rosy dawn light the perfection of a pallid breast full and round and wonderfully adorned by a nipple as neat and pink as a new clover blossom.

How long he remained thus familiarizing himself with her beauty Wyatt entertained no notion but presently he sank back and relapsed into a deep and restful sleep.

After blowing the coals into a blaze, Wyatt observed, "I have been thinking that, once we have waited out our time here in the hills, we had best travel down to London."

"London! Oh, Harry, no! I would be *that* terrified!" She looked swiftly up from plaiting her hair into slim twin braids. "I've never seen a town larger than Huntingdon."

"So is everyone the first time they enter London. And small wonder. Near two hundred thousand souls, so they say, live and have their being in and about London. Certainly 'tis the best place quickly to snatch at power and fashion a fortune." Eagerness entered his voice. "Now that Sir Francis Drake is readying a fleet to sail against Spain there will be opportunity and to spare for a brisk young mariner with ambition, a new wife and a measure of gold in his purse."

"Sir Francis Drake! Oh, Harry, yon *is* a name to conjure with." Kate smiled and set about lacing up what she called a privy coat—in reality a clumsy corset fashioned of buckram and wooden splints. Suddenly she noticed that her feet, revealed by the morning sun, were none too clean, so, blushing, she concealed them under her petticoats. "At every fair and every tavern one hears songs and new tales about this Golden Admiral of the Queen's. Here's one of the latest."

In a rich, untrained contralto she sang:

"*You brave heroic minds*
Worthy your country's name,
That honour still pursue;
Go and subdue!
Whilst loitering hinds
Lurk here at home with shame."

When he had done applauding softly—he wanted no untoward noises emanating from their glen—she turned in a wren-quick motion.

"Is't indeed true that Sir Francis is a veritable giant possessing the strength of two men?"

"Lord love you no, dear. Why, I stand a full head taller than he, but there is that about those fierce blue eyes of his and something in his manner that would lend truth to such reports.

"I vow 'twas amazing to witness how those popinjay courtiers, great noblemen and even state councillors bowed low and scraped their toes when Sir Francis passed. You'd have laughed, too, the way the painted ladies at Court fluttered and cast sheeps' eyes in his direction, for all that he's new married to Elizabeth Sydenham."

Wyatt's enthusiasm mounted even as he set about skinning a rabbit taken in his springes. "You should hear the wondrous tales concerning his voyage around the globe, how he put down mutineers in his crew, fought cannibals and finally captured the great *Cacafuego*, otherwise the *Nuestra Señora de la Concepción*, the Governor of Peru's treasure carrack."

"Then 'tis true no lie that he fetched back a million pounds in gold and silver?"

"Yes, it is true. Everywhere Spaniards quake at the mere mention of him they call '*el Draque*', and King Philip rages over huge losses suffered at his hands." He jerked the gory hide from his quarry and flung it into the bushes. "But what has gone before is as a pale shadow to what our Golden Admiral now will accomplish against the Papists. You should have watched Sir Francis' expression, Kate, when Foster and I recounted that foul treachery attempted aboard the *Primrose*."

"Sir Francis, then, must be rich in his own right?"

"Aye. He's become one of the richest men in all England but keeps his money at work. Hardly a venture sails for foreign lands but counts at least one Drake-owned vessel among its number."

Wyatt carried the rabbit's pink carcass indoors then reappeared to pour water over his bloodied hands. "He already owned Buckland Abbey, Sherford and Yarcombe manors in Devon when he married Sir George Sydenham's daughter and now is lord over still vaster properties by consequence."

"Then surely this famous gentleman must be high and mighty of manner." Inexplicably, Kate ran over to fling arms about him and kiss him on a V exposed by his unbuttoned doublet.

"Nay, Sir Francis' nature is to the contrary," Wyatt smiled, patted her head. "As a rule he is among the most unassuming of men, except when he brags of what he has done, and will do, to the Dons. Is it not amazing to recall that, scarce fifteen years ago, he had little to his back and nothing in his purse? To prove to you that my ambitions towards owning my own craft are not moonshine, I'll remind you that Sir Francis is not alone in wresting fortune and glory from the sea."

"Who, for instance?"

"Sir Walter Raleigh, Sir William Winter, Sir Richard Grenville and the two Hawkinses, John and William."

He placed an arm about Kate, ever amazed and delighted at the firm softness of her, then turned her about that he might gaze full into her wide grey eyes. Gravely he informed: "What these men have accomplished is not beyond me. I vow to you, Kate, you shall live to see me knighted and lord over a fine manor. I further promise you," he spoke softly, soberly, "that the Queen, someday, will be pleased to receive Lady Wyatt at Court."

Her vivid lips curled into a smile of ineffable confidence, blissfully unaware of the enormous hazards he must overcome. "I believe that you will, Harry. I, too, have dreamed large dreams for us."

After breakfasting they wandered out into the glen and sat under the beeches watching various birds busy with their small affairs. When Kate coaxed him into describing his voyages Wyatt made her see and smell a number of the hot and malodorous ports at the Mediterranean's eastern end, caused her to marvel over the great crumbling buildings of Constantinople where the Grand Turk ruled, and to shudder over the wickedness of Marseille. In her turn she entertained him by singing any number of old country songs as they bathed, mother-naked, in a pool found below a miniature cascade. And so on wings of sheer delight commenced their week of hiding.

CHAPTER XIV

LONDON TOWN—1585

JUST two days after the *Primrose* had sailed off down the Thames on her way to Plymouth, dusty and road-weary Henry and Kate Wyatt tramped through Moorgate and became engulfed by restless and burgeoning London.

For a night, and quite honestly, too, at the Red Knight they occupied a room as man and wife since they had been married at Bedford in the county of that name. That all-important ceremony had been performed by a kindly but doddering old rector of a parish church who had not proved unduly curious over their sunburnt and travel-stained appearance, and so had joined them in Holy Matrimony and had recorded the marriage of this sturdy, red-haired young man with the steady, dark blue eyes and the handsome, golden-haired young woman who seemed so completely serene and confident,

Happily, their sixty-odd-mile journey down to London had been enlivened by but one mischance; a pair of burly fellows had plunged out of a thicket to snatch at the bridle of that sumpter horse upon which Kate's pillion and their slender baggage had been slung. The merest prick of Wyatt's dagger had caused one of the robbers to lumber off howling and nursing a dripping arm, while with the quickness of a ferret the other became lost amid the tangle from whence he had emerged.

Once Kate had been safely installed, Wyatt set off for the waterfront and re-experienced the thrill he had felt on first viewing the maze of yards, topmasts and gaffs created by the dozens and dozens of vessels of all rigs and twenty nationalities anchored in the Pool, off Billingsgate, or tied up near Her Majesty's Custom House.

At a chandler's loft in Buttolph Lane favoured by Captain Foster, he ascertained, first, that the *Primrose* indeed had sailed, and second, that due to King Philip's embargo, nearly a hundred English merchantmen had failed to return from Spanish ports. Also he had reaffirmed news that Queen Elizabeth was mustering a great army to fight the Papist Powers in the Low Countries.

Through one Nicholas Spencer, a ship rigger and an acquaintance of long standing, Wyatt made inquiry as to where might one, for a modest, a very modest, sum hope to purchase a small sloop, a hoy or even a bugalet. The vessel he desired might be of small tonnage provided she was capable of keeping the sea for a month and could be navigated by—say seven mariners and a Master?

"Now, friend Wyatt, what you bespeak is not easily come by," Spencer replied, fingering his beard. "Although many craft have lingered in the river since the Spanish embargo, even more are under charter first, to transport the Earl of Leicester's forces across the Narrow Sea, and then to keep his poor dogs of soldiers in victuals. But let me see, let me see."

Spencer, a wizened, brown-faced fellow bearing a broad purplish scar across his left cheek, meditated briefly, then spat on to stinking mud exposed by an ebb tide. "I mind a paunchy Dutchman I encountered at the Bell Inn yesterevening. Being fat and lazy, he's 'feared to risk a slave's chains aboard some Spanish galley. He owns an old hoy that *might* serve yer purpose and should be sold cheap, I'm thinking."

Pieter van Kleykamp proved to be a huge, fan-bearded barrel of a man possessing no visible neck and a bright red moon of a face. *Ja.* A hoy he owned in the Pool. How old was she? Well, the *Katrina* was no longer as young as once she had been. But then, who was? Kleykamp bellowed at his own wit. How old? Well, maybe she had slid down the ways fifty—maybe sixty years ago. But, by St. Michael's lance, the *Katrina* still was well-found, sound as a nut.

They inspected her and, as Wyatt had anticipated, she proved to be almost round—her length being just twice the measure of her beam and therefore allowing ample cargo space. But the hoy was, beyond a doubt, very, very old and leaky. Worse still, Mynheer van Kleykamp obdurately refused to consider a groat less than fifty golden pounds for his craft—hull, spars, and running gear.

Hopeful and desperately wishful, Wyatt inspected the Dutchman's vessel from her stem to the weird, whipstaffed rudder by which she was steered. He found it encouraging that van Kleykamp offered no objection when he dug his dagger's point into each and every one of the hoy's ribs, knees and sheathing. The Hollander only noisily swilled beer and grunted when, occasionally, Wyatt's blade sank in with suspicious ease; he knew that, in the present market, he would win his asking price.

In the end Wyatt decided that, despite her venerable appearance, the *Katrina* essentially was sound and that her hutch of a forecastle would just about accommodate the crew he had in mind, although they must sleep pretty much piled on one another like pigs in the sunshine. Aft was the Master's cabin, low ceilinged and furnished with only a narrow bunk and a drop-leaf table.

"Now, as to her sails?"

The Dutchman's massive shoulders rose in a shrug. "Oh, mine canvas haff I sold alreadys."

Wyatt glowered at this infuriatingly placid, moonfaced fellow. "But, Mynheer, you gave me to understand that my fifty pounds would cover rigging and sails."

"*Nie.*" Van Kleykamp scratched at his hairless pate. "Hull, spars and running gear you vill haff. I said nothings about sails."

The young mariner swallowed hard—nothing *had* been said about canvas, but the purchase of a suit of even hand-me-down sails would leave Kate Wyatt with precious little on which to subsist until he fetched home the first profits earned by the *Katrina*.

Caustically, Wyatt thanked Mynheer van Kleykamp, had himself rowed ashore and for two more days ranged the waterfront from Paul's Wharf to Swan Pier; from Smart's Key all the way downstream to Galley Wharf in the shadow of the Tower. His arms and back ached from rowing endlessly it seemed, between one craft and the next. Spencer had been entirely correct; vessels were greatly in demand, especially those suitable as transports or victuallers in trans-Channel trade.

"Surely you will come across a better craft?" Kate encouraged as they sat in their tiny bedroom, her needle flashing to repair rents in his second-best galligaskins—full and unpadded breeches. A long time would pass ere he could afford others of similar quality.

Wyatt frowned, slowly beat one fist against its fellow. "The kind of ship I want 'twould seem is as scarce as crowing hens. Worst of it is, if I'm to sail from Plymouth along of Drake's squadron I must leave within the week. He's gathered a powerful fleet and waits only the arrival of some victuallers and I *must* sail with him, sweeting. Yonder lies my great opportunity."

Her pale lustrous hair gleamed in sunset light beating through a window nearly as small as the one through which he had escaped Huntingdon jail. "What was the most seriously amiss with that hoy you mentioned the other day?"

"Her age—and the price I'd have to pay for her," he admitted despondently.

"Is she rotten?"

"No. The *Katrina's* timbers seemed sound enough wherever I could test them, but, because of ballast, I couldn't examine her bottom and I can't afford to have it removed, or to have her careened." Again he beat his fists together—a mannerism he had when perplexed, Kate noted. "I expect I'll end by purchasing her though I'll have to go into debt for a suit of sails—and that I don't fancy."

He then explained that a set of sails, even of old canvas, would require another fifteen pounds.

"Surely your friend Nicholas Spencer will accept a written promise for a part of the purchase price?"

"Likely he would," Wyatt agreed. "But plague take it—'tis a poor thing for us to start off in debt."

"You shouldn't look at it that way, Harry," Kate commented, bending her bright head to bite off the thread. "Consider that you are merely hiring money, as you would a pack horse—you are paying for the use of it."

In the end he bought the hoy, then dickered with Nicholas Spencer for the necessary sails and certain other supplementary gear. That bluff and genial individual proved quite ready to advance the necessary sum provided that Mistress Kate added her signature to a letter admitting the obligation. This was only customary, he added in some embarrassment, when the principal maker of such a note would be leaving the jurisdiction of the Queen of England.

Because of his nearly depleted purse, Wyatt decided to recruit for the *Katrina*—odd and perhaps lucky that his first command should bear the same name as his wife—five men instead of the seven he originally had contemplated. Therefore he exerted every effort to secure and sign on only strong, young and likely hands, of which precious few remained about the Port of London.

So at the end of the week the *Katrina* swung to her moorings with sails bent on, with her standing gear freshly tarred, and showing bright new planks here and there along her long-unpainted sides.

In the matter of picking up a cargo for Plymouth Wyatt met with no trouble at all. There was plenty of freight such as canvas, barrels of biscuit and casks of salted beef destined for such of the Queen's ships as were outfitting in the town of Plymouth.

"An I find Sir Francis already sailed, I'll be back within the month with enough profit to pay off Nick Spencer and careen the hoy, too," he promised, drawing Kate closer to him and trying to ignore the suddenly stricken look of her. "I'll not want for return cargo. 'Tis said that merchants in the coastal traffic are fighting for space."

Sated and slaked of their urgencies, Wyatt and his wife lay abed in Dame Foster's little spare room—the Captain had bespoken it for his former Mate—and sleepily watched a succession of small clouds dim the face of a gibbous moon. Kate murmured, stirred, pressed a smooth, damp cheek to his. "What odd shapes they assume. Do you recognize the one which suggests a silvery battle flag streaming in the wind?"

"Aye," he whispered. "To me it looks like a banner flown in victory." But even as he spoke the moon disappeared and in a trice the omen vanished as if snatched away by some revived enemy.

Kate shivered. "Oh-h. That *was* unchancy!"

"It signifies nothing, my heart. 'Tis silly to credit omens."

She turned again to him and when the moon presently reappeared neither of them noticed the fact.

Book Two

"TO ANNOY THE KING OF SPAIN"

CHAPTER I

H.M.S. *BONAVENTURE*

ADMIRAL SIR FRANCIS DRAKE roused to the sound of drums rattling on deck. He yawned, half sat up but settled back against an enormous feather bolster at the head of his elaborately carved four-poster bed—a bed which was clamped to deck and side. Idly, he watched the bright reflection of wavelets dancing on the vermilion-and-gold-painted beams above. Through the stern ports—they were larger than the windows of many a country church and as tastefully decorated but with their designs done in clear glass—Drake could see certain of the vessels composing his slowly increasing squadron.

Tall and stately at her anchor swung Rear-Admiral Knollys' *Galleon Leicester*, the bright flags at her mastheads curling gently to an onshore breeze. Beyond her lay the *Tiger*, commanded by Lieutenant-General Christopher Carleill—a capable fighting man he was thankful to have along on this little matter. Kit Carleill knew how to handle troops ashore, he did, and, praise God, he wasn't one of those block-head generals who fought only according to the rule book. Often he had proved he could improvise tactics to meet a given situation on the spot.

"Pray God Her Majesty don't change her mind again, or that Burghley, the timid old goat, persuades her that real peace with Spain remains possible."

Reaching out, he summoned a page by ringing a silver bell. While he waited for the boy to appear he got out of bed and, with flowing night shift billowing about his sturdy and slightly bowed legs, went over to stand staring out of the stern ports. It was fine to see Plymouth! He first had beheld this pretty little port as a boy when, with his father, he had fled Papist persecution in Tavistock, his birthplace; then, as an apprentice seaman, a yellow-haired youth, smallish but possessed of an enormous ambition. Here he had collected ships and recruited men for several of his most devastating raids into the Caribbean. It was in here that, on a sunny September afternoon in 1580, he had sailed the *Golden Hind* to complete his dazzlingly successful circumnavigation of the world.

Idly Drake watched a small boat come pulling over from the *Primrose*, she of Bilbao fame now was refitted as a stout little man-of-war and sailed under the command of crusty old Martin Frobisher. Whom was she fetching over to the flagship? Surely the Vice-Admiral would not so far anticipate the General Council called to meet aboard the *Bonaventure* at nine of the morning?

"A fine morning, Sir Francis," a fresh-faced page, wearing Drake's crest embroidered on his doublet, advanced offering his master a sparkling clean shirt, fresh hose of plum-coloured silk and breeches, which were now becoming the fashion, together with a stiffly starched yellow ruff. "A fine morning, sir," he repeated, "and Captain Fenner would like a word with you most immediate."

"I'll receive him as soon as you have trimmed my beard." Drake stepped out of his night shift but lingered a moment to permit cool air to come bathe his diminutive but powerfully constructed figure.

Eight or ten old wounds had left reminders in the guise of white or purplish scars. Most noticeable of all was the one he had taken during that all-but-fatal attack at San Juan de Ulúa back in 1568 when Don Martin Enriquez, Viceroy of Mexico, had fallen upon John Hawkins' little fleet quite as treacherously as the Corregidor of Bilbao had attempted to seize the *Primrose*. On that day Francis Drake had achieved a deep and undying hatred for Spain, Rome and all that they stood for.

Even as the page rolled up the Admiral's hose and slipped on high-heeled pumps of yellow Spanish leather decorated with large rosettes, he could hear mariners and soldiers being summoned for prayers. Apparently Sir Francis had decided he would not this morning offer prayers at Divine Service, although it was his invariable practice when at sea to conduct either the morning or evening religious observances required upon any vessel or vessels he commanded.

The page noted that an opened Bible lay on a table beside Drake's bed. Not for nothing was he the eldest son of Edmund Drake, who at Gillingham Reach, the Tudor navy's home port, had been appointed as Bible Reader to the Ships. For this pious duty Drake's father nevertheless had received so meagre a pittance that he and his swarming brood of twelve sons had been forced to camp aboard a hulk abandoned on a malodorous mudflat in the Medway.

Once the page had tied Drake's ruff into position the Admiral adjusted his belt, then knelt and, together with his page, prayed to Almighty God that He would favour certain bold moves he was contemplating in the service of his Royal mistress—also that the fleet might speedily conclude its provisioning.

His devotions at an end, Drake sprang lightly up and almost ran out of the cabin. A soldier outside his cabin door hurriedly presented his arquebus.

"Good morning, Archibald."

"And a fine morning to you, sir. Captain Fenner's that anxious to see you, sir. He's brought tidings from London."

News from London? God send it was not some contradictory command from the Queen!

Drake's small bright blue eyes narrowed. When he appeared on deck it was to find Captain Fenner in anxious conversation with a pair of merchant officers both of whom pulled off their hats and bowed as the resplendent little figure advanced. They had come to report, the merchant masters explained, that the main supply of gunpowder forwarded by John Hawkins from the Tower had been delayed by a fierce storm which had come swooping up out of the Bay of Biscay to wreak severe damage in the Thames Estuary and all along the south-east coast of England. The magazine ships, Fenner's companions swore, had barely been able to fight their way into Southampton and were so badly battered that at least three or four days' work would be required to render them seaworthy again.

"Indeed, sir," declared one of the visitors, "it were a main bad tempest. Many are the poor fishermen whose widows are red-eyed and whose children go hungry."

"Plague take it!" This was the nearest to profanity that Drake customarily would allow himself—indeed a strange affectation amidst a generation of the most tremendous swearers in all English history. "More delay."

Presently Vice-Admiral Martin Frobisher's small boat was rowed up under the *Bonaventure's* counter and that white-bearded, weather-beaten individual came scrambling up the side, nimbly enough for all that he was about fifty, to report that, during the night, the *Barque Bonner*, one hundred and fifty tons, had sprung so serious a leak that undoubtedly she would have to careen before putting to sea.

Drake listened, paced agitatedly about his quarter-deck, a thick gold chain slung below his ruff flashing to his short and jerky stride. His brow fell into the wrinkles of frustration. Every delay now was like a thorn entering his flesh and, more lately dread presentiments had been nagging at his peace of mind like the incessant clamour of a scolding wife. Suppose that the Queen, at this last moment, took it into her head to transfer the supreme command upon some highborn

Court favourite? She had done so in the past, God wot. Suppose that Spanish agents in London or in Plymouth, for that matter, had caught wind of his true intentions and were preparing a deadly welcome? Aye, the sooner he could get to sea, the better.

More and more small boats commenced to appear alongside, and, having shipped oars, trailed astern of the *Bonaventure* like ducklings clustered about their mother.

At length, all the leaders of the fleet appeared aboard, including privateer captains and those who commanded ships belonging to, and fitted out by, the City of London. In fact, only two of the Queen's own vessels, the *Bonaventure* and the *Aid*, would accompany this expedition.

Drake's own vessel, the *Thomas*, at that moment came sailing out of the inner harbour to drop anchor before a new fort being constructed under Drake's direction. He had bestowed the command of her to his younger brother, Thomas Drake—a youth from whom he was coming to expect a great deal. Not to be outdone, Will Hawkins had sent along the *Galliot Duck* and had named his nephew, young Richard Hawkins, to be Captain over her.

All in all, twenty-nine ships flew the Cross of St. George in addition to a variety of gaily hued banners bearing the arms of gentlemen serving aboard them.

Drake's Captains created a curious pageant as they collected on the *Bonaventure's* quarter-deck. These offered a series of paradoxes in that they affected modish fripperies and elegant, but generally tasteless, costumes, while their faces were weather-stained, hard and sometimes downright brutal.

"Gentlemen, I deem the moment proper," Drake declared, his gaze swinging from one bearded face to the next, "to disclose privily to you the object of this venture upon which we are presently to embark.

"Most of you are aware that the Catholics, through the Jesuits and the Guises of France, time and again have plotted the murder of our Gracious Queen, that not six years ago the League's troops under Doctor Sanders invaded her realm of Ireland, and that Papist Princes for ever bestir Scotland to make war upon us."

The Admiral was talking rapidly, persuasively. "You all will recall the plottings of Francis Throckmorton and that the Dutch Prince of Orange was murdered by an assassin hired by this unholy League. Gentlemen, even Lord Burghley has become convinced that Her Majesty must act promptly, or our Protestant friends in the Low Countries and in the west of France will be most cruelly exterminated.

"The Queen, therefore, has undertaken to defend the United Provinces," Drake's voice rang out, "by landing a strong army under the Earl of Leicester and has decided that, without actually declaring war, we are to render Spain impotent to attack us."

Martin Frobisher's untidy white beard lifted and fell under a puff of wind as he snorted, "Without declaring war? Sooner can one pass a porpoise through a ring bolt!"

"And how, Sir Francis," queried Knollys grimly, "can this, our weak and ill-equipped squadron, be expected to render Philip of Spain and his great fleets unable to undertake their vaunted *Empresa* against us?"

Crowding in, they strained to catch Drake's reply. "How? Here is the grand plan. We are to fight Spain in the name of Dom Antonio, Pretender to the Crown of Portugal. As you know, Philip has seized his realm so Her Majesty's Councillors feel that, without risking a declared war, she can allow Englishmen to fight in this fashion at the same time attracting to his cause Hollanders, Swedes and Huguenot French. Such a combination would take the form of an international company to which the Queen will grant commissions to fit out, to victual and to sell booty in England. In return for this licence, the Royal Treasury will receive a generous share of the spoils."

Amazement, satisfaction and doubt variously became registered on those fierce, red-brown faces now revealed in every detail by the brilliant sunlight.

Lieutenant-General Carleill spoke first. "God's toenails, Sir Francis, we, already assembled here in Plymouth, surely ain't expected to tarry until a parcel of foreigners can be recruited?"

"Not if I can prevail!" Drake returned warmly. "Through certain friends in Spain, Sir Francis Walsingham has ascertained the fact that two *flotas*, the one in Lisbon, the other Cádiz, are being collected, armed and supplied for King Philip's *Empresa*, or conquest of England.

"Now on our part, so the Lords of the Navy Board declare, we too need time, time in which to build war galleons and great-ships for our defence and to cast cannon and train crews for them."

"How much time?" demanded the hoarse accents of Captain Edward Careless of the *Hope*.

"All of two years," came Drake's prompt response—he lent the impression of knowing all there was to know about this matter. "Now, gentlemen, you will readily understand the urgency of our mission.

It is in all ways to harass and impoverish Spain. We are to deny King Philip munitions and naval stores from abroad, we're to harry his fisheries." His expression kindled and those piercing blue eyes flickered from face to face. "Best of all, we've permission to harry the Spanish King's *own* ports!"

"God above!" burst out Captain Fenner. "*Attack Spain herself?*"

"Aye," Drake replied easily. "Also, we're to excite rebellion in Philip's colonial possessions and," he almost licked his lips, "place them under tribute."

Captain Careless' leathery features fell into a grin. A neat phrase that "place them under tribute". What he really meant was to sack, plunder, burn and otherwise destroy the great treasure-producing ports of the Spanish Main.

"By thus hamstringing this fellow Philip"—Drake injected a world of contempt into his tone—"we can win scope in which to build a fighting fleet and so stand ready when the *flotas* of Spain and Portugal finally sail to attack us."

The Admiral might have added, but did not, that a deal of this apparently native philosophy had been evolved by John Hawkins, who for many years had advanced the strategy of carrying the war to Spain herself and ever had held out against the folly of squandering English gold and lives on the Continent.

It was true enough, however, that he and John Hawkins had seen eye-to-eye on insisting that Philip could be defeated by the creation of a blockade which would deprive him of many vital munitions which could not be produced in his kingdom. Dreaming old dreams anew, they had pointed out that the loss of treasures from America would cause the Hapsburg's already shaky economy to collapse.

After taking a brisk turn down the quarter-deck Sir Francis bore down upon the council as if he were attacking it.

"I further charge you, gentlemen, to complete your provisioning and the fitting out of your vessels at top speed. See what can be done to procure food immediately, fill water butts today—but with sweet water. I wish to be gone before an order comes from Whitehall bidding us delay against the arrival of foreigners. Now, my good friends, get you gone about your occasions."

CHAPTER II

THE SURVIVORS

ON THE day following his summoning of the General Council Sir Francis Drake commenced to feel somewhat encouraged over a quick departure from England for the magazine ships had not been so severely damaged as reported and, granted luck and a fair breeze, should come sailing into Plymouth's crowded harbour within the next forty-eight hours.

By dint of promises, bonuses and threats, mounds of supplies collected on the little port's fishing piers grew steadily higher. Everywhere barges, whalers and all manner of small boats were pulling out to ships whose mariners were busy reeving new tackle, cutting gun ports or bending on canvas.

Now that he had conducted the vesper service aboard his flagship the Admiral settled himself comfortably to a table set upon the quarter-deck and applied himself sparingly to a flagon of cool Canary wine while a secretary laboured to keep up with his master's preparation of a report. Feet thumped up the poop-deck ladder and the Officer of the Deck appeared doffing his cap. "Sir Francis, a hire boat lies alongside bearing a brash fellow who insists that he be permitted to address Your Honour in person."

Drake glanced up from under bushy yellow brows. "He gave his name?"

"No, sir, but he claims your friendship and consideration."

Because his mood was mellow, Drake nodded. "Does he now? Well, direct the rascal aloft, but he's to remain only a moment, mind."

"Aye, sir. I'll fetch him prompt away."

"Stab me!" the Admiral burst out when before him appeared the dark red head, coppery complexion and solid figure of Henry Wyatt. "If it ain't our young cockerel of out the *Primrose*."

"Aye, Sir Francis, and my humble thanks for receiving me."

Drake ran an eye over the visitor and decided that he must have fallen on to hard times being barefooted and clad only in a sadly stained shirt and ragged pantaloons. Moreover, there was about his dark blue eyes an anxious, almost stricken, look which previously had not been there.

"Well, my lad, and what would you of me?"

"Sir," he looked at the Admiral in the eye, but the words fell heavily from his lips, "I came to learn whether you can find me a place among your company."

"Oh? So our fine young cock has altered his views about entering Her Majesty's service? How flattering. Belike you've squandered the Queen's gift money and now must win your bread?"

A painful flush surged into Wyatt's cheeks. "No, Sir Francis. There is more to it than that."

"More?"

"Aye, sir. I bought me an old hoy in London—the best I could afford, and was fetching supplies for your fleet, but last week a great gale sprang up and—well, the *Katrina's* bottom could not have been sound—I'd not the money to have her careened—all at once she commenced to leak like a market basket."

"She sank?"

"Aye, sir, and took three of my crew with her," was Wyatt's miserable admission. "The rest clung to the wreckage and were picked up by yonder hulk."

Drake's expression softened and that singularly winning smile of his warmed Wyatt's heart. "It is a sad thing to lose a ship, especially your first. I know. I have lost ships, even have had to sink them myself as I once did off San Bernardino." He was thinking of a certain critical day off Nombre de Dios nearly fifteen years earlier. His fingers commenced to tug at a lustrous pear-shaped pearl in his ear. "So you are ruined?"

"Worse than that, sir," Wyatt admitted bitterly. "I am in debt, and—and I now have a wife to support."

"Wife? Dear God, man, you *have* been busy since last we parted. Guy," he beckoned a serving man. "Fetch up imminently a cup of wine and a plate of food, I warrant my friend here has dined neither well nor regularly in some time. That will do, Foulke," he informed his secretary. "We will resume later. Pray relate to me, Master Wyatt, all that has chanced since last we met."

Between gulps of Canary and attention to the leg of a cold capon nicely garnished with truffles, Wyatt described as best he might the tragic fate of the witches of St. Neots, his escape from jail and lastly the glory of Kate Ibbott's courage and constancy. "So you see, sir, 'tis hard for me to picture my fortunes at a lower ebb." He straightened his shoulders, forced a smile. "Since the hulk which rescued me was for Plymouth, I bethought me of your parting words."

Thoughtfully Drake fingered a diamond and pearl pendant suspended from an ornate gold chain. "How many hands were saved along with you?"

"Three stout fellows, sir, and they find themselves in little better case than I."

"Instruct them to go aboard the *White Lion.*" Briefly Drake's jewel-loaded fingers caressed his golden beard. "As for you, Master Wyatt—um, well, my Sailing Master's Mate met with an accident two days ago. You will report to my Flag-Captain, Thomas Fenner. Your wage will be ten shillings each month. An you prove the handy mariner I take you to be, why, perhaps I'll find you a new command at the Spaniards' expense."

CHAPTER III

THE QUEEN'S DARLING

DESPITE the repeated dispatch of gallopers and swift pinnaces along the coasts of Cornwall and Devon to hurry the assembly of essential supplies, Sir Francis Drake's small squadron was forced to linger day after day in the pretty harbour of Plymouth, all the while defiling its water with chips, garbage and less attractive flotsam. Worse still, certain crews commenced to desert, lured by the promise of high wages paid aboard merchantmen engaged in coastwise traffic.

Seemingly futile were Admiral Sir Francis Drake's appeals to the Privy Council and especially to the Corporation of the City of London which had underwritten a majority of the ships under his command. That small man's temper grew ragged at the appalling slowness with which certain new guns, demi-cannon and perriers, were being mounted. Every day's delay was terribly costly and the chief expense of this expedition was borne by himself and other private investors. The Queen's Treasury did not share in this—her Treasury thus far had advanced not a penny. Only grudgingly had Her Majesty lent the *Bonaventure* and the *Aid* for this cruise, and even their crews were paid from the private purses of the investors.

As for Henry Wyatt, the delay meant even greater torment. He could picture Kate thunderstruck, bewildered and discouraged by the letter he had painfully scribbled upon arrival at Plymouth. To be sure, there was no certainty that she would receive his missive since he had had no choice but to entrust it to the sober-appearing pilot of a dispatch pinnace. For all Wyatt knew the fellow might have thrown away the letter and got drunk with the shilling paid to ensure its delivery. How bitter it was to be so comparatively near to Kate and yet so far. Possibly by now Captain Foster had completed his first voyage to the Low Countries in a new cromster he had bought with the *Primrose's* sale money.

Poor Kate! What a blow she must have suffered on reading about the loss of the *Katrina*, and with that hoy the bulk of her self-selected dowry. How easy to be wise in retrospect! Cost what it might, he should have taken time to careen the *Katrina* and so inspect her bottom foot by foot and plank by plank.

And now the urgent necessity of repaying Nicholas Spencer those fifteen golden pounds he had borrowed hung like a millstone about his neck. God above! Would Drake's squadron never stand out and shape a course for the Bay of Biscay? How long must he await the opportunity to prove himself, and so gain a new command?

Of the Admiral, Wyatt saw little yet; whenever he did, the yellow-haired hero of England invariably treated him to a friendly nod and that smile which, magically, generally converted bitter enemies into staunch friends. There had been many a tempestuous debate in council during which various Captains hurled oaths and insults at each other until Sir Francis Drake appeared, ready to understand each and every man's problem, and yet insistent that every officer give in two points to gain one. In an age where short tempers and long daggers were the rule his patience proved to be monumental.

Nothing amazed Henry Wyatt more than that discipline Drake insisted on enforcing aboard his flagship and all those under his command. Heretofore, crews had been known to ignore their Captains' commands when it suited them and on many a long voyage mutiny had been the rule rather than the exception, consequently many an expedition had come to disaster.

On his epoch-making voyage around the world Drake had come within an ace of disaster on the bleak shores of Tierra del Fuego. He had tried, dined, and then very politely indeed had executed one Thomas Doughty as the moving spirit of disunion.

True, certain veteran sea dogs like Frobisher, Borough and Bromley grumbled incessantly against this new order and spared gentlemen serving under them as much as they could of their duties as mariners.

At length the missing ordnance arrived and was hoisted inboard piece by piece. A party of armourers from Deptford Naval Yard made sure that the guns were properly mounted and disparted. They begrudged the time, being busy in arming certain vessels which John Hawkins was building against that day when English men-of-war must stand out to sea in the defence of the Realm.

Nearly every day ships made port describing impressive preparations undertaken by King Philip's Admirals, especially the crafty and battle-wise Marquis of Santa Cruz. All Spanish and Portuguese colonies, cities and towns of consequence were under levy. In addition the shipyards of Lisbon, Cádiz and Barcelona had become hives of activity. There, the keels, ribs and frames of gigantic carracks, galleons and galleasses were rising by the waterside.

Wyatt found no difficulty in keeping busy. The *Bonaventure's* Sailing Master, Humphreys, was able, intelligent and energetic, but crippled by rheumatism and often seized by strange low fevers contracted while slaving on the east coast of Africa.

Not long after he had entered the Queen's service Wyatt made friends with Captain Tom Moone. A gruff, famously blasphemous individual, he had accompanied Drake on his epoch-making world-encompassing voyage in the *Pelican*, which during the voyage had been rechristened *Golden Hind*.

Now he captained Drake's private venture and night after night regaled wide-eyed patrons of waterfront taverns with weird tales concerning the Anthropophagi—a race of men who, possessing no heads at all, saw from eyes set as nipples in their chests and ate through their navels. Further he described great, bellowing sea elephants and vicious sea stallions which, granted an opportunity, would bite a man in half. He spoke also of those slothful, gentle Aborigines the Globe Circlers had found to inhabit a great land-locked bay on the western coast of North America.

Wyatt, listening, thought of Peter Hopton and their encounter at the Red Knight. What fate had overtaken that lusty, carefree cousin of his?

"Aye. When we raised the Spice Islands," Moone was saying, "ye could smell them five leagues out to sea, so rich are they with groves of cloves, pepper and sugar." Nearly toothless, Moone spluttered while talking like a miniature waterfall, indeed his spittle sprayed in all directions, especially when he warmed to stout ale offered by eager admirers.

"Cappen, be they women about those Spice Islands?" inquired eager admirers.

"To be sure, ye vast ninny," Moone snorted. "Although the inhabitants o' the East Indies are peculiar, their young are born of women, just as here, and not hatched from eggs as I have heard certain lying voyagers declare."

"Be they comely?"

"Aye. They're gentle, sloe-eyed and brown as a tinkler's butt. Ye should have beheld our Admiral on the Island of Mocho that day the natives turned traitor. 'Twas yonder the Naturals slew and then ate poor Tom Flood and Tom Brewer entire. Aye, 'twas bad. The Admiral himself was shot i' the face. An ye consider him closely ye'll note a scar where the arrow penetrated just below his right eye near the nostril of his nose.

"There numbered nigh on two thousand," Moone continued, "all howling like witch-wolves. Because of a contrary wind and tide we were forced to lie offshore and watch our poor mates stripped naked and secured hand and foot. Then the savages sang and danced about them awhile; finally, these monsters would bend over the prisoners and cut gobbets of flesh from their living bodies. These they tossed in the air to be caught and eaten by the dancers."

"Sure, and there must have been something ye could do?" insisted the Corporal.

"Aye, we fired a broadside but the range was too great and when we tried to land for a rescue, why, their arrows fell thicker nor raindrops during a thunderstorm. So, in a rage, the Admiral ordered our anchor raised and we sailed away from Mocho wi' our water-casks and belts emptier than ever."

"Do such wonders as mermaids really exist?" demanded a tar-splashed rigger.

"Aye, me lad. I've clapped eyes on such my own self, mostly near the mouths o' great rivers which do flow into the sea from South America. In an truth these creatures are not beautiful as some would have you believe, being near hairless and of a grey-brown complexion. All the same, they do carry their young about under their arms and suckle them even as they swim."

"Tell us o' that treasure ship ye took off Peru."

Plain gold ear-rings glinted as Moone tilted back his shaggy head the more easily to consume a prodigious draught of ale. "Why, in truth, friends, the matter was no such heroic deed so the ballad writers would have it. Spanish ships in the Pacific regions sail quite unarmed; we found but seven arquebuses aboard when we took *Nuestra Señora de la Concepción*, known to us English as the *Cacafuego*. We went over this great treasure ship's side yelling like demons threatened wi' a shower of Holy Water and had only to wave our weapons a few times before the Spaniards fell on to their knees and screamed for quarter."

"You slew them all, no doubt?"

Thomas Moone turned his battered head and fixed the speaker with a baleful gaze. "Ye be but a poor, ignorant lout not to know that our Admiral is a gentleman o' rare mercy. Never once did he sell a prisoner into slavery or put him to the torture. Whenever we had plundered a prize it was his custom to banquet her officers in his cabin and then, after making them presents from among their own goods, to return them courteously aboard their vessel."

"But in God's name, wherefor?" demanded a voice from the rear of the tap-room. "Don't the curs'd Spanishers burn and torture our men made prisoner by them? Didn't pore John Oxenham suffer the tortures o' the damned 'fore the Viceroy o' Peru had him hanged in Lima?"

"You speak true," growled Moone. "Me, I'll never ken why Sir Francis deals so dainty wi' the Papists."

To all this and much more Henry Wyatt listened, saddened by his memories of Peter, but, like everyone else, his eyes narrowed and his breath quickened when Captain Moone described how the holds of the *Cacafuego* had yielded bar upon bar of the purest silver and gold, how into the *Golden Hind's* strong-boxes had been emptied many small sacks of pearls, emeralds and those great yellowish diamonds for which the mines of South America were celebrated.

What prompted Wyatt to glance up just when he did he could not have explained, all the same he noticed a group of three men quietly entering from the stable court. One, clad in bottle green slashed in scarlet, obviously must be a gentleman of considerable distinction, and the other two of lesser rank, although not belonging to the serving-man class.

There was a certain aloof bearing to that vital, dark young gentleman, something about the way his light-brown beard was trimmed in the Italian fashion which seemed familiar. All at once, he recalled that afternoon at Hampton Court and Drake's clipped voice saying, "And yonder stands that paragon, Sir Philip Sidney, so-called soldier, poet and for the nonce our Queen's darling."

That the Queen's darling was also Master of her Ordnance and therefore stood near the top in military matters was another fact which impinged upon Wyatt's consciousness. *Why* should the Master of the Queen's Ordnance thus almost furtively enter Plymouth? Quickly and unobtrusively Sir Philip traversed the back of the tap-room on his way to a private chamber, guided by the landlord who was all humble bows and delighted smiles.

Quite without formulating any definite plan Wyatt pulled on his round, visorless leather cap, inched to the edge of the crowd and stepped out into the courtyard where half a dozen saddle horses stood steaming to be cooled down by a trio of varlets who evidently composed the rest of Sir Philip's company. To Wyatt's experienced eye there could be no doubt that these animals had been ridden far and fast.

One fact emerged paramount in his mind. Like everybody else serving aboard H.M.S. *Bonaventure*, he was aware that Sir Francis Drake lived in mortal dread of being superseded or embarrassed by the presence aboard of some Court favourite very like this same dashing Sir Philip Sidney.

At the waterside Wyatt, on impulse, paid a waterman two farthings to row him out to the flagship, which galleon appeared positively tremendous lying on the grimy waters, her rigging etched sharply back against a violet-and-blue evening sky.

The Admiral was playing at draughts with Fenner, his Flag-Captain, when an aide declared that a certain member of the crew was almighty insistent on having a word with Sir Francis. Drake, who prided himself on being always accessible to officers and other ranks, nodded assent.

"So 'tis you again, Master Wyatt?" he snapped. "Always, it would seem, there is drama in the air when we do meet."

Anxiously Wyatt crumpled the brimless cap before him. "Aye, sir, but this time I may have been in error troubling you."

The chill blue eyes hardened. "God help you an that's the case. Speak up, man. What is it?"

"Why, sir, do you remember a courtier you pointed out when we were at Hampton Palace?"

"There were many."

"Why, sir, 'twas a very handsome young man with a forked brown beard." His eyes directed a sidewise glance at Captain Fenner. "You named him 'the Queen's darling'."

Drake's jaw shut with a click. "Sir Philip Sidney! He is in Plymouth?" His words might have been so many strokes on a taut drumhead.

"Aye, sir. I just saw him arrive. He is put up at the Trident Tavern."

Fenner rapped out a lusty oath. "God's fiery eyeballs! 'Tis just as we feared!"

Drake bent a penetrating look on Wyatt. "Did Sir Philip arrive in state? Had he many companions?"

"Nay, sir. He must have ridden hard and fast he was that hot and muddied and he had but two gentlemen in his company."

It was easy to see that Drake was thinking hard. He jumped up and took several quick steps back and forth while Fenner growled in his beard and sulphurously lamented that the squadron had not long since cleared Rame Head.

Drake suddenly snapped his fingers. "I'll warrant that romancing young hot-head has slipped the Queen's silken fetters and is come to volunteer." He tugged hard at his little pointed beard. "Stand by," he directed Wyatt and bellowed up the companionway for his secretary.

When Foulke Greville appeared Drake dictated a shrewd but humble-sounding letter to Sir Francis Walsingham urging that this challenge to his authority be recalled at once to Court.

" 'I simply cannot countenance Sir Philip Sidney becoming one of my company," he concluded, "especially under the circumstances I have related. Her Gracious Majesty will never credit, unless you speak to her in all haste, that I did not coax her favourite into joining my expedition.'

"Send that off to Greenwich Palace, Greville, and spare no expense. You, Master Wyatt, will be our post rider and travel with all speed. I entertain not the least desire of viewing the world from a cell in the Tower."

CHAPTER IV

AT MRS. FOSTER'S

"AND SO, poppet, I delivered the Admiral's missive into Sir Francis Walsingham's hands. When that great man had read it his face flamed like a sunset." Wyatt, seated on a stool, was warming hands at a tiny fire in that spare bedroom of Mrs. Foster's which had become their only home.

"You see, Kate, 'twas a most touchy business. Sir Philip Sidney is espoused to Walsingham's daughter, Frances. 'The fool,' railed My

Lord Councillor. 'Oh, the romantical, blithering idiot.' And he laid such hard terms upon his son-in-law I blush to think on 'em."

"Small wonder," Kate commented while deliberately combing those honey-white tresses which ever were her husband's chief delight.

The Queen, he explained, had yet to learn that her favourite not only had disobeyed orders directing him to depart for service under the Earl of Leicester. Much like a naughty schoolboy, he had played the truant in a fit of pique because the Queen had deemed him too dear for so rugged an expedition as her Admiral contemplated.

Hollow-cheeked and sunburnt after two days on the road, Wyatt rejoiced because, in parting, Walsingham had flung him a small purse. "Take this, my good fellow, and pray commend me to your Admiral. I trust your speed and his promptness has saved himself, Sir Philip, and me from a most grave disaster."

"And how does Sir Francis Walsingham appear?" Kate obviously was pleased to find her Harry figuring in affairs of state. Her wide, grey eyes fairly shone.

"He is above fifty, long of nose and a little bent through rheumatism."

"The purse?" she said smilingly and held out her hand. " 'Tis a Godsend, my sweetheart, what with that golden pound the Admiral gave you, I—well, I need not worry so."

"Alas, Sir Francis' pocket was near empty," he sighed. "A single gold piece and a few silver coins." He pulled her on to his knee. "I had hoped it might contain enough to pay off that accursed bill Nick Spencer holds against us and perhaps serve you comfortably until I return." He glanced about. "Where is my good green cloak? And where are your necklace and comb?"

His wife forced a stiff smile. "News of the *Katrina*'s loss was not long in reaching London. Nicholas Spencer was most kind, but certain other creditors brought bailiffs and stripped us of everything. For a fact, Harry, they left me little more than this gown in which I stand."

Slowly Wyatt beat his fists together. "My poor darling! Surely 'tis an evil thing that so early in our marriage such a mischance should have befallen us."

From her position on his lap Kate reached out and used a bare and none-too-white toe to thrust the end of a faggot back into the fire.

"Life, dear my heart, I have been told is naught save good and bad luck befalling in varying degrees. Perhaps 'tis better that our ill luck should come when we are young. And we are not without good fortune." She turned her head and looked up into his level blue eyes.

"Good fortune?" he repeated dully.

"Yes, sweeting." Her lips brushed his hard cheek. "When you return from the expedition, which, under your able Admiral I am sure will prosper, you will find two of us here to love and make much of you."

"Oh, Kate, Kate! Are you indeed sure?"

"Beyond any question," she replied simply. "Mother Foster says so and she has had much experience in such matters."

After he had done kissing her he sighed, "Oh God, and to think I must sail so far distant and leave you all but penniless. Surely, Kate, you must rue the night I tapped on your shutter?".

"Never!" she burst out passionately. "Never for a single moment. You are leaving in the morning?"

"Aye," he admitted. "The Admiral will want assurance that I have seen Sir Francis Walsingham."

"'Tis just as well," she murmured. "Should your creditors learn you have returned it might go hard with us, so it is best that you leave in the early hours. But until then . . ." She loosed her shift until it slipped down into her lap and glanced over a gleaming white shoulder at their narrow and uncomfortable bed. She smiled serenely.

CHAPTER V

SEPTEMBER 14, 1585

NOT much time was required for the good villagers of Plymouth in the County of Devon to learn all about an express messenger who came galloping down from London. It was reported that he had killed two horses with the urgency of his travel. Soon it became bruited about that this galloper had fetched three letters—one directed to that gallant young knight, Sir Philip Sidney, bidding him return instantly to Court; one to Admiral Sir Francis Drake who had heaved a vast sigh of relief on receiving direct orders from Her Majesty that under no circumstances was Sir Philip Sidney to accompany his expedition; and one instructing His Worship the Mayor of Plymouth to clap the Queen's darling into prison if he even so much as hesitated in departing for London.

Poor Sir Philip was perplexed. How had the Queen so quickly learned of his attempted truancy? It was reported that that poor romantic young knight had raged like a madman on reading Gloriana's curt and peremptory order to present himself forthwith at Greenwich Palace.

Once the "Flower of Chivalry" had been seen safely on the road back to London by Sir Francis Drake and his subordinate Admirals, all the while weeping crocodile tears, the harbour of Plymouth became the scene of almost ludicrous, scrambling haste. One after another the supply ships, caravels, hoys, hulks and cromsters alike were towed or warped to the quaysides and on to them were tumbled the first stores that came to hand.

No sooner did one vessel become laden than another presented her lade board—later larboard—side to the wharves. So great was the Admiral's haste that nobody knew what stores went into what ships. He would not even tarry to replenish water-casks depleted by incessant delays. The crews, *and* gentlemen—the latter already had begun to observe Drake's steadfast dictum that they must "hale and draw with the mariners"—worked themselves red in the face.

Indeed, the Golden Admiral went so far as to post parties of sailors along the London road and station a picket boat off Yarmouth under orders to alert him and delay any messenger the Queen might dispatch. All day long during the twelfth and thirteenth of September Drake's squadron swallowed armaments, victuals and other equipment.

It might have been a false alarm but when Drake's lookout on the London road came tearing into Plymouth at dawn on the fourteenth, gasping that a Queen's messenger had paused for a meal and a change of horse at Tavistock, the Admiral turned to his Flag-Captain. Aware that the wind blew fair, although the sky was grey and patched with rain clouds, he snapped, "Make immediate my signal to weigh anchor. 'Fore God, I'll not be denied!"

Villagers came crowding down upon the Barbican, lined the various wharves and even walked out on a half-finished mole. Those aboard coasters and other vessels not accompanying the expedition watched canvas break out aboard one after another of the twenty-nine vessels comprising Drake's squadron. Most of them looked tiny and indeed were so—being of less than a hundred tons burthen.

In fact getting under way out there were but three really sizable ships—the *Bonaventure* flagship, of six hundred tons, flying Drake's pennant and the Cross of St. George, the *Galleon Leicester* of four hundred tons, showing the flag of Rear-Admiral Knollys—a cousin of

Gloriana herself—and finally, the Queen's ship *Aid*, two hundred and fifty tons commanded by cantankerous Captain Edward Winter. It was, the wiseacres gloomed, a weak and pitifully small squadron with which to challenge the might of Spain and Portugal, hitherto undisputed rulers of the Seven Seas. Any one of these great carracks now outfitting in Lisbon and Cádiz could show more guns than any six of Drake's most powerful men-of-war.

"To be sure his ships are small," observed one rugged Master Mariner, "but mark the names that sail them—Frobisher, Winter, Knollys, a Hawkins and two Drakes!" He was right. With this squadron were sailing men whose constancy, fortitude and endurance were to shape not only the destiny of Europe, but that of all the world for centuries to follow.

One by one they slipped out of the harbour, their sails lifting and falling until the offshore breeze filled them steadily and whipped out those white flags marked with the blood-red Cross of St. George. Also it drove out to sea the smoke of salutes fired by each ship as she passed a little castle guarding the Barbican's seaward end.

Aboard ship the men looked eagerly out to sea and only a few cast so much as a backward glance at the steep hills and green meadows of Devon now diminishing astern. Did not the wealth of Spain and of the Indies lie beyond their bowsprits? Whenever their duties permitted mariners and gentlemen directed glances up to the *Bonaventure's* quarter-deck where stood a small, erect figure in brilliant blue. At long last they were off with the Golden Admiral, off to learn what fate awaited them in those far lands beyond the horizon.

CHAPTER VI

OFF VIGO BAY

UNDER an increasingly hot sun, Sir Francis Drake's armada—landsmen were continually surprised to hear how often Spanish and Portuguese nautical terms were regularly employed aboard the Queen's ships—ploughed across the ever-fickle Bay of Biscay. Two days previous it had encountered a roaring gale which had scattered the squadron and had driven the pinnace *Speedwell* right back to Plymouth.

It being Sunday H.M.S. *Bonaventure* showed all her flags while the

Admiral did some mighty impressive preaching from the break of his quarter-deck.

Among those gentlemen who listened was one Hubert Coffyn, Esquire. His companions deemed this young gentleman gay, witty and yet shrewd because in his estimation the Golden Admiral stood only a trifle less omnipotent than God Almighty.

Possibly because Wyatt and he were almost of an age and absorbed in learning all they could concerning the art of navigation, a mutual regard developed between them. It was mostly from young Coffyn that Wyatt gained invaluable knowledge concerning the management of ordnance and the manner of preserving discipline. For instance, Coffyn described how, when a battle was joined, arquebusiers and pikesmen were sent to man the galleon's towering fore- and stern-castles, while certain lusty bombardiers armed with grenadoes jammed themselves into fighting-tops hardly bigger than beef-casks.

"Aboard this man-o'-war and most others, the sailing officers are"—Coffyn erected a long brown finger—"the Captain, you'd call him 'Master' aboard a merchantman—the Boatswain, the Boatswain's Mate, then the Gunner and the Gunner's Mate."

Although Henry Wyatt long since had arrived at this information, he kept quiet. "Then there are the seamen; generally they are divided into petit officers and those mariners who manage the sails. They get all of ten shillings a month. Under them are ranked the younkers, or ordinary seamen; then the grommets or apprentice mariners and, last of all, those luckless dogs' bodies called the ship's boys."

"Aye. But 'tis concerning our ordnance I am the most curious," Wyatt stated as they lingered near the base of the galleon's lateen-rigged mizzenmast. There was a second, and smaller, mizzen stepped slightly aft of the first, and, because this was the first of the Queen's ships in which such a second mizzen was raised, it would become known as a "*Bonaventure* mizzen".

Yielding to the flagship's lift and heave, they crossed the deck to view other ships of the squadron or "armada", as Coffyn insisted on calling it, strung out in a long irregular formation. They ploughed through the Bay of Biscay's dark blue waters, their sails appearing unnaturally clean in this brilliant sunlight.

"Gunnery? Friend Wyatt, you have come to the right man," laughed Coffyn. "I am a gunpowder man first, last and all the time. Say what the old gaffers will, the longbow has had its day; it is with this that wars of the future will be won."

He patted the chace of a long-barrelled piece and explained

seriously: "Here we have a demi-cannon which will throw you a thirty-pound iron ball some 1700 yards. To be sure you cannot tell just where you will hit at such a range," he added, slacking that plain cloth neckband he wore at sea in place of the ruff. "But 'tis a prodigious distance for a ball to carry. Is't not?"

"Aye. How many men are required to serve such a piece?" Wyatt ran his eye over a bewildering pattern of tackle and lines securing the gun to deck and side.

"Four Gunners," came the prompt reply. "Of course, there should be six Gunners to the heaviest cannon we now mount." He turned and pointed. "Now there, friend Wyatt, we have a culverin, a most useful piece of ordnance which will hurl a seventeen-pound ball about 2500 yards."

"Why, that's above half a mile!" Wyatt gasped, then his bright blue eyes grew suspicious. "Surely, friend Coffyn, you are funning me?"

"Nay. Tomorrow you shall have proof of what I say for I warrant by then Sir Francis will have ordered a gun practice. Of course the other Captains will growl like hungry bears and the gentlemen will curse and pout about. Although we be not so heavily armed as those new ships we hear are building at Deptford, yet we mount eight demi-cannon to each broadside."

"And what are called those small cannons mounted on our poop and forecastle?"

"They are cannon perriers that fire balls of stone. The next largest are demi-culverins. All these are called battering ordnance, being of short range but throwing heavy shot. Then we have murdering pieces such as those sakers you see mounted along the rail and falcons guard our waist. These weapons load by the breech and have very short range because they are designed principally to repel boarders; much of their force is lost through the ill-fitting locks on their breeches."

Coffyn's instruction continued until Wyatt's head was swimming with unfamiliar terms; nonetheless he set himself to memorize them one and all.

This September day was one such as sea-going mariners like to dream on; the air was warm and yet not hot; aloft yards creaked a soft accompaniment to the wind thrumming in braces, halyards and shrouds. Rightly or wrongly the word was circulating that tomorrow the coast of Spain would lift above the horizon. Therefore gun drills and target practice would take place.

"Wait until you serve aboard some of our other vessels," Coffyn remarked. "Then you'll come to understand wherein Sir Francis is wise by insisting that men of varying duties shall keep to their part of the ship and that unfailing obedience shall be the rule. God's Mercy! Aboard practically any other ship you'll encounter any amount of quibbling and bickering over an unpopular order; sometimes the mariners simply ignore such a command and go unrebuked.

"It was that way on the *Black Bear* in which I ventured to the west coast of Africa for John Hawkins. The gentlemen aboard would have naught to do with common mariners and held themselves aloof, refusing to undertake any manner of work concerning the sailing of the ship—'twas their business to fight her, said they. Worse still, most of them maintained varlets and serving men who were forbidden to lift a finger in the vessel's management even though their very lives hung in the balance."

A flourish of trumpets sounded upon the poop deck whereupon groups of brilliantly attired gentlemen departed to partake of their afternoon meal. In this squadron, as in most others, but two repasts were served each day while those of lesser grade themselves cooked rations when they listed over fires kindled on sand boxes situated just below the break of the forecastle.

As usual, whenever the sea permitted, Sir Francis Drake dined in state. Openly he enjoyed the fact that a poor parson's son could eat with a page waiting at either elbow, one ready to pass his food or offer a brass basin into which he could rinse his mouth, the other to replenish a wine goblet of pure gold the minute it became empty.

In a great chair of carved wood and embossed leather the Admiral appeared almost diminutive, especially when at his right sat the towering figure of the Sergeant-Major, Anthony Powell, a gigantic and dark-visaged Welshman. To later generations the Sergeant-Major would be known as a Major-General Powell. Present also were Drake's two Corporals of the Field—later to be known as Brigadiers. Lieutenant-General Carleill with interest was noting that this afternoon it was essentially military officers who had been bidden to the Admiral's table. Of course it had caused Drake no small satisfaction to find himself in command of both the naval and military elements.

For the moment the Admiral was silent, occupied in chewing a chunk of decidedly tough beef and wondering whether these others even suspected his anxiety over the next few days. To be sure they had beheld the vast power of Spain on land and sea, as demonstrated in the Mediterranean and in the Low Countries, and to a man they were aware of the terrible fate in store for heretics captured fighting against His Most Catholic Majesty. Hardly a man at this table but had lost some relative or close friend to the Inquisition.

Nonetheless, Drake's heart lifted at commanding the greatest naval expedition ever to depart from the shores of England. Not that this would be the last such squadrons, or the most powerful, for, come another two or three years those great ships and galleons John Hawkins now was designing and laying down with infinite skill and imagination and foresight would become available. Who should command those magnificent new men-of-war but a certain Francis Drake? Might not an earldom lie within his reach, should certain present plans and calculations bear fruit?

Drake put down his table-knife and, employing his courtesy fingers, the thumb and third finger of his left hand, raised the last bit of beef to his bearded lips. He found lantern-jawed Christopher Carleill studying him with a quizzical look in his steel-coloured eyes.

"I warrant I can read your thoughts," Drake smiled over the soft strains of viol music rendered by a pair of musicians stationed in the companionway. "You are thinking 'a pox and a murrain on the Admiral for keeping mum concerning his intent'?"

Carleill's slash of a mouth relaxed. "Prettily conjectured, Sir Francis. Indeed, your Corporals of the Field, the Sergeant-Major and I need time to consider landings and the tactics to be attempted."

"Aye," Sampson nodded in harmony with the *Bonaventure's* easy pitching. "Exactly what is our undertaking, Sir Francis?"

"First I intend to win the unconditional release of our countrymen and their ships and goods," came the ready reply. "Also I shall inflict what damage we may to Spanish shipping." He frowned. "Alas that my orders forbid us to burn their ports."

"Of course we can plunder them?" demanded Powell. Because of a great purplish birthmark disfiguring his right cheek the Welshman's eyes shone extra blue by contrast. He wore his beard forked and it looked as thick and coarse as the fur on a bear's back.

"Aye, we are permitted to plunder, but not above half a league inland under any circumstances. As you may wot, friend Powell, the troops we'll fight in Spain herself will prove vastly superior to those poor fever-ridden devils we've met so often i' the Spanish Main."

One after another the guests shoved back their stools and from heavy leather cases produced clay tobacco pipes which they filled from a casket of gilded lead offered by one of Sir Francis' pages. Drake smiled to himself. Anyone could tell neither Sampson nor Powell really enjoyed smoking. Even Christopher Carleill handled his pipe clumsily and frequently spat into a ewer placed beside the table; but since it was the mode to smoke tobacco, he smoked, coughed and wiped furiously watering eyes.

"Good friends, I intend to strike at Bayona on Vigo Bay," Drake announced simply. "There is good anchorage in Vigo where we can sort our stores—God knows we've the need—and allow your troops to stretch their legs."

Carleill spat, nodded emphatically. "The sooner the better, say I. All our ships are vastly overcrowded; a man to every two tons of burthen is over-risky. I've kept my fingers crossed lest some pox or plague break out. Why, Knollys declares that aboard the *Aid* the troopers are so jammed 'gainst one another that many are unable to lie full length upon the deck."

"Why Bayona?" Sampson was a man of few, and generally blasphemous, words.

"A goodly number of our impeached ships lie there and are held in the other ports about Vigo Bay."

The Sergeant-Major grinned while wiping sauce from a grey-streaked beard. "Does it not chance that in Bayona is a rich cathedral and several great churches and monasteries?"

At the words 'churches and monasteries" a speculative and hungry expression appeared on those leathery faces ringing Sir Francis Drake's dinner-table.

"Aye," the Admiral admitted easily. "I seem to have heard of such. But because of this overcrowding Kit here mentions we stand in need of further supply vessels. Those we have brought from England would serve for a short voyage, but——" He broke off short, quite deliberately leaving his subordinates with the impression this cruise might prove long indeed. Already he could imagine their debates as to whether the expedition was destined to sweep suddenly into the Mediterranean and so fall upon and sack unsuspecting ports on the east coast of Spain, or whether their armada would strike south in an attempt to intercept gold- and spice-laden carracks beating up from the west coast of Africa.

"Once we lie off Bayona," Drake informed Carleill through a haze of rank grey tobacco fumes, "one party will land to the north and another to the south of Bayona. Meanwhile I will lead a third party into the town itself."

The assembled officers stared a little. Drake was speaking as casually as if he were contemplating a bear-baiting rather than an impudent and quite unprecedented assault on the King of Spain's own realm. Why, his bearing suggested that he was about to lead a mighty army against a weak and ill-defended fortress rather than a badly disciplined and poorly organized force less than a thousand sea-worn men against the most powerful and best-led army in Christendom, or in all the world, for that matter.

CHAPTER VII

CERTAIN OCCURRENCES IN VIGO BAY

HAD an army of Cyclopses suddenly emerged all dripping from the sea the inhabitants of the Province of Galicia could not have been more thunderstruck than when they beheld a strange armada numbering twenty-six sail standing shorewards from the direction of Cape Quejo. When the word was passed that this squadron was English and commanded by no less a demon than the terrible *el Draque* himself a wild clangour of church bells sounded an alarm and terror gripped the countryside. Utterly panic-stricken, merchants, nobles and wealthy householders loaded their most precious merchandise and possessions some on to mules, others into little row galleys which conveyed them up the Vigo River or into the hills.

Off Bayona the English ships expertly furled sail, let go their clumsy anchors, then watched Lieutenant-General Carleill in the *Tiger* set off leading three other small vessels in pursuit of the fugitive row galleys.

Curiously, the English studied the town, yellow-walled and red-roofed for the most part, lying sprawled along the waterfront. Behind Bayona a row of hills bare and treeless looked parched, seared and of a curious brownish hue, different indeed from the soft blue-greens so typical of the south coast of England. Everywhere over there small boats were scurrying about like frightened waterbeetles on a millpond.

Pinnaces were brought alongside the larger ships, gigs and long-boats were lowered and the Admiral's own blue-and-gold galley manned and armed and otherwise held ready.

Wearing a steel cap and a jerkin of tough leather which easily could turn a spent arrow or a glancing swordblow, Henry Wyatt waited to take his turn among the soldiers and lamented that at his side hung not that handsome bilbo he had lost in Huntingdon Town but a clumsy shortsword which was Coffyn's second weapon. Before long, Wyatt swore, he intended to replace this borrowed blade with something more suited to his taste.

Loud were the boasts of what was about to chance ashore; of what prodigies of valour John Simpkins or Watt Black were about to perform.

"Icod! Already I can feel a pair o' gradely gold candlesticks i' my fist," grunted a broad-faced fellow who spoke with a heavy Yorkshire accent.

On the *Bonaventure's* tall but narrow poop deck had collected a knot of officers. They lingered there briefly with vari-coloured morion plumes whipping in the breeze and with the sun glancing off their black-painted cuirasses. Some of them had been enriched by designs done in gold, or by silver ornaments which glittered like ripples in a sunset. This was the only touch of colour. Put away were the gaudy garments of yesterday—sombre greens, blacks and russets predominated aloft. As for Sir Francis, he had donned a morion heavily crusted with gold captured during the sack of Venta Cruz back in 1573. In it he wore an ostrich plume, a panache of blue and white, his favourite colours.

Men were to be seen tumbling over the sides of the other ships and the landing force was ready to go ashore when a long, low barge flying the King of Spain's red-and-gold standard came pulling out from Bayona at a speed which must have had her oarsmen gasping. The emissary proved to be a very frightened English merchant who, obeying orders from Don Pedro Romero, Governor of the town, had ventured out to learn the purpose of this squadron now holding Bayona under the menace of near a hundred cannon. Conducted before the Admiral, he took oath that all the seized English ships had been released some time earlier.

Drake fixed the renegade with a chilly blue eye. "Methinks, sirrah, you are but a poor rascal forced to bring such a message in the interest of our countrymen held prisoner ashore." He swung about to his Corporal of the Field, Captain Sampson, and spoke in a metallic voice that many on board had not previously heard. "Take my galley and a guard, seek His Excellency the Governor and demand from him plain answers to two plain questions."

"Aye, aye, sir." Beneath the dented visor of a heavy casque Sampson's hard brown eyes commenced to glow.

"First, you will inquire of His Excellency, Don Pedro, whether Spain and England are at war."

"Aye, aye, sir."

"Second, if our countries are not at war, then why have our ships been impeached?"

"Aye, aye, sir." Captain Sampson bowed, beckoned Coffyn, a trumpeter and six stalwart arquebusiers.

"Out upon it!" growled Vice-Admiral Frobisher. "What boots it to delay our attack?"

Drake shot the grizzled old fellow an impatient look—there never had been much love lost between them. "There will be time and to spare when I receive answers to my questions. If indeed we are at war my tactics will be sharply altered."

He turned aside, pretending not to hear disappointed oaths arising from small boats loaded to the gunwales with men fiercely impatient to be ashore and at the pleasant task of parting Spaniards from their wealth. The sight of long lines of bullock-carts crawling off into the hills, of little caunters with patched brown sails scudding off across Vigo Bay did little to soothe their disappointment.

"God's blood! Yonder gravy is dripping right through our fingers," snarled a veteran sergeant. "We'd have no such niceties were old Frobisher in command."

Wyatt, too, burned with impatience. At anchor in the harbour of Bayona lay half a dozen fine barques all infinitely superior to that *Katrina*, with her ungainly leeboards and worm-eaten strakes.

Shortly Captain Sampson returned to the flagship together with a deputation of English merchant captains trading in Bayona. These Drake received courteously on his quarter-deck and questioned them sufficiently to learn that certain of the confiscated ships and cargo had indeed been released. No state of war existed reported the Corporal of the Field—or so the Governor Don Pedro Romero had sworn. Further, he had declared that although a hostile force had in fact invaded the realm of His Most Catholic Majesty, he felt himself much too mean a subject to assume the responsibility for opening hostilities.

The Governor, Captain Sampson grinned, was utterly astonished that a warlike expedition from the miserable little fogbound island of England should have dared to invade one of King Philip's ports with guns run out and matches burning. The eruption of a volcano could not have been more astounding. Certain it was that, by now, couriers must be pounding southwards bearing intelligence of this incredible affront to the dignity of Spain.

"You say 'certain of the impeached ships'," Drake pointed out, staring at the tallest of the Englishmen; "then not *all* of our ships and cargoes and men have been released?"

"No, Your Excellency. They have released those of us who affirm we will remain here and continue trading as before."

"So?" The pointed golden beard assumed an aggressive tilt. "General Carleill, pray order your troops ashore. I intend to call upon this lying fellow, Don Pedro Romero."

As loud cheers rose from the waiting boats Henry Wyatt felt his spirits soar. He looked about. Even though these were regular troops maintained by Her Majesty's Government yet there was no uniformity either as to their equipment or to their clothing. However, a good many dirty white surcoats bearing the Latin Cross of St. George lent the suggestion of uniform. Otherwise, longbows, pikes, arquebuses and tacks, clumsy and unpredictable pistols, were the order of the day. Most of the officers standing in the stern carried pikes, but a few, like Coffyn, favoured either petronels or wheel-lock muskets.

The arquebusiers had already ignited slow matches which, fixed to an S-shaped arm, would, when the trigger was pulled, raise a pan cover and thrust the glowing match onto a bed of priming powder. Further, the arquebusiers carried a fork-shaped rest, their fourteen-pound weapons being much too ponderous to fire off-shoulder lacking support of some kind.

Sweating, barefooted and generally half-naked mariners pulled for the City of Bayona so hard that presently this flotilla's lead boats commenced to cut off fugitive caunters and rowboats. This phase of the operation proved disappointing. These Spaniards were not of the fighting sort; they merely wept and wailed like lost children when these red-faced and generally fair-haired strangers came pulling up alongside.

Bayona fell without even a token resistance, much to the disappointment of certain fire-eaters among the gentlemen. None the less the intaking proved an exhilarating business to former merchant sailors such as Henry Wyatt. How curious and thrilling it was thus to tramp as invaders and conquerors through a succession of deserted streets, to gaze up at shuttered second-storey windows with the certainty that behind them cowered handsome young wenches all a-trembling for their virtue.

"Faugh! This is but pale sport," grumbled shaggy-headed Captain Thomas Moone. "A pox on all this caution. Look." He flung a hairy arm aloft, indicating a window from which unwisely peered three pairs of limpid and lively black eyes. "Were this Santa Margarita or

San Juan, why, lads, I'd have had yon door down in ten seconds and be stripping yonder beauties inside o' a minute. God knows what's come over Sir Francis."

Here and there the thud-thudding of improvised battering-rams busy at various warehouse doors reverberated through the hot and dusty atmosphere; once in a while a thin rising scream sounded to attest some undisciplined lout must be amusing himself contrary to orders. On the whole, however, the troops behaved well; they only seized goods found in the Royal Warehouses and those of larger merchants.

Presently, drums and cymbal music were heard, then out onto the cobbles of Bayona's principal plaza clattered a resplendent figure astride a spirited black stallion.

A half-company of halberdiers attempted to keep step behind this dignitary, but they moved in ragged ranks and appeared apprehensive. Clearly the nearness of *el Draque* was bearing upon their spirit with crushing effectiveness.

Where might the English Commander be found? When certain among the English Captains pointed out General Carleill, Don Pedro's lean features relaxed. At least he would not be called upon to address that demon incarnate, Sir Francis Drake.

He dismounted and stalked towards General Carleill, then, a few feet short of that hard-bitten officer, he pulled off his conical hat and brushed the street with its plumes. He was, the Governor declared, intrigued by this curious visitation from a supposedly friendly power. Would General Carleill condescend to accept some wine, oil and possibly some grapes and marmalade delivered to his encampment?

Carleill appeared to look clean through this swarthy little man. "Aye, sir, we'll welcome your supplies if with them come such of our countrymen as yet linger in your dungeons."

Don Pedro thereupon swore upon the honour of his mother and called assorted Saints to witness that all English prisoners had been liberated.

To General Carleill this was proving a most unsatisfactory parley, especially since the sky had begun to darken and gusts of wind were commencing to stir spirals of dust about Bayona's ancient market place. Up from the waterfront ran a messenger from the *Bonaventure*. The weather looked ominous, therefore the Admiral required the landing-party immediately to return aboard their vessels.

Over waves turned lead colour and showing ever-larger whitecaps, the pinnaces and small boats struggled back out to the squadron beginning to wallow clumsily at its anchorage. The wind freshened so quickly that many small boats were hard put to disgorge their human cargo and one or two were swamped ere they could be hoisted inboard. Under a livid sky the gale rose towards a shrieking crescendo and hurled down torrents of rain which chilled luckless Englishmen huddled upon decks and extinguished their cook fires.

Barely in time sail was made and Drake's squadron went reeling out of Vigo Bay and towards the comparatively safe Bay of Biscay.

CHAPTER VIII

THE TRUCE

For three whole days the gale beat upon, drenched and dispersed the English squadron whose crews and troops no longer could boast a dry shred of clothing. As usual faint hearts in Drake's armada cursed their fate and clamoured for a swift return to England.

Two of the smaller ships were never seen or heard from again. Undoubtedly, they had become overwhelmed during a black and wind-filled night.

"Surely the Admiral will return to Plymouth?" opined the *Bonaventure's* Master Carpenter. "He must, since our water-casks are nearly dry."

"You know not Sir Francis Drake," the flagship's Assistant Gunner growled. "He will return to settle his business at Bayona."

His prediction proved to be correct for, on the morning of October 1, 1585, Drake's armada sailed back into Vigo Bay and cast anchor in a well-protected anchorage above the city. On this occasion the Spaniards seemed disposed to offer resistance since considerable bodies of troops could be seen marching along roads paralleling the sea.

It now being certain that, despite Don Pedro Romero's protestations, many English seamen remained prisoner in the Bayona dungeons, General Carleill was granted free rein ashore. Meawhile Drake ordered his Captains to capture any and all vessels attempting to escape. Many coasters and slow-sailing carracks were overhauled and such Spaniards who attempted to protect their property promptly were trussed up or cut down if they showed any inclination to fight.

It was in one of these fleeing carracks that the sacred vessels of

Bayona Cathedral were discovered. Hungry eyes considered the size and perfection of a huge, gem-encrusted golden chalice, of many diamonds flashing on the Bishop's crozier and from his mitre. That piece of spoil which brought something of a satisfied smile to Drake's features was a huge cross of massive silver, double-gilt and beautifully adorned with a profusion of emeralds and rubies. Captain Moone, who professed himself something of an expert on the subject, estimated this prize of the loot as at least 30,000 Venetian ducats.

"It's mere table scraps you've here, my lads, and no more," Moone rumbled. "Wait till we take the city itself!"

Wyatt from his post on the steerboard side peered across sunset-tinted waters. How very ancient seemed this port with its time-mellowed walls, with its weather-beaten cathedral towers and sagging warehouses. A fortification of some sort crumbled on nearly all of the hilltops in sight, among them the inevitable Roman watch-tower and the arches of a long-broken aqueduct.

The citizenry now engaged in bearing their most treasured possessions inland suggested columns of ants. Such a sight had not been seen in Spain since Ferdinand and Isabella's armies had driven the last of the Moors across the Straits of Gibraltar back to Africa from whence they had emerged hundreds of years earlier.

Coffyn, licking sun-cracked lips, predicted, "Tomorrow we'll e'en sample fine wines in place of spoiled beer and dine on fresh fruits and young lamb rather than on this rancid beef." He winked. "Mayhap we'll also find pleasanter bedfellows than these flea-ridden troopers of Carleill's."

Wyatt nodded, but thoughts of her who so uncomplainingly occupied that cramped and lonely bedroom in Captain Foster's cottage remained uppermost in his mind.

As events turned out, the Governor of the Province of Galicia dispatched a herald to request a parley and to point out that he now commanded some three thousand seasoned veterans, battle-hardened, and was quite ready to oppose any attempt upon Bayona.

Sir Francis Drake therefore donned his most resplendent armour and instructed his gentlemen and officers to present as brave an appearance as lay within their power.

A parley between the Governor and Drake took place aboard a barge anchored well out on the river. "Just what is it," inquired Don Pedro, "Your Valiant Excellency, the Admiral of the English Queen, has come to obtain?"

The Governor struggled to remain urbane despite the humiliation of being forced thus to treat and parley within the borders of King Philip's own realm.

Drake spoke straight out, the instant release of all English prisoners and the right to water and to trade for provisions. Don Romero further must agree to an exchange of hostages. On the other hand, he, the Queen's Admiral, agreed to return the captured church possessions and promised that Bayona would not suffer from further violence or depredation. The Governor bowed a balding head, departed pale with humiliation.

Thus it came about that on that same afternoon the sun warmed a noisome column of prisoners. Hollow-eyed, shaggy and bearing festering fetter scars on their wrists and ankles, they danced feebly and with joy. When they reached the waterfront and faced their deliverer many attempted to kiss the hands of that short but commanding little figure in blue and white. Although patently pleased, Drake would not permit such homage.

From the King's Aduana and Warehouses were fetched what remained of the looted cargoes and English ships sent flying up the river before the seizure of Bayona were brought back.

During the next seven days prevailed a curious situation with Queen Elizabeth's troops, in a time of peace, occupying a Spanish port. There could be no doubt but that the Golden Admiral and his squadron indeed were temporary masters of Galicia. Wyatt found it curious to behold sunburnt, yellow-haired Englishmen under arms walking about the streets and market-places of Bayona and mingling quite affably with the swarthy and generally less robust troops of the Royal Governor. Devils, however, peered from their officers' dark eyes, these haughty fellows having long been accustomed to lording it over Europe and half the world. It was inescapable that, bitterly, they resented their present humiliation and such an unheard-of affront to Spanish prestige. Yet they were so well disciplined that there was not one instance of brawling with the hated *heréticos Ingleses*.

A revelation and warning, too, it proved for men to witness the amazing precision of the Spanish drill and to note the care they devoted to their excellent armaments.

When officers of the opposing forces chanced to meet, both sides proved punctilious about bowing or lifting their caps. During the chaos of the Middle Ages, military salutes had fallen largely into desuetude, but now they were being revived by King Philip's tough veterans.

In a placid reach of the Vigo River above Bayona English ships, as if manipulated on a chessboard by some invisible hand, were towed hither and yon in order that stores tossed aboard helter-skelter in Plymouth might be sorted out and reapportioned as they should have been some three weeks earlier. To round out perishable items Spanish farmers, surprisingly, brought produce down from the hills in big two-wheeled carts drawn by huge, fawn-coloured oxen the yokes of which were gay with fringes and streamers of every imaginable colour.

When it became evident that the Protestants did not intend to ravage and lay waste the countryside and would pay good coin for what they needed, every imaginable kind of food was forthcoming. There was even a brisk undercover trade in small arms for all that the sellers were well aware that very likely these swords, daggers and bilboes would soon be employed against their brethren and fellow Catholics.

Most important of all to Sir Francis Drake was the refilling of his water-casks. Never had he forgotten the tortures of thirst suffered aboard the *Golden Hind*. He was seriously concerned also about the overcrowding aboard his vessels. Although his Captains stormed and argued, he, mindful that no state of war as yet existed, refused to impress any of the Spanish craft in Bayona's harbour; no more would he force any of the rescued English Masters to serve under him.

It came as something of a shock to Sir Francis that so many of the local English merchants refused either to enlist in his squadron or return home. Indeed, these easygoing expatriates—mostly Catholics—preferred to continue businesses built up over many a long, lean year. Many of them were winning fortunes in supplying the *flotas* under construction in the naval arsenals of Lisbon and Cádiz. These contemptible varlets, as Rear-Admiral Knollys termed them, knew full well that such ships were intended for but one purpose—the invasion of England. Curiously enough, it never occurred to most of the English rank and file to criticize; were there not just as many Spaniards living and trading in England? Neither they, nor the local merchants, paid much heed to the weathercock of international politics.

"I'll be hanged, drawn and quartered before I comprehend their intent," Hubert Coffyn admitted on the third evening of the fleet's reoccupation of Bayona. "'Fore God, an Englishman to my mind should be English in all things, and a Spaniard, Spanish. A pox on these greedy fellows who first run with the hares and then chase with the hounds!"

Coffyn and Wyatt were strolling along a broad, tree-shaded

promenade paralleling the water's edge and casting curious eyes on the rows of narrow-fronted, red-roofed dwellings interspaced by tiny orchards and gardens. Occasionally their path would swing inland, thus allowing space between it and the water for some well-built house and a wharf which projected a short distance into Vigo Bay.

The strollers were studying one of these when a manservant came out, bowed low and said in clear but heavily accented English, "*Señores*, my Master Jenkeens would be honour' eef you care join heem een one cup of wine."

"Well, I'm damned!" Coffyn grinned. "Did you say his name is Jenkins?"

"*Sí, señor*. My *padron* is Engleesmans from Brees-tol."

Wyatt nodded acceptance, being curious to converse with one of these inexplicable expatriates—especially one who evidently had fared so well. They followed the yellow-jacketed servant through a small gate and, in a miniature orchard, encountered a plump, jolly-appearing and red-faced fellow who jumped up and offered his hand.

"Roger Jenkins at yer service," he declared. " 'Tis indeed a vast and a rare honour to welcome countrymen o' gentle blood to me humble abode." His clothing was rich and of modish cut, as was his full brown beard. The merchant looked just a trifle apprehensive as he invited his guests to seat themselves under some carefully trimmed almond trees.

The personification of assurance, tall young Hubert Coffyn sauntered over to a bench and straightened his sword alongside him. After seating himself he pulled off a flat, dark green cap. "You would appear to do yourself well here in foreign parts, friend Jenkins," he observed, running an eye over the façade of yellow-grey stone of Jenkins' house. Espaliers of pear and peach softened its outline with their upreaching arms.

"Aye. To be sure. I do moderately well in ordinary times, but for the last three years trading is become very risky and difficult."

"In what do you traffic?" Wyatt inquired. Who knew but that sometime, when war was less imminent, this same Master Jenkins might prove a valuable acquaintance?

"Why, young Master, I do export wines, cordage—I sell only the best cable made in Spain," he stated proudly. "My hemp is fetched all the way from beyond Africa. I vow there's a fortune to be won in such. Of course I also export *bacalao*—salted codfish."

"And you import?" Wyatt prompted, sinking into a comfortable corded chair and swinging his sword across his lap.

"Why, good English woollens, hides, and"—Jenkins licked full lips—"ordnance whenever I can come across some." His bloodshot grey eyes lost their casual look, became calculating. "I'll tell ye these Spaniards hunger for cannon, especially since *el Draque* has driven them into arming their colonies i' the Americas."

He chuckled. "God's blood! Your Admiral is my patron saint, you might say. The more he flogs the Spanish, the better my business. Hardware of any nature is scarce—iron chain, for instance. Why, right now I could make rich any man who would sell me two hundred fathoms o' stout, forged chain." He bent slightly popping brown eyes on Wyatt. "By chance, ye'd not list where I might chance on some, would ye, sir?"

All three turned their heads when a door opened releasing a flood of yellowish light into this darkening garden in which crickets and tree frogs had sounded tentative evening chirps. It was not the man-servant who appeared, but a dark, big-bosomed girl of some nineteen winters.

Jenkins straightened, obviously irritated. "Paula, what do you here?"

She curtsied a trifle awkwardly. "Why, *Padre*, I would greet and speak to these our countrymen." She sniffed. "Mama and Teresa still array themselves. They will come out soon."

"Ye should not have ventured out uninvited," Jenkins complained, but there was no anger in his voice. "So long as yer here ye might as well make yourself useful. Fetch a pitcher out o' that winepipe from Fayal and fill the gentlemen's cups. Then ye'd best hunt up some almonds—not those wi' the worms, either. Ha! Ha! The best and nothing else is for our English guests."

When the girl Paula returned, Coffyn observed she seemed in no great hurry to retire and prolonged her pouring of the wine. In serving she bent so low in presenting a heavy silver goblet that not only could he peer full into her smooth, olive-tinted features but also into the front of a voluptuously well-filled gown. Her subtle and effective exposure of swelling, pink-pointed breasts rivalled the arts of the most accomplished coquette at Court.

There was nothing stiff or formal in Paula's manner, nor did constraint mark the bearing of Mistress Jenkins and a second daughter, Teresa, a buxom lass who had inherited her father's jolly manner, light brown hair and ruddy complexion.

Soon it became known that Mistress Jenkins was of Portuguese descent on her father's side and English—from Hampshire—on her mother's. Obviously, the whole Jenkins family was happy and at home here in Spain as they never could have been in England.

Hubert Coffyn drained his cup of Fayal, a wonderfully mellow amber fluid, in two long gulps, then thrust legs out before him and settled back to contemplate in admiration more enthusiastic than delicate the buxom figure of Paula Jenkins. Smiling, he inquired, "You have visited England?"

"No, sir. Only *Padre*."

"Have you no ambition to see our country?"

"Oh-h so much. I should like to see the so-wonderful city of London," Paula admitted, then her smile faded. "But of course we would not be made welcome there."

"Why not? Your father is English, is he not?" He peered through the dusk at the full, squarish outline of her mouth and found it infinitely provocative.

Paula sighed. "Yes, he is English, but also a Catholic. We all are Catholics. No, I do not think we would be made very welcome in England."

Hubert laughed, shook his fair head. "Nonsense! In England there remain almost as many Catholics as Protestants, especially in the northern counties and in Scotland, and there are several famous Catholics at Court, so you really should see London. There's a lively city for you."

With a second and third goblet of tawny Fayal tucked beneath his well-filled belt Master Jenkins settled back more comfortably in a beautifully carved chair.

"Paula, *chiquita*, why don't you show Coffyn your tame swans?" He turned to his plump, dark-featured wife. "Luisa, go prepare us a little supper. Teresa, *vaya con su madre*."

It surprised Wyatt not in the least that Hubert Coffyn should evince a deep interest in swans and presently followed Paula through the merchant's house towards the river into which Master Jenkins' wharf projected far enough out to berth a stout galliot. Her decks were still piled high with merchandise Jenkins had selected to save when the hostile squadron had first appeared.

Jenkins refilled his dark-visaged guest's goblet of fragile Venetian glass. "Women are decorative, but I prefer to drink without the clack of their tongues in my ears. You say you are a Merchant Master? Do you command your own vessel?"

"I did." Wyatt leaned forward, elbows on knees to sketch aimless designs with a stick in the dust before him. At length he cast his host a quizzical glance through the twilight. "You just now mentioned a great demand for ordnance?"

"Aye. In Cádiz and Lisbon stout brass guns will bring near their weight in silver."

Gently Wyatt beat fists together, drawled: "An you be truly as hard-pressed for cannons belike I can discover a few among certain foundries in the South of England. I have a cousin who casts them," he lied.

Master Jenkins' round stomach trembled to his sudden sitting up. "Have ye, indeed? Nay, friend Wyatt, jest not. Not longer than three days past the Master of the Royal Arsenal in Toledo offered me"—he checked himself—"a truly princely price for as many long guns, demi-cannons and culverins as I could supply."

A surprised whistle escaped the red-haired Master Mariner. "But I had thought that Spanish gunners preferred pieces casting a heavier ball."

"So they do. It seems, however, that forts guarding San Domingo, capital city of Spanish America, stand in dire need of long guns. Apparently the principal fort there has just been completed but its embrasures remain empty. This officer I speak of was nigh tearful because his superiors were threatening him with disgrace for his failure to find such cannons."

Jenkins leaned far forward and lowered his voice. "Could ye but get quick permission to return to England I could furnish ye with a stout neff of one hundred tons burthen and a letter of credit drawn upon a certain Genoese banker in London."

"How can you be sure, friend Jenkins, that such cannon will not already have been found?"

The merchant snorted impatience. "They will not be found—the King's Admirals are seizing all ordnance in the realm. Now here is what can be done. A friend and agent o' mine, one Richard Cathcart, dwells in San Domingo and there directs my commerce with the Spanish Main." Eagerness entered his voice. "Could ye but lade these cannon aboard my neff ye could steer straightaway for San Domingo under English colours during the first half o' the voyage and King Philip's colours for the balance.

"Consider, young sir, that above the tremendous profit we would derive on the purchase in England, the Royal Governor in San Domingo also will pay a great bonus, so fearful is he that the English will come sweeping in from the east. What say you?" It was odd to hear this Hampshireman referring to his countrymen like foreigners.

"I must mull the matter over," Wyatt temporized. "For all that what you offer sounds a most promising piece of traffic."

"Whilst *el Draque*—er, Sir Francis Drake I mean—remains here, pray consider my house as your own." Jenkins winked. "Should you desire to amuse yourself ashore as mariners are wont, why ye've only to tip me the word and tell me yer fancy by way of a wench be she white, brown or gypsy. What wi' this infernal drought, the port teems with comely wenches eager to bed for the sake o' a well-filled belly."

CHAPTER IX

FOREIGN INTELLIGENCE

ADMIRAL SIR FRANCIS DRAKE received the ill news aboard his private row galley concluding an inspection of his squadron. Personally he wished to make certain that all casks were full of fresh water. A watch-boat of his on duty near the entrance had been able to capture and bring in a coaster on her way from San Lucar in the south to the port of San Sebastián near the frontier of France.

The captive Captain, a truculent, olive-skinned *Malagueño*, refused to sell his cargo of salt fish, so it was confiscated. Still shouting defiance, the *Malagueño* was then brought aboard that little galley where Drake sat on a scarlet cushion, concentrating upon a set of muster lists just presented by Sergeant-Major Powell. The *Malagueño* even taunted his captors with an item of news which rendered English faces longer than a day without bread.

"Sir! Sir! There's tidings of great import," Thomas Drake called out.

"Eh? What's amiss? Can't you see I'm occupied?" Drake flung at the young Master of the *Galliot Thomas*, who for all the world might not have been his own brother.

"Sir, we've a foreign monkey aboard who gloats on certain ill news for you."

"Well, Thomas? Well? Bring the clod aboard." When, struggling and kicking, the Spanish Captain was produced, he spat defiantly onto the deck at Drake's feet, whereat the Admiral sprang up and seized the fellow by his beard. Thrice, four times he wrenched the Spaniard's head violently back and forth and then he dealt him two smacking buffets on either cheek. Then, having uttered not a word, Drake resumed his seat.

Young Thomas Drake forced the prisoner to his knees and, pressing the point of a poignard against the back of the fellow's leathery neck, growled, "Now speak up, you surly dog."

The captive's eyes rolled dazedly but he gasped out: "Satan's burning curse on all *demonios Ingleses*! You accursed heretics have sailed in vain. The Holy Virgin and Her Angels guard our coasts."

Martin Frobisher came pulling up in his longboat, ragged grey beard a-flutter in the onshore breeze. "About what does this ape chatter?"

Young Drake could not restrain himself any longer. "What this lying lout says is that last week the Plate Fleet from Mexico entered safely into San Lucar harbour."

Drake's face flamed and he stiffened as if stung by a pike's point. "Impossible! This swine is lying! The Viceroy's *flota* is not due for another two weeks. Most certainly I will intercept it off the coast of Barbary."

Tom Drake was the picture of dejection; although dark and slight, he resembled his illustrious brother not a little about the eyes and mouth. "I fear, sir, that what this garlic-eater claims is but too true. For my officers and I have questioned certain of his crew separately. Their description of the galleons, their names and the exact hour of the *flota's* arrival are all of a piece."

Sulphurous were the oaths that circulated the English armada. Sir Francis Knollys fairly excelled himself; was he not a champion curser? As for Drake, he stared fixedly out over Vigo Bay, hard brown hands clenched so tight that their numerous rings dug into his flesh.

"Dear God," he rasped, "but for those delays caused by that popinjay Sidney, I would have cruised off San Lucar in time."

Eventually he roused and spat over the rail. "Alack, gentlemen, what is done is done, and there's no more mending a piece of bad luck than in putting wise words in the mouth of a fool."

Few guessed that to Drake the *Malagueño's* news was an especially heavy blow. Perhaps without realizing it, he had been counting on the capture of the Plate Fleet to finance the construction of several new merchantmen.

And then, too, his share of the *flota's* treasures should have helped defray the heavy costs of that elaborate household over which presided his new wife, Elizabeth, *née* Sydenham. Again, it was costing a deal more than he had expected to maintain his pages, secretaries and lesser servants in addition to an extensive wardrobe and the good table he insisted upon setting.

As soon as the bad news became known ashore, church bells commenced exultantly to peal in Bayona.

It was therefore scarcely the most propitious moment for Henry Wyatt to request an interview with the Admiral; how could he know Sir Francis was plunged into one of those savage black moods which, fortunately, seized him but seldom? He was full of enthusiasm, having planned to the least detail a most audacious project. At the moment he carried letters of credit from the wealthy Roger Jenkins and the offer of Jenkins' fastest neff to convey him to England. There, cannon would be purchased in the interests of the Governor of San Domingo, but faulty ones calculated to burst at the first discharge. It was a mighty deep and clever plan Wyatt had figured out, one which he confidently expected would meet with the Admiral's instant and enthusiastic approval.

To his amazement those penetrating blue eyes gleamed hostile as sword points. "Well, sirrah, why do you thus dare to intrude upon me again? God's blood! Have I not done you enough favours but you must come whining for more?"

A gasp escaped Wyatt, so very different was this from the reception he had anticipated. "I regret, Your Honour, thus to trespass on your time and good nature, but whilst ashore I learned somewhat of interest and have evolved a plan for your approval."

"You evolve a plan? Who bade you, you blundering sprout, to thrust your addlebrained schemes upon me?"

Drake's cold rage was formidable, his beard bristled and his nostrils opened and shut like the gills of a stranded fish.

Although fairly choking with disappointment Wyatt set his jaw and stood his ground. "None the less I crave your indulgence, sir. Methought you should know that the defences of San Domingo in Hispaniola——"

"A plague on you, sirrah! I know where San Domingo lies. Do you presume to instruct me in geography?"

Desperately the red-haired Master shook his head. "Never, sir, but I'm told the forts guarding San Domingo lack all manner of heavy ordnance."

"A likely tale! Get you hence and do not again seek my company unbidden."

The amazing injustice of Drake's reception brought angry tears to Wyatt's eyes, the first since that terrible, sleep-haunting day in Huntingdon Town market place.

God alone knew what substitute measures Master Jenkins might adopt when he failed to appear in his role of deserter. Silently, sullenly, Wyatt resumed his duties as Sailing Master's Mate, and on the eighth of October, 1585, the English fleet upped anchors, made sail, and vanished into the vast expanses of the Atlantic.

CHAPTER X

THE JOURNAL OF HUBERT ·COFFYN

DESPITE an unaccustomed sense of lethargy and the throb of a mild headache, Hubert Coffyn prepared to make an entry in that journal he had vowed to maintain throughout the voyage. That he was a miserable penman any one of his masters at Eton College would gladly have attested; also that his spelling would forever remain an abomination in the sight of educated men. Nevertheless, Coffyn unstoppered a small leaden ink-bottle, selected a quill from the brass case he kept at the bottom of his sea bag and, making use of a table upon which the gentlemen of lesser degree usually dined, commenced laboriously to write:

December ye third. On ye evening of November ye sixteenth our squadron did come to anchor in ye Bay of Santiago in ye Cape Verde Islands ye same pertaining to ye Crown of Portugal, now usurped by that Man Philip. During this same night our Admiral-General did cause Lieutenant Generall Carleill to land above a thousand Soldiers upon a little Cape which lieth some distance to ye eastwards of ye town of Santiago. This force he did then divide into several small companies, which did march to an emminence lying near two miles from ye city. Here our Lieutenant-Generall rested his troops until dawn then re-forming them into three divisions, he advanced against ye flank of ye city, which was equipped with many strong batteries and high walls. To our vast surprize no shot was fired and no voices called down from ye battlements. Wherefor ye enemy should have fled from very strong positions and so abandoned their ordnance—excellent long cannons and demi-cannon of bronze and ye same fully charged is passing strange. Yet it was so. Corpo'ls of Ye Field Barton and Sampson were ordered with a small body of men to make a reconnoitre. They found ye city empty as well as ye forts, so General Carleill did order hoisted ye Great Flag of St. George so that ye fleet should see it and know that ye town had fallen into our hands.

It being November ye seventeenth and ye birthday of our Most Gracious Sovereign, we did discharge a salute from all ye ordnance to be found in ye deserted city. To which ye fleet did respond with broadsides. Much disappointment was found among our ranks that ye enemy had proved so cowardly!

Young Coffyn paused, passed a hand over his eyes and noticed that their backs were sweaty. He rose and sought a nearby scuttle from which he drew a piggin of water taken on at the Cape Verde Islands. Two or three officers off duty lay sleeping, curled in their cloaks about the deck, pillowing their heads on sea bags. Their weapons and armour, suspended from pegs driven into the *Bonaventure's* bulwarks, clinked and clashed softly to the galleon's monotonous rolling.

Heaving a sigh, Hubert Coffyn picked up his quill again and decided to cut short his manuscript by omitting to mention that the loot taken in Santiago had proved nearly as scarce as inhabitants:

We did pursue ye Governor and Bishop and ye inhabitants to a small town inland lying named San Domingo. This place was found to be deserted. Our Admiral-General did then utter a message demanding a ransom, but no reply being received ye City of San Domingo then was consigned to ye flames.

However, considerable supplies of wine and fresh provision having been discovered, and Sir Francis might well have spared ye city saving that a ship's boy was most foully murdered during the night. Our Admiral being greatly enraged did then order Santiago put to ye torch and a merry blaze ensued. Because thus far they had won nothing in ye way of booty, grumbling did arise among mariners and troops alike on ye last day of our stay in those profit-less islands. Our Admiral-General therefore did cause his whole army to be paraded, together with crews from ye ships, and did cause them to swear a mighty oath of fealty to Her Majestie's cause and to ye authority conferred on him by her.

A growing nausea which for some hours had been plucking at Coffyn's throat grew stronger. Sweating heavily, he forced himself to scrawl:

And so on November ye twenty-sixth we did charge aboard our armada all good ordnance discovered in the Portuguese Islands, they being much pressed for ordnance. Some say we now are sailing for one of ye West Indies, God and our Admiral alone knowing whether this be so.

Quite an effort was required to put away quill case, ink-bottle and manuscript but Coffyn just managed to do so before, suddenly, he retched and vomited all over the deck.

"Curse you for a swinish clod!" roared an aroused sleeper.

Others, nauseated by the resultant foul odours, joined in his abuse. Coffyn clung to the rail, slobbering: "Your pardon, gentlemen. 'Tis passing strange but my hands are as of sand and—and——" He broke off to spew.

" 'Tis clear you have been taken by a fever," presently mumbled the flagship's Chirurgeon, one Nathaniel Godwin, "and 'tis aggravated by a flux I fear." The stricken young gentleman, already racked by spasm of nausea, now became tormented by diarrhœa, which doubled his malodorous misery. At the end of a few hours Coffyn's mind commenced to wander. He raved of casting of monster culverins, of the manufacture of corn powder, then babbled weakly of Bideford in Devonshire where conies and rabbits scampered about green-crested white cliffs.

Ever longer grew the expression decking Chirurgeon Godwin's smallpox-pitted countenance when a similar fever struck down two more gentlemen and nearly a dozen forecastle hands and soldiers.

"I have met wi' this curs'd Cape Verde fever before," the Sailing Master declared. " 'Tis deadly in most cases and oft leaves those who recover addled in their wits. God knows why the Admiral chose to put in there."

"For water," Wyatt supplied as, quietly, he attempted with wet cloths to cool Coffyn's burning forehead.

"Aye, but 'twas bad water," gloomily commented the Boatswain. "The stream, I noticed, ran below the town and was very foul."

Wyatt nowadays was more silent than usual, being preoccupied with thoughts of Kate pregnant, alone, and all but penniless. Worse still, although Drake's squadron had been at sea for over two months now the Assistant Sailing Master's purse was no heavier and he had won command over not so much as a pinnace. Considering his last interview with the Admiral, there seemed little likelihood of any such advancement for all that Drake, as was his custom, made it a point always to greet by name not only his officers but even the humblest of the ship's boys. One of these hapless lads lay expiring on a sodden tarpaulin, his breathing stertorous and his face gone a ghastly yellow-green. Wyatt went over to hold a gourd of water to the boy's fluttering lips for all he knew that the soothing fluid be vomited a moment later.

Day after blazing day the stricken armada continued on its westward course and so ran before the wind. Meanwhile the contagion spread until only two vessels, both little caravels, remained free of this mysterious and virulent epidemic. Now men were dying every hour for, thanks to overcrowding below and on deck, it proved impossible to keep the ships in anything approaching cleanliness. At the end of a week the *Bonaventure* gave off so intolerable a stench that even an insensitive nose could have recognized it at half a mile's distance.

In the beginning the dead were slipped overboard to a reading of the burial service by the Admiral's Chaplain, some officer or even by Drake himself, but now, no sooner had a stricken man's spirit departed than certain able-bodied mariners dragged his corpse across the deck to heave the hideous thing into the sparkling blue sea.

Worried to distraction, Vice-Admiral Frobisher at the end of a fortnight appeared aboard the *Bonaventure* to suggest that the squadron stop running free and change course so that a wind from off the beam might blow between the decks and so perhaps abate the epidemic.

Sir Francis Drake listened attentively but ended by shaking a sun-bleached yellow head. "Nay, Martin, I've met with such fevers before and it is not to be blown away by any wind, no matter how sweet or powerful. We will hold to our present course and beseech God that we raise one of the Indies before too many poor wights are sped."

Wearily obedient to the Admiral's inflexible will, the plague ships continued to plough on towards the Caribbean with the north-east Trades singing through their rigging and hurling diamantine spray over their starboard quarters. Because of these trade winds the squadron practically sailed itself, which was well, since the remaining able-bodied men became largely occupied with tending delirious companions who lay about the decks moaning for death, water or some loved one.

Henry Wyatt devoted most of his time to Hubert Coffyn who, though terribly weak and emaciated, yet clung stubbornly to life, his once-powerful chest rising and falling in febrile rapidity. In desperation Chirurgeon Godwin ordered sulphur to be burned, also saltpetre, which for a while alleviated that awful stench 'tween decks but had no effect upon the epidemic. Now, every masthead, day and night, held a lookout straining for the sight of an island and a haven on which the sick could be landed and the hale enabled to cleanse their vessels and themselves.

More than two hundred and thirty corpses had drifted astern of Drake's armada before a lookout aboard H.M.S. *Aid* raised that hail which everyone had anticipated with a passionate intensity. Wyatt supported Hubert's gaunt head on his knee, eased a few spoonfuls of broth into his mouth and announced, "Land's been sighted, so now, friend Hubert, certainly you will live to dip your arms elbow-deep in treasure."

The wasted figure's bloodshot brown eyes wavered up and he managed the faintest imaginable nod.

Wyatt added, "And somewhere out here I'll find me a stout caravel for my own." Hubert blinked, nodded once more and then settled back against an old topsail, closing his eyes. Wyatt lingered, passing broth about in the malodorous gloom of the gun deck and trying to forget the delirious moaning of a big Gunner who endlessly called for a girl named Dolly.

The land sighted proved to be Dominica among the easternmost islands of the Leeward group, a fact which proved that the Golden Admiral had lost none of his skill as a navigator.

The Indians of this island, having recently revolted against intolerable Spanish cruelties, came paddling out and waving green branches as signs of peace and welcome. Their bodies were painted yellow, red and blue and looked uncommon garish against the Caribbean's vivid blue-green waters.

With them they fetched along a few miserable captive Spaniards through whom they became able to converse with Drake's officers. Eagerly they begged the Englishmen to land, all the while fervently assuring them of friendship, but Drake, with the nearly fatal treachery on Mocha Island deep-rooted in his mind, curtly silenced the growls of his Captains and refused. He did, however, order trading for tobacco and cakes made of cassava root, the which, veteran crew members insisted, were potent in curing this particular fever.

The foul and noisome ships then set sail northwards and, two days later, entered a spacious and well-protected bay in a deserted island named after Saint Christopher, little guessing that in the years to come the great fleets of Drake's successors, Hood, Rodney and Nelson, would shelter in these same waters.

CHAPTER XI

THE NEXT VENTURE

ST. CHRISTOPHER—later St. Kitts—proved to be ideal for Sir Francis Drake's purposes. The island was beautiful beyond imagination while affording abundant supplies of wild fruits and tobacco—that great antiseptic. What an indescribable relief it was to be off the cramped and stinking *Bonaventure* thought Wyatt as he helped to bring the sick ashore and range them in rows beneath cool shelters fashioned of green palm fronds. Within a day the stricken ceased dying and commenced to mend and, best of all, the infection ceased to claim new victims.

Because the island was uninhabited and no danger of hostile attack existed no guard was kept beyond lookouts among the hills. The bearded crews grew strong again through feasting on the meat of those wild cattle and pigs which roamed the island in great droves.

"In this at least the old Dons were wise," remarked Lawson of Dover, Coxswain of the Admiral's little row galley and a dependable individual well regarded by his mates and officers alike. "As fast as the old-time Spaniards seized an island they at first opportunity would land a few beeves and swine that castaways of their nation might not starve. On Hispaniola, foı instance, I have seen wild cattle numbering up into the thousands feed along the sea coast."

On this garden of an island there were also quantities of wild pigeons, beautiful greenish-grey birds showing a wide black band on their tails and so tame they could readily be killed. Further food was found by the capture of ugly lizards which, when properly cooked, proved to be as succulent as capons.

Many of the sick men quickly recovered strength. Although Chirurgeon Godwin paid small heed, to Wyatt it proved interesting that those who rallied the most swiftly in the past had suffered some heavy sickness. Such individuals were up and about long before invalids who had enjoyed good health up until the Cape Verde fever had seized them.

Well men, in this beneficent atmosphere, filled out and soon resumed their full vigour. Readily they entered into such rough games as were initiated by their commanders. All along the smooth white beaches wrestling matches took place and tall pikemen merrily cracked each other's pates in quarterstaff bouts. In shady glens formed by tall cieba and mahogany trees archers set up butts, and bowstrings rapped against bracers and clothyard shafts flashed through the warm sunlight to accompanying shouts of "God save the mark!"

A measure of Wyatt's discouragement departed and, as he knelt to his prayers each night before slumber, he praised a merciful God that he had been spared that terrible fever, that he remained strong. Because of this he had learned many arts and refinements concerning navigation and seamanship since leaving Plymoth Hoe below the horizon.

Christmas Day was celebrated by special games of football, cudgel play and musketry, for which unusually lavish prizes were furnished from the Golden Admiral's private treasure chest. The only gloomy note was struck by great gaps in the ranks of contestants and an absence of familiar faces that would never again laugh or offer a coarse jest.

Together with other convalescents, Hubert Coffyn reviewed a parade offered by Carleill's troopers in honour of their beloved Queen. Comfortably enough, the invalids looked on from the shade of palm-frond lean-tos.

At the end of a fortnight the adventurers had regained their spirits and a large part of their strength. The fresh air, the leg room and, above all, fresh meats, fruits and vegetables had filled them out, while ceaseless drills had rendered them letter-perfect in their tactics and musketry.

Unfortunately, not a few continued sickly and, as the Sailing Master had predicted, a number of them never regained their right minds after the fever had left them. Of course, the ancient quarrel persisting between the archer who could speed a dozen shaft while an arquebusier was recharging his cumbersome weapon flared up anew and only the prompt infliction of punishment averted serious trouble.

As for Sir Francis, he seemed to be everywhere at once—the epitome of brisk vigour. Those that knew Drake best claimed that he was plotting his next move in which he would combine past experiences with innovations calculated to deceive and outwit the Spaniards.

Whatever he intended, Drake kept his plans to himself until the fleet had been at sea four days.

To Henry Wyatt's uneasy surprise he was abruptly summoned to the Admiral's handsome red-and-gold cabin from supervising the replacement of certain worn sheetlines and halyards.

The day being uncommon torrid, Sir Francis, like most of his men, had exchanged hot and tight-fitting hose, breeches and doublet for a muslin shirt and loose pantaloons such as the enemy affected in these latitudes. Scattered over a wide table were many charts, maps and other drawings more beautifully executed than any Wyatt had ever beheld. Foulke Greville, Drake's principal secretary and "loyal Achates", sat busily preparing lists and drawing up requisitions of varying kinds.

It was so hot in the flagship's cabin that already perspiration had begun to drip from the end of Vice-Admiral Martin Frobisher's bulbous and claret-coloured nose, whilst Lieutenant-General Carleill had stripped to the waist, thus exposing a great mat of black hair on his chest and a long purplish scar running along his ribs. Drake used a cambric handkerchief to mop his forehead then impatiently pushed back yellow hair cut quite short since Bayona.

"Here is Master Wyatt, sir," announced Flag-Captain Fenner.

The piercing blue eyes swung up to bore into Wyatt's coppery features. "Does my memory mistake me, Master Wyatt," he demanded curtly, "or did you not upon that accursed day we departed Vigo Bay make mention of Hispaniola?"

Desperately uneasy lest Drake might yet be considering his offer as an impertinence, Wyatt replied in the affirmative.

"Did you not mention an absence of long cannon in the forts protecting San Domingo?"

"Aye, sir." Wyatt was conscious of an intent scrutiny from a dozen pairs of eyes. "But because of the delay attendant upon our cruise to the Cape Verde Islands it is now impossible to be certain that none have arrived there."

A slight flush stained the Admiral's sun-darkened cheeks; obviously he did not relish being reminded of that fruitless and well-nigh disastrous diversion to Santiago. "In other words you cannot be certain that those forts on Hispaniola are still destitute of heavy ordnance?"

"Yes, sir. Surely the Spaniards long since must have suspected that you intend to strike in this direction."

One of Drake's bushy yellow brows climbed a trifle. "That is well reasoned. Tell me what you know of the city."

Wishing that his tongue did not feel so thick and clumsy, Wyatt replied, "I *know* nothing concerning the city of San Domingo saving what Master Jenkins has told me."

"And that was?"

"That San Domingo is the capital and seat of Spanish authority over all their possessions in this Western World. He swears 'tis beautifully situated and handsomely constructed of stone and much fine marble. Yonder dozens of churches and monasteries are to be found. The capital is in fact reputed to be by far the richest town of Spanish West America."

Drake nodded and smiled at various of his Captains. "That is no lie, gentlemen. San Domingo should prove a plump sweet plum if ever there was one. Now, gentlemen, let us consider how best we can shake King Philip's tree in order that this plum will fall surely within our grasp."

Immediately the Admiral pushed forward a great map of San Domingo and launched into a dissertation upon the strategy and tactics to be adopted. Since, apparently, he had forgotten Wyatt's presence that uneasy individual commenced to edge towards the cabin door. Drake, however, lifted his hand.

"Nay, pray bide here, Master Wyatt, for I intend dispatching the *Galliot Duck* to reconnoitre and Captain Hawkins is like to find himself so busy with observations that he'll need a handy sailor along of him." The Admiral then went on to describe his intention of landing emissaries to secure an alliance with his old friends the Maroons, fugitive Negro slaves, for on Hispaniola, as elsewhere, the Spaniards' insensate brutality was about to reap a bloody harvest. Various voyagers had reported to Drake the presence on Hispaniola of hundreds of desperate blacks and Indians who longed for the day when they might exact a ferocious revenge.

Rear-Admiral Knollys, ever lean and saturnine, declared himself opposed to the inclusion of unknown and probably untrustworthy allies; in this he was warmly supported by Captain Edward Winter of H.M.S. *Aid*.

"Out upon it, Sir Francis. There's no telling what course these blackamoors might adopt should the luck o' this affair turn against us."

Drake's small, sweat-soaked figure abruptly straightened itself and he spoke succinctly: "They'll not turn. Are they not those who must face the wrath of Spain if we are defeated? Which God forbid! At Venta Cruz and Nombre de Dios I found them loyal and valiant although my luck was out. No, these poor blackamoors will never turn from us."

A Greek trader, captured by one of the squadron on patrol duty and now serving the expedition as pilot, was presently led in. Although the renegade seemed all smiles and bows obviously he was fearful that his poor little barca and its cargo of young olive trees might be seized and that he himself would dangle from some Englishman's yardarm.

A few reassurances from Drake were all that was required to set the fellow to sketching a crude but recognizable plan of San Domingo's new forts and batteries. The old Greek's eyes rolled and he muttered directions to himself while his brush outlined a long sandspit jutting out to sea from the eastward end of San Domingo. To the westward the onlookers perceived that here the island described a broad curve ending in a low promontory.

"Between the point of this spit, *señores*, and this headland to the west lies a bar which may safely be crossed only in moderate weather. Here, beyond this bar and within the range of long cannon lie the limestone walls of the city," he declared. "Alas, *señores*, the only point suitable for disembarkation within the harbour lies at this spot."

"A great lot of good such a landing-place will do us," growled Frobisher, "if those two stars this garlic-stinking fellow has drawn represent forts."

"Inquire if those marks indeed indicate forts," Drake directed, "and if so how many guns they mount."

The interpreter chattered in Greek then informed: "He swears he has not visited San Domingo in many months, but at that time they mounted only fifty cannons. He noted, however, many embrasures yet empty and awaiting the arrival of ordnance from Spain."

"Has this smelly rogue heard whether these missing guns have arrived?" Knollys cut in.

"No, sir. He declares he has not visited the city in half a year but was on his way thither when the *White Lion* took him prize."

"Let him proceed." Conscious of the attention of these great lords, the withered old Greek explained that the city lay completely encircled by high walls of stout limestone and that a pair of castles guarding the sea wall had been built by Royal Engineers and recently he had heard of these forts being manned by Spanish regular troops.

"Where then can we land?" Wyatt heard Carleill's harsh deep accents demand.

Drake spoke up. "I have learned that some ten miles west of San Domingo lies a shallow bay with a beach suitable to our purpose—but it is guarded by two watchtowers kept by volunteers from the city."

"Ten miles, eh?" Carleill drawled, fingering his heavy black beard.

Meanwhile the Greek pilot eagerly expatiated upon the richness of the houses, the number of great warehouses and the vast wealth accumulated in the churches. The city teemed with noblemen, wealthy merchant princes and officials high in the colonial government. What was the population? Why, 'twas numbered close on sixteen thousand not counting slaves and transients, of which there were many because this was the crossroads of the Spanish King's American possessions. No. It had never before been attacked, the Greek declared, and its inhabitants, because of their forts and the valour of the troops, were convinced that it never would be. After all, was not the cream of the Spanish colonial army there to protect them?

CHAPTER XII

THE MAROONS

THANKS to the navigational skill of one Eric Parker, an English mariner who, unlike a majority of his ilk, had elected to quit Bayona after having dwelt and trafficked there for years, the *Galliot Duck* was enabled to sail boldly into San Domingo Harbour, slipping confidently among a bevy of tall merchantmen and two large men-of-war there at anchor. The *Galliot Duck*, briefly rechristened the *Santa Teresa de Gloria*, claimed to have sailed over from the Presidency of Cuba bearing a cargo of cured hides, or so Parker, her pretended Master, averred in flawless Spanish.

Small cold ripples of excitement descended the length of Henry Wyatt's back when the stubby little galliot's bows nosed into the busy and varicoloured harbour of San Domingo. To think he was actually viewing those great fortifications so graphically described by Master Jenkins under a certain almond tree back in Bayona!

Wyatt was wearing only a pair of ragged knee-breeches and had become so burnt that with his naturally deep complexion he could readily pass for a Spaniard. He studied a long series of embrasures let into towering battlements looming yellow-grey above the filth-dotted but still clear green waters of the harbour. The muzzles of cannon showed in almost all of them!

Unfortunately the galliot was forced to sail so close under the parapets that it proved impossible to estimate the probable weight of the pieces glinting so threateningly up there. Sure enough, yonder lay that cobbled landing-place described by the old Greek—many canoes and small boats lay drawn upon it. It was situated at the innermost extremity of the harbour and was so dominated by batteries that any enemy attempting to land must inevitably be blasted into rags and tatters. High in the air numbers of buzzards soared about the lacy twin towers of that great cathedral in which reportedly reposed the bones of Cristóbal Colón.

"Will ye look at the size o' their accursed cathedral?" muttered a younker by the name of Jackson. "I warrant we'll find some tidy pickings in there."

That no hint of the English squadron's presence thus far had reached this pleasant colonial capital was unmistakable. The little galliot made port in the early afternoon because Captain Richard Hawkins, a turbulent and often quarrelsome individual, had selected this hour when a vast majority of the inhabitants would be plunged into their customary siestas.

The *Duck*, propelled by a light breeze, tacked across the harbour and in so doing ascertained that two men-of-war present must be undergoing extensive repairs. One huge galleon of about six hundred tons and French-built by the look of her, the other a gallizabro or small, swift-sailing galleon. This last represented a new class, designed by Admiral Menéndez especially to cope with assailants of the King's Plate Fleets. If fought with any skill and courage this gallizabro alone would be more than a match for the *Bonaventure*.

Quite deliberately, the spy boat then picked her way through a maze of anchored ships, two of which, if one were to judge by the nauseating odours they gave off, must be slavers fresh in from the Guinea Coast. Rigs of all sorts were to be recognized such as zabias, pataches, frigates and carracks and inter-island traders. Scattered along the waterfront was a row of truly imposing structures which included the Aduana or Custom House, the King's Warehouses and the Captain-General's palace. Further on was what Parker identified as the King's Treasure House where bullion was collected and guarded until the Plate Fleets should set sail for Cádiz. The whole seaward façade of this structure, as in the case of the other Royal buildings, was adorned by elaborate carving and showed King Philip's coat of arms in gigantic scale.

How many poor devils of slaves, Wyatt wondered, had languished and died under this same lashing sun to create yonder lovely stone tracery?

Set among what must be extensive gardens and at the crest of a low hill dwarfed by the mountains beyond it lay the Viceroy's palace, all white and shimmering under this blazing December sunlight.

"That old Greek spoke the truth," grunted Richard Hawkins while fanning away a halo of flies. These and other insects came pouring over the side like enemy boarders.

Only a very few Negro bumboats put out to meet the pseudo *Santa Teresa*, their long canoes gunwale-deep under heaps of coconuts, oranges, limes and other fruits such as sailors fresh in from the sea were given to craving.

Upon the battlements no sign of life was visible beyond the head of a single somnolent sentry who had removed his steel cap and leaned his pike against a wall to linger in a patch of blue-white shade. Indolently he was fanning himself with a frayed palm leaf.

Once, twice, the galliot made a circuit of the harbour as if in search of a suitable anchorage, but when the harbour began to rouse now that the sea breeze commenced to blow and the shadows to lengthen, Hawkins worked his craft in an erratic course back towards the harbour's mouth through a fleet of yellow-sailed fishing-boats bowling in in company with a couple of clumsy caravels. These, apparently, must have come over from Mexico for they raised the Towers and Lions of Castile and Aragon and fired a salute when they passed a castle on the eastern side of the entrance.

To Wyatt, young Hawkins directed tensely: "Contrive to cast a lead as we pass over the bar. Let us make certain our vessels won't break their backs under the Spanish guns."

A certain tenseness prevailed over the galliot. If anyone had bothered to watch the so-called *Santa Teresa* during the past hour surely they must become suspicious. Wyatt and young Jackson, as they handled their sounding leads, viewed the battlements and noticed considerable activity up there. Steel glimmered and a hoarse braying of trumpets came beating over the water, then a cannon roared.

"God's eyeballs," snapped Hawkins, "yonder clods at last have taken alarm! Make all sail!"

"Your pardon, sir," Wyatt called. "Yonder castello only returns the salutes. To crowd on canvas at this moment would arouse suspicion."

Richard Hawkins bit off an angry retort. "You may be right."

Quite boldly leads were heaved when the emerald waters beneath the galliot's keel paled to a yellow-green and a sigh of relief escaped Wyatt when he recorded a good three fathoms. There was water and to spare for any and all ships in Drake's armada.

One of the inbound caravels sailed by so close that her crew shouted greetings. Parker waved and leisurely bade them welcome. "She's the *Santa Ana de Vera Cruz*, fresh in from San Juan de Ulúa," Parker grinned, "and just in time for a real party on New Year's Day."

Thanks to her complete insignificance the *Galliot Duck* remained apparently unnoticed and, unchallenged, passed among the inbound fishing craft who greeted her with cheerful shouts.

Once well out to sea the galliot steered west until at dusk she sighted the entrance to a small bay dominated by two sturdy watch-towers that guarded a magnificent and well-sheltered beach.

It was, Hawkins announced, the very place to throw ashore six or seven hundred troops with a minimum of delay—provided the watchtowers first were overwhelmed.

Just as if she had not the least interest in this bay the spy boat cruised on by, her yellow-brown sail bellying under a crisp breeze. Off yet another bay lying perhaps a league beyond the guarded beach, Captain Hawkins ported over his helm and when the first stars commenced to take on that white-hot lustre of the tropics steered his craft into within thirty yards of the shore, came into the wind and there dropped anchor.

"Show two lanterns from the spritstay, the one above the other", Hawkins directed. "And you, the red-haired rascal, get your men ready to shove off at an instant's notice."

"Aye, aye, sir." Wyatt could sense the young Captain's hostility. Hawkins needn't go taking on so about a perfectly proper suggestion; he wished that it had been somebody else with whom he had apparently locked horns. As John Hawkins' son, he was invariably accorded more deference than was warranted by his command over the smallest vessel in the English squadron.

Presently the galliot's cockboat was slipped over the stern and Captain Hawkins had himself rowed ashore. He sat stiff and proud in the sternsheets while Wyatt steered for a sloping stretch of shingle. Then, for half an hour, while mosquitoes made merry with the rowers crouched miserably over their oars, waiting, waiting, Hawkins would not go ashore or even close to that dark jungle in which all manner of monkeys and night birds were now raising their eerie calls.

"Avast!" young Hawkins snapped suddenly. "Here they come."

From among the shadows an English voice called in recognition signal, "Gloriana," to which Hawkins replied "God save the Queen." Then emerged upon the shingle Vice-Admiral Martin Frobisher, Sergeant-Major Powell, Captain Moone and a young cornet, together with a dozen of the most hideous-appearing humans Wyatt had ever dreamed of beholding.

The Maroon chieftains wore necklaces of wild hogs' tusks interspaced with human knucklebones and displayed crescent-shaped pieces of ivory stuck through their earlobes and the septa of their noses. They wore in addition a weird variety of headdress set upon sable hair as frizzy as a hedgehog's back. Bearing a varied assortment of javelins, bows and clubs, they came trotting silently down to the water's edge.

By the strong starlight their flat, sable features took on a faint bluish tinge and Wyatt noticed that many of them had filed their teeth into sharp, dog-like fangs. All were naked save for a belt from which was hung a species of lustrous sea-shell into which had been thrust each Maroon's private parts, obviously as a protection against the thorns and brush of the jungle.

Jackson whispered, "Ben't they like very fiends out o' the Pit?"

"That they are," Wyatt softly agreed. "I'd scarce admire the lot of any Spaniard who falls into their clutches."

Thomas Moone, he who had accompanied Drake on several previous expeditions, apparently found no trouble in conversing with the Maroons' simian-appearing paramount chief, although the Negro seemed to emit nothing more complicated than a series of clicks and grunts.

" 'Tis agreed," he informed tough old Martin Frobisher. "Before dawn our savage friends will overwhelm the watchtowers guarding our landing-place and I trow we'll meet wi' some gruesome sights once we come ashore."

"No doubt, *if* they succeed in surprising the Spaniards," grunted the Vice-Admiral, "but God help us if they fail."

CHAPTER XIII

SHOW OF FORCE

DURING the dawn of New Year's Day, 1586, Sir Francis Drake's fleet heaved up their anchors. There was no longer any point in pretending that its presence had passed undetected. Too many pirogues and zabias had sailed into sight, only to put about and scurry off towards that Pearl of the Antilles called San Domingo.

One by one the English ships set flags and banners to flying, trimmed sail and headed for two blue-green mountains looming above the horizon. Lieutenant-General Carleill's troops gave a last-minute inspection to their harness and sharpened swords and pike points. The archers tested their bows while arquebusiers made sure that their corn powder was dry and that their matches were fit to be lit at a charcoal brazier which never went out in the 'tween decks.

Bravely from all mastheads fluttered the Cross of St. George and, following ancient custom, gentlemen of coat armour slung wooden shields, purely heraldic now and of no use in battle, over the poop-deck rail that their enemies might recognize who was coming to fight against them.

Although he remained far too weak to take a part in the impending battle, Coffyn caused his father's old-fashioned morion and dinted cuirass to be brought on deck.

As usual, no one knew for sure what course Sir Francis Drake contemplated, and his gentlemen kept directing glances at that stubby, erect figure standing near the poop-deck's rail.

Because of losses through the epidemic, the ships no longer were overcrowded, and the survivors appeared eager as staghounds to be slipped of restraint and hurled against that big, white, yellow and grey city commencing to loom large below the mountains ahead.

Drake stood apart, staring over the sunlit sea. What fate awaited him yonder? Much like this he had come bowling down upon Santa Marta, San Juan de Ulúa and Nombre de Dios. Scattered rain-squalls lifted over the horizon and wandered about the sky briefly to drench ship after ship and caused archers to curse and hide their bows under waterproof cases. But the showers were light and, within a few minutes, the hot sun beat down as before.

Although it was mid-afternoon, few siestas were being enjoyed in San Domingo for troops of cavalry could be seen cantering near the shore while straggling bodies of troops toiled along roads leading into the capital. It would seem, the officers concluded in grim satisfaction, that here there would be no repetition of that pusillanimous and baffling refusal to fight which had spoiled their attack on Santiago. A few small ships could be seen scurrying out of the harbour and in frantic haste fleeing off down the coast.

"A pity. There's no catching them now," Drake growled. "They're certain to be heavy-laden with valuables."

Henry Wyatt, posted beside the *Bonaventure's* pilot because of experience gained in the *Galliot Duck*, now found the city of San Domingo even more imposing in appearance than before. Recalling his failure thus far on the expedition to win so much as an escudo, he quite unconsciously licked his lips. Surely in this rich town there must be waiting to be won treasure enough to secure for sweet Kate and the child which certainly would greet his return a home of their own? And not too humble a one either.

In his deeply tanned face teeth glinted when he considered the quantities of ships now penned in yonder harbour. While the flagship bore steadily down upon the bar he could see puffs of grey-white smoke begin to spurt from the battlements of that massive castello guarding the harbour's western entrance. Undoubtedly these were no more than signal guns. Now to every tower climbed brilliant flags—those of the King, the Viceroy, or that of some powerful noble.

For the life of him, Wyatt could not comprehend why the troops had not yet been landed on that beach the galliot had reconnoitred. Aware of a rising tension in his being he glanced along the flagship's waist, crowded now with bearded, sun-bleached men in steel caps and wearing white surplices marked with the Cross of St. George. Hard fellows to a man, the troops cracked coarse jokes.

"Lay you two ducats, Will, I'll be frolicking wi' a wench afore you do," one boasted.

"Aye. Ye'll tumble some poor black i' an alley."

The first arquebusier spat onto the deck. "Nay, I'll ravish no nigger but some dainty pale-skinned damsel o' the best blood in Spain."

"Why boggle, lads? Grandee lady or nigger wench—they're all the same i' the dark," cackled another.

"Ye can keep your pale-skinned females," grunted a tall, gap-toothed spikeman. "Me, I fancy a big black lass wi' the sweat dripping off her teats like suet from a well browned roast."

Thanks to the *Duck's* reconnaissance, the *Bonaventure*, flaunting Drake's personal banner from her principal mizzen, headed confidently for the bar. All the same, her steersman cast Wyatt a searching look. "Ye'd best be right about these soundings else you'll find yerself flayed alive and rubbed with salt in some Spanish dungeon."

Wyatt's dark red brows converged. "All will go well provided you bring yon cupola on the King's Custom House in line with the cathedral's right-hand tower."

When the water paled and shoaled silence descended upon Drake's armada, enabling the crews of its twenty-five vessels clearly to hear a furious rolling of drums and the bray of trumpets along the battlements. Sir Francis Drake, gilded helmet agleam, came striding across the poop deck, supple and easy.

"Very presently now, Master Wyatt, we will discover whether those long guns you spoke of have arrived or no." He shot the younger man a curious, almost apologetic look. "If we're struck 'tis none of your fault. You warned me early enough."

The mariners gathered on the forecastle anxiously scanned that opalescent pale green line identifying the harbour bar's inner edge.

As, steadily, the *Bonaventure* bore down upon it, Captain Fenner commenced to curse. " 'Twill be a near thing—a damned near thing." Bits of swill, floating out of the harbour, commenced to slide past the flagship's dark blue sides.

When the bar glimmered beneath the *Bonaventure's* sprit, Drake, perhaps involuntarily, gripped a shroud and braced himself. Everyone aboard felt the flagship's progress slow as she entered the shoal water, and she seemed to squat on the sea for an eternal instant. A tumultuous cheer broke out. The *Bonaventure* had crossed the bar.

Singly, or by twos and threes, the other English ships, painted yellow, red, brown or blue, followed Drake's lead until presently they all were across except that notoriously slow sailer the old *Galleon Leicester*.

Obedient to their Admiral's signal the squadron put over helms and, in a long and irregular line, commenced to parallel the battlements. This manœuvre, as Hubert Coffyn pointed out, was executed at so discreet a distance that only a long cannon could have ranged the English ships now sailing in line ahead.

"Hoist my signal to open fire," Drake quietly instructed his Master Gunner. A blue-and-red-striped flag promptly soared to the galleon's signal yard and at once the eight heavy demi-culverins composing the *Bonaventure's* lade board or port battery roared in succession. Undulating billows of grey-white smoke drifted lazily off towards the besieged city but, as Hubert Coffyn had fully expected, not one of the armada's shots fell better than a hundred yards short of the castellos to raise brief, impressive spouts of shimmering spray.

One after another other English warships followed suit, making the whole red-roofed city resound and reverberate to the thunder of their guns. Presently the reports came rumbling back as echoes from among those mountains beyond the port, and sent great clouds of sea birds, such as terns, cormorants and pelicans, into terrified flight.

The Spanish western castle now opened fire, but with equally negligible results. As for Drake and his senior officers, they kept their attention on that great battery which defended the harbour landing-place. Were any long cannon emplaced up there among the ordnance? Everyone could see gunners carrying handspikes, rammers and swabs hurrying about.

"Lucifer's curse on 'em!" snarled Winter. "Why don't the bastards open fire and let us learn the worst?" It was a tense moment, for if there were even demi-cannon mounted yonder the invading squadron would suffer a bad, if not a fatal, mauling. The Spanish commander obliged scarcely a minute later. Some ten guns in the main battery let fly, spewing out great ring-shaped patterns of smoke into a rain-squall which came scurrying in from the sea. Quite distinctly Wyatt could see the enemy cannon-balls go arching up, up into the sky. Coffyn suddenly grinned and dealt his leg a slap of satisfaction. "They've mounted nothing better than demi-culverins or perriers."

"How can you tell?"

"Consider the parabolas their balls describe." Even General Carleill thrust his black beard far out over the rail in order to study the flight of the approaching cannon-balls.

The conditions described by Master Jenkins of Bayona evidently still prevailed, for the castello's broadside plunged into the surface of the harbour a comfortable two hundred yards short of the *Bonaventure's* steerboard rail.

Presently Drake ordered his armada to cease fire and thereby diminished the din by half. The English cannonade, however, had not been entirely devoid of effect. A carrack was seen to be heavily ablaze and one of those caravels Wyatt had watched making port the day before was so far down by the head that her foremast leaned crazily out over the water.

In leisurely fashion Drake then anchored his squadron just inside the bar, but far enough out to avoid Spanish artillery and the danger of a surprise boat attack.

CHAPTER XIV

IN-TAKING

ONE by one at first and then in clusters, the yellow-red lights of the town blinked out in San Domingo and, as if to relieve them, a myriad stars commenced to glow so brightly that the outline of the castellos was easy to discern even though there was no moon.

Henry Wyatt, obedient to a signal from Flag-Captain Fenner, ordered brought alongside the Admiral's row galley which, together with the *Bonaventure's* other small boats, had been trailing astern. As quickly and as silently as possible arquebusiers, archers, pikemen and such mariners as were detailed to accompany the expedition clambered down into the waiting small craft.

Although a strong offshore wind should blow most sounds out to sea it formed no part of Drake's intent that the Spaniards be warned of his impending strategy. Meanwhile boats from the other men-of-war appeared, urged along by the land breeze in addition to their oars.

Wearing an unadorned steel cap, breastplate and a short black cloak, the Admiral-General nimbly descended a rope ladder to be joined by General Carleill and his two Corporals of the Field.

It was a bitter disappointment that Wyatt's duties detained him aboard the *Bonaventure*. He and Hubert Coffyn, also cursing his fate, were left peering into that darkness which swallowed the flotilla of small boats.

"D'you think they in the forts will suspect what's afoot?" Coffyn queried, slumping weakly onto an empty powder keg, for, once more aboard ship, the invalids had ceased to improve, while not a few went out of their heads.

"No, I don't think they'll twig," Wyatt replied. "With this breeze off the land I doubt if they have heard aught alarming."

Soon the wind blew stronger and to render those left behind more miserable the rain came pelting down out of a lightless sky. Eons and eons seemed to drag by. The anchored vessels sullenly pitched and wallowed, their spars and top hampers whining as if irked by this unwanted inactivity.

Now that time hung heavy on his hands Wyatt, as usual, attempted to guess what might chance with his beloved Kate. By now she must have grown almighty big with their offspring, undoubtedly conceived in that heavenly little vale in the forest above St. Neots.

St. Neots! In the darkness his lips tightened at recollection of what had chanced there and in the Huntingdon Town market place. Undoubtedly such abominations as witches and warlocks did exist. Every man jack in England would admit it, but to accuse poor disfigured Meg and his gentle, overly curious and impractical father of such dreadful practices was absurd! As for his mother—in his mind's eye he saw again that ghastly attenuated figure with the ragged grey hair swaying against the noonday sky.

"Some day," he silently resolved, "I'll face up Sir John Addison and force him to recant. After all, 'twas he who roused the authorities and pressed the accusations." Besides, it occurred to the Assistant Sailing Master that he must have his own conviction set aside. For a fact, at this moment he was but a condemned criminal, fugitive from the Queen's justice.

He was only half aware that Coffyn was talking on and on. "Aye,

Harry, I can scarce wait till we assault the city." He lowered his voice. "You see, my family's grown poor through services to the Crown. My sire was hard-pressed, almost to his last shilling, to arm me against this voyage. Pray God we discover King Philip's treasure-house well stocked." He turned a pallid face that shone with rain under the galleon's great stern lantern. "Aye, Harry, and you'll pick up certain baubles in the interest of that sweet Kate you forever prate about and your family."

"Saving Kate, I have no family," Wyatt replied bitterly. "However, I mean to collect my fair share of the booty *and* a certain caravel I saw stand in to San Domingo yesterday. 'Fore God, Hubert, she looked fast, had clean lines and seemed well constructed."

All during that period in which the fleet sidled and rolled to its anchors men were talking in a similar vein, while wondering just what scheme the Golden Admiral had invented to bring about the capital's reduction. Veterans among them realized that San Domingo must prove a very hard nut to crack. Its castellos were powerful and it was now rumoured that near a hundred and fifty cannon of all sorts defended them. Furthermore the Spanish King's troops would be fighting from the protection of battlements—if their leaders really possessed the military capacity they were reputed to enjoy.

It lacked but a couple of hours to dawn before a scattering of small boats could be discerned pulling stealthily back towards their ships out of the gloom. They rode high, being no longer weighted down with troops and their fighting gear. When a bumping sound alongside was heard Captain Winter himself sought the head of the ladder and called down into the wind-filled dark, "Is all well, sir?"

"Aye," Drake's voice replied, strong and distinct. "My Maroon friends to a man massacred guards in the watchtowers. Handy fellows, they made a regular dog's breakfast of them," he added while swinging up the *Bonaventure's* side, the dark cloak blowing clear. "The Dons indeed are infatuated to slay, torture and otherwise persecute their poor slaves. And now, let us to our rest for, at sun-up, we stand in against the city."

Long lines of shaggy brown pelicans, looking like survivors of some antediluvian age, commenced to beat past Drake's ill-assorted squadron on their flight to sea. Gulls and other sea birds began to scale and dip about the tops when the English fleet commenced to bestir itself. Anchors were raised, dripped slime over battered sides. Canvas, but by no means full sail, was spread as, one by one, various elements of Drake's command fell into an irregular line behind the *Bonaventure.*

The Admiral-General once more had arrayed himself in that splendid suit of black, gold-mounted armour which he had worn off Bayona. On his breastplate were depicted striving tritons and giants, while Sir Francis' high-combed morion and its familiar clump of blue-and-white ostrich feathers lent him the illusion of greatly increased stature.

On Fenner's command trumpets commenced to sound in the flagship's waist where gunners blew on their linstocks and crouched tense beside their cumbersome demi-cannon, sakers and falconers. Under a stiff onshore breeze smoke from burning matches whirled off across the deck together with the usual coarse jokes. High above the maintop snapped the red and white pattern of the Cross of St. George.

Over from the castellos floated an answering blare of bugles and a loud clashing of Moorish cymbals. Flags, brilliant as butterflies and infinitely varied as to colour and design, appeared on nearly every tower and battlement. Long since, all Spanish craft had crowded into San Domingo's inner harbour and had become so tightly packed that there could be no possible way of manœuvring them. As for those two fighting galleons Wyatt had noted, they now lay protecting the entrance to the inner harbour with guns run out and battle flags a-flying.

Nearer and nearer to the forts sailed Drake's flagship, her half-naked crew taut and sweating with expectation. At length the English vessels drew so close that their companies could distinguish individual figures, for example a tall Captain wearing black and scarlet plumes and a yellow surcoat. The gleam of pike heads, armour, and the flash of matchlock barrels shone in ever-increasing detail.

At last Drake gave a sharp tug to his little yellow beard and, crossing the break of the poop, called down to his Master Gunner. "Open fire, Master Alwin, and make sure your men aim high rather than low."

The *Bonaventure* heeled over under the recoil of her ladeboard battery and so touched off a cannonade which continued unbroken for nearly an hour with the English armada slowly circling the outer harbour and battering the fortifications with their heavy guns. Happily, the enemy ramparts proved to be nowhere near so durable as they appeared. Quite often, when a thirty-pound ball from the demi-cannons struck a battlement, a whole segment of it would fly up into the air leaving a raw white gap.

The Spanish fire, however, was far from ineffective. Again and again Drake's ships were hulled and men were killed or hideously mutilated by flying splinters. Yet until near high noon the English ships kept on describing their deadly circle. When at last they drew off, some of them had had topmasts carried away and their carpenters had nailed sheet lead over wounds gaping near their waterlines.

Once the fleet had returned to its anchorage practically every able-bodied man remaining aboard raised an outcry, brandished weapons and otherwise did their best to create an impression that Drake's entire force was about to land on some swampy land to the west of the city. Drake strode about the poop deck taking short, quick steps—much like a gamecock in his walk, thought Hubert Coffyn.

Obviously, the Admiral-General was on tenterhooks to learn whether the Licentiate Don Juan Fernández de Mercado would be able to resist a sally; would he sense an opportunity of annihilating the cursed *heréticos* on this open ground where his Spanish-trained regulars would be at their most effective?

"Ha! 'Tis as I hoped," Wyatt heard the Admiral grunt, for no sooner had the small boats pushed off towards the swampy ground than one of the two gates piercing the west wall protecting San Domingo swung open, and out galloped a squadron of handsomely caparisoned and accoutred cavalry. Next appeared a body of musketeers, followed by a dense column of pikemen.

These forces turned southwards and formed up on the edge of that swampy lagoon towards which Drake's mariners were now pulling. Plumes jerking to the beat of oars, Drake stood in his row galley's sternsheets shading his eyes and peering steadfastly into the jungle behind the swampy land ahead. Had Carleill been able to complete his circuitous ten-mile march up the coast in time? What was contemplated was so daring a manœuvre that no professional commander of the day would ever have attempted it.

Tugging anxiously at his beard, Sir Francis gave orders for the flotilla to rest on its oars out of range from the shore for never had he entertained the least notion of flinging ashore his scanty force of poorly armed mariners. Meanwhile, more and more troops trotted out of San Domingo at the double—pikemen, crossbow men and quite a few matchlock bearers. Soon some six or seven hundred Spaniards stood drawn up in grim expectancy.

Smoke from that Spanish ship which had been set afire during the morning drifted lazily over the city walls and wandered along the beach, casting irregular bluish shadows over the richly garbed *caballeros* on horseback.

Taunts and insults and promises of painful annihilation began to ring out over the water. The English were cowardly dogs, yelled the enemy. Were they afraid to come ashore? What else could be expected from the perjured followers of that heretic whore who occupied the Throne of England? Aboard the flotilla English faces commenced to redden and weapons were handled in eager anticipation of having done with this nonsense.

All at once trumpets sounded from the direction of a dense wood situated between the Spaniards and their city's gates, and there swung into sight the vanguard of a solid, steel-clad column playing field music and bearing at their head a huge Cross of St. George flag.

Swiftly the two companies of fire—the archers and arquebusiers—then deployed under guidons and red-and-white-striped banners. Behind them Carleill's three squadrons of pikemen formed a dense triple line.

The Spaniards raised an astonished shout and wavered a moment, then their cavalry brandished ten-foot pennon-tipped lances and wheeled. Astride small but powerful horses they charged headlong at this second English force which so mysteriously had appeared on their flank and rear. Faster and faster rode the *caballeros*, their surcoats and plumes streaming bravely in the wind.

A scattering volley from Corporal of the Field Sampson's men emptied a dozen and more saddles, then the famous clothyard shafts which had decided Poitiers, Agincourt and Cressy began whirring through the tropical sunlight. Horse after horse went down, screaming and threshing wildly. Others, stung beyond endurance, bolted, throwing their fellows off-stride or literally bowling them over.

On command of General Carleill the archers and the arquebusiers turned and ran back through the files of waiting pikemen, there to reload or to select fresh shafts.

On rushed the Spanish cavalry, bravely enough, for among them were numbered some of the best and noblest Spaniards in the New World. In their ranks rode the Licentiate Balthasar de la Villa Fane, the Auditor of the Royal Council, Fiscal Licentiate Aliago and the Licentiate Arero of the Colonial Council. The President-General himself had begun the attack, but, unfortunately, he and his horse had stepped into a bog, requiring a party of riders to drag him out.

Thus far, not one Englishman had been killed or even wounded, but at least fifteen or twenty *caballeros* lay crumpled in death or writhing in pain before the English position. When, at the very last moment, the Spanish horses sensibly refused to impale themselves upon those murderously gleaming pike heads, the cavalry wheeled and streamed back to re-form behind crossbow men and arquebusiers advancing to crush Carleill's force, wearied as it was by its long march under a searing sun.

Once an appreciable number of Spaniards had swung away from the beach in order to face the threat presented by Carleill, Drake ordered the boats back to their ships. The mariners complied but reluctantly, swearing by all and everything holy that they had been meanly cozened out of an opportunity to teach the Dons who was, and who was not, a whore. "Besides, those fornicating troopers will have sacked the goddam place 'fore we can get ashore," snarled a one-eyed Boatswain.

From his position aboard the Admiral's galley, Wyatt obtained a clear impression of what was chancing on shore. At the moment arquebusiers of both sides were running forward, planting their musket yokes and banging away on practically even terms. What decided the outcome of this struggle—and probably for the last time in English history—were longbows.

Drake's archers were able to loose a dozen shafts while the enemy's crossbow men were, with ponderous windlasses, cranking back their powerful steel bows. Faster and faster under those deadly clothyard shafts the yelling Spaniards commenced to fall.

The instant he perceived a wavering General Carleill ordered forward his squadrons of pikes. Before their silent, steady advance the Spaniards broke in headlong rout towards the city; many of them, however, took shelter among tangles along the road and so improvised a series of ambuscades which were not eliminated without considerable loss.

Further, the defenders adopted a favourite Spanish tactic. Their horsemen rounded up a great herd of semi-wild bulls and oxen and goaded them towards Carleill's troops in the hope of disordering their order of battle. It turned out that no amount of pricking with lances and swords could force these bawling creatures to face a blazing fire from English muskets. Those beeves which were not slain turned and lumbered off towards the safety of the jungle, bellowing their fear and trampling the few courageous Spaniards who sought to control them.

Once the enemy was in full flight and only their gasping and groaning wounded remained, Lieutenant-General Carleill ordered a halt, removed his morion and employed a water-soaked sponge, set into its top for coolness, to mop his heated features. Thus far matters had proceeded well enough, he concluded, and, despite the fact that his men were weary from the long march up to San Domingo, they looked ready and steady enough. Best of all, his total casualties thus far amounted to less than twenty.

Too experienced a commander either to permit the loss of his own momentum or to grant the enemy an opportunity to rally, he turned his hawk's face to Sergeant-Major Powell. "Do you take half our men and assault that gate towards the forest whilst I lead an attack upon their portal nearest to the sea. Wi' God's help we will soon meet together in the principal square of San Domingo."

"Aye, aye, sir." The dark-browed Welshman turned away shouting commands that were readily obeyed because everyone could glimpse Spanish soldiers beginning to reappear on the walls.

On this landward side were many empty embrasures, but into them small murdering pieces such as minions, sakers and falconers were hastily being dragged.

For a space the invaders helped themselves to richly ornamented weapons and other equipment dropped by those who had fled from the shore, then, their arms clattering to a jolting double-quick, the English troops started in pursuit, sweating in streams and cursing under the weight of their arms. Sword in hand and yelling like a fiend from the Pit, Carleill charged the San Domingo's eastward gate at the head of his men. As usual the Spaniards had built their landward walls somewhat lower and had armed them less heavily than those facing the sea.

After skilfully deploying his force, Drake's General granted it but a brief moment to catch breath before he strode out in front, silver-plated armour flashing bright as a meteor and a clump of scarlet-green plumes atop his morion tossing like a palm frond in a gale. In one hand Carleill carried a dag—or a heavy wheel-lock pistol—in the other a sword.

"Forward!" he bellowed. "Forward, and win glory for our Queen!" He had taken but two steps before a ragged volley sounded on the ramparts. Carleill's aide stumbled and sank forward onto his face, to lie with quivering fingers digging at the warm brown earth.

Other Englishmen fell under that murderous leaden hail ere they gained shelter under the wall and began heaving each other up onto the parapet; they had no intention of affording the defenders an opportunity to reload and better organize themselves. A few petronels and wheel-locks boomed, then the struggle grew comparatively silent as swords and pikes got to work.

Burly, yellow-haired Captain Edward Careless of the *Hope* leapt down amidst a knot of screaming, dark-faced Spaniards collected directly behind the disputed gate and cut down two before the rest took to their heels leaving him free to unbar and fling open the valves. Through it and into an empty cobbled street pounded scarlet-faced, deep-shouting English pikemen, their weapons flashing in the afternoon sun.

Off to their right they recognized the sounds of a furious engagement which argued that Sergeant-Major Powell was in the act of carrying the other gate. Thus it was that Lieutenant-General Carleill and his men, panting like winded runners, gained the market place first. There he commenced hurriedly to re-form his company lest they become broken up into ineffective little plunder-hungry bands. Indeed, this city proved so huge that, very easily, it could engulf the seven hundred men at his disposal.

Presently, sounds of conflict grew louder to the north and soon bands of Spaniards, wild-eyed and fleeing panic-stricken, appeared in the market place and thus found themselves caught between two fires. Most of them at once flung down such arms as they retained and, kneeling, implored mercy while others raced off down alleys and into houses. A mere handful attempted to cut their way through to that castello which guarded the inner harbour.

At four of the afternoon Carleill ordered a Cross of St. George displayed from a cathedral tower to inform Drake's armada that the victory was theirs. The victory, but not yet the city.

CHAPTER XV

THE SACK OF SAN DOMINGO

DESPITE the fact that his men had not enjoyed a full hour's sleep during the past thirty-six, Lieutenant-General Christopher Carleill hesitated not a moment before attacking both castellos guarding the harbour; nor was Admiral Sir Francis Drake any less prompt in recommencing a bombardment of those same forts. Leaving a handful of exhausted and wounded troops to hold the great central plaza of San Domingo, Kit Carleill led forward the rest, hollow-eyed and drag-footed. Meanwhile men from the ships swarmed again into small boats, burning to be in at the kill and so earn some measure of glory that might stop the mouths of the soldiers when the time came for boasts.

Just before dusk the mariners landed on that very beach towards which they had demonstrated earlier. Jaws working with excitement, Drake himself led them. Wyatt could now appreciate how much it had cost that fiery individual to remain personally aloof from the battle—as became a good commanding officer.

A combined attack upon the principal castello had been set for ten or so, Hubert Coffyn averred as he and Wyatt waded ashore. He was using a short pike as a staff. He was further armed with a petronel, or light musket, and a poignard, but he wore neither breastplate nor helmet, his strength being still incapable of supporting such weight.

At half after nine the fleet, under the temporary command of Rear-Admiral Knollys, recommenced its bombardment and the night throbbed to vivid flashes from the artillery of both sides. On this windless night the cannonade sounded positively thunderous as, for a first time, Henry Wyatt found himself marching into battle, aware that before him lay a well-armed enemy ready to fight for his life.

During the affair aboard the *Primrose* he had, of course, faced hostile swords and had slain his first and second man, but this trudging over fine sand towards those thundering guns was something different. He trembled gently and felt a powerful desire to urinate.

Behind him a ship's boy began chattering like a demented person in a transparent effort to conceal his fright. Pretending that the lad had stumbled, Wyatt extended a hand. "Take my fist, youngster, this accursed beach is full of holes." At once the boy's incoherent chatter ceased, and his hand when it crept into Wyatt's was cold and trembling.

Nearer and ever higher loomed the castello's machicolated battlements; in this half-light they rose to the very stars. If anyone abroad on the ramparts noticed the mariners approaching they raised no alarm. An explanation lay, perhaps, in the fact that at this moment Carleill's troops were launching a furious assault against the far castello's barbican.

Calm now, Admiral Drake paused a moment, gazed up at the walls, then said almost casually, "Let's get up there, lads. Give me a shove on your shoulders." Being small and light, he was swiftly boosted up onto the parapet where he stood a moment outlined against the glare of houses burning deep in the town.

To his last hour Wyatt would never forget the impression he received of the Golden Admiral silhouetted thus against the sky, his powerful profile pencilled in gold and red.

By the dozen, and then by the hundred, mariners, screeching

obscene threats, swarmed over the wall. What resistance appeared was as futile as it was brief.

Side by side, Ned Jackson, the young Boatswain's Mate from Greenwich, Wyatt trotted past a row of cannon and, at the head of a flight of steps, found himself confronted by a party of shadowy figures. He heard his sword-blade rasp over the bulge of someone's breast-plate, then more English, howling like demons dipped in Holy Water, came running up. Although the Spaniards yelled for quarter, precious few of them were granted such mercy and a majority were cut down where they stood, or driven over the battlements.

When, shortly before midnight, both castellos had been stormed, Drake ordered bonfires to be kindled on the parapets to inform anxious Rear-Admiral Francis Knollys that, at last, the city of San Domingo had been completely conquered.

Only because they were restrained by a discipline peculiar to the followers of Sir Francis Drake was the sacking of prosperous San Domingo postponed by his troops until the following morning. After the surrender of the battery and castellos Kit Carleill's men bivouacked in the square and gorged themselves on victuals from the nearest houses.

Alas, they were so few as to be all but powerless in preventing a headlong exodus of those inhabitants who had not already fled during the squadron's demonstration before the city on the preceding afternoon. These took no shame in their flight; after all, had they not the President-General's example? That windy poltroon on being pulled out of the swamp had galloped inland, leaving the defence of the capital to the Licentiates and a certain Don Diego Orsinio, Captain of the flagship on this station.

When dawn broke restraint no longer was imposed, so, with sword and pike in hand, Drake's men proceeded to make themselves free of the city according to the brutal fashion of that age.

A row of imposing, stone-fronted residences attracted pillagers who proposed to ravage that quarter nearest the sea. Wyatt, jubilant at the prospects of loot, found himself carried along with a throng of half-naked seamen and joined in using a section of broken yard-arm as a battering-ram with which to break down the iron-clamped door of a great house which boasted an imposing coat of arms above its portal. This scene was being duplicated all up and down the street.

When the heavy door was finally battered down shrill feminine screams sounded within. Young Jackson of Greenwich, grinning in fierce anticipation, led a band of mariners inside. The first person

Wyatt noted was a big Negro in yellow livery and swinging a cudgel. At sight of these hairy, sunburnt fellows the slave dropped his weapon and fell prostrate, all the while chattering prayers for mercy; no one paid any attention beyond dealing him a contemptuous kick.

Wyatt paused to gape, open-mouthed, upon magnificent tapestries, rich furniture and the glowing panelling of a great reception hall. At its far end row upon row of books with finely tooled and gilded backs gleamed in the dawn's rosy glow. Over a floor of diapered black and white marble flooring Wyatt made straight for a heavy, iron-bound chest guarded by a cumbersome, ponderous padlock.

A cursory inspection warned that nothing short of a heavy hammer would make the least impression upon it. Accordingly, he tucked under one arm a pair of huge silver candlesticks. A snarling sound as of ripping cloth attested the fact that one of his companions was engaged in tearing down a curtain of glowing, ruby-coloured velvet.

"Icod! Won't this make my Polly so fine a petticoat as ye'll spy about Cold Harbour?" the younker grinned, bundling the material under his arm. Other invaders were penetrating what appeared to be a dining-room and commenced to shovel solid silver plates, cups and other tableware into sacks improvised from tapestries hacked into convenient squares.

Wyatt, bearing in mind Kate's desperate need, considered the contents of that iron chest and loked about for a lever of some sort. A red-headed gunner, lacking all but a few teeth, waved a bandaged hand, "Come along. Methinks I hear pretty white mice squeaking aloft."

Through barred but glassless windows sounded bursts of gunfire, the crackle of smashed wood and shrill shrieks mingled with bursts of uproarious laughter.

No heavy implement coming to hand, Wyatt turned aside to join a surge of sweating, ill-smelling men up the stairs.

Opposite to the landing was a door of highly-polished cedar. It swung open just as Wyatt and his companion reached the second floor to disclose a frail, light-haired old gentleman wearing a dark red doublet and carrying a naked sword.

The apparition made no effort to guard himself, only offered his weapon to Wyatt hilt foremost. In almost perfect English he said, "Since for me to defend my household is impossible, señores, I surrender at discretion and implore you not to harm my wife and grand-daughter."

"You will pay ransom for them?" demanded Wyatt, accepting

the sword. At the same time he noted to his momentary satisfaction that its guard and hilt were beautifully chased in gold and set with a multitude of small precious stones.

"Yes, gentlemans, an you molest them not."

"We'll not harm an old gaffer like you. You should learn that Sir Francis Drake——"

The old man's silvery jaw dropped. "*El Draque commands you?*"

"None other."

The old man turned and called out in the reedy accents of advanced age: "*Gracias a Dios!* You are safe, my loved ones. Despite all that is said, *el Draque* is a merciful man and does not make war upon women. This I learned some years ago in the Pacific." He bowed towards the knot of half-naked men. "Señores, I am Don Juan de Antón, my King's General of the Western Sea and presently your prisoner."

Jackson chuckled. "'Fore God, then we're in luck! This old whiskerado will supply us wi' a tidy ransom!"

A broad smile relaxed Wyatt's heated features. Here at last was luck. "You are well informed, sir. Our Admiral has directed that all persons of quality and honour suffer no harm so long as they offer ransom and offer no dispute. You say that you once met Sir Francis?"

"*Si, si.* I was aboard *Nuestra Señora de la Concepción*—the galleon you call the *Cacafuego* when your Admiral captured her off the coast of Peru."

"Very well. Keep your women upstairs and they'll come to no harm. Meanwhile these lads and I will cast a look about."

Don Juan de Antón commenced to protest, but still more mariners came clumping up his broad stone steps wearing segments of tapestry and hangings as raffish cloaks and gulping wine from ornamented silver goblets.

Wyatt and Jackson kept on down the corridor until they encountered a large bedroom and noticed two females, a dame whose hair was quite as white as Don Juan de Antón's and a slender, raven-tressed girl of perhaps seventeen. Both were kneeling before a private shrine upon which gleamed a row of candles. Even when the door crashed back the two black-clad figures moved not at all, except to count beads on their rosaries.

Accompanied by his spindle-shanked host, Wyatt tramped over to a dressing-table upon which stood several small ebony caskets.

Don Juan quavered, "Upon my sacred word, señor, all our jewels lie here—do not torture us."

While other invaders swept on down the corridor grabbing up whatever met their fancy, Wyatt drew Don Juan aside. "I want a key for that iron chest below."

Don Juan de Antón sighed and from a wallet strapped to his belt produced a heavy key. Young Jackson strode over to those kneeling, black-clad figures and unclasped a heavy gold chain from about the old lady's neck. She moved not a muscle, only continued to whisper fervent appeals to the Holy Virgin. The younker then plucked from the old dame's hair a tall tortoiseshell comb set with pearls, which, being removed, permitted a heavy lock of silvery hair to escape.

"*Puercos Ingleses!*" Don Juan drew a hissing breath and, drawing a dagger from his doublet, lunged forward. Wyatt grabbed the old man's wrist in time and easily took away his poignard.

"Let be," he advised. "Jackson's not harming your dame."

Now from the rear of the house were raised screams redolent of terror. Serving women had become aware that the doors to their bedrooms would soon fall open.

Delighted oaths resounded. " 'Fore God, this cream-brown kitten looks just my size." "Gi'e us a lusty buss, poppet, we be been to sea near four months." "Hold still, ye little hellcat, whilst I slice yer petticut strings. Ye'll get yerself cut, else." "Icod! Look, lads, this one's got teats bigger nor Franklin Potter's spotted heifer."

Once Don Juan de Antón's bedroom had been thoroughly ransacked, Wyatt, in deep satisfaction, hefted a pillow-case bulging with very choice loot. Next he dropped Don Juan's sword clattering onto the polished snakewood floor and planted his heel on its blade with the intention of snapping it off.

A harsh laugh escaped the old man. "That blade is of the best Toledo temper. You will never break it."

"Why then, old man, I'll keep it," Wyatt laughed. "Where's its scabbard?" Which, being produced, proved to be a handsome affair of red morocco stamped with many gold arabesques and boasting a ferrule and lip of solid gold.

"Have you food and water up here?" Wyatt then demanded, sobering.

"*Si, señor.*"

"Then barricade this door till I return. Meanwhile, I'll post some reliable fellows outside." He bowed under the sack of plunder. "You and your ladies will not be further molested."

"May the Virgin bless you—heretic though you be!" The old *caballero's* deeply lined, pinkish-grey features quivered. To Wyatt it was strangely moving that a pair of tears should creep down those withered cheeks. Clearly, Don Juan had expected that his womenfolk would suffer that fate which was befalling his servant girls.

"Now, by Lucifer," young Jackson cried, "let's go see what the old goat keeps in his strongbox."

Once Wyatt knelt to unlock the iron chest, half a dozen mariners collected, their wine-heated faces and borrowed finery emphasizing that wild disorder which had befallen this stately mansion. Some of the more drunken had donned parts of female garments, the delicacy of which afforded an absurd contrast to hairy legs, broad, bare feet and muscle-knotted arms.

Like so many evil small boys the looters yelled when the padlock clattered onto the floor and Henry Wyatt raised the treasure chest's ponderous lid. Everyone could see that inside were gold ornaments, plates, goblets and all manner of jewellery set with huge pearls and diamonds from which the sun, beating through wrought-iron window bars, drew maddening flashes. Jackson snatched up one of several small leather bags, jerked impatiently at its drawstring and so spilled a double handful of golden ducats to jingle and roll over the red tile floor and cause an almighty wild scramble.

"Now's the time, lads, to help yourselves to a choice item or two," Wyatt invited.

The men's elation faded. "'Item or two'? Is that all?" snarled one. "Curs'd if I'll surrender what I win to any Royal Auditors."

"None o' that!" Wyatt warned sharply. "You know it means the gallows for the first man-jack who keeps back more than a few trinkets out o' the public impound."

A party of younkers, having satisfied their carnal desires in a more or less violent fashion in the servants' quarters, reappeared, dishevelled, somewhat sheepish and scratched, to gaze incredulous on this first of the New World's fabled wealth. One after another they shuffled forward, sunburnt and unshaven, to scoop up and finger a handful of gold coins; each made a single selection from among the precious ornaments.

Wyatt, visualizing the effectiveness of a sapphire brooch on Kate's pale bosom, selected a lovely piece of jewellery all encircled by alternate seed pearls and baguette diamonds. For himself he preempted a heavy gold medallion and chain. If worse came to worst, one could always dispose of such a treasure link by link as the need arose.

Even when the last of the raiders had taken his share, Don Juan de Anton's strongbox appeared to have been but little depleted, so there was some grumbling when Wyatt replaced the padlock and tucked the key into his belt.

In the morning he decided he would seek the harbour and learn what had befallen that Mexican caravel which had challenged his interest.

CHAPTER XVI

ROSEMARY

DURING that triumphant, brutal and lustful turmoil which attended Drake's capture of San Domingo, Hubert Coffyn willy-nilly became swept along amid a band of pikesmen bent on garnering the fruits of their efforts. Hubert went along unwillingly, aware that his slender supply of strength was fast ebbing. That accursed fever seemed to have robbed his legs of so much strength that he was forced heavily to seat himself on the rim of a fountain and linger there, painfully aware of heaving ribs and a spinning head. When eventually his distress lessened he found he could discern, outlined against the morning sky, the cathedral's towers and the long low roofs of the Royal buildings.

"This is a dawn ever to remember," he advised himself while viewing the flare of torches and the furtive movements of figures flitting like embodied ghosts from one alley or garden to the next. "Poor devils of householders," Coffyn muttered. Nearly all of these apparitions carried a chest or lugged a heavy bundle. Few were under arms of any sort.

On the far edge of a little plaza fronting the fountain before which he was resting Coffyn saw a party of broad-shouldered younkers out of H.M.S. *Aid* overhaul a trio of burghers who foolishly tried to put up a fight. In an instant they were cut down. Shouting like schoolboys the younkers then forced the lids of certain caskets carried by the three Spaniards.

Desperately Hubert Coffyn wished to get up and secure a share of his own somewhere. After all, that ancient castle of Norman origin which, for near ten generations, had sheltered his family's varying fortunes near Bideford in Devon stood urgently in need of repairs. Besides, Hubert was determined some day to buy back certain of

Portledge's original fields and forests, sold by his grandsire in order that he might be able to support good King Harry's quarrel with Francis I, suitably equipped.

Wars, the weary young man reckoned, would some day prove the final undoing of the Coffyn family. Right now he and two younger brothers were the last remaining males in their line and the manor, descended through the centuries from Sir Hughe de Coffrefort—who had been one of Rufus the Red's most trusted councillors—was in a parlous state.

Although his legs now felt somewhat steadier, he still had to lean so hard on a half-pike that he didn't dare trust them yet. Every now and then shouting bands of marauders appeared in the plaza, trailing pikes and directing rapacious glances on such warehouses and residences as yet stood with doors intact.

Towards the centre of San Domingo some musketry could be heard when Carleill's dog-tired troops encountered occasional points of resistance. Presently a conflagration broke out behind Coffyn's fountain and soon the whole plaza became smoke-filled and heated by the leaping brilliance of flames. The three dead Spaniards lay where they had fallen, and meandering rivulets of blood crept out from beneath their bodies to create tiny, ruby-hued puddles among the cobbles.

The capital's very vastness seemed to have absorbed the invaders as water does a sponge, and for many minutes not a single Englishman appeared in the plaza, only terrified townsfolk, their slaves and a few priests shuffling along on sandalled feet in a vain attempt to carry off some precious item of church service.

The splashing of water behind him suddenly reminded Hubert of a consuming thirst, so he held his mouth to the cool, spouting stream a long moment. Feeling surprisingly refreshed he stood up and uncertainly looked about. Whither should he go in search of loot? He recalled Wyatt's saying that the most imposing residences appeared to be situated along the waterfront.

Leaning hard on his support, Hubert had entered a wide, palm-tree-shaded street where gracious, handsomely carved façades were the rule when suddenly off to his right he heard a woman's terrified scream.

"Spare me, kind sirs! Oh, for God's sake, spare me! I'm as English as yourselves!" The plea was ending in another nerve-rasping cry when Hubert shuffled forward at top speed. As nearly as he could decide the cry had originated in a handsome house facing the sea and designed in the Moorish fashion. Elaborate wrought-iron grill-work protected its ground floor windows, but its door sagged drunkenly on its hinges.

Unsheathing his sword, Hubert stepped over the remains of a splendid door of cedar bound in brass. A red-eyed soldier waved an amiable invitation. "Come in, sir, come in! Plenty o' plunder for everyone, and a fine assortment o' wenches up on t' floor above." The speaker had slung a baldric of green velvet elaborately embroidered with seed pearls and gold thread over one shoulder, and wore a gorgeous Spanish helmet sporting a long white heron's plume thrust onto the back of his head. Obviously he was very drunk. The increasingly hot daylight revealed a puncheon of brandy standing on a heavy refectory table and dripping amber fluid onto a waxed stone floor set in yellow and black chequers.

From upstairs sounded more screams then the sound of a blow and the tinkle of broken glass and many drunken guffaws. Bolts of brocade, tossed headlong down the staircase, created vivid streams of colour leading up to the second story. More shrieks distracted Hubert from his hurried inspection of a sideboard loaded with massive silver plate. That English voice again was imploring help, between cries of indescribable anguish.

At considerable cost to his slender store of strength, Hubert climbed an elaborate staircase and found himself confronted by a long, dimly illumined corridor. This house obviously belonged to some powerful official or wealthy merchant.

He was crossing the limp body of a servingman, lying huddled at the top of the stairs, when there sounded a wild pattering of feet and out into the corridor ran an entirely nude, brown-skinned young woman. Her eyes were huge and starting in terror and long brown hair streamed out behind as she fled from a half-dressed younker marked by bloody scratches on either cheek. Cursing like a madman, the looter threw his quarry over one shoulder and lugged her, kicking and screeching, back into that apartment from which she had escaped.

Sobbings, cries, and futile pleas sounded in various rooms all along the corridor. Coffyn raised his voice, cursed the lecherous dogs within and reminded them of the Admiral-General's terrible wrath and inevitable punishment.

A crash of overturned furniture behind a door immediately facing Hubert prompted him to investigate. When he flung open the portal it was to discover a slender, black-haired girl struggling furiously in the grasp of a grey-haired arquebusier. Clad only in the remnants of a bloodstained shift and wearing an expression of indescribable horror, the victim fought on, gasped: "Oh, God save me! Is no decent person about?"

"Leave be!" Hubert shouted and, reversing the half-pike, prepared to use it as a club. Somehow the struggling pair tripped and fell at Hubert's feet. The attacker was up in a single bound and spouting incredible obscenities. The fallen girl reached out and in desperation grasped one of Hubert's ankles. "Help! Help me!" she gurgled.

"Back, you dog! Back, I say!" Hubert whirled the pikestaff about until its point once more was presented.

"A black pox on 'e! Ye'll not rob me o' my sweetmeat!" roared the grizzled ravisher, and lurched forward.

Precisely Hubert drove his pike's point deep into the fellow's left shoulder. Raising a howl of anguish the latter reeled back with blood spurting from between the fingers of that hand he clapped over his wound. Had he but known it, the arquebusier could have exacted prompt vengeance, for indeed the whole house seemed to revolve about Coffyn's head and it required a deal of will power to order the fellow out into the hall. He went, bawling to know what in hell had become of his pike. "Icod! When I find it I'll spit this whelp o' the nobility like a capon."

"Close-bolt door!" he gasped to the nearly nude girl now lying half across the threshold.

" 'Tis too late," she moaned without looking up. "In all mercy, sir, run me through."

The wounded man apparently had found a pike and reappeared in the passageway, roaring like a spiked bull.

By a superhuman effort Coffyn wound fingers in the girl's glossy black hair, hauled her clear over the threshold, then slammed and bolted the door barely in time.

Then all the world dissolved into a fiery spiral and Hubert collapsed senseless across the ravished girl's quivering legs.

The sun was hot and high and outlining the window in cruel intentness when Hubert regained enough consciousness to realize that although he still reposed upon the floor a cloth had been thrust under his head. A water-soaked cooling clout traversed his forehead and helped immeasurably in restoring his senses until he became aware of the odour of wood smoke, the reek of stale blood, the occasional resounding boom of some cannon fired in the distance. For a space he could only sprawl supine.

Gradually his eyes focused themselves on the very handsome

furniture of what appeared to be a study or library, then a slight motion attracted his gaze to the figure of a slim girl. Of about nineteen years, she hovered across the library, looking fearfully down upon him and clad in a flame-coloured velvet ceremonial cloak which must have pertained to some order of chivalry for to its left shoulder was appliquéd an elaborate badge.

Her covering, very effective beneath wild-streaming black hair, was so long that it was not until she took several steps that he noticed she remained barefooted. To secure the cloak she had belted it about her with a length of tapestry bell-cord.

At the moment this great-eyed girl was, in listless fashion, plaiting her hair into twin braids. The next thing he noticed was that his own poignard lay beside a celestial globe on the desk beside her. Through half-opened eyes he seized the opportunity to study his companion's piquant features. Seen in profile, hers was a narrow, slightly upturned nose, a short yet rather full upper lip, a small, well-rounded chin and a rather long and slender neck. Her complexion was of a curious golden-rose hue, while her hair was the lustrous blue-black of a raven's wing. At her feet, discarded, lay that tattered and bloodied garment he first had seen half-shrouding her nakedness.

He drew a deep breath and tried to speak but all that emerged was a muffled croak. The girl whirled so rapidly that her mantle parted sufficiently to attest the fact that, beyond this flame-coloured cloak, she wore nothing at all.

Her great black eyes stared down fixedly upon him, then her golden-rosy features commenced to quiver and her hand groped out to close over the dagger.

"Nay, be not afeared. You can very readily slay me. I'm weak as a new-born puppy."

The girl drew a succession of deep breaths. "You mistake me, sir. 'Tis not you I would slay, but myself, rather. Had I possessed the courage I would have done so long ago. However, I surely shall find that courage when you, or any man, lay so much as his finger upon me."

Somewhere Hubert found strength to struggle up on one elbow. "Be assured it remains my eternal sorrow that this morning I was too late to spare you such grievous misuse. Can you but point out your —your ravisher surely he will be hanged."

"That," she cried, "would greatly please me. I am sure I can point him out since I well and truly scratched both cheeks. But, you— why are you so weak?" On naked feet she pattered over and sank on to her knees beside him. "Even while those wretches tried to batter down this door you lay like a dead man."

He described the Cape Verde fever and its ravages in the fleet.

"Would to God it had scourged your whole armada!" she sighed, and eyes so dark a brown that they appeared black closed wearily. "To think that all these years I have boasted to my friends of English ancestry. Pah! I even swore that although Turks, French and Portuguese might rape and loot, no Englishman would ever defile a truly virtuous woman."

He forced a wan half-smile and was aware of a multitude of flies swarming in through the glassless window. "It would seem that you know little concerning fighting men and their ways, no matter what their race or realm. Tell me," he continued hurriedly, "how is it you speak thus in the purest of English?"

"Because I, Rosemary Cathcart, am purebred English," she announced with a return of pride. "My father is Richard Cathcart, a merchant of this city, and formerly of Hull."

Wincing a little, the girl seated herself upon a cushion beside him and explained how her father's affairs had prospered in the trade between Spain and her American Colonies for all that, to begin with, he had been a Protestant.

Her mother, the girl related, had exacted a promise that, come what might, her daughter Rosemary should be reared in the Protestant faith. The merchant captain had clung to his oath, although not long afterwards he had espoused a wealthy Spanish woman and so had become converted to the Church of Rome. As a result the rest of Richard Cathcart's children were half Spanish and Catholic. Rosemary spoke less tensely now and rearranged the cloak about her.

Next she told how, once he had turned Catholic, Captain Cathcart had been able to secure licence to trade all manner of leather goods between Spain and her dominions in the New World. In fact, he had become a leading licentiate in the capital. Where was he now? Occupied with business matters in Cádiz, so until the arrival of Drake's ships her stepmother had ruled this house.

"I'm sure she was"—she began to weep—"slain this awful morning." When at length the girl's sobs died away Hubert quietly explained his name, military rank and station in life. After a while he begged a drink from an *olla* slung in a corner—it was a jar of coarse red clay which, through constant evaporation, kept water sweet and cool at all times.

For a space they listened to various comings and goings in the street, but the house itself sounded silent as a sarcophagus. At length he got up and announced his intention of seeking food. The quest proved a grisly one for the murdered servingman's body still lay at the head of the stairs attended by clouds of flies.

Another dead body was sprawled by the foot of the staircase—a grey-haired fellow who, to Hubert, seemed faintly familiar. Recognition came when he noted that the dead man had been run through the left shoulder and that a triple line of scratches marked his ash-hued features. Apparently the pike's point must have penetrated deep enough to sever an artery and so drain the life from Rosemary Cathcart's despoiler.

CHAPTER XVII

PEARL OF THE ANTILLES

WHEN, early on the morning of January the third, 1586, Sir Francis Drake sent ashore certain heavy guns captured in the Cape Verdes, he ordered them mounted on the battlements. Next he summoned certain obdurate strongpoints in San Domingo to surrender and when they refused his big cannons so battered them that their capitulation was prompt and unconditional.

Once the entire city lay in his hands the Queen's Admiral-General ordered a survey to be made and learned, as many had predicted, that hundreds of the wealthiest inhabitants and Government officials had escaped into the mountains. For many their flight proved futile since they perished in agony at the hands of the Maroons. These, in strong war parties, were ravaging the entire coast and far inland as well. Often they gutted the very estates upon which they had been held in servitude and exacted a ghastly revenge.

Elation commenced to evaporate among the leaders of Drake's armada on discovering that both the Royal Treasury and King Philip's Custom Houses were as bare as old Dame Hubbard's cupboard. To Drake, especially, this ill news proved a bitter pill, for thus far the expedition remained a very long way short of even paying expenses. Unless matters mended he well know that certain gentlemen back in London would make trouble for him with a Queen who would not tolerate failure, especially when it touched her moneybags.

On the bright side of the situation there lay, bottled up in the inner harbour, behind three ships deliberately sunk to bar its entrance, a very handsome French built galleon of 600 tons, practically new, and much the finest vessel in that part of the world for all that she laboured under an absurd and delightful name, the *Grand Guy*. This appellation clung to her long after her captors had, ironically enough, rechristened her *New Year's Gift*.

It came as a severe disappointment to Henry Wyatt that that caravel he had picked out to replace the lost *Katrina* proved to have been sunk during the bombardment. Consequently there remained nothing for it but to survey the contents of the inner harbour, an easy matter since the vessels were deserted save for rats, and so closely jammed together that it proved an easy matter to climb from one rail to the next.

At length the sweat-bathed young Master Mariner boarded a stoutly-constructed Venezuelan barque of about one hundred and twenty tons burthen. Although she would never be speedy, she would do, he concluded, after a thorough examination. Certainly *La Virgen de Compostella's* deck beams seemed strong enough to support the weight of a battery of demi-culverins that would throw a shot weighing ten pounds a distance of twenty-five hundred yards. Undoubtedly he would discover what was needed to complete the barque's battery either in King Philip's handsome arsenal or mounted somewhere upon the castello's battlements.

Permission to confiscate and assume command would have to wait, Sir Francis Drake being much too occupied in computing the ransom for sparing the city. Eventually the Admiral and his Captains sent off their demands to that village where the Royal Governor quaked in his boots. If 100,000 ducats were not immediately forthcoming, why then, San Domingo, known as the Pearl of the Antilles, would be burnt and levelled street by street and quarter by quarter until this sum was raised. Once Drake's summons for ransom had been drawn up by the clever pen of Foulke Greville, it was entrusted to the Golden Admiral's Negro valet because he not only spoke Maroon and several Indian dialects, but also could converse in excellent Castilian Spanish.

Drake the next day was superintending a temporary restoration of the city gates when from the direction of the mountains appeared a limping, staggering figure. It was his valet. The poor creature was barely able to reach his master's side than he fell, bleeding fatally from a lance-thrust through his chest.

One of Drake's rare cold rages seized him on listening to an account of what had chanced. It appeared that an officer from the

Grand Guy became infuriated that the English Admiral's messenger should prove to be but a common black. This valiant had then snatched a lance from a trooper and, spouting outrage, had run the poor blackamoor through the side.

Yellow beard a-quiver, Drake turned to Corporal of the Field Sampson. "Ride into the town and select two friars from among the prisoners. Corporal Bowen, rig me a pair of nooses from yonder fig tree," he snapped as he arose from offering a prayer for his dead servant's soul.

Half an hour later the two clerics, having been granted leave to shrive one another, were hanged and left to swing for the delectation of certain black-headed buzzards. An armed party then departed in search of such Spaniards as still lurked among the suburbs of San Domingo. While a white flag fluttered from Corporal of the Field Sampson's lance-shaft, these brown-faced gentlemen were informed that until he who had murdered Drake's body-servant was handed over, two more prisoners would be executed every day.

Six unfortunates had perished before a party of *caballeros* came galloping down from those mountains, so lovely blue-green behind the captured capital, with a grey-faced prisoner in their midst. With jaws set and bright blue eyes a-glitter Sir Francis rode out to the gallows tree.

"Now, hang him yourselves," he snapped to the prisoner's escort.

"But—Señor General," jabbered the cornet in command, "your messenger, he was only a black, surely——"

"Poor Diego had as much of a soul as you and was foully murdered. Get done with this matter. Only then will I consent to negotiate for the city."

"Small wonder the Cimaroons worship Sir Francis and would make him king," grunted Knollys.

"Aye," nodded Frobisher, "when, ten years gone by, he fought on the Tierra Firma 'twas said he could always raise a black army to his aid."

Drake ruled from the Viceroy's palace and, gradually, something approaching order was restored in the Pearl of the Antilles. Many claimed Drake was inclined to take permanent possession of San Domingo, feeling positive that this rich city could be held to the greater glory and honour of his Queen. Not only Frobisher but Carleill and Knollys then pointed out that the fever had so reduced the English force that enough men could not be spared if the contemplated expedition were to be pursued.

When the demanded ransom was refused, Drake announced that he would commence levelling San Domingo. He proved as good as his word, but his men soon discovered that a majority of the capital's buildings, being solidly constructed of stone, would not burn satisfactorily, and could only be pulled down at the cost of considerable manual labour.

When at length one whole quarter had been flattened, Drake, very sour of mien, reduced his original demand of 100,000 ducats, and indicated that the payment of a mere 75,000 ducats would cause destruction to cease.

He was the more disposed to be liberal because careful exploration of various wells, garden plots and false walls had yielded a surprising golden return. Further, churches, nunneries and monasteries were yielding salvers, candelabra, ewers and cups which would, for generations to come, grace many a sideboard about London and in southern England.

Another time-consuming activity was destruction of religious images—a duty not to be evaded. Under the impact of mauls and sledge-hammers a multitude of stone saints lost their hands, heads and arms and most of the English rejoiced to see this purifying task so thoroughly accomplished.

Also it soon became evident to the conquerors that, as was so often the case in Spanish possessions, these great buildings in San Domingo served as a false front to disguise a diminishing economy. In so many of their provinces, presidencies and colonies mines were no longer worked, due to an insensate extermination of native labour.

Every day another segment of the city was handed over to destruction although the fugitive Governor, the Archbishop and a group of principal merchants swore by all they held holy that there was no possibility of their raising so enormous a ransom.

"We can wait," Drake informed their emissaries. "Yours is a pleasant town and there is plenty of food."

During this enforced delay the Admiral-General devoted much attention to the refitting and revictualling of sound vessels and the replacement of worn-out craft. From the care with which he armed these his subordinates deduced that, in the immediate future, no course would be shaped for home. Not that they grumbled. The unpalatable fact remained that, thus far, the expedition had failed to realize even a third of its golden ambitions, even though it had far from failed in its other purpose—that of hampering and embarrassing the King of Spain.

If the squadron's descent upon Vigo Bay had dealt a bitter blow to the arrogance of Philip the Second, surely the capture and occupation of the Pearl of the Antilles, his capital in the Western World, must indeed prove a truly shattering blow, leaving him humiliated and defeated in the eyes of his enemies—especially in those of the Grand Turk still brooding over his bitter memories of Lepanto.

One evening, Henry Wyatt, having completed the faithful discharge of duties aboard the *Bonaventure*, judged the moment auspicious for approaching Sir Francis about the command over a certain bluff-bowed barque named *La Virgen de Compostella*. Drake he discovered comfortably ensconced in the viceregal palace but guarded by numerous smartly turned-out sentries and as alert and omniscient as ever.

The Admiral-General's compact figure, seeming more diminutive than ever, was seated on the Viceroy's gilded throne. He was listening to music rendered by a string orchestra of some thirty pieces and appeared to be refreshed and in high good humour as he puffed at a long-stemmed pipe. Obviously Sir Francis had found pleasure in a report just presented by red-nosed old Vice-Admiral Frobisher for, smiling, he toyed with a ruby pendant from his left ear.

"Well, well, Master Wyatt," he commented. "Long since I've expected you to come begging. Pray seat yourself after taking your pick of yonder goblets." He pointed to a table upon which stood ranged row on row of silver drinking vessels of all sorts.

Wyatt's broad features went darker still, as always they did when he entered Drake's presence.

"I—I thank you, Your Excellency, but—but——"

"Tush! Go on, man, go on." Drake waved a bejewelled hand. "Pick one of the best as an earnest of my apology. There *were* no heavy guns here and had I but listened to you back in Bayona I would not have squandered that afternoon in testing their batteries." He frowned a little, tugged at his pointed yellow beard. "That afternoon cost us a lot, eh, Frobisher?"

"Aye, that it did," growled the Vice-Admiral, bending a rheumy eye on this broad-shouldered young fellow with the dark red hair. "We granted these Spanish whoresons time to pack up and bolt like frightened hares. Aye, those were six very costly hours."

Drake's never-very-friendly Vice-Admiral presented an incongruous appearance. His battered features and pulpy red nose framed in ragged white whiskers, together with a freckled bald scalp, contrasted oddly with many gold chains, emerald earrings, rich hose of

Venetian silk diapered in black and yellow, a scarlet doublet and a Flemish ruff so enormous that he could manage his pipe only with difficulty.

Once Wyatt had made his selection—a beautiful chalice, the stem of which was modelled as a sea-horse rearing to support a bowl of gilded silver—Drake sat forward. "I presume you have sought me out again—despite my prohibition—to demand a ship from among our prizes?"

A breath, quickly drawn, steadied Henry Wyatt's wildly-beating heart. In the next few instants he would know whether a step had been taken towards that manor house and the knighthood for which he yearned and towards the commercial barony he meant to erect for Kate and their children. "Yes, Your Excellency," he replied, looking Drake steadily in the face, "I am told that the *Vantage* is no longer seaworthy."

" 'Tis true enough," Drake replied through a cloud of drifting smoke. "But already I have given stout John Rivers a sturdy carrack in her place."

At Wyatt's chopfallen air Sir Francis grinned suddenly and exerted all that seemingly irresistible magnetism which had raised him so high into the nation's esteem and on occasion in Her Majesty's favour. "However, friend Wyatt, I'll not deny that I can find use for another sumpter vessel, being minded to remove from this place the best cannon and all the powder that comes to hand. What vessel had you in mind? 'Tis not by chance a barque called *La Virgen de Compostella*?"

At Wyatt's thunderstruck expression Frobisher burst into booming laughter that echoed through the halls of the palace like the roar of an old lion. "Nay, look not so amazed, young sir. Sir Francis and I watched you yesterday from the battlements examine her every spar, line and sail."

Sweat broke out on Wyatt's brow at reflection upon his presumptuousness.

"You may have her," Drake said cheerfully over the strains of music. "But on two serious conditions. First, I will receive a one-third of whatever your command is allotted as her share during the balance of this voyage. Second, being short-handed, I can spare you not one man of my company. You, therefore, must undertake to man, supply and arm this barque, although the last two should pose no great problems."

"Aye, sir. I'll see to that." Wyatt uttered a shout of joy, and suddenly kissed the Admiral's well-perfumed hand. He was so youthful, so radiantly happy, that the Admiral-General laughed.

"You understand, Captain Wyatt"—by God he had employed the military term for Master!—"that this barque will become your whole property only at the end of this voyage?"

"Aye, aye, sir, and may God bless your generous heart."

"See, then, that you sail your new command to the greater glory of our Queen and in stout defence of the true religion."

CHAPTER XVIII

LA CALLE DE LA TRINIDAD

BECAUSE, like the so many other invalids, Hubert Coffyn was required to remain ashore, he became able to resume duty towards the end of that month during which Sir Francis Drake ruled San Domingo. His assignment posted him to be second-in-command over troops guarding the Royal Mint. Here captured gold and silver was being melted down into ingots, or short, wedge-shaped bars easy to pack in chests. Only jewellery and the most beautiful and unusual examples of plate were spared Drake's smelting kettles.

He found it pleasurable indeed, after a hot day's duty, to make his way towards Richard Cathcart's handsome residence in the Calle de la Trinidad, across from that same palm-bordered square where he had rested on the morning of the in-taking.

Thanks to the resilience of youth, Rosemary Cathcart now was nearly recovered from the horror which had numbed her, although her stepmother and stepsisters had vanished as if engulfed by an earthquake.

An aged maternal aunt appeared to beg shelter since her home had been battered down to enforce the payment of ransom. With her tears and lamentations Doña Elena brought a retinue of mulatto servants which supplemented survivors of Cathcart's staff and restored Rosemary's home to a semblance of order. All the Negroes either had enlisted in the English service or had wandered off to join the Maroons.

Both to assure Rosemary's safety and to gratify his own inclinations, Hubert installed himself in the absent merchant's cool and spacious quarters.

In the evening it proved pleasant to linger amid a grove of umbrella pines in a garden overlooking the bay. Out there the great stern lanterns of Drake's squadron glowed and wove a continuously changing pattern whenever they swung to their moorings.

The city remained quiescent, still, save for an occasional song or some tune played upon a guitar for, after their initial outburst of violence, Drake's men indulged in no more indiscriminate looting and no further violence was offered to inhabitants so long as they remained respectful and subservient. In fact, many householders came streaming back into San Domingo from the country circulating accounts of tortures and depredations committed by the Maroons.

"Pray tell me more concerning England and especially about Devon," Rosemary pleaded, busily stitching a slashed tapestry together. "Father will speak of little saving the Humber's mouth, East Riding and Lincolnshire." She smiled faintly and briefly regarded him over a length of thread she was about to snip off. "Why, I could vow I have visited there, but of Devon I know nothing, save that it is that part of England which means home to you and to your Admiral."

"Devon," Hubert explained readily, "the West Coast, I mean, is possessed of a peculiar beauty. Picture, an you will, many wild windswept cliffs rising so high above the sea that one discovers difficulty in descending to the beaches, as, for instance, at Clovelly, from which my home lies but a few miles inland. Because it rains often we boast wonderfully green meadows divided by flowering banks and hedges. Thanks to a great warm current which sweeps in close to our coast, much fruit is grown. 'Tis even claimed that palm trees will thrive along our southern shore.

"Inland lie many fine domains, manor houses and rich estates for through the little port of Plymouth now streams much wealth from the Levant, West Africa and," he smiled, "more recently from America. Our people differ largely from the rest of England both as to speech and appearance."

"Why so?"

"Certain learned men do testify that survivors of the original inhabitants of the island fled to Cornwall and Devon, first before the invading Saxons and then to escape my Norman ancestors. Therefore we of Devon hold ourselves to be of the very purest English blood."

Warming to his subject, Hubert then described the ancestral domain of the Coffyn family, from an ancient keep—built to withstand marauding Norsemen and Moslems—to its great dining hall and once extensive stables. These last were ruinous now, he admitted simply, and stood empty save for work-horses and a few palfreys to mount his much younger brothers and sisters, of which he had two each.

A slight sigh escaped Rosemary. "Do you imagine I could ever feel at home in England?"

"Why not? Are you not English-born?"

"But it is a land of which I know naught saving its language and somewhat of its history."

"I am convinced of it." Earnestly he bent forward, studied her cleanly-sculptured golden-white features and found fascinating the rich carmine of her lips.

"Perhaps I can persuade Father to send me there?" She nodded sadly. "Before he would not, but now"—she reddened, bent further over her sewing—"since I am no longer virgin, no *caballero* would dream of espousing me even were Father to offer him the half of his wealth for my dowry."

Hubert imprisoned her hands between his. "That evil which befell was against your will. You fought until strength failed, and he who assaulted you is dead. I am glad that it was I who slew him. Rosemary, can you not rid yourself of that——?"

"No," she declared firmly. "No, not ever! On my return to England I think I will enter a convent of the Church of England. And now, shall Enrique fetch you a cup of chilled Canary?"

CHAPTER XIX

THE *BARQUE HOPE*

NEVER since he had been a lad snaring his first rabbits in the forests near St. Neots had Henry Wyatt been so completely absorbed and so thoroughly contented. After all, had he not prevailed upon certain Englishmen and French Huguenots liberated from the dungeons of San Domingo to help him sail his new barque on the promise of shares?

He had rechristened his new command, not at all originally, the *Hope*, and had her worked around to a berth at a small pier in the outer harbour belonging to Richard Cathcart; this on the advice of his friend Hubert Coffyn, who was now filling out again and losing the last of his invalid's pallor. Apparently the care and shy affection bestowed upon him by Mistress Rosemary Cathcart had played no small part in this improvement.

When first he heard her father's name he had stared, recalling that pleasant evening in Bayona beneath Master Jenkins' almond tree. Icod! It *had* been a Señor Cathcart with whom he had been meant to deal in the matter of those long cannon. How differently might this adventure have turned out had Drake been minded to listen! Well, that was water down the millrace.

Once he discovered his friend's lodgings, Wyatt took to dining there of an evening, listening to current rumours, furnishing a few of his own and discussing problems which, once inconsiderable, now loomed large in his immediate future.

It was well that he had approached the Admiral-General just when he did for now the golden aspect of this expedition was beginning to wear thin. Day after day elapsed without a ransom offer from those cowardly but obdurate Spanish authorities. Sir Francis Drake's temper grew short when, reluctantly, he ordered the city's ransom reduced next to 50,000 ducats and finally to a paltry 25,000. Although every day a further section of San Domingo collapsed into a tumbled heap of ruins, the Governor swore upon the honour of his mother and, more important, upon the sanctity of all the Saints in the Decalogue that such an amount simply could not be found.

Proof was afforded that, indeed, Sir Francis had abandoned hope of extorting a satisfactory sum when careful revictualling and re-arming of the English armada became the order of the day.

A leather-faced Master Armourer indicated to Henry Wyatt that he must find room for no less than fifteen demi-cannon in his barque's hold. Their great weight, he pointed out, would furnish the *Hope* with excellent ballast and so stiffen her against any and all storms. The Armourer would offer the Captain—Wyatt now wore the dignity of this purely military title—free permission to help himself for his private benefit to any of the enemy's small ordnance; there were fine sakers, falconers and minions going begging, he averred.

Thus the new Captain was able to lower into his hold some two dozen sakers, falconers and murdering pieces. These, he reasoned, would be in great demand towards equipping men-of-war now being completed in the shipyards of John Hawkins. Undoubtedly all these pieces would serve their turn against King Philip's *Empresa* if and when Spain's well-nigh-overwhelming sea power might sail against England.

Having observed from his experience with Master Foster that a diversified cargo earned the surest profit at the end of a voyage, Wyatt reluctantly sold the sapphire brooch he had selected during the sack. A pity that never would it adorn the white perfection of Kate's bosom, but with that bauble he succeeded in bribing the Keeper of Captured Stores to sell him an enormous supply of small arms, deemed antiquated or otherwise unfit for service aboard Drake's men-of-war.

He loaded these purchases into a cart and spent the last two days of the English occupation in driving to a point beyond the walls at which the Maroon chieftains had established a plunder exchange. Here the big sable warriors, clad in tawdry finery and wearing necklaces of human fingers and ears, would barter the goods looted from the great inland estates and, because they hungered for weapons with which to ward off Spanish reprisals once Drake's sails had disappeared over the horizon, Wyatt was able to close many an advantageous bargain.

So, evening after evening, his mule cart returned to town with two brawny Negro slaves standing guard over food staples such as yams, coconuts, manioc, tapioca and much smoked beef. Further, he obtained sacks of cocoa beans, ground logwood and cochineal, the last two being precious as essential to the dyers' trade.

Occasionally the *Hope's* Master yielded to temptation and purchased, as speculation, some magnificently carved chests, a tapestried chair or a whole window of richly-hued stained glass. In the main, however, he invested in fine leathers and cloths which he knew something about.

"This," he would often say to himself, "I am buying for Kate." He also purchased for the expected infant a supply of toys, miniature ships, wooden animals, bright red balls, and a beautiful poppet wearing a brocade gown—just in case the child he expected to find upon his return should prove to be a girl.

Often it was near midnight before he dismissed the two burly Negro slaves he had received as his share from the general pool. To be exact they were slaves no longer in that he had manumitted them on condition they serve aboard his barque for a year and a day.

According to grade every officer of the fleet became owner of two or more blackamoors. The three Admirals and Lieutenant-General Carleill, of course, received ten choice Negroes as their share. The chiefest of Wyatt's problems was that of securing twenty hands who must not only sail the *Hope* but serve her battery as well.

Despite all efforts he failed to secure Drake's permission to obtain the services of that gentleman-adventurer named Hubert Coffyn; particularly since the ravages of the plague the Admiral remained adamant that the complement of his original squadron should not be weakened.

Yet it was through Coffyn's efforts that there appeared aboard the *Hope* one Michael Henderson, for four years a prisoner in San Domingo and once master of his own vessel. Tall, grey-eyed and scrawny as a bittern, he proved not only quite willing to sign articles as Master's Mate but bespoke the services of one William Tompkins, a fellow prisoner who understood the serving of cannon and could speak fluent Portuguese and Spanish.

The next additions to the barque's company were a trio of hollow-eyed French Huguenots—liberated after near five years' imprisonment. They spoke yearningly of La Rochelle and the good wines of France. Eventually Wyatt rounded out his crew with a party of Genoese and Venetians who had been pressed into serving aboard the *Grand Guy*.

These comprised the European element of Wyatt's crew. For the rest he selected volunteers from among the Maroons, powerful fellows who claimed to have done a deal of seafaring. No one could understand their language saving Will Tompkins because he had escaped from a galley and then had dwelt among these savage folk for over a year.

Wyatt trusted best of all his English Mate and Gunner, then the Huguenots, next the Maroons, and finally the Genoese and Venetians. These, although they clung to their Catholic faith, swore loudly that they would render loyal service.

On the twenty-fifth of February, 1586, Wyatt surveyed his barque with satisfaction for now the *Hope* lay with water-casks filled, battery mounted and her cargo of captured cannon so stowed that at the Admiral's command they could be broken out without loss of time.

In the forward hold and in the Captain's small cabin were stowed the precious dyestuffs, the cocoa and well-dressed leather and other private cargo. What furniture he had brought aboard would have to take its chances upon the ballast under the *Hope's* diminutive fore-castle. Of corn meal, olive oil, bacon and salt fish and meat, various lockers held a plentiful supply.

Michael Henderson soon proved his worth through his clever distribution and stowage of the cargo, while Will Tompkins selected various hands and drilled them in the service of the barque's two sakers and six minions; as a considerable innovation he mounted two falconers for bow chasers.

. . . . .

On the brilliantly sunny morning of January twenty-ninth a pinnace came sailing over from the *Bonaventure* and rounded up to where lay the *Hope* with rigging freshly tarred, new yards slung and showing a number of raw new planks along her waterline for Captain Wyatt intended that never again should there be a repetition of the *Katrina's* loss.

When the boat from the flagship came bumping alongside Wyatt was busy down in the forehold with his mate occupied in tallying such trade goods as were owned by Tompkins and Henderson since, with his customary open-handed generosity, Drake had allowed all released English prisoners, according to their stations, a share in the plunder.

"Ahoy, Cap'n Wyatt, below there!" Tompkins' round red face, gleaming like a miniature sun, appeared framed in the hatchway. "We've a pinnace from the *Bonaventure* alongside, sir. His Excellency the Admiral requires yer immediate attendance—and be well turned out, says he."

What could be brewing? Something of considerable moment, Wyatt deduced. Possibly the squadron was about to sail for her next objective? Rumour spoke of this as Nombre de Dios on the Tierra Firma, or mainland of South America. Possibly, possibly not.

On second thought Wyatt decided against so simple an explanation. Although his own water-butts were abrim many in the armada remained unfilled and the Golden Admiral was notorious for his qualms on the subject.

Henry Wyatt found pride in the fashion his four shiny black rowers bent to their oars and drove his gig shooting through the outer harbour's chip and refuse-littered waters. Certainly a ceremony of some sort must be under way aboard the flagship; lines of soldiers in the usual wide variety of costume stood drawn up in ranks, pikes and arquebuses a-gleam and their pointed steel caps bright through polishing.

"Captain Wyatt? Pray proceed to the poop," directed an officer of the deck once Henry Wyatt had saluted a plain wooden cross nailed to the break of the quarter-deck.

From the maintop the Admiral-General's blue and white personal flag lazily curled and uncurled and cast restless shadows upon the recently cleansed deck. Two splendidly clad officers stood expectantly before a crimson-cushioned chair placed behind an ornate table upon which three scrolls of paper lay beneath a sheathed dagger, placed there to keep them from blowing away. Wyatt recognized Knollys, Frobisher, Winter and several other senior Captains of Drake's armada standing to one side and talking in undertones.

Almost at once the new arrival guessed the meaning of this ceremony because, to his right, stood Captain Robert Cross appointed to command over the new galleon—she who had been the *Grand Guy* and was now the *New Year's Gift*. Beyond stood burly John Rivers about to captain a carrack replacing his worn-out *Vantage*.

A blare of trumpets caused all gentlemen present on the quarter-deck to remove their hats while pikemen and arquebusiers presented their weapons. Accompanied by his aides, Lieutenant-General Carleill and Flag-Captain Fenner, Drake emerged from his cabin garbed in resplendent doublet of black-and-gold brocade slashed and puffed in scarlet.

Quite solemnly he greeted his officers, then bent his head and, kneeling upon the deck, offered a prayer for the success of the ships now being added to his command. Then from each of the commanders over his new ships he exacted a mighty oath that they would submit to his discipline without question, fear God and ever fight valiantly to the glory of their Sovereign. This ceremony having been accomplished, a Cross of St. George banner was presented to each of the new commanders, who then departed mightily elated, each to his own vessel.

"If only Kate could have witnessed this hour!" thought Wyatt, smiling happily in the stern sheets of his little gig, for under his arm crackled a document commissioning the *Barque Hope*, owned by one Henry Wyatt, as a ship of war and presently under lease to the Crown of England.

Surely the expedition from now must go well for Henry Wyatt of St. Neots; he scarce could fail to return in triumph to London Pool. Mercifully, Providence refrained from revealing to him the results of certain foreordained events.

CHAPTER XX

ON THE SEA WALL

A LAND breeze bringing with it the sour-sweet odour of tropical jungles commenced to blow stronger, whereupon the lights of Sir Francis Drake's fleet commenced to waver and dance over the harbour's inky waters. In brilliance and number they now rivalled those of San Domingo, now nearly half destroyed. A week earlier

Drake, wearied and perhaps convinced by the Royal Governor's insistence that he simply could not produce more than 25,000 ducats, had ordered his thoroughly disgusted crews from their task of pulling down these magnificently-built stone houses.

That sea wall which fronted one side of Richard Cathcart's property having proved deserted, Hubert Coffyn pressed close to Mistress Rosemary's side and guided her towards an empty embrasure where he spread his mantle upon an overturned gun carriage. He was grateful that enough daylight persisted to reveal in its delicate purity the outlines of Rosemary's features and the limpid quality of her dark eyes.

This evening the girl had parted her glossy hair over the centre of her forehead and there had suspended from a crimson ribbon a single pearl. He noted this fact with delight because this was the first time she had worn even a trifle of jewellery. "Tomorrow, Hubert," she observed softly, "you will return aboard your flagship."

"Aye, but there's no telling when our Admiral will weigh anchor. Everything depends on wind and weather."

In a quick, bird-like motion she gazed into his still thin features and laughed gently. "La, sir, you now make almost two of he whom I first met."

"God send we forget that meeting," he murmured, slipping an arm about her shoulders.

"I would I could, too." Her gaze sought the low outline of her father's residence and her voice faded until he could scarcely hear. "Recently I—well, I have had reason to feel sure that there will be no fruit of that dreadful morning, other than the hurt to my honour and the pain in my soul."

"Bless the all-merciful Lord for that! Still, had you—well, had you conceived—that mischance would not in the least have altered my determination that we shall, one day not too far distant, be married—an you will have poor Hubert Coffyn."

She looked at him wonderingly, then the dark, warm curve of her lips parted in a radiant smile. "So you really desire me despite my deflowered state? I do believe you are set upon it, which is well. When you become set upon a thing, Hubert, I note that you are given to attaining your object."

From his wallet Hubert produced a carnelian bearing the Coffyn coat-of-arms and mounted as a ring. It proved so large that the circle of gold would only fit over her thumb. He kissed her with passion, yet tenderly, too, while the warm land breeze rippled the cloak about their legs and the distant discordant howling of Maroons revelling about their camp-fires came beating through the gathering darkness.

After a while he straightened his little standing ruff whilst she pushed back a stray lock of sable hair.

"You promise then, my sweeting, to board the first vessel for Cádiz?"

"There should be little difficulty in securing passage," she assured him gravely. " 'Tis after I reach Europe I foresee our troubles. And they will be grave."

"For example?" he laughed.

"I fear that Father, although English born and bred, will wax very wroth over the murder of my stepmother and sisters, over the looting of his home and the seizure of all his goods here." A frown merged her delicately straight brows. "Alas, Hubert, I do foresee it will not be easy to obtain his consent to my marriage with one of Sir Francis Drake's officers. And"—her fingers tightened in his—"his consent *I must have*. Father and I have ever been very tender towards one another. You understand? I could not bear to deepen his grief by any deed of mine."

Gravely, gently, he argued against her decision but, to his dismay, he could not shake her will.

"Nay, even though it rends my heart, I'll never come to you lacking Father's blessing. Provided he does soften his heart towards you—how will I get to England? Surely, once the news of *el Draque's* plundering here becomes known war will break out 'twixt England and Spain."

"Nonetheless, it should be possible for you to obtain passage in some vessel sailing from Cádiz with supplies for Spanish troops garrisoned in the Lowlands. Once there it shouldn't prove vastly difficult to obtain passage on one of those little vessels which always ply across the Narrow Sea in war as in peace."

Finding an eloquence hitherto unsuspected, he again pictured the warm welcome surely awaiting her at Portledge near Bideford and assured her he entertained not the least doubt that crippled old Sir Robert would receive such a reserved, well-bred and lovely young female into the family, for all that Richard Cathcart's family possessed no patent of nobility beyond one naming him a Knight of Malta, in return for devoted services rendered to Holy Church and to the Crown of Spain.

Rosemary stirred. "Were Father to consent," she stiffened a trifle, "would your sire object to a truly modest dowry? You see, your precious

Golden Admiral has raised such havoc with Father's property there's no telling how much remains to him."

"Lord love you, no! Hubert assured. "E'en though we at Portledge be poor as church mice these days."

They embraced among shadows wrought by the sea wall then, taking his face between her hands, she turned it so that the light of the half-moon could illumine it, and remained staring upward as if indelibly to impress upon her memory every detail of his features. She memorized just how his brows almost joined above wide-set, but rather small, light brown eyes, how the plain gold rings in ears that lay flat to his head gave off fugitive flashes, how powerfully modelled was the jaw beneath his close and curly brown beard. His moustache recently had been trimmed short, chiefly because Drake himself had done so, and in this he followed an example set by nearly all gentlemen in the armada.

Suddenly he swept her off her feet and carried her into an embrasure where in turn he held her so that the lunar effulgence could reveal the serene beauty of her pointed face. Because she seemed so light he guessed his strength must be fully restored. Then he reslung his cloak and guided Rosemary to the house in the Calle de la Trinidad.

The black who admitted them had sufficient wit to plant his torch in a sconce and then pad away on calloused bare feet.

"Within the year, my love," he whispered fiercely, "either you will come to me in England or I shall go to Spain in search of you."

A look of terror convulsed her features. "No, no! Promise that you'll never come to Spain."

"I'll give no such word," he insisted gently. "So you must seek me in England."

"God help me I will, if there's any earthly way of obtaining Father's consent."

Once young Coffyn had departed she remained in the vaulted hallway, staring blankly upon a crude, temporary door hung to replace that which had fallen before the fury of Drake's marauders. Then, venting a slight shuddering sigh, Rosemary plucked up the torch, paused briefly to gaze on a certain dark stain on the lower step. Mechanically, she spat upon it and went up to her own room.

CHAPTER XXI

TO HER GRACIOUS MAJESTY, REPORT

Now that the coastline of the Tierra Firma had merged with the Caribbean's dark blue lustre, Sir Francis Drake betook himself to the shade of an awning rigged on the *Bonaventure's* poop deck and cast a critical eye over his squadron as it bowled along under a favouring slant of wind. Big and little, all his vessels were showing "a bone in their teeth".

A smile of grim satisfaction curved the Admiral's features, grown thin because, following his capture of Cartagena, he had suffered a touch of fever which had sapped even his astounding vitality.

Somewhat wearily, he sent for Foulke Greville, that able and observant young gentleman who was so facile with his pen. When the secretary arrived lugging a portable writing-desk under one arm, the Admiral relaxed upon a settle and fixed an uneasy eye upon the Queen's blue, red and yellow standard fluttering from his mizzen-top.

Before commencing to dictate, Drake moodily considered the *New Year's Gift*, noted how bright a big Latin cross painted on her fore-sail appeared when seen against this ultramarine ocean.

Foulke Greville arranged himself as comfortably as possible while balancing the writing-case upon his knee and selected a number of well-sharpened quills. Across the top of a sheet of foolscap he inscribed the date—March the thirtieth, 1586—then glanced over to the settle and the small, languid figure upon it.

Thoughtfully Drake ran fingers through hair cropped shorter than it had been in many a long year; the heat of Cartagena, in addition to the fever, had rendered the wearing of long hair unbearable. He commenced to dictate:

"Upon quitting the Island of Hispaniola and the great Capital City of San Domingo there, I did set my course across the Carib Sea towards the Tierra Firma, or Main Land. It had been my first intention to destroy Santa Marta and then raid those pearl fisheries which lie on Margarita Island, but alas, God sent me contrary winds so I determined to make for Cartagena in the Spanish Presidency of Venezuela.

"Although I possess as true and excellent charts, both of Cartagena and of its approaches, as are known to exist, I craved a pilot to conn in my flagship. Yet such a man I could not come upon albeit I searched everywhere because I was loath to risk my vessels among the most treacherous rocks and channels which do lead into the Cartagena Bay." Drake plucked reflectively at a beard now so sunburnt that it appeared white in colour and selected his words with care.

"Wanting a pilot, I therefore did determine myself to conn in the ships. I arrived off Cartagena, Capital town of the Spanish Main, on the third day of February near four o'clock of the afternoon. Cartagena, Your Majesty must know, is second only in importance to San Domingo which I captured and half destroyed to your fame and glory. But Cartagena greatly surpasses that city in commercial importance for it has made a great commerce out of Spain and a new colony named New Granada. Also, Cartagena trafficks with all the Indies as well as with Peru and all the coast of the Firm Land and even of those who fish for pearls at Rio de la Hacha.

"That Your Majesty may comprehend the difficulties confronting me, I must state that Cartagena is greatly protected with powerful forts and by the strength of Nature. Such ordnance as my ships could bring to bear could have had but small effect. One end of this town faces westwards towards the open sea and there is no approach to be made from this direction. Northwards, a great marsh extends until it is secured by high ramparts. For Your Gracious Majesty's convenience I append a plan of this vastly rich city."

Drake broke off and swallowed a long pull from a mug of watered rum and lime juice. "Foulke, make certain a fair copy of that map prepared by Master Guevara be appended."

"Aye, Sir Francis. Already I have ordered a miniature in preparation."

"Two entrances there are into the Lake or Lagoon of Cartagena. The one is named La Boca Grande which is the usual entrance into the lagoon, the other, La Boca Chica or the little mouth. At the southward end of Cartagena Lake lies the harbour proper, divided from the lagoon by a sandspit upon which is reared a stout fort mounting many cannon. Also barring entrance unto the harbour proper is a great chain the which can be anchored over to pilings on the mainland.

"Spies reported that behind these barriers lay two great galleys of war and a huge galleass belonging to the Spanish King's Navy. Leading from the harbour is an inlet which retreats and circles back into that marsh I spoke of which borders the sea.

"Cartagena thus stands secure upon an island and the only access to it is over a wide causeway above three hundred yards in length at the city end of which stands a barbican and a drawbridge commanded by a fort mounting heavy ordnance.

"Think you I make myself understood, Foulke?"

"Aye, Sir Francis, admirably, if I may say so." The other seized this opportunity of switching pens and dipped his new one into a small, leaden ink bottle.

"On the afternoon of February the ninth I did make a demonstration against this city with some twenty-five vessels of all sizes. I approached close enough to cause cannonading from the fortifications but to this futile discharge I did not deign to make reply."

Drake paused, took a sip from his pewter mug then wiped suncracked lips on the back of his hand. "Having made pretence to be greatly dismayed by the strength of their fortifications I then stood back out to sea until I arrived off the entrance to that most treacherous channel which is called La Boca Chica.

"Through the Grace of God and my skill as a navigator I was able to lead my vessels safe through this little passage and presently emerged upon the waters of Cartagena Lagoon. After deploying my ships I then came to anchor about half-way down the length of this placid body of water and facing the inner harbour.

"Once darkness had fallen, I caused all the pinnaces and boats to be filled with armed men, which under General Carleill did land without the least loss upon the sandspit at a point near unto the sea. This peninsula of sand is covered by jungles and scrub wood and in my judgment did offer the weakest link in the chain of defences securing Cartagena, for it runs straight and level near three miles and leads into the very streets themselves.

"Upon nearing the town, however, this peninsula narrows to something less than one hundred and forty yards and across this place entrenchments had been dug and armed with six great cannon."

Again the Admiral paused, casually to follow the course of some flying fish; gleaming silver-blue, they rose out of a long, sapphire-hued billow and went skittering across the water only to vanish with magical suddenness.

"Of these defences I had become aware through questioning prisoners taken at San Domingo. The excellent and valorous General Carleill and I therefore determined to wait until the tide should be low so that your soldiers might pass around the end of this formidable defence. In the blackest of darkness your valiant General—Carleill is truly valiant, mark you, Foulke, I have met none braver anywhere—did lead his troops along the aforementioned sandspit.

"Corporal of the Field Sampson commanded the archers and pikemen, and Corporal of the Field Goring the companies of fire with which marched General Carleill. Behind this Sergeant-Major Powell led four companies of pikes which constituted my main force of assault. Captain Morgan did command my rear guard.

"Once your Army had circumvented the fortifications and divers sticks smeared with poison, General Carleill did signal me that he was about to attack the fortifications commanding the sandspit. At this time I did cause Vice-Admiral Frobisher to sail forward and engage those forts guarding the boom between the two harbours. This I counted would sufficiently distract the garrison from General Carleill who was successful in marching his troops along the low water-mark, they being protected by an earthen bank not only from the cross fire of two war galleys lying in the lagoon, but also from cannon mounted on entrenchments, because this ordnance could not sufficiently be depressed to cause them harm. Our musketeers did raise a cheer for Your Majesty then fired a volley and pressed home the charge.

"Here was no repetition of San Domingo for the enemy stood their ground with the utmost constancy and had they but been protected by steel corselets, as were our men, instead of mere jackets of quilted cotton, our advance might have been driven back. A very pretty bicker then ensued but ended with the Spaniards in full flight. In the course of it Corporal of the Field Goring did seize and hold personally one Alonso Bravo, the Spanish General commanding in Cartagena. Captain Edward Winter took his full share of cut-and-thrust at the side of your most excellent General Carleill. Alas that Corporal of the Field Sampson here did suffer a most grievous wound.

"Every man of one part as of another came so willingly onto the service that the enemy were not able to endure the fury of such hot assault.

"Your troops, Most Gracious of All Sovereigns, following my direction, granted the enemy no respite but in the instant rushed their earthworks from behind. Yet it was not until they won through to the central market-place of Cartagena that the fight slackened and came to an end when General Carleill's own sword cut down the Spanish ensign bearer. Thus, dear my Lady, has victory and glory again crowned your arms."

Drake sighed, swallowed another sip from his posset into which cinchona bark had been grated, then turned again to study his squadron all strung out behind the flagship as she ran northwards. A reminiscent smile curved his lips as he recognized the bluff outlines of the *Primrose*—saving her near capture he never would have been here.

"The city, however, was not taken free of cost. Above twenty-eight stout soldiers fell, not counting the wounded—God knows they were a plenty," he added in an aside. "How many do you suppose survived their hurts?"

Foulke Greville frowned, scratched his ear. "Perhaps one in four, Sir Francis. Certainly not more, so excessive was the heat." He dipped his pen, waited for the Admiral's next words.

"On the morrow I advanced my fleet to engage the castellos guarding the boom and causeway. To my great joy these hoisted the white flag and fell into my hands without a shot being fired. Thus was captured Cartagena, King Philip's great Capital city on the Spanish Main."

The Admiral broke off, rose and strode across the sun-splashed poop deck towards that point where Flag-Captain Fenner with paradoxall compass, astrolabe and sextant was engaged in determining the degree of latitude. The accurate calculation of longitude would have to wait nearly a hundred years more. On becoming aware of the Admiral's presence Captain Fenner tucked the sextant under one arm and bowing, doffed that flat, broad-brimmed felt hat he invariably wore at sea.

"And how do we sail, Will?"

"We make capital progress to the nor'west, sir, but I doubt whether we will sight any vessels. Since our sack of San Domingo there has been time for alarm to spread the length and breadth of this Carib Sea."

Drake shaded his eyes and scanned the sky. "What think you of tomorrow's weather?"

Fenner shot his superior a quizzical but admiring glance. It was uncanny how surely Drake seemed able to scent a brewing tempest. Not for nothing was he renowned the world over as a consummate navigator and seaman.

" 'Fore God, Sir Francis, the aspect seems fair enough to me."

"Maybe so, maybe so. All the same pray signal my Captains to come aboard this afternoon rather than tomorrow."

"Aye, sir. The signal will be made directly."

On returning to his bench Drake only half settled himself upon its edge and sat leaning forward with hands locked and elbows on knees. Clearly, he took small satisfaction in that which must now be included in his report.

"When the question of ransom for sparing Cartagena from the flames arose I determined upon a million ducats as the proper sum, but, alack, the Bishop and the Religious Orders had been warned of our coming and so had fled together with the principal merchants and their choicest properties so far into the interior that I could not come up with them. I therefore reduced my demands to one hundred thousand golden pounds but pillaged many goodly cargoes of dye-woods, fine raiment, linens and silks.

"To persuade the enemy of my zeal in your interest, dear my Lady, I did order burned several rich outlying districts; when at the end of a month I had received no offer and because a virulent fever again had commenced to afflict my crews, I trust you will not deem me remiss in that for ransom I accepted"—he grimaced—"the sum of 110,000 ducats, which in our currency amounts to about £37,250. To this however must be added a thousand Florentine crowns obtained through sparing of certain religious properties situated outside the walls of Cartagena."

He jumped up and, yielding to the galleon's pronounced pitch, commenced to stride back and forth, all the while fingering a jewelled dagger he never went without.

"My fleet being ready to take the sea again I did summon a Council of War—there being matters of grave concern to be considered. First, my soldiers and mariners felt sharp disappointment that they should receive so small recompense for all their hardships and travails, particularly since they were volunteers, receiving no wage from Your Majesty's Treasury. I beg Your Majesty therefore to judge how rejoiced these honest soldiers were to learn that the Lieutenant-General and his principal land officers had agreed to forgo their share in the ransom of the city they had captured with such gallantry.

"The example being set, my sea Captains could do no less for our poor mariners; verily, we wished with all our hearts the sum to be thus divided would have been a more sufficient reward for their loyal endeavours.

"We touched also upon the wisdom of mounting heavy cannon on the walls of Cartagena and of leaving there a permanent garrison to serve both as a base of operations against the enemy and as a new colony to the profit of Your Gracious Majesty. Alas, that our numbers had become so reduced and with fevers again raging throughout my ships, it seemed to me to be unwise to plant the colony at this time."

Drake's nether lip disappeared between his somewhat irregular and stained teeth. "This decision proved the most painful of my career in Your Majesty's service."

The Admiral-General broke off, strolled over to the rail and there remained, apparently absorbed in the antics of a school of porpoises but in fact forbidding himself to speak what was in his mind. Quite clearly he was recalling a certain interview with Walsingham, who had warned him of the Queen's political inconstancy, of her failure to see that a bitter and decisive war with Philip was inevitable. Elizabeth, he had explained, still believed that she could go on indefinitely refusing to levy taxes necessary for a proper defence of her realm. No, Drake decided, he had been well advised in not colonizing Cartagena; not so long as Elizabeth, still wooing the phantom of Peace, was entirely capable of sacrificing the officers and men who held that city in her name.

Returning to his seat under the awning, Drake concluded, "I therefore, on the thirtieth day of March after a stay of six weeks on the Tierra Firma did lead my armada out of the Boca Grande and set sail northwards for the Channel of Yucatán."

Foulke Greville flexed stiff, ink-stained fingers when it became obvious that the Admiral had finished his dictation.

"Do you wish to peruse your report as I have penned it, sir?" he demanded perfunctorily; he being well aware that Drake abominated all manner of paper work like the Devil himself.

"Nay, but after I have affixed my seal make me a fair copy which is to be sent aboard the *Aid* and placed with the rest."

Towards sunset the wind faltered and then died out while, at the same time, a sickly, yellowish-green tinge crept over the rim of the sea until it corrupted the healthy blue of the sky. The aspect was one to fill the sea Captains with misgivings as they swung up a treacherous rope ladder rigged in the *Bonaventure's* waist. Henry Wyatt, soberly clad and serious of mien, stood with the rest in a loose semicircle before the Admiral's wiry, supple little figure and paid close heed to his instructions, for Drake's so-called Councils of War were nothing of the sort. He seldom asked opinion but merely stated his own determinations.

"Gentlemen," he announced briskly, "you will shape your courses for Cabo San Antonio at the western point of Cuba. There we shall expect to take on fresh provisions and water. Thence," he ran his eye over the leathery and red-brown features ringing him around, "we will steer for Florida in North America and there reduce the Spanish forts at St. Augustine and St. Helena.

"Of their strength I presently know nothing, nor of their importance save that they lie so situated that they command the Florida

Channel, through which King Philip's treasure *flotas* of custom pass on their way to Spain."

Those bright blue eyes swept the gathering, noticed how the words "treasure *flotas*" had kindled various degrees of anticipation.

"Later, God willing, I will pay a visit to a colony established by Sir Walter Raleigh on an island called Roanoke. In return for certain information most useful on this our expedition, I have passed Sir Walter my word that I will stop to learn how his people fared and to spare them anything I may in the way of succour or sustenance."

Into Wyatt's mind's eye flashed a vision of that grubby tavern back in London where Peter Hopton had in such glowing terms described the vast area now becoming known to Englishmen as "Virginia". Poor Peter! What had become of him?

On his way back to the *Hope*, like the rest of the squadron, rolling sullenly, motonously over a succession of oily swells, Wyatt cast an apprehensive eye at the sky's sickly hue and determined that once aboard he would make certain all guns and gear were lashed down to withstand another of those formidable storms, or *tornados* as the Spanish termed them.

Book Three

THE WEROWANCE

CHAPTER I

LADY DEXTER'S PRECEPTRESS

To Mistress Kate Wyatt it seemed that never in her life had she felt more utterly weak, weary and dispirited than when she glimpsed the towers and chimney-pots of London from the crest of a low hill she had just ascended. She sank on to a grassy rock beside the road and tried to find consolation in the fact that she would not have to walk so far as the city proper. She still wondered at her failure to regain strength after her long ordeal attendant upon the birth of little Henrietta one icy night nearly two months gone by.

A first baby, an old midwife had cackled, was always the most difficult. Kate prayed that this was the truth, for even now she winced over recollections of those awful searing, rendering pangs, of Mistress Foster, and her ancient and very dirty midwife friend, hovering about and murmuring useless encouragement. At the last there had ensued a series of haemorrhages which had all but wafted her away for ever from this world—and Henry Wyatt.

Presently Kate drew a deep breath, struggled to her feet and retrieved a bundle in which she was transporting such odds and ends of broken food as she could salvage from gay and giddy Lady Dexter's table. Soon there came into view the thatched roof of that little cottage she was sharing with Master Foster's widow. Built long ago, before London had commenced to spread out, engulfing field after field and copse after copse, this ancient cottage's walls were sagging and in its moss-covered thatched roof swarmed whole colonies of mice so fertile that not even a long-furred cat from Turkey could keep them in check.

"Dear Lord!" she asked herself. "Shall I never again enjoy silence?"

All week long she had laboured to instruct the arrogant and boisterous progeny of Lord and Lady Dexter in the art of playing the lute and the viol. They seemed for ever to be shrieking, weeping or tormenting each other. And now she faced the prospect of the various forms of din raised by John Foster's five orphans, the eldest of whom had not yet attained her eighth year.

Consisting of only two rooms this draughty old cottage offered no privacy whatsoever. Kate, her infant daughter, and the two youngest Fosters were forced to share one room while Polly Foster, her baby and the two older children slept in odd corners of that chamber which served also as a living-room, dining-room and kitchen. Dear God, how piercingly cold it had been in the cottage, for all that the older Foster children industriously scavenged along the Thames' banks and various backwaters for bits and pieces of driftwood.

Until the news came that big, hearty John Foster had been cut down during a clash with French privateers off Calais, Kate had never realized how crushing a blow it was to a woman to have her family's provider snatched away. In the course of but a few weeks, Polly Foster had been reduced from a modest but comfortable living to this squalid existence, eked out by washing and mending for such seafaring friends of John who, hearing of her plight, would trudge the mile and a half up from Billingsgate to give her employment.

For once, and a wonder, the Foster children were not racing about, even though the afternoon had turned fair after almost a solid week of fog and cold dismal rain. Kate brightened though at the thought that little Henrietta, so softly pink and white, soon would lie cooing or wailing in her arms. It was providential that John Foster's widow was still suckling little Timothy since her own breasts had failed almost at once; the midwife attributed this to excessive loss of blood in childbirth.

Alas, Henrietta also had not escaped unmarked by their joint ordeal. There was a purplish patch, which refused to fade, on one of her arms, caused by the wise woman tugging too hard at that tiny limb and Kate hoped it was only imagination to fear that one of her infant's feet seemed to curve slightly inwards. Whenever she bathed the baby, she hoped to find the foot straighter, but thus far her right foot persisted in toeing in to an alarming degree.

"—And to think that I should be weak and trembling after a walk of only four miles," she reproached herself while trudging along over mud often ankle-deep. "Lord's mercy, and I used to think naught of walking into Huntingdon Town and back in a single day."

To rest herself Kate paused to pluck a sprig of apple blossom which she started to put into her pale hair but it proved too wet so she tucked it into her bundle instead, along with a clump of bluebells she found nodding above a patch of violets. They looked so wonderfully fresh and fragrant after the rain.

Sighing, she once more slipped fingers under the knot securing her bundle. This week she had been unusually fortunate in securing a scrap of loaf sugar, half a flitch of bacon and two whole loaves of slightly stale rye bread apart from the usual eggs and vegetables bestowed by a kindly gardener on the Dexter estate. The Foster children would undoubtedly make short work of them.

A spiral of grey-blue smoke was rising above the cottage's mouldy, grass-grown thatch, and beyond it loomed the forbidding outlines of the Tower and the less austere tower of St. Katherine's Church. Out on the Thames' yellowish waters two tall war galleons were beating their way upstream towards their anchorage off Lyon Key. Experienced now in such matters, Kate recognized these for two of those low-sided, handy vessels such as John Hawkins had designed most especially for service against the Spaniards and any other enemies of Her Gracious Majesty Queen Elizabeth.

"Somewhat must have gone amiss," Kate worried, then hurried her dragging feet. "Else the children would be tussling and playing about out of doors like so many two-legged puppies."

Perspiring slightly, the young woman breasted a low rise on a muddy cow-path leading up to the cottage. When she recognized a man's deep voice her heart leapt like a stag stung by an arrow.

"Harry, Harry!" she thought. "My Harry's returned." Dropping her bundle, she commenced to run, all the while calling out his name and fighting to restrain tears of overwhelming joy.

At the sound of her voice the various ragged and dirty young Fosters appeared, and with them a man, a dark bearded fellow who not in the least resembled her husband. Kate halted, buried her face in her hands and commenced to sob out her anguished disappointment. She wouldn't have done so had she not been so dreadfully weary and discouraged. Straightening, she rallied, waved and then turned back to retrieve her bundle, and, by the time she returned to the cottage most of her tears had been staunched.

Beaming proudly, Polly came bustling out, slapping aside such of her young children as impeded her progress. "Oy, ducky, 'tis me brother Harold. Made port only yesterday."

Kate tried to respond to a burly, black-eyed fellow who, apart from wearing an enormous, bristling black beard, lacked his left ear, which lent him a lop-sided appearance. Surprisingly, Harold Matson grinned, lumbered forward and relieved her of her bundle after crushing her fingers in an honest if vice-like grip.

"Uncle Hal's been to the New World—the New World," chanted the oldest boy. "New World—New World," chorused Mistress Foster's brood. "He's been telling us about the Naturals there. Uncle Hal says that all children, even girls, there go naked—naked—naked—in America."

"America?" Kate forced a smile to lips no longer that deep cherry hue so admired of Harry Wyatt. "You mean the Spanish Main?"

"Nay," said Matson, leading along a bevy of nephews and nieces, "I speak of the Isle of Woccocan which I visited whilst serving Sir Richard Grenville." He shrugged, smacked his sister on her ample bottom. "Woccocan to my notion is but a poor land, so, since we fell in with no Spanish ship, Pol, I've fetched you only a pair of little pearls—but of good lustre. Would to God I had brought you a bagful, now that poor John's sped.

"Pearls!" gasped Polly Foster. "Did 'e say *pearls*?"

"Aye, and here they be."

Both women and the four children peered delightedly upon those tiny iridescent, cream-coloured globes lying lonesomely in the vast palm of a hand marked by many callouses and more than a hint of tar.

"How truly beautiful!" breathed Kate, at the same time conjecturing whether, perchance, her Harry might by now have garnered something similar—wherever he might be. No one, it seemed, had heard whither Drake had sailed once he had left the Cape Verde Islands behind.

In Whitehall, Greenwich and about London one heard rumours and to spare; the Golden Admiral was attacking rich Portuguese stations in the Indian Ocean; he was headed for the Moluccas and the vast wealth of the Portuguese East Indies. Just as solemnly it was bruited that Drake was making for the Straits of Magellan with intent of repeating his dazzling successes against King Philip's possessions in the Western Ocean. Many were the voices which proclaimed that, beyond a doubt, Sir Francis' armada had sailed for the Carib Sea. No one really knew anything for certain, Harold Matson included.

"Bless 'e, Hal," Polly sighed. "These pearls will put a steady fire under me kettle and somewhat in it for many long weeks to come. Yer main kindly wi' yer poor sister." After her lips had brushed her brother's weatherbeaten cheek they were damp with tears of gratitude. Then, noticing Kate's woebegone expression, she brightened. "Take cheer, duckling. Yer Harry's bound to return soon, well laden wi' all manner o' wealth and finery."

"What makes you so sure?" Kate could not help asking.

"Why, never have any o' Sir Francis' people returned empty-handed, an he bore himself faithfully and well."

"Would to God I'd sailed along o' Drake instead o' that skinflint curmudgeon of a Sir Richard Grenville," grumbled Matson, settling himself before the tiny fire which, being kindled with damp driftwood, gave off little heat while filling the cottage with acrid blue smoke.

The mariner fumbled suddenly in a wallet lashed to his belt by a length of tarred cod line and produced a tiny silver coin. He beckoned the oldest lad, John, a runny-nosed urchin of nearly seven. "Do you and your sister Helen trot down to 'e crossroads and wi' this sixpence purchase me a tender and juicy roasting fowl. Wait!" He held up a restraining hand. "And have the publican fill to the brim, mind ye, yonder jug wi' the best ale to be had."

CHAPTER II

HOME IS THE MARINER

THE Foster household feasted that evening and the youngsters, together with their elders, listened round-eyed to Matson's tale of how, as Mate in one of seven vessels dispatched by Sir Walter Raleigh to the New World under command of Sir Richard Grenville, he had voyaged to that same section of coast where, the year previous, a certain Captain Amadas and his crew had met with a most friendly reception at the hands of Naturals inhabiting the Island of Roanoke.

While the black-bearded fellow enlarged his tale, Polly Foster's biggest iron pot bubbled comfortably and rich yellow fat from the chicken soon arose to the surface to be skimmed off and poured over a mess of peas and beans.

"And where d'ye hail from, ma'am?" Hal Matson inquired of Kate, busily slicing one of the loaves she had fetched from Lord Dexter's. It was lucky, too, that she had pre-empted the heel of cheese.

"Why, I'm from a small village you would scarce have heard of, in Huntingdonshire."

"Huntingdonshire?"

"Aye. From the village of St. Neots." She tried not to weep amid smoke blowing back from the ill-constructed fireplace.

Matson raised a cow's horn full of ale to his bearded lips. "St. Neots? Now out upon it! Where have I heard speak of yon village?" Hal's hairy Adam's apple rose and fell thrice before he set down the horn. " 'Fore God, I remember now. 'Twas one of the colonists we set ashore on that miserable sandbank off Virginia. He hailed from such a place. Ye wouldn't call to mind a powerful, tow-headed fellow who is ever full of fun and laughter?"

"You'd not remember his name?" Kate demanded, wrinkling the smooth white expanse of her brow. After all, she had known, or heard of, every soul who dwelt in that part of Huntingdon for nigh on fifteen years.

Hopefully Hal eyed the pot, thrust feet, bare now because his new boots hurt, out towards the hearth, whereupon the long-furred cat from Turkey went over and viewed them with no great approval.

"No. Curs'd if I can. Ye see, ma'am, there were nigh on a hundred men. We had little traffic wi' em save to set the poor wretches ashore and help them fight a battle wi' the Naturals afore we sailed for home."

Rapidly Kate ran over in her mind who might indeed have gone to America from St. Neots. Suddenly she burst out, "Did you say this fellow was yellow-haired and uncommonly strong?"

"Aye. He were the strongest man i' Governor Lane's new colony."

"Then," she declared, "you must mean Peter Hopton."

The mariner stared, then grinned. "Ye've hit the nail on the head, ma'am. 'Tis indeed Hopton of whom I speak."

"Oh, if only Harry were here!" Kate clapped hands in gentle enthusiasm. "You see, Master Matson, this Peter Hopton you speak of is my husband's first cousin. Tell me more of him. Is he well? Is he married? Has he taken up a great grant of land such as we hear are promised to settlers?"

"Now as to whether he be married or no I'll not vouch for, but I wot well that neither he nor anyone else i' that plagued land had as yet set themselves up as landlords when we departed."

He sniffed hungrily and waggled his bearded jaws until the children screamed with laughter. "God's gullet, Pol, is not yon wretched fowl ready? At the moment I could eat a horse then chase its driver."

After supper came the most exciting moment of that memorable evening when from a small sea bag Hal had left in his chest in London he produced a small leather pouch filled with what appeared to be finely chopped brownish leaves, also a curious white object fashioned of clay. After stuffing the brown matter into a bowl at one end of this mysterious equipment the mariner with calloused fingers plucked a coal from the grate and held it over the clay instrument. Presently he drew a deep breath, then from his nostrils gushed a vast cloud of grey white smoke. The children shrieked in alarm.

"God's mercy!" screamed little Helen. "Uncle Hal's caught afire!"

and before Kate or her mother could prevent her, she dashed a pitcher of water full into her uncle's ruddy features. Roaring like a bull of Bashan, he sprang up and would have spanked his niece's bare bottom had he been able to catch her but she had darted out of the open door with the speed of a rabbit pursued by ferrets and only ventured back when Hal Matson's wrath had been assuaged and his pipe rekindled.

After sundown when Polly's brother had departed, swinging off down the lane towards London, Kate revelled in the luxury of fondling her infant. Did the tiny thing's slightly twisted foot seem straighter? By the half light she thought so.

"Things will go better for you now, at least till your man comes home," promised big-bosomed Polly Foster. "Tomorrow, e'en though it be the Sabbath, I'll risk a trip into London. I mind a certain Jew in Blackfriars of whom my John spoke as honest. I'm sure he'll not wait to traffic for these pearls on the Holy Day despite the risk."

"Oh, no, Polly. The pearl money is for you and yours; I'll not touch a farthing of it."

The widow treated her young companion to an exasperated look. "God's Body, and who are you to be so uppity? You poor, whey-faced half-ghost. Nay, I'll neither have you nor your babe go hungry whilst we feast."

She placed a powerful arm about Kate's slim shoulder. "If you're set on't your Harry can make it up to me when he makes port, and for sure he'll return fair laden down wi' wealth. So"—she winked broadly—" 'tis a fair risk I'm taking. Now let's see, what think you o' yer babe? Methinks she's filled out during this week. God send my milk flows another six months. It should. It always has, even as long as two years."

While speaking Polly unlaced her stays, fetched her own infant from its place in her bed and attached first one and then the other of the babies to a large, brown-ringed nipple. Comfortably she settled in the only chair worthy of the name in the cottage. "Now tell me how you fared at Dexter Hall this past week? Did the Honourable Francis have you as before?"

Angrily, Kate flung a faggot on to the blaze. "To be sure. The wretch twice got his hand up my petticoats ere I could fend him off." In the firelight the girl's fair complexion darkened. "For a cockerel of seventeen years he's learned too much and too readily from his precious father and his second wife—Guinevere. They're two of the most shameless creatures ever to tread God's earth," she continued bitterly. "Even at Court their conduct is held to be utterly shameless."

"Then why not leave my Lord Dexter's employ?"

"Would that I could! But where else, dear Polly, can I earn two whole shillings a week and have my board and keep, such as it is——five days of the week? Where else can I bide within walking distance of Harry's infant?"

As expected, Polly could offer no alternative, Dexter Hall being the only manor house in the immediate vicinity. With a rueful smile Kate lifted her skirt and three petticoats to expose a slender white thigh, the perfection of which was marred by three livid spots.

"These pinches," she explained angrily, "were bestowed by Lord Dexter himself when his wife's back was turned, though for that matter I doubt he'd hesitate to tweak me in her presence."

Next the pallid-haired girl slid up the sleeve of a wrinkled, grey kersey dress until she disclosed four finger-marks sketched in brownish-blue. "And this is what happened when the Honourable Francis did waylay me yesterday eve on the stairs to the destitute gentlefolks' gallery."

"You'd better leave before worse befalls you," Polly advised, handing over tiny, doll-like Henrietta that Kate might belch her whilst she performed a similar service to her own sturdy boy baby.

Kate fondled the baby's incredibly soft neck an instant. "God knows I intend to leave the first instant I can find another situation."

CHAPTER III

DEXTER HALL

RAINDROPS dripped from a gloomy double row of cedars leading up to the main portal of Dexter Hall.

As yet these cedars did not stand very tall since Lord Anthony Dexter's new manor house had been completed but a scant two years earlier, an edifice made possible by profitable investments in an organized trading company which had penetrated the frigid waters of the White Sea to traffic with the barbarous Russians for furs—an enormously lucrative undertaking.

Kate Wyatt felt inexplicably depressed as she passed under the portal and the florid inscription upon it: "Through this Wide opening Gate None come too Early or Stay too late." Once inside she turned at the shortest wing of the house which stood out like the middle arm of an E. The floor plan presently was in great favour since it reproduced Elizabeth's initial. Here Lord Dexter's steward and bailiff kept their offices and transacted business.

Only by sheer persistence had Kate gained the right thus to enter Dexter Hall through its main portal. Others of comparable social standing such as Mr. Skipworth, the younger children's tutor, the Reverend Parker, who was this noble family's private chaplain, and various impoverished relations, of which there were now a round dozen—poor, timid folk who suffered constant reminder that they now existed in comparative comfort only through the largesse of big, hawk-nosed Lord Dexter and his empty-headed and lascivious but lovely young wife—were graciously accorded the honour of passing through the main portal.

Lesser personages were required by a pompous major-domo to enter by the servants' door along with gardeners, candlemakers, sheepshearers, gamekeepers and such.

Her sense of depression was the heavier because such foul weather meant that Lord Dexter's offspring would grow restless through being kept indoors. Worse still, Lord Dexter and his foppish son by an earlier marriage to a violent, dark-visaged lady of Norman descent could not go hunting. Kate, of course, long since had got dripping wet and the hem of her best gown splashed with clay and mud. Nor did it help her peace of mind while hurrying upstairs to hear voices raised in angry dispute. Apparently, Woolton, the steward, and Greene, the bailiff, were beginning another of their interminable quarrels.

She hurried along to the great hall's gallery, feet scuffing over a thick layer of rushes, freshly cut, thank Heaven, and no longer reeking of fermenting scraps of garbage overlooked by the numerous dogs and cats which roamed freely about. At this moment the great hall appeared singularly dismal with its long rows of bare wooden tables and plain benches. Here was where all the household, saving Lord Dexter's immediate family, consumed their meals. Each sat according to his or her station above or below the salt.

Almost never, except on holidays, did Lord Dexter and his lady occupy handsomely carved chairs arranged about a table set upon a dais before a bay window at the hall's western end.

Because of the cloudy sky next to little could be appreciated of some stained-glass windows imported from Venice at vast expense. As she hurried along towards a staircase leading to the gentlefolks' quarters, Kate's eyes automatically sought Dexter's imposing coat of arms—three black bulls' heads sable on a field argent divided by a chevron gules.

She had often wondered whether the family motto—*Fortis Amor Est*—had been prepared by a cleric.

A wry smile curved Kate's lips, still blue with cold. How aptly this motto described this line of barons descended from Sir Geoffroi du Droit, one of the Bastard's favourite henchmen.

Fortis Amor Est. Kate was still silently repeating the motto when at length she reached her cubicle, a sorry little affair lacking a fireplace but equipped with a not uncomfortable trundle bed and a battered chest to contain her pitiably few garments. With a cloth she rubbed, as best she might, her numb and aching feet, then stripped to change into her only other gown, sorry garments such as Franklin Ibbott's daughter would have scorned little less than a year ago.

After rebraiding her hair and tucking it up under a modest white cap, she summoned courage and hurried to the nursery where Eloise and Gilbert Dexter awaited her arrival with no appreciable anticipation. It would be nice though to be able to toast her chilled hands before a crackling fire and to feel this penetrating chill leave her.

Kate Wyatt's worst fears proved justified—neither Lady Dexter nor her lord was in evidence, having departed for Court where he was enlisting patronage for another venture to the White Sea.

The children, aged twelve and fourteen years, were dressed in exact miniature replicas of their parents' gaudy garments and were playing at cup and ball with the Honourable Francis, their half-brother.

"A pox on such luck," piped Master Gilbert when Kate entered. "We've been hoping you'd tumble into a bog and drown."

Kate forced a smile. " 'Tis not the fault of the road makers that I did not."

The Honourable Francis rose, as darkly handsome and languid as ever. "Mend your manners, you little imp; you, too, young lady." He scowled at his half-sister. "We have all plagued Mistress Wyatt long enough."

Had one of those stiff portraits on the wall commenced to speak, Kate could not have been more astonished, especially when the Honourable Francis fashioned a perfectly charming smile and advanced, extending a well bejewelled hand.

"Mistress Kate," he lisped, "yestermorn, my sire read me a homily upon courtesies due to a lady. I vow I'm contrite for my plaguing of you last week, and trust you will find it in your heart to forgive me."

Kate donned her most winning manner while opening the cabinet in which were kept a viol and a lute. "There's naught to forgive."

"When you have done with these moppets," Francis smiled, "I've an Italian dulcimer to show you. 'Tis a thing of beauty and just arrived from Naples."

"A dulcimer!" Enthusiasm entered Kate's voice. "I have often heard of such. Is't true one can strike half notes and three full octaves upon it?"

"Aye. 'Tis a most lovely instrument of ebony, all inlaid with ivory. Perchance you could instruct me in the rudiments of its use? Eloise will show you to my cabinet."

Completely dumbfounded over such unexpected interest in music—of which the Honourable Francis possessed less knowledge than a snowbird although, for a young gentleman of fashion, the playing of at least one musical instrument was a prime requisite.

The music-room's pleasant warmth, in addition to a long draught of ale sent up by her firm friend Cuthbert, the butler, went far towards dispelling Kate's gloom and she became Patience personified while guiding Gilbert's grubby fingers over the strings of his lute and schooling Eloise to sing.

Accordingly, the two-hour instruction period seemed to pass with astonishing rapidity and the moment came when Gilbert could toss his lute into a corner and, yelling like a pig stuck under a gate, bound off down the hall to join the other lads of the manor in a rough game of Saracens and Crusaders.

Once her brother had departed, Eloise smiled sweetly and smirked, copying from her mother's Court airs. She declared herself pleased to show her music mistress the Italian dulcimer and, brocaded skirts and miniature farthingale swinging, for all that they weighed nearly ten pounds, tripped off down that tremendously long gallery overlooking the great hall. At length Eloise entered into the Lord Dexter's family quarters and came to a handsomely carved oak door.

Kate hesitated. "Oh, really, my dear, I shouldn't come here. It isn't——" But Eloise was already pounding on panels which promptly swung inwards. It was reassuring to observe that this apartment was indeed a work cabinet lined with dozens of books and boasting a terrestrial and an astral globe to either side of a brilliantly burning fireplace.

Indeed, this seemed a cheery apartment for expensive wax candles burned in tall gilt candlesticks and a brand new gonfalon bearing the family's coat of arms glowed richly above the mantelpiece.

Sure enough, on a writing-table stood the dulcimer, its ebony case richly inlaid with designs executed in ivory, mother-of-pearl and silver. Of trapezoidal shape, this wonderful instrument boasted many metal wires for the striking of which two little hammers tipped with padded kid were provided.

"Oh, how lovely, how very lovely!" she cried.

Then the Honourable Francis passed her the strikers. "Here, Mistress Wyatt, pray see what you can accomplish with these."

The instrument gave off such clear singing notes as she had never previously heard; it required no time at all to pick out a simple air.

Meanwhile, the Honourable Francis, brave in a wine-coloured doublet slashed in canary yellow, fetched out two lovely goblets of Venetian origin—delicate and wondrous affairs of glass with vari-coloured dragons constituting their stems. From a pitcher, also of Venetian glass, the heir to Dexter Hall filled both goblets with tawny yellow wine.

"Sup a little," he invited. "You must be weary after your stint with those young fiends. I vow your patience is beyond belief."

"But I have already drunk a measure of ale."

"Try this wine," he insisted gently. " 'Tis very mild and is imported from the Island of Málaga." He laughed easily. "The Dons may be idol-worshipping Papists, but they can at least produce excellent wines."

Kate hesitated then decided against affronting his offer of friendship so accepted the goblet. He indicated a big chair before the fire and spoke at length of life at Court and of the wars being fought in the Low Countries.

"I mean to join Leicester before long," he announced, fingering the beginnings of a moustache. "But I must wait until my sire raises a half-troop of horse."

Kate made an inward sigh of relief. So the Honourable Francis soon would leave for the wars? Perhaps then she would be spared lingering glances such as he now was directing at her breasts, so very unfashionably rounded and full due to her inability to afford stays.

"I wish you well on your military ventures."

"Do you, indeed? I am glad of that because, Kate, my dear, I find you confounded distracting and desirable," he drawled, fingers tightening on the arms of his chair. "An you kiss half as well as you play the viol you'll prove a paragon among mistresses."

Kate leapt to her feet but was not quick enough. His arms were about her and his nearly beardless face pressed avidly to hers. Despite her best efforts he managed, amid a reek of strong perfume, to plant a moist kiss on her mouth. In desperation she wrenched herself away, struck out and brought her hand hard across his cheek. With the violence of her motion her skirt knocked one of the Venetian goblets crashing on to the floor.

"Let me go!" she gasped and made for the door.

To her surprise the Honourable Francis made no effort to interfere, only drawled, "By God, that I'll not!"

Dark eyes baleful and young powerful features flushed dark as the wine spread over the floor, Lord Dexter's heir eyed her.

"Touch me once again and I'll raise the house!"

"You'd best not," he warned. "Your first wail will land you in a debtors' prison."

A breathless laugh escaped her. "Bah! What cheap threat is this?"

Then he started forward again, dark blue eyes aglow. Kate drew her breath, whereupon he in the yellow doublet halted, offering momentary encouragement. "You deem me a liar, eh?"

"Yes. Among other detestable things," she raged and began sidling towards the cabinet door.

A shrewd look calmed the Honourable Francis' manner. "D'you recall one Nicholas Spencer—a ships' chandler?"

"To be sure. My husband outfitted his vessel from his stores. What of that?"

"Do you remember going surety for certain supplies?"

"Aye, but—but—Master Spencer would never jail me for a debt contracted by my husband—who is also his good friend."

The tall young fellow laughed easily while testing the scarlet marks left by her fingers. "Perhaps old Spencer would not press for payment."

"Then what is this all about?"

"A matter of fifteen pounds."

"Master Spencer promised faithfully to wait for his balance until my husband returned."

The Honourable Francis Dexter stooped, picked up the largest segment of his shattered goblet and eyed it petulantly. "Aye, but that was before the Spaniards captured two of his hulks and so drove him to the verge of the debtors' prison. Old Spencer proved only too glad to sell me the surety you signed, especially when he—er—learned of the deep attachment I have conceived for you, my sweet Kate."

"And now—now you press me for your payment?"

"Nay, be not so blunt—let us say that with you in my arms I can forget all about the matter."

Debtors' prison! Waves of despair engulfed Kate. Hardly a jail in England but held its share of such forlorn and penniless wretches; if destitute of family and friends they either starved until death came or the deadly prison fever shortened their sufferings.

Often when marketing in Huntingdon Town she had, as a charitable deed, stopped by the prison to bestow stale bread and other scraps of food upon the inmates, long-haired, filthy and gaunt creatures who rattled their chains to attract attention and then attempted to sell pitiful bits of their handiwork. Female prisoners, especially if young and comely, sold their charms in exchange for food and favours from the jailers, brutal, uncouth fellows none too choosy about their bedfellows.

"You would not dare to force me," she faltered. "Some day my husband will kill you."

"I doubt it," the youth drawled. " 'Tis much more likely that I would slay him. I am an excellent fencer."

"Have you no—no pity?"

He must have been overjoyed at the crumbling of her defiance, a crumbling prompted by the fears for Henrietta. She commenced to tremble and stared piteously across the cabinet at the Honourable Francis Dexter as he refilled the surviving goblet.

"I'm not such a bad fellow," he announced. "So I'll permit you to discharge your debt upon terms which should prove easy and agreeable."

"And—and your terms?" She could feel a sensation as of hot waves beating at her breasts and thighs.

"Until I depart for the wars you will comply with my wishes, whatever they be."

Kate gasped and her pointed features flamed to the pale blond braids encircling her head. "You'd not drive so unworthy a bargain!"

"Would I not? Come, be reasonable, my sweet Kate. Is not this cabinet more comfortable than a jail?"

Because strength seemed suddenly to ebb from her legs Kate collapsed, rather than sat, upon an uncomfortable oaken armchair of that sort which had been fashionable during the reign of the present Queen's father. Dear God! How could so young, so handsome a youth prove so evil? There was no doubt about it. With little Henrietta to consider, she was trapped as neatly as any vixen. Alack, that she could not appeal to her father.

"Then you will—you will enter into the bargain?"

Dully, she demanded, "What certainty have I that if—if I yield you will surrender my surety?"

"The word of a gentleman," he replied with all the hauteur of Lord Dexter himself, then went over to shoot the door's bolts. "And now, my pet, let me see what glories that ugly gown of yours conceals."

"I accept your attentions because it appears that I've no choice in the matter," she said and, with quivering fingers, commenced to undo her bodice. "But again I warn you that, as surely as the sun rises, my husband will slay you when he returns."

CHAPTER IV

ROANOKE ISLAND

THE afternoon of April the twentieth, 1586, proved to be as lovely as could be imagined in that part of Virginia which is now known as North Carolina. The waters of Roanoke Sound shone bluer and less muddy than for some time. On Roanoke Island, as well as on the mainland, birches, beeches and maples were garbed in the soft, shiny foliage of spring.

Governor Ralph Lane's settlement, however, benefited little from this solar glory. The sunlight served only to reveal how mean and poorly constructed were various huts and cabins sheltering Sir Walter Raleigh's little colony. Without mercy it betrayed how shakily stood palisades designed to defend this miserable collection of hovels in which the remnant of Governor Lane's men had survived almost a year's fighting, hunger and bitter toil.

When a bell, small and of petulant timbre, commenced to toll invalids sprawled on the coarse white sand never even bothered to turn their heads. Not only were they completely incurious but also too weak to afford such an effort.

Down upon the beach, however, a group of colonists engaged in repairing a pinnace cast brief, inquiring glances over their shoulders. So, too, did a party of rag-clad soldiers engaged in driving long birch saplings into the mud to fashion a clumsy imitation of weirs in which the Indians trapped shad, sea trout and other delectable fishes.

The work parties dropped their tools and commenced wearily,

reluctantly, to return to the stockade while from various cabins appeared shaggy, heavily bearded individuals, many of whom were clad in the remnants of once-rich raiment. A majority of these scarecrows were garbed in cloaks and breeches of deerskin and a weird miscellany of sailcloth garments reinforced by leather. The colonists moved slowly, like the half-starved creatures they had become.

Because of Peter Hopton's kindliness towards Chabak, a young Natural captured by him during the preceding winter, and the Monocan's skill in the use of snare and fishing spear, the big gunner did not present quite so cadaverous an appearance as his fellows.

"Why, in God's name, did Lane and Grenville decide on this place?" Peter grumbled to himself. "Such sandy soil grows nothing and requires a deal of effort to walk upon." Long since he had set aside his steel cap and breastplate, but invariably he wore a dagger and carried that longbow which he much preferred to an arquebus issued in June of last year when Richard Grenville had set ashore Sir Walter Raleigh's boisterous but bewildered colonists.

Recently Peter had come to understand that here on Roanoke had been planted no true colony, despite the presence of scientists, metallurgists, smiths and cabinet-makers. The only husbandmen here were present by chance, humble fellows who had tilled the ground before fate or adversity had made them into soldiers. Truly, Sir Walter Raleigh must have much misinterpreted the burden of Parson Richard Hakluyt's *Discourse on Western Planting*.

Farm bred, Peter quickly saw why this colony had come to grief, why there were so many graves scattered among the dunes beyond the palisades. What Sir Richard Grenville's seven ships had set ashore was a colony in name only, and was in fact, merely a military expedition accompanied by a few deluded scientists and artisans. The reef upon which Sir Walter's venture was about to founder was as simple as life itself.

Peter now could appreciate the honest error into which Captains Philip Amadas and Arthur Barlow had fallen back in 1584, when, briefly, they had visited on Woccocan Island. They had chanced to land there during the summer when the Naturals had just brought in their harvest. Improvident as always, the Werowans—or chiefs among these people—had decided that since there was food and to spare, plenty should be bestowed gratis upon the strangers, especially because their medicine men declared these white-faced folk to be the returned spirits of long-dead warriors.

Last winter had proved that, after an autumn season of downright gluttony, the inhabitants of this country really went hungry through the winter months, eking out a precarious existence with such shell-fish, fish and game as fell before crude spears made of stingrays' tails and stone-tipped reed arrows.

It had soon become evident that the Secotas could not, even if they would, share their scanty supplies with these arrogant outsiders who gave every indication of remaining permanently, and whose murderous "firesticks" were driving the game far inland.

Right at the outset, Naturals in the vicinity had been astounded and outraged by Sir Richard Grenville's stern measures in burning their principal village on Roanoke to enforce the return of a small silver cup. This measure proved to have been a blunder of the first magnitude, for the Secotas, a tribe inhabiting Roanoke Island, veered from diffident friendship to such downright hostility that they made peace with the Monocans, their traditional enemies on the mainland.

On drawing near to the Council House, largest edifice on the island, Peter nodded to fellow Council members, many of whom leaned heavily on staffs or proceeded dragging feet.

Now the outline of that crude frame structure known as the Council House loomed a few yards distant. Converging upon it appeared more and more gaunt apparitions. Peter Hopton knew nearly all of them intimately. The well-born amongst them—mostly younger sons of indigent noble families—invariably seemed to have fared better than their humbler companions, probably thanks to superior intelligence.

Yonder came Peter Ludlow, still limping because of an arrowhead which could not be dislodged from his thigh. Although of but twenty-three years, he looked, after this fearful winter, like a man twice his age. And then there was Hubert Wolf, thin as a rail and with his skin turned the colour of a lemon peel. He was tottering along in defiance of a fever which had all but carried him off.

The soldiers as a whole presented a more robust appearance than the colony's luckless artisans and scientists who had proved themselves unable even to determine which fruits and roots were edible and which were not.

The Council House occupied a slight eminence commanding a view of the sound, over which at the moment multitudes of gulls, grey-and-white terns and other sea birds were flying. In the middle distance, two black specks attested the fact that certain members of the garrison had gone fishing.

To the number of fifteen, the Governor's Council filed into the

Council House in which Governor Ralph Lane also lived and attempted to administer this forlorn colony. Because there were no stools, let alone chairs, in evidence, various Councilmen sank onto their haunches, imitating the Naturals of the mainland. A few coughed and spat onto the log flooring, waiting for Governor Lane's entrance.

From his post near the door Peter Hopton could survey the proceedings with ease. Recently he had been appointed a Corporal of the Field by Captain Philip Amadas who bore the resounding, if empty, title of "Admiral of the American Coast". Not a single vessel, beyond two decrepit little pinnaces, sailed under his command.

Of late two parties had sprung up within the colony; one comprised of such gentlemen-adventurers who sided with the policies of Governor Lane. The other included those who followed fiery Sir Thomas Cavendish, Leader of the Opposition.

In silence the two groups disposed themselves on opposite sides of the Council chamber and crouched on their heels to glower morosely upon each other. Only Sir Thomas Cavendish and Humphrey Bolton, Esquire, had taken the least pains with their attire. The other Councilmen wore greasy, food-stained shirts and ragged doublets that no one had even attempted to mend. Nearly all boots and shoes in evidence gaped in hopeless disrepair.

At length Sir Thomas Cavendish growled, "What has become of our noble"—what a world of sarcasm he injected into the title—"Governor? Hanged if I'll wait on His Lordship's pleasure much longer."

More muttering and stirring took place before the Governor strode in, thin red nose running as usual and eyes watering from a severe cold which he could not seem to shake off. He jerked a bow to the assembly and came quickly to the point.

"Captain Amadas, you are in charge of our supplies. How does the commissary stand?"

"It stands not at all," broke in John White's hoarse voice. "It lies flat, lacking even a single barrel of flour to prop it up."

Employing a smooth, round stone the Governor rapped sharply on the wooden table before him. "I require you gentlemen to bid for permission to speak or else maintain silence. We must proceed in an orderly——"

"Oh, for God's sake!" burst out Philip Askew, a surly former army officer. "Don't stand there wagging your silly forked beard at us prating order. Had you but exercised the wits of a loon and the courage o' a louse last winter we'd not be in the desperate pickle we now find ourselves."

"Avast there!" roared Captain Amadas, a towering giant of a man, "I be no happier over this miserable business than the rest of ye but I'll enforce respect for Governor Lane. Next person interrupts will answer to me."

Blinking nervously, Governor Lane considered the gaunt and fever-flushed faces thus pitilessly revealed by bright spring sunlight. "I believe I inquired, Captain Amadas, how long will what remains in the public storehouse keep our bodies and souls together?"

"At the rate our men are perishing," Amadas declared bitterly, "we retain about enough half rations to last a fortnight—but only provided some sturgeons swim into our weirs."

"Which have been ill placed," cut in Andrew Gosnold. "Had you listened——"

"Peace!" thundered Amadas.

"Surely Sir Richard Grenville must shortly return with plentiful supplies of all manner," continued the Governor. "He gave me his knightly word that he would."

"He's two months overdue," querulously broke in Thomas Hariot, historian and surveyor to the expedition. He looked so frail that a puff of wind might readily send him rolling off down the beach like a clump of dried seaweed.

"Knightly word, my arse," broke in Cavendish and jumped to his feet. "Grenville has ever been a tyrant, a domineering, self-seeking dog. I tell you, Ralph Lane, as I have said before, that he and Sir Walter intend for us to rot here! Your precious Grenville at this moment most likely is looting the Caribbean along o' his friend Sir Francis Drake."

"A pox on Raleigh, Grenville and all the rest o' those nobs back in London!" snarled another voice.

Peter's hands tightened on the haft of his pike. The new speaker was one Shamus O'Downs, a fierce, dark-visaged Irishman; fugitive chief of one of those piratical clans infesting the Shannon's estuary. "I've had a plenty o' this starving because our old woman of a Governor insists on coddling the beast-like Naturals."

Face after face swung in O'Downs' direction as, in vain, Governor Lane hammered and Captain Amadas roared for order.

"Let him speak! Let Shamus speak out," chorused the Council.

The Irishman jumped up, jaw out-thrust and wicked little grey eyes agleam.

"I say let us have done with this timorousness. Since the Naturals won't traffic wi' us, let us take what we require. I've heard it vouchsafed that in Namontack, Werowance Chapunka's capital, lies laid up ample stores o' smoked fish, venison and corn."

" 'Tis not so," broke in a member of the Governor's party. "At this time of year the Naturals have scarce enough to feed themselves. Always they starve from the moon of the New Year till their next crop is made. You, Shamus, should realize this truth had you but wit enough to think beyond the range o' your arquebus."

Even more bitter wrangling broke out, attracted listless artisans who had nothing to do, and soldiers too weak to participate in an unremitting and ill-rewarded search for food.

"Go on, O'Downs!" roared Cavendish. "Maybe, Ralph Lane, you will deny that the natives of Namontack wear many ornaments fashioned of copper so rich with gold it scarce requires refining?"

"That is true enough," wearily admitted the Governor. "But, gentlemen, one must take a long view. We are weak and greatly reduced in numbers while the Naturals are numerous, proud and as fierce as hungry mastiffs." He elevated thin and very dirty hands. "Can you not perceive, gentlemen, that, come what may, we must not further antagonize either the Secotas on this island or the Paspeghs and Monocans on the mainland? Until our supply ship appears, we indeed lie at their mercy."

Once more Ralph Lane reminded his followers of the dire consequences attending Sir Richard Grenville's folly when the colony had scarce set foot ashore. During a feast some Natural pilfered a little silver cup. It had been but a very insignificant loss, yet, when the fiery Grenville had demanded his property in vain, he had donned corselet and morion, and, marshalling all the troops, had marched to the nearest Secota village which he pillaged and proceeded to have burnt to the ground. Next he had ordered his men to hack down several fields of green maize which later would have served to feed the infant colony during many a lean month.

"Aye. We've heard the tale full many a time and oft. But now we stand in a different case." Cavendish got up. Instantly O'Downs, Bolton and several others followed his example. "I tell you, Ralph Lane, Grenville and Raleigh have abandoned us. Therefore, as General of the Land Forces, I intend to lead all able-bodied men against Chapunka, Werowance of the Monocans, and, by the glory of God, we'll wring food and pearls and belike some gold out of that stiff-necked old savage and his painted crew."

In vain the Governor hammered on the table then turned in helpless appeal first to Philip Amadas and Thomas Hariot, and then to the other two or three councillors who had adhered to his policy of peace, patience and moderation.

Cavendish's party constituted an overwhelming majority and nothing remained but to heed their suggestions.

"I've devised a plan," O'Downs announced, staring truculently at the Governor's lean, black-clad figure. "Ye've all heard no doubt o' the famous Oke or idol so vastly venerated by the Monocans of Namontack? To the Naturals this Oke is more holy than a splinter from the True Cross, Christ's shroud and the Holy Grail combined is to us." The Irishman swaggered forward, a tall, gaunt figure upon which sorry garments hung loosely and in wrinkles. "Me, I'm for storming Namontack by surprise and then holding this Oke to ransom for all the grain and gold we need."

Utter dismay clouded Ralph Lane's drawn and sensitive features. "Nay! I forbid you to even contemplate such folly! Such an act would cause the immediate extinction of this colony. This Oke of which you speak is sacred not only to the Monocans, but to the Pamunkeys, the Secotas, the Paspeghs, the Kecoughtans and many other tribes. To violate their sacred place would bring them like ravening wolves upon us." He looked desperately about. "Besides, I swear unto you that my spies report the granaries of Namontack to be near as empty as our own."

Peter, watching breathlessly, sensed that a turning point in the fate of Sir Walter Raleigh's first American colony was about to be attained. Although he could understand the Governor's reluctance to make war upon Chapunka, he nonetheless yearned for a full belly once more, and to have something further in his wallet than the four or five freshwater pearls protected by a little nest of down plucked from the breast of a wild duck.

"Bah!" thundered Cavendish, aggressively thrusting out a great brown beard. "You'll believe anything that spares you a fight."

"Nay! I am Governor over this colony and speak in the Queen's name."

Bolton shook his big, bullet head. "Out upon it! Yer no more fit to rule over this colony than a country schoolmaster. Let the majority rule, say I. Now, who's for sitting here sucking our thumbs and starving until a ship may, or may not, appear?"

Only the Governor, Hariot, Captain Amadas, and Andrew Gosnold held up their hands.

"Now who's for making those bloody Naturals prance to our tune? Who's for forcing them to trade? Who's for exacting vengeance for the slaughter of our exploring parties?"

A shout which would have been louder had the colonists not been so weak caused the Council chamber to resound. Peter found himself yelling as loud as Shamus O'Downs—not that he fancied that glib, black-visaged Irishman in the least. He and O'Downs undoubtedly remained the two most powerful men among the seventy-three-odd who had survived the winter, a fact which inevitably threw them into rivalry of various sorts.

In the end Governor Lane submitted to the will of the majority. "God help us," he cried bitterly. "I have done all that I might and I will not grant my consent to so mad a project which will surely end with us dead or writhing at Chapunka's torture stakes. But I will not forbid you."

The Council raised a brief cheer, then, for further consultation, the leaders followed Sir Thomas Cavendish back to the hovel he occupied among the dreary, grey-white dunes of Roanoke Island.

CHAPTER V

NAMONTACK

ALEXANDER PORTER, Peter Hopton's cabin mate, a tired little stonemason originally from Norwich, with fevered eyes watched the blond young giant's preparations for General Sir Thomas Cavendish's expedition against Chapunka's town. Porter had been thinking of home more than usual lately, his strength for a month now had been ebbing as obviously as an equinoctial tide.

Peter encouraged: "Just rest, my good friend, and I will fetch you back some real provender—maize cakes and perchance a young deer or a rabbit that will restore you greatly. Besides, soon a ship will come."

Porter sighed and turned fretfully onto his side. "But our supplies are now two months past due, and many are the dangers from the Spanish and tempests. Oh, Peter, what would I not give to watch the maids of my village dancing for a garland and the lads shoot arrows at a clout on May Day."

The sick man rambled on and on while Peter drew forth and

inspected each and every arrow from a waterproof quiver. Now and then he would reject a shaft. Not for him a clumsy arquebus among these grey-green tangles on the mainland. Let him who would sweat with firelock and prop along the narrow and twisting game trail which alone led to Namontack, lying some ten miles inland.

Quoth the dying stonemason, "Pray carry my bow, Peter, 'tis somewhat shorter than yours and therefore handier in underbrush." Porter sighed a long, sibilant sigh. "It's a good bow, lad. With it I once won a silver arrow at my Lord Howard's Christmas Day shoot."

"Why—why——" Peter was genuinely touched. "I'd not think on it."

"Nay. I've the notion poor Alex Porter will ne'er again find use for it," and he broke into a series of spasmodic retchings such as were draining away the last remnants of his strength.

Peter clapped him gently on the shoulder. "Why then, Alex, I'll take and make use o' it, but only because 'twill aid me to bring back good food to restore you. Mark my words, you'll live to build full many a fine wall i' this country yet—and 'tis a fine, rich country where, in times to come, will grow a great nation."

The invalid spat blood, then smiled wanly. "You're daft on the subject, Peter. Now go and let me rest."

Being aware that the colony and its palisade were always under observation, Sir Thomas Cavendish decided upon a ruse. All the invalids and injured men able to move were escorted, to a loud beating of drums and sounding of trumpets, down to the shore and embarked aboard the larger pinnace, which hoisted sail and steered southward along the Sound in the general direction of a great bay known as K'tchisipik, a huge body which in due course would become known as Chesapeake Bay. Such a move would seem logical to the Monocan lookouts.

The white men were known to be mad for treasure and gold mines were believed to exist near the Chesapeake's headwaters; there pearls the size of radishes also were to be picked up for the bother, or so the Naturals themselves had heard. Several times Governor Lane's men had attempted to explore that fabulous body of water but always something had prevented.

Hidden within the houses thirty-five of the strongest Englishmen watched their pinnace diminish in the distance and prayed that their feeble companions could summon sufficient strength to sail her back after dark.

Once night had fallen, inky black because low clouds were piling in from the direction of Cape Hatteras, the little expedition formed up on the beach to board their leaky lesser pinnace. Here Cavendish and Shamus O'Downs personally inspected all weapons, then made certain that each man carried the single handful of maize and chunk of badly-smoked sturgeon which would have to support him until the capture of Namontack, or whatever other fate awaited him on the mainland.

A pair of Paspeghs, succumbing to the dazzling bribe of an antiquated wheel-lock and a very undependable petronel, seemed eager enough to be on the trail to Namontack and led off through dripping woods. It was hard work keeping up with them so easily did the Naturals bend and twist around low-flung live oak branches and the ghostly streamers of Spanish moss dangling from them.

Because of their famished condition Sir Thomas Cavendish's men were slow in reaching a dense pine forest blanketing a hill behind the town of Namontack and dawn had already begun to brighten the tallest tree's tops. Robins chirped, jays scolded and quantities of brilliant little warblers viewed this bearded and haggard little column of Europeans with bright and inquisitive black eyes.

Presently General Cavendish decreed a halt. "Our guides," he informed his followers, "inform me there are but two gates let into the walls of Chapunka's palisade; therefore Captain O'Downs with the ten men already selected will make all speed towards the east gate. The rest, saving six who will remain outside to deny the savages exit, will fight with me into the town."

Sir Thomas' always dark and penetrating eyes in this half-light seemed cavernous. "You'd best recall 'tis not only for your very lives and those of our sick, as well, we fight, but also for the honour and greater glory of our Gracious Queen. Therefore I conjure you to strike hard and often, showing no mercy to any man saving Chapunka and all of his family."

"Saving yer presence, Sir Thomas," O'Downs broke in, "ye'd best remind these lads 'tis their Oke which must be captured at all costs."

A final inspection of firearms marked a resumption of the march. Peter brushed a layer of wet leaves from his cuirass and wished that his conical steel cap did not weigh so infernally heavy upon his straw-coloured pate. Because of a chilling drizzle which had persisted throughout most of the night he could not yet uncase Alex Porter's bow nor yet uncover the mouth of his quiver. Instead, he hefted a half-pike equipped with a heavy, leaf-shaped blade which had a slim crossbar fixed below it, designed to prevent its point from penetrating too deeply in the heat of battle. Many a good pikeman had died, so his father had claimed, through inability to clear a pike-head hung up in some enemy's body or gear.

At the edge of the pine woods light was increasing when Captain O'Downs led off his ten men at a dogtrot to circle that rough palisade which protected Chapunka's capital. They were half-way to their goal before a sleepy squaw, hawking and spitting, shuffled out to fill her gourd at a spring. She spied the strangers, emitted a startled shriek and raced back into Namontack yelling like a pig about to be butchered.

Cavendish sprung out of the underbrush, rusty mail a-gleam in the dawnlight. "Now! Let us upon the idolators; show them no mercy!" His arquebusiers went crashing down the slope, dragging Y-shaped musket props and deployed until they were ranged in a scattering line before the west gate. Through this had commenced to pour a howling, nearly naked mob of warriors.

At Sir Thomas Cavendish's command the English firelocks roared and with devastating effect, for at such a range each of the heavy, ten-ounce leaden balls slew or crippled as many as three men. The crashing reports of this initial fusillade having created an expected confusion and terror among the scarcely wakened Naturals, Peter Hopton's archers planted a handful of arrows handily in the earth at their feet then nocked shafts over broad thumbnails and commenced remorselessly to pick off any and all Monocans who dared show themselves.

Sir Thomas then advanced his musketeers over the writhing wounded and through the gate into Chapunka's big wooden town. A second volley was delivered with deadly accuracy at the yowling Naturals who, utterly panic-stricken, rushed senselessly about.

Stark-naked women and children cowered in the lodges and screeched like fiends from the Pit. Only a few spear-thrusts and a handful of arrows were directed against Cavendish's ragged little band, then a ragged fusillade from the far side of Namontack attested the fact that Shamus O'Downs' men were delivering their assault. The arquebusiers having reloaded, Cavendish raised his family war cry, led the way deeper among the bark-roofed cabins, his long sword flashing like summer lightning.

Having restored Porter's bow to its case, Peter tightened his belt, pulled up the half-pike out of the ground and made sure his dagger was free in its sheath. Something went *clank!* against his breastplate, then a stone-headed arrow, its shaft shattered, dropped at his feet.

Running but a scant stride behind Sir Thomas and young Bolton, Peter felt his heart lift when he levelled his pike at a screaming warrior distinguished by a blue turtle painted on his breast. He lunged straight at the centre of that design and felt the pike's head jar against bone then slip in until its crossbar checked the thrust and blood came spraying into his face. Someone dealt him a shrewd blow on the head with a club, but his helmet saved him and he pressed on, thrusting and stabbing at a howling mass of weirdly painted demons before him.

Again and again sounded the curious rasping noise caused by a stone weapon being turned by steel morions and cuirasses. Hoarse oaths and panting shouts raised by the English contrasted oddly with the thin and high-pitched war cries of Chapunka's warriors.

Ever deeper towards that temple in which the Oke was worshipped pressed the attackers. It seemed to Peter Hopton that he had been thrusting and slashing for hours. His pike shaft had become hard to handle, so slippery had it grown with warm and sticky blood that had run down it. For a time it seemed as if he and his companions were fighting their way through a solid wall of bodies. He heard someone cry, "Oh God! I'm sped."

In the press he must have slain women as well as men, the turmoil being so furious that it became impossible at the last instant to deflect a thrust.

All at once the Monocans raised a mournful howl, dropped their weapons and ran to fling themselves over the palisade or to squirm through openings between its pointed logs. Many of the Naturals were cut down from behind, but many more succeeded in gaining the safety of the pine forest. Sheer weakness prevented a complete massacre of the women and children remaining within the confines of Chapunka's capital, but without compunction or delay, without exception, the throats of the wounded and male prisoners were cut.

The earth had begun to spin about so Peter was forced to drop on to a log to recapture his wind. The weapon-littered ground literally was carpeted with painted brown bodies and tangles of black hair sprawled amid widening pools of brilliant carmine.

Less than half an hour after the first arquebus had boomed Namontack village lay helpless in the grip of the English, and Chapunka's favourite wife and her two sons were prisoners, together with a good half of his harem. To joyous shouts a dozen weather-beaten rascals dragged the Oke from its altar in a circular bark house erected to shelter it.

"And to think 'e bloody Naturals worship so hideous a thing!" grunted Gosnold, wiping bloodied sweat from his cheek.

The Oke proved to be a curious idol, human in form but boasting the mask of a wild-cat for a face. Affixed to the Oke's back was a pair of big bird's wings; electric blue, they certainly must have originated from some place much further south. One of the men who had served with Hawkins declared them to be from a macaw, a bird native to distant Mexico and Guatemala. The legs of this idol ended in fish tails instead of feet. Happily, the victors noted that the scales on these seemed to have been fashioned from pure gold.

"To me," observed Askew, one of the scientists, "there exists a significance to this idol. Their Oke expresses the sum of God's creatures—the beast, the bird and the fish."

"A pox on their foul idol," growled Captain Humphrey Bolton. "Let's on to the granaries and fill our bellies."

Resounding and fervent were the curses which broke out when but three deer-hide sacks of that essential staple, corn meal, were discovered. The only supplement was a good supply of edible roots, some with sheaves of dried fish and a few smoked haunches of venison. In various huts smaller stores were discovered but, from a supply point of view, the storming of Namontack proved less than satisfactory.

CHAPTER VI

THE WEROWANCE CHAPUNKA

FOR three days following the return of Sir Thomas Cavendish and his ragged train of soldiers, hostages, plunder and food the settlement experienced a rare wave of optimism. True, five more invalids, including Peter Hopton's cabin mate, perished even as a nourishing broth was offered them.

It chanced that at this time a strong gale drove great numbers of fish into the weirs and that hunters on the island slew several does and their young fawns—to the outrage of the few remaining Paspeghs—so, for the first time in many months, full bellies rumbled in and about Sir Walter Raleigh's sickly little colony. Only far-sighted men like Ralph Lane, Thomas Hariot and Captain Philip Amadas looked beyond this enjoyable but inevitably brief period of plenty.

Bonfires blazed outside the palisade and the slender remaining stock of beer and wine was recklessly lowered. Why not revel? demanded Bolton and O'Downs. Did the colonists not hold many strong male slaves captured in the woods? Besides, there were full baskets of food reposing in the community storehouse. Of course, most of this provender was perishable and would soon spoil, but what of that? There was plenty for today and tomorrow.

Not one of the adventurers but had fetched back at least two brownish-skinned maidens cowering, frightened half out of their wits, and clad in aprons of finely tanned skins that fell apron-like before and behind. Their fringes, however, failed to conceal tempting brown thighs and the captive ladies who wore their glossy hair in bangs in front and in a short pony's tail behind wore nothing above the waist saving necklaces of bone and seed and intricate designs tattooed about their upper arms.

Little girls under ten went stark naked save for a girdle of thongs which supported a pad of soft moss between their thighs.

All in all the female slaves proved to be bright, merry creatures, not in the least concerned with the future.

To Peter Hopton's lot had fallen two straight, supple and comparatively light-skinned wenches of about fifteen or sixteen. Certainly they must be the daughters of some Natural werowance else they never in the world would have borne themselves so proudly. Their smooth young bodies, innocently uncovered save for pearl-shell necklaces and fringed split skirts of well-tanned lynx skins, glowed copper-brown where they had not been rubbed with chalk. According to the tribal mode they thus marked their foreheads, cheeks, chins, arms and legs.

At first the captives had proved intractable and had spat and scratched like a wild-cat's kittens. Alas, that poor Alex Porter had been much too far gone for the enjoyment of these comely, if greasy and rancid-smelling maidens. A series of well-directed cuffs and a birch switch smartly applied to the elder girl's bare bottom quickly persuaded Seikanank and Cocushon more gracefully to submit to the lot of females captured wherever wars are fought.

Having long been deprived of wine, a mere half flagon of Rhenish wine from Sir Thomas Cavendish's private supply set Peter's head to reeling and when, before a victory bonfire, the successful raiders celebrated, he like the rest caused his two captives—for convenience renamed Jane and Jill—to dance about the fire wearing no further adornment than a string of lustrous mussel shells and a clump of cardinal and blue-jay feathers tucked into their raven tresses. Icod! Peter grinned in the dark while listening to the last drunken yells fade in the starlight. " 'Tis main wonderful to find a tidy and loving wench bedded on either side o' me, especially when cold winds come booming in from the Atlantic."

Now that Alexander Porter rested among other wasted cadavers in a shallow grave amid the sand dunes, Hopton had their cabin to himself and was glad of the extra space. It was amazing how readily, how cheerfully, these young Monocan females adapted themselves to their new status. Why, they actually vied in winning even so little as a kindly word, an extra bit of food, or even a friendly pat on the buttocks.

Indeed this was a time for hearty, if ephemeral, rejoicing, and a week passed before a solitary war canoe, burnt out of a single log, came paddling over to Roanoke from the mainland. A young warrior sat in the bow waving a green branch while two lesser Naturals applied their paddles. The fellow was clad in a glossy marten-skin mantle and displayed a pair of dried, stuffed tanagers tucked through slits in his earlobes. He was handsome and betrayed his noble lineage in cleanly modelled and quite pale features. Cautiously the canoe hovered just out of arquebus range while the herald shouted that the great Werowance Chapunka begged leave to treat for his god and family with the famous white princes from beyond the sea.

"Tell the puppy to come ashore," called Shamus O'Downs, who chanced to be Officer of the Day. "We'll not talk else." The youth was allowed to land and though empty-handed was immediately cuffed and spat upon. Peter never forgot the detached pride with which the young savage endured a series of indignities showered upon him until at last the Irishman conducted him before Governor Lane who sat sad and apprehensive for all his white-plumed hat and a splendid scarlet cloak.

Through Chabak, Peter's man slave, the emissary spoke briefly and to the point. His uncle, the Werowance, he described as the mightiest warrior in all the Land of Pomeiock; he ruled over a dozen lesser kings called weroans and spoke directly to Machecomuck the Great Spirit who ruled in Popogusso—Heaven. The white princes, Chapunka had decreed, might do as they pleased with all captives saving only his royal wives and children. For the safe return of these he was prepared to pay much tribute and more for a surrender of the Oke.

To begin with, the King of the Monocans would furnish two canoes loaded with those copper ornaments which the Englishmen appeared so to admire and would produce three weasel skins full of fine pearls when the Oke was returned undamaged. The speaker then grew excited, warned that tribes as far north as the next bay above the Chesapeake and as far south as the Sea Islands were collecting huge war parties to capture the Oke by force if necessary.

While interviewing this splendidly-muscled stripling—he was so light-coloured as to appear Spanish or Italian—Ralph Lane slowly stroked his ragged grey beard and hoped that the state of his garments, all torn and salt-stained, beneath the splendid silver and scarlet cloak had gone unnoticed.

"To your uncle, the great Werowance Chapunka, I send greetings," said he kindly. "Say that for the safe return of his wives and children I will accept no reward."

An angry roar escaped Captain O'Downs. "The Foul Fiend fly away with you, Ralph Lane! You'll not return those savages ransom-free; the old savage will deem you more witless than you are——"

Through the interpreter, Governor Lane continued as if there had been no interruption. "Tell your uncle, the great and famous warrior Chapunka, that for his idol I will accept neither pearls nor ornaments, but instead"—he hesitated, as if mentally computing—"twelve large canoes so loaded down with maize meal, nuts, terrapins and other good provender, that not a hand's breadth shall separate their gunwales from the water."

This time it was Cavendish who broke in, "Now, by the Gullet of God, Lane, you go too far! We'll accept the treasure. There's more food to be found where we won this. I know of three villages not a day's march distant, as big or bigger than Namontack."

At last the Royal Governor was stung into action and jumped up white with rage. "Silence, you undisciplined rogue," he shouted in a trembling voice. "I bear the Queen's commission and on my head, not yours, lies the success or failure of this colony. I say *food we must have*, food above ornaments and pearls."

Peter was astonished that this customarily mild and sedate individual could break into such a tirade as followed. "Are you so bemused that you cannot foresee that, from now on, no one of us will dare place foot on the mainland by day, or outside yonder stockade by night?" He levelled a quivering forefinger at Roanoke's roughly pointed palisade. "We must gain, right here and now, food sufficient to last us until the ship arrives from England. Without this provender

I demand we shall perish surely unto the last man. Now hold your tongue, Sir Thomas Cavendish, else I'll have you in irons. Drake knew how to deal with Doughty and your sort, and so can I!"

Perhaps it was sheer astonishment that held Cavendish and O'Downs silent long enough to allow the Natural emissary to incline his head towards Lane and state in all earnestness: "Believe me, my Father, to the Monocans and Secotas in this season remain not so many as three canoe loads of such food as you bespeak. But pearls, ornaments and fine furs you shall have in abundance."

And so it came about two days later that the garrison stood to arms with the stronger sick men amongst them to receive an impressive flotilla from the mainland. Some canoes contained as many as fifteen hideously painted and befeathered warriors. The Werowance must have known that two demi-culverins and four falconers—all the ordnance the colony possessed—and a triple dozen of arquebuses were trained upon him when he stepped ashore.

Involuntarily, a reconnaissance, or advance detachment, which had descended to the sound's edge, presented their pikes—such was the dignity of that tall savage who, under a tall heron's feather sweeping back from his forehead and with two more sticking straight up from behind his ears, stepped ashore holding aloft a branch upon which clumps of pink and white blossoms nodded and danced.

Because the old king's left eye no longer existed its lids were puckered in on it like lips about a toothless mouth. Both on his chest and belly showed dozens of small scars caused by blood-letting during sickness. About his shoulders the Werowance wore a mantle of some rare silvery pelt which Peter Hopton could not recognize. Through the lobe of Chapunka's left ear, pierced and distended to receive such an ornament, was thrust the bright plumage of an indigo bunting, while to his right upper arm was secured the skin of a goldfinch.

Offshore, awaiting the signal to advance, lay the ten or twelve canoes deep in the water with ransom. Lean, sun-cracked lips were licked and the gaunt garrison nudged each other to see the four foremost canoes each conveying a heap of glowing copper ornaments. Behind these floated other canoes heaped high with golden meal, the glossy pelts of otter, beaver, wild-cat and cougar.

Governor Lane stepped forward, raising in greeting a staff of ebony topped with a gold and ivory knob. He tried as best he might to inject friendliness into his greeting as, through the interpreter, he declared himself honoured by this visit of Chapunka, greatest of all the Indian kings in Virginia. He regretted the necessity of slaying so many of Chapunka's subjects, he declared, but the Monocans had failed to discharge their treaty obligations to supply the colony with maize and venison.

Twice the Werowance's features, painted in vertical yellow and red stripes, contracted as if to speak, but he remained silent at the water's edge with ankles still awash and arms folded over his scarred chest.

"I come as a defeated warrior bringing ransom for my god, my wives and children," Chapunka announced at length. The sun picked out the line of his high cheekbones and the stripes of paint traversing them; his one eye glittered bright as that of a healthy gamecock. "Where is the Oke?" he demanded impatiently.

"It shall be restored to you," Lane declared, standing very straight and solemn. "When you have sworn a great oath that peace shall reign between us, your people and mine, at least until the first snow shall have flown next autumn."

The Werowance hesitated, glanced at the dark throng of warriors manipulating their canoes offshore, but at length inclined his head. The heron feather made a rippling motion. "There shall be peace between us, O Prince among the White Men."

"Tell the old bugger to fetch the ransom ashore," O'Downs grumbled. "I trust these villains not a thumb's length."

When the last deer-skin sack of maize—there were only six in all—the last pelt and ornament had been heaped upon the beach, Peter Hopton's men escorted Chapunka's wives and their offspring down on to the cold, firm sand. While they embarked the onlooking warriors made no sound and remained some fifty yards or more offshore, patently aware of those arquebuses held ready on their yokes.

When the Oke was brought forward on a sort of stretcher, a great cry rang out over the sound's silver-grey water. Then a pair of sorcerers leaped from a canoe and came wading in to accept the sacred object. Meanwhile the Werowance, his wives and children prostrated themselves upon the damp sand.

Once the idol, promptly decked with garlands of fresh flowers, had been secured aboard the largest canoe, the Werowance Chapunka turned and faced his enemies. Deliberately he flung the flowering branch into the water, then in silence splashed out to be assisted into the royal canoe.

At once paddles backed water, then, turning their craft towards the mainland, the Naturals paddled away at speed.

CHAPTER VII

STATE OF SIEGE

NO ONE, not even Governor Lane, was sufficiently fatuous to imagine that Chapunka would honour his promise not to wage war until snow flew. As it was, during two weeks peace prevailed over Roanoke Inlet, just long enough to lull the colonists into carelessness. Then the Paspeghs, Secotas and Monocans struck with merciless savagery. A party of seven men hunting turtles' eggs along the beach were pounced upon and either killed or captured. Among the latter was Captain O'Downs, although he defended himself with desperate valour.

Swarms of savages in full war paint came howling over the dunes but bolted just out of cannon-shot to watch others of their number run down and board the larger pinnace. Terribly piercing were the death screams of her crew. Fortunately, a puff of wind filled the other pinnace's sail and sent her downwind faster than the enraged Naturals could paddle.

From that hour no Englishman dared to put foot outside the palisade unless he went fully armed and with a heavy escort. Night after night, the Monocans and their allies brought prisoners to be tortured to death within sight and earshot of the beleaguered and dangerously depleted garrison.

They reserved O'Downs for the last, probably because of his great strength and unbending defiance. Ghastly were the Irishman's howls and screams while, using clam shells, Chapunka's squaws joint by joint hacked off his fingers and toes then slit his nostrils. They then held burning brands to his private parts before cutting off his eyelids. At least fifteen hundred savages danced, howled and tossed their weapons into the air when, at long last, the black-haired Irishman slumped lifeless in his bonds. They then literally cut him into little pieces.

So overwhelming in numbers were the Secotas, Monocans and Paspeghs the garrison could do nothing and no one heeded Sir Thomas Cavendish when he called for volunteers to make a sally.

" 'Tis sheer suicide," declared Captain Amadas, standing to arms among the all-too-few able-bodied men.

Bitter indeed were the reproaches levelled at the Cavendish party when the siege was continued by relays of the enemy who continually passed back and forth to the mainland. It became unmistakable that Chapunka's force on the dunes was augmented daily. Sentries on the palisade could see canoe after canoe arriving from the south end of the sound; undoubtedly an attack in force would soon be delivered.

The garrison would have strengthened its palisade but no wood remained beyond that obtained by pulling down huts and cabins. Banded together in their cramped enclosure, the colonists enjoyed no privacy, and the stench from the fouled earth grew ever stronger.

Peter Hopton had grown unmistakably fond of Jill and Jane, his fawn-tinted handmaidens. They proved to be merry little creatures, ever ready to smile or to anticipate his least desire. Adoringly their large and limpid black eyes followed him when he went about his duties—which required not much time since no longer could any fishing or hunting expeditions be sent out.

A month from that day upon which Sir Thomas Cavendish had fallen upon Namontack the storehouse stood just as empty as it had been for, lacking even a semblance of discipline, the colonists had gorged themselves during those two deceptive weeks of peace.

Jill exposed sleek brown thighs crouching over the one iron kettle in which Peter's little *ménage* cooked all their food. Mournfully she inspected a tiny chunk of dried venison which, with a handful of maize and few clams, would go towards making a weak gallimaufray or catchall stew. All the same she grinned as she patted her stomach which had lost considerable roundness; so, too, had her firm little breasts.

Peter was thankful that his harem had not followed an example set by certain Indian women slaves who insisted on donning parodies of European female costumes fashioned out of old mantles or worn-out sail-cloth. Wisely, Peter's prizes refused to wear more than fringed and abbreviated aprons of deer-skin.

For his portion of ornaments included in the ransom, Peter had had the foresight to select bracelets, anklets and necklaces fashioned of rich, gold-red copper. He had a bad time at first, it being manifestly impossible to ornament his handmaidens with gifts of identical value. Jill had flung herself on Jane and had wrenched off a copper ear-ring which, mistakenly, she deemed to be more desirable than a little silver bangle set with a turquoise.

On the whole, though, while the food held out the three dwelt happily together. Peter would lie with head pillowed on Jane's lap while Jill gently explored his rangled and oily yellow locks for such insects as she might find. Not a soul in the colony but had harboured vermin of varying species since embarking at Plymouth almost exactly a year earlier.

When the stores were almost exhausted, Lane, being one of very few colonists to remain celibate, delivered a long harangue in which he urged that all captives should be set at large. This, indeed, caused threats of open mutiny.

"What difference makes it?" snarled Andrew Gosnold. "We are bound to perish come a few days, so let us sleep warm until then."

"But the ship may come."

"The ship?" Shouts of bitter laughter arose. "Damned if I'll surrender my Susan—I'll eat her someday soon."

The Governor, as usual, stormed, threatened and in the end gave in.

Peter told his handmaidens a couple of nights later, "I'm thinking this will be the last night we'll frolic together."

They, understanding not a word he uttered, nodded brightly, smiled and slipped smooth brown arms about his neck. All they grasped was his intonation of the word "frolic".

That night it seemed as if Peter's premonition was justified for, in their encampment among the dunes, Chapunka's warriors lit huge bonfires, thundered their drums and howled like winter wolves. Clearly, they were working themselves up towards a grand assault. All night long the tumult persisted whilst haggard Englishmen marched the parapet and recalled O'Downs' dying screams.

"Most likely the Naturals will attack us come dawn," Peter predicted to his sleepy bedfellows. " 'Tis ever the fashion of yonder warriors."

To render the embattled colonists' situation even more precarious a light fog arose before dawn which blotted out the landscape but left stars visible if one looked straight upward. Peter polished Alex Porter's bow, readied his quiver and then unwrapped the lock of his arquebus and lit a slow match at a campfire glowing outside his cabin. He thrust the match into place in that metal arm which, when the trigger was pulled, would force up a pan cover and so bring fire into contact with his priming charge.

How lonely he felt up there on the parapet, for all that every man able to bear arms was crouched staring intently into the shifting, eddying mists. Still no warning was raised by pickets Cavendish had posted some hundred yards beyond the palisade gate.

Would to God he were still in his cabin where Jill and Jane lay snuggled together like puppies. Well, this might very well prove to be his last morning on earth; certainly he had not sensed the presence of

Death so strongly since that fateful day in Huntingdon Town market place.

Um. What might have chanced with Henry Wyatt? Had he been slain by the Sheriff's enraged pikemen or had he suffered death by hanging? Certainly he had killed that archer by the gallow's foot. Poor devil! How horrible a home-coming had betided Harry Wyatt. Did such ill creatures as witches really exist? He fell to wondering. After all, was it credible that the Devil could transform himself into a black goat, dog or cat and then converse in a human voice?

He shifted, wished that the chill caused by his corselet would diminish. He overheard conversation interspaced between fits of coughing from behind the two demi-culverins. Their crews nervously were arranging and rearranging a scant supply of cannon balls.

It was growing gradually lighter; soon out of the gloom should arise yelping war cries.

The sun must then have peered over the horizon for, all of a sudden, the fog assumed rosy-pink tints.

"Why don't 'e bloody savages attack and have it over with?" muttered someone.

"They'll be on us soon now," opined Captain Amadas. "The mist is fast thinning."

But still sounded no squalling war cries, no thud of bare feet upon the damp sands of Roanoke Island.

The tension became almost unbearable. Suddenly the mist lifted like a curtain and a startled voice yelled: "My God! Look, look out to sea!"

Through the last tendrils of fog out on the Atlantic could be seen the white glimmer of a sail. "The ship! The ship! No, by God's Glory, two, three, a dozen at the least!"

Peter passed a shaking hand over sunken eyes. " 'Tis witchcraft," he warned himself. "There cannot be so many ships out there." But there were. For over an hour more and more vessels came sailing into Roanoke Inlet showing the Cross of St. George at their topmasts.

"By God, 'tis Drake!" cried Captain Amadas. " 'Tis his own colours fly at that biggest galleon's mizzen."

CHAPTER VIII

ROANOKE INLET

BECAUSE the *Hope* drew very little water Captain Henry Wyatt was able to sail his command so close to Roanoke Island that the splash caused by his anchor frightened dense flocks of yellow-legged shore birds into frantic flight. He found it pleasant to observe how smoothly, how efficiently his crew now could discharge their duties. The Portuguese and Genoese laid out on the yards and clewed up the mainsail and topsail quite as smartly as the topsmen aboard the *Aid* and *Bonaventure*.

Already Will Tompkins and his gunners were drawing charges from their pieces. The ship's cook began kindling his fire in a sand-box at the foot of the mainmast and scolded the Captain's two Negro boys into baiting fish-hooks.

From the *Hope's* poop Wyatt studied that frail palisade which surrounded what seemed a motley collection of cabins and jerry-built huts. So these white sands, slate-grey waters and dark green forests constituted that country over which Peter Hopton had rhapsodized in England? At any rate, his cousin had not lied on one point: America *was* huge. Since leaving Florida Drake's armada had paralleled an ever-changing, but unbroken, coastline for near two weeks.

The reduction of St. Augustine had cost valiant Sergeant-Major Powell that life he had preserved during the Voyage of Circumnavigation and in near a hundred hard-fought battles. Now his bones mouldered in a rank Floridan swamp.

While forts protecting St. Augustine were being dismantled and their ordnances removed Wyatt had seized his opportunity to explore inland for the golden cities of Cibola.

Of course he had come upon no such town and had been unmercifully taunted by fellow Captains upon his return. Still, as Peter had averred, this land was unbelievably fertile. Here grew forest on forest capable of furnishing the finest woods imaginable for shipbuilding. Game and wildfowl were so abundant in Florida that even a very unskilled hunter found no trouble in keeping himself well fed. On the whole, Peter *had* told the truth—to serious listeners.

Carefully, the *Hope's* Captain restored a fine new backstaff and kenning glass to their cases. So this bleak-appearing island was the paradise Peter had visited nearly three years ago—or had it been Woccocan? For the moment Wyatt took small stock in Roanoke Island, so poor-looking with scrubby pines and lonely dunes sparsely crowned by clumps of beach grass and sea grapes.

Across the sound and well below that point in the inlet at which the armada was anchoring could be seen great numbers of canoes paddling for the mainland. Apparently the Golden Admiral's arrival had put to flight a most formidable array of Naturals.

Diverting his attention to the fort, Wyatt noted how a gate now stood ajar. Through it a straggling line of men were heading down to the water's edge and shouting something. By cupping a hand to his ear, he heard: "Food! For the love of God fetch us food!"

Following an example set by young Thomas Drake of the *Francis*, Wyatt ordered broken out a box of sea biscuit, some yams and a chest of smoked beef. In a burst of generosity he even sacrificed a jug of amontillado from his private store.

By the dozen boats from the squadron began putting out from various men-of-war and pulling towards that pitiful group capering weakly along the shore.

A broad grin spread over Tompkins' ruddy features once the *Hope's* cockboat drew near to the island's broad silver-grey beach. "Icod! Those rascals hev women among 'em, by God. Look, Cap'n. Them is Natural women or I'm a monkey."

Wyatt, his body swaying to the rhythm of the oars, squinted in the sunlight. What Tompkins said was so. Waiting on the strand were almost as many half-naked, dark-skinned creatures as there were tattered scarecrows.

The colonists could not wait for the boats to be beached but went floundering out, waist-deep, to meet them. Soon the beach was thronged by Englishmen clapping one another on the back, laughing and greedily gulping drafts of wine and beer. The captive women congregated shyly to one side, pointing, giggling and staring in wonder upon these hale, red-faced fellows so different from their gaunt and pallid masters. News, queries about home, and boasts from the newcomers filled the air. Was war with Spain yet a fact?

Once his cockboat's keel grated on the sand, Wyatt sprang ashore to gaze with incredulous amazement upon these emaciated scarecrows. Surely *these* men could not have found Virginia to be the paradise Peter Hopton had depicted. Suddenly he stiffened. That great frame, that tawny mane and yellow beard! So thin had his cousin grown he could not be sure that indeed Peter Hopton stood yonder until he raised a delighted shout and came running forward. A moment later the two were hugging each other, volleying questions without waiting for answers.

Later, while Jane and Jill, obviously much impressed by Wyatt's coppery complexion, dark red hair and short beard of the same colour, giggled over the stew-pot, well filled for a change, Peter forced a rueful grin.

"For true, Harry, ye were born under a lucky star," he declared. "After all you suffered at home 'tis only meet that ye should command so trig a little barque."

"She's handy," Wyatt admitted, "and were she twenty tons bigger I'd be loath to change from her. But she's too small for my purpose." He then went on to describe his cargo of cannon and the trade goods and furniture. Later still, when the amontillado had commenced to work, he even mentioned a certain little coffer of gems and gold coin locked beneath his bunk.

"Despite everything, I'll not wholly envy ye," Peter laughed. "Not so long as I've my little playmates here." He smacked first Jane and then Jill on their buttocks and winked. "Harry, yer welcome to either, you, or any good friend. Ye'll have had a long celibate spell I'm thinking."

Wyatt directed a quick glance at the *Bonaventure* faithfully mirrored by the glassy waters of the sound.

"I would my good friend Hubert Coffyn, from Devonshire, were able to come ashore. You would fancy him, Peter."

"What ails him? Did he take a buboe at Cartegana?"

The *Hope's* red-haired master shook his head. "Nay. The poor devil's once again in the grip of a fever which has much afflicted us since we tarried in the Cape Verde Islands. 'Tis a mysterious malady which, after having seemed to quit a victim, returns from time to time. Not a few of our sick have lost their reason, but Hubert, praise God, remains clear-headed."

Peter laughed. "It's a vast shame because, mayhap, he would enjoy the company of these my dusky handmaidens."

Wyatt hesitated. During the sieges and in-takings it had proved more than difficult not to fall in with the almost universal practice of bedding a likely wench or two. He hadn't yielded, despite coarse conjecture on his reasons. There was Kate—Kate to whom he certainly wished to return without the Spanish pox and possibly a half-brother or sister to their child. If all had gone well her baby must now be about three months of age, he calculated.

A fierce impatience seized him for it was now known that, having discharged his promise to look in upon Walter Raleigh's colony, Sir Francis Drake intended to shape a course for home.

Trailing pinnaces and small boats behind them—even at sea such were seldom hoisted inboard—the squadron for three days swung to their anchors in the roadstead of Roanoke Inlet. Drake fancied neither this anchorage nor the situation Sir Richard Grenville had chosen for Raleigh's colony. Too many mudbanks and sandbars criss-crossed the inlet, and should a gale come whooping in from the south-west why, his ships must either drag ashore on Roanoke Island or fight their way out to sea through a very narrow inlet—no mean task for ships rigged as were his.

The weather continued fair, however, and the colonists waxed fat again and their Councilmen recaptured enough energy to bicker fiercely over two courses left open to them by Drake. He would, the Golden Admiral declared, provide Governor Lane's people with all manner of supplies, ammunition and enough heavy cannon to build a proper fort. Further, he would even detach for their use two of his small vessels on which Lane's men might conduct further explorations of the coast.

On the other hand, the colonists were welcome to come aboard and abandon this unchancy settlement. A fresh start, Drake pointed out, might well be made at some more auspicious place.

The usual stormy scenes in council became re-enacted but, in this instance, Governor Lane's views prevailed, probably because Drake was here and ready to enforce the Queen's authority. In the end the colonists voted to stay where they were, if reinforced by volunteers.

Accordingly, the *Francis* and Wyatt's *Hope* were designated to remain with the colonists until Grenville's promised supply ship put in an appearance. Guns stowed in the *Hope's* forehold, Drake pointed out, should serve to defend the island. He agreed also to leave for their service a number of trained gunners.

With a sinking heart Henry Wyatt acknowledged orders placing him and his barque at the disposal of this querulous Governor who, so far, had made such a miserable botch of things. Now he could scarce hope to be reunited with Kate before the mid-autumn.

Of late he had suffered anxiety over her means of livelihood. Certainly that scanty sum he had left with her must have become exhausted. Suppose his creditors had become impatient, as certainly they would when Drake had returned without him? Suppose Nick Spencer demanded his money—what then would chance? A shiver ran down his back at the answer—debtors' prison. There was nothing for it, however, but to obey Drake's orders, so the *Hope* and the *Francis* were towed close inshore with hatches unbattened that unloading might commence in the morning.

To celebrate the colonists' decision to remain steadfast, an almost elaborate repast was tendered the Admiral-General in the Council House. After the feasting on stores fetched from Florida, ballad after ballad was bellowed out, and liquid loot from Santiago and cities along the Caribbean was downed in such Homeric quantities that full many a Captain had to be overpowered or assisted, reeling, down to the beach.

In fact, Captain Robert Cross of the *Bond* swore he would spend the night ashore, and Captain Jonas of the *Primrose* by mistake sent his own boat back to the ship without him. In a befuddled rage he then commandeered Wyatt's cockboat while that individual was still exchanging gossip with his cousin.

What orders Jonas, a very senior Captain in the armada, had flung at the *Hope's* boat crew Wyatt could not ascertain, but when a full hour had passed and there was still no sign of his cockboat's return, he yielded to Peter Hopton's bibulous insistence that he share his hut. Wyatt accepted only reluctantly, being far too alive to certain temptations offered by those eager and copper-brown bodies so intimately near; especially with all this málaga and amontillado resting comfortable and warm beneath his belt.

Towards dawn a violent wind suddenly sprang up and commenced to tear at the slab roofs of the huts. It whistled through chinks in the logs and sent fine sand to dancing in miniature whirlwinds along the beach. Momentarily, the gale's velocity mounted; lashing over from the mainland, it screamed over the waters of the sound and caused Drake's ships lying quite unprotected in the open roadstead to begin to wallow like so many pigs roused unwillingly from slumber.

Scarcely twenty minutes after those first uneasy puffs had set low-flying clouds to scudding over the mastheads, a full gale was blowing and the "weigh anchor" signal had appeared on the *Bonaventure's* signal halyard. In a frenzy of anxiety Henry Wyatt ran barefooted along the shore, shouted and waved at the *Hope*, but at the same time was aware that he couldn't possibly make himself heard aboard his command.

All through the fleet white puffs of storm sails were breaking out in an almighty hurry. Not a man out there but realized that it would be touch and go whether their high-sided craft could be manœuvred through the inlet.

Sick at heart, Wyatt stood in the surf and, through the flying spindrift, watched his men lie out on the *Hope's* yards. He could distinguish Henderson's gaunt, wind-whipped figure clinging to the mizzen shrouds as he got the barque under way. Because the *Hope* lay so close inshore, Wyatt hoped his mate would realize there was no time for heaving in an anchor. Henderson did and, to Wyatt's vast relief, rigged a buoy and slipped his cable. In a frenzy of anxiety the *Hope's* Captain watched his barque's lateen sail snap full, then, gradually, her hull commenced to cruise parallel to the shoreline. Yellow hair streaming wildly, Peter raced up, buttoning a jacket about him.

"God above!" he yelled over the tumult and shielding his eyes from flying sand. "We've ne'er seen anything the like o' this afore."

"It'll be a near thing, a near thing, by God." Through eyes nearly blinded by wind-caused tears, Wyatt strained to judge the leeway his vessel was making. Would she be able to weather a treacherous sandspit he knew to lie but a quarter mile distant? The *Hope* must be considered as good as lost if she grounded.

By now all the ships, big and small, were scrambling down the inlet with flags standing out as if starched and sails stiff under the wind. Spray flew high over their rails as the shallow waters of the sound became tormented into short, muddy, frothing billows.

Spindrift quickly dimmed the outlines of lesser ships and soon even the largest galleons became lost amid blinding rain which descended like a waterfall. All that Wyatt and Peter could see was that at least a majority of Drake's ships had weathered the sand bar and now were plunging, reeling out into the Atlantic.

Heart in mouth, Wyatt pelted along the beach, shielding his eyes and watching the awful struggles of his little barque to stay afloat and away from the spouting sand bars. He emitted a ringing shout of delight when, with only a few yards to spare, the *Hope* cleared a silvery welter of waves marking the last hazard and, under straining topsails, stood out to sea. After all, the *Hope* represented the difference between a return to abject poverty and the foundation of a modest fortune. His barque looked dreadfully, pitiably small amidst this fury of winds and waters, Wyatt reflected, but surely Master's Mate Henderson would fetch her safely back once the storm had abated.

CHAPTER IX

MAN PROPOSES

DURING three whole days and nights the colonists and such elements of Drake's armada as had been caught ashore posted lookouts who strained their eyes seawards. It was only towards sundown on the afternoon of June the thirteenth that a topsail glimmered above an ocean once more smiling and of a brilliant blue beyond a grey margin of silt caused by storm-stained fresh water.

One by one, various ships came limping back—the *Tiger* minus a foremast, the *Galleon Leicester* showing only the jagged stump of her mizzen above her bulwarks. Hardly a vessel in the squadron but in some fashion betrayed the ordeal she had survived.

On the fifth day all vessels had been accounted for save the *Francis*, Captain James Erizo's *White Lion*—and the *Hope*. It seemed as if an invisible band had become fixed about Wyatt's chest, a band which grew tighter and tighter as the uneasy hours laboured by.

Patiently, Henry Wyatt, together with his cousin, patrolled the beach, shouting or rowing out to each new arrival in hopes of learning what had chanced with his barque. No one seemed to know anything, which was not surprising since the great gale had scattered Drake's ships far up and down the coast of that land named for the Virgin Queen.

"She's bound to turn up," Peter reassured. "Ye say yer man Henderson's capable?"

"None better. He'd commanded a ship of his own afore the Spaniards took her from him."

"Then keep up hope, Harry. She'll turn up. Now let's go see what Jane and Jill have stole for our supper. I'm in the mood for a jolly little tumble tonight."

Even as he fell silent a shout of "Sail ho!" arose from the lookout tower. Sure enough, the setting sun revealed a tiny speck of white making for Roanoke Inlet. After a little it became apparent that not the *Hope*, but the *White Lion* had been sighted. The little galleon was limping along under jury masts and was steered by a great oar because no trace of her rudder was to be seen.

Captain Erizo, although nursing a broken arm in a sling, had himself rowed directly for the flagship, aboard which Drake was pacing like an angry terrier. Of no small concern to him was the fact that still missing was the *Francis*—his private venture and commanded by his own brother.

In an agony of suspense Wyatt loitered near the gangway, and watched Captain Erizo hoisted inboard in a bosun's chair since his crippled arm prevented his customary use of the *Bonaventure's* rope ladder. As he stumped aft everyone noticed how sunken and bloodshot were Erizo's eyes and that a great blue-brown bruise showed on his forehead. When Wyatt stepped forward and plucked at his sleeve, the *White Lion's* Captain turned a haggard countenance.

"For God's love—what of my barque?"

"I've bad news for ye, Wyatt," he said. "The *Hope* was fighting main hard on a northerly course when the hugest billow I've seen broke over her. She capsized, filled, and sank like a stone."

Although the other Captains crowded about murmuring words of comfort and encouragement, Wyatt could only stand dazedly clutching a shroud and staring out over Roanoke Inlet.

"The *Hope's* lost," he muttered. "The Queen's great cannons—all my goods. Oh, Peter, what have I done to deserve this? Poor Kate—poor babe. What can I do now?"

He allowed Peter to row him ashore, grimly silent; his despairing, dark blue eyes fixed themselves on dirty water sloshing about in the gig's bottom.

The loss of their supply ships *Hope* and *Francis* proved too much even for the most determined of the colonists. So, in due course, Ralph Lane set his jaw and signed a decree directing Raleigh's men to destroy their settlement by fire and then board the Golden Admiral's ships for passage homewards.

Book Four

LA EMPRESA

CHAPTER I

PORTSMOUTH

ALTHOUGH pennons, St. George flags, and personal banners streamed bravely from every masthead in Drake's armada and his guns roared salutes to Portsmouth Castle, although multitudes of small craft came sailing out to cheer the victors the Admiral's leathery features betrayed no trace of elation. In fact that doughty individual was not in the least anticipating a certain conference inevitably to be held with Lord Burghley and Sir Francis Walsingham.

Of course he had more than bettered his instructions "to annoy the King of Spain", had temporarily wrecked Spain's colonial economy and had shattered forever the myth of Spanish invincibility. Still, the unpalatable fact remained that, from a financial point of view, this cruise had proved the most disappointing of any he had undertaken since his very earliest days at sea.

Drake calculated that he and his backers stood to lose at least three shillings in each pound invested, despite those carefully guarded gold ingots carried aboard H.M.S. *Aid* and *Bonaventure*.

Today Drake had donned his favourite blue-and-gold doublet and had clasped about his short, thick neck a magnificent collar of rubies, diamonds and emeralds whilst tear-shaped rubies swung below his ears and on the tang of his rapier's hilt glowed the vivid green fires of a massive emerald.

Yes. He must brace himself for stormy interviews and some caustic comments at Whitehall. For example, why had he failed to complete his mission by the capturing of Panama City and its fabulous wealth? More pertinent still, why had Havana, that fortress which lay squarely athwart the Plate Fleet's homeward route, remained unattacked? And was not Nombre de Dios yet welcoming those jingling mule trains of treasure which, twice a year, arrived from Panama City? What were the reasons for not at least fortifying and holding Cartagena?

Could the Queen and her Councillors be made to understand that the keen edge of his weapon had been irreparably blunted by that fever taken in the Cape Verde Islands? They must be made to understand that, by the time his armada had won Cartagena, less than half of Carleill's troops and his own mariners remained alive, and that many of these were unfit to man the rigging or to stand against the enemy.

Mechanically, Drake watched the Lord Mayor of Portsmouth's pinnace, brave with bunting and welcoming flags, put out from a jetty and head for the *Bonaventure* now furling sail and rounding up to her anchors.

Of justice at Walsingham's hands Drake felt confident; surely the astute statesman would perceive that, in a non-commercial way, his expedition had been no failure? After all, had he not taken and sacked four Spanish towns, and, more important, stripped two of the principal cities in New Spain of all means of defence? Had he not defeated regular Spanish infantry and flouted the King of Spain in his own country?

Despite the loss of the *Hope*, he was fetching home two hundred and forty heavy cannon, the majority of them of brass. This captured ordnance should prove most useful in arming those swift fighting galleons John Hawkins had designed and which now were taking shape in the shipyards of such master builders as Peter Pett of Deptford, John Apslyn, Richard Merrit and others.

He was not unaware that the hurt he had caused Spain was being discussed from the frozen wastes of the White Sea to the steaming jungles of Africa and Spice Islands beyond, and that now the name of Francis Drake was ringing like a trumpet-call throughout the known world.

Even Drake failed to appreciate the full extent of the fear inspired in Philip's sailors by the mere mention of his name. It was reported that when *el Draque* was known to be in the vicinity, the entire crews of Spanish ships were given to deserting. It was solemnly averred by the Spanish that since no true Christian could so overcome the forces of Spain, *el Draque* certainly must have sold his soul to the Devil. He was reported to keep in his cabin a magic mirror which revealed the whereabouts of Spanish ships, the number of their crews and all that happened aboard of them; also he had discovered the power of loosing gales, or of ordering calms to suit his purpose.

Well might Lord Burghley write, "Truly, Sir Francis Drake is a fearful man to the King of Spain." Yet, in what light would he appear before those cold-eyed merchants in the City of London and to the officers of Her Majesty's Treasury? Of course, the fact that he, Frobisher, Carleill and other leaders of the expedition had taken nothing out of the common fund should stand in their favour and incline Her Majesty to grumble less over the comparatively lean pickings he was bringing back this year, but there was no guarantee that his ever-capricious Queen might not incontinently order him to the Tower.

It was therefore with silent misgivings and wearing a taut smile that the Admiral-General greeted His Worship the Lord Mayor of Portsmouth. That worthy appeared, red-faced, sweating and adorned with a heavy golden chain of office and a heavy, sable-lined black cloak.

Suddenly Drake's smile became genuine. Into his agile brain a wonderful new scheme had sprung full-fledged, one which this time certainly would pour vast riches into the ever-yawning coffers of Her Gracious Majesty. This scheme was far more audacious than that one from which he was just returning, yet it was entirely possible of being put into execution. The question was, would he be allowed to pursue it?

CHAPTER II

REUNION

DURING this past year of 1586 the City of London had grown faster than in any five years previous. The success of various ventures to the Russias, to Africa, to the Levant and to German ports had enabled lucky or successful merchants, mariners and speculators to build a multitude of new homes, each according to his taste.

The Widow Foster's ramshackle little cottage therefore no longer was removed by a brisk half an hour's walk beyond the new borough of St. Katherine's and the nearest house. New homes, modest ones to be sure, now stood above the strand less than one hundred yards distant. There they were afforded a fine view of steaming mudbanks and miscellaneous rotting hulls, the ribs of which shone as stark against a sunset as the bodies of felons hanging, stiff and sun-dried, from the gibbets at Wapping.

The afternoon was sultry, humid, and smoke from the chimney-pots of London, thickened now by a new fuel called "sea coal", imported from Newcastle, hung low over the glassy, fawn-coloured Thames, so little Henrietta Wyatt wailed persistently. At length, Kate Wyatt interrupted the laundry over which she was toiling and flicked suds from her fingers then picked up the infant.

Again she was dripping wet, so, sighing, Kate commenced the oft-repeated task of changing her baby's ragged and stained swaddling clothes. Because of this humid heat, such of the Foster children who had remained at home were quiet, for which Kate was infinitely thankful. An hour ago the Widow Foster had tramped off to market, a shapeless chip basket dangling from one powerful red arm.

"Oh, do be good!" Kate implored the whimpering infant. "I know 'tis hot as well as you, poor lamb, and better."

Using the back of a hand she pushed a limp strand of white-gold hair up the damp contour of her forehead. Beyond a doubt her advanced pregnancy caused her unduly to notice the humidity. How she yearned just to repose quietly on a pallet bought shortly after the handsome and gallant Honourable Francis Dexter at last had ridden off to the wars.

She supposed that, according to his lights, the heir to Dexter Hall had acted with becoming decency and consideration. A day before his half-troop of horse had mustered on a green behind the manor house, he had cheerfully bestowed upon the mistress he was about to dismiss a purse containing all of five pounds in coins of various denominations and mintage. But he also had bestowed, which was more precious by far, that sheet of foolscap upon which was recorded the fact that Henry Wyatt and his wife, Katherine, admitted indebtedness to Nicholas Spencer, who, in the presence of a notary, had transferred said testimony of debt to the Honourable Francis Dexter.

For once genuine tenderness had supplanted ill-concealed lust in Francis Dexter's smile. "By all God's shining angels, Kate Wyatt, yer a rare fine wench," he'd said. "It pleases me that my bastard shall have so fine and lovely a mother." He had swung up into his saddle, clothed in yellow velvet. "Call on me for his or her care an you will. I swear I'll not deny the by-blow's mine."

Kate had stared up at him—young, handsome and dark, astride a grey battle-trained charger which could rise on its hind legs and strike out with its front hooves as shrewdly as any boxer.

"Go," she said in a low voice tinged by a bitterness and hatred too pointed for expression. "Go, and when your enemies surround you, when your arm fails and Death looks you in the face, remember that my curse lies heavy on your head. Remember, also, an you are spared in battle, that Henry Wyatt some day will lay your arrogance low."

The Honourable Francis had turned a little pale but while gathering his reins he had managed a strident laugh. "Gramercy for your fine farewell, Mistress Wyatt," he had cried, had struck spurs to his charger and had gone galloping off, leaving her standing there for all the world like a pregnant, unwanted whore, clutching his purse and Harry's note of indebtedness.

All this came to mind while Kate was securing fresh swaddling clothes about Henrietta's tiny hips. Anxiously, she inspected the infant's malformed foot. Praise God, it did appear somewhat straighter. Perchance patient rubbing and stroking might restore it to its originally intended position?

"Come, you sweet little monster," she cried gently and plucking up the baby, carried her over to the shade of a pear tree where a chance zephyr from off the Thames possibly might reduce a rash staining that tender little neck and limbs. She was placing the infant in a rush basket doing duty as a cradle when a shadow cast on to the grass beside her caused her to wheel and gaze upwards in alarm—nowadays London Pool had grown so busy all manner of men came tramping towards the city in search of employment aboard Her Majesty's ships or in the Thames Side's busy dockyards.

Instinctively Kate clutched Henrietta to her and the infant commenced to squall.

"Harry!" There he stood, thinner, more sinewy than of yore, but the same steady light shone in his dark blue eyes, his hair was the same deep chestnut-red that had thrilled her in St. Neots.

"Kate! My own sweet Kate!" cried he and flung wide his arms.

His radiant expression faded when Kate shrank back from his embrace as from a beggar hideously afflicted by some disease. "Oh, Harry, Harry!" she wailed. "Is it indeed you?"

"Of course. Why do you draw back? Is this not *our* child you hold?"

"Aye, *she* is, but—but——"

His glad look faded when he noticed how her swollen abdomen lifted an apron of patched brown kersey.

He started forward again. "Buss me, my darling, 'tis been so cruel long since——" Surely she had merely gained weight? But again she retreated until the branches of the pear tree barred her further retreat.

"Kate," his voice assumed a taut, harsh quality. "Kate, why do you stare on me so strange? Why do you draw back?"

"Oh, H-Harry! 'Tis that no—no longer is it meet that I rest within your arms or f-feel your d-dear mouth on m-mine."

He dropped a small vellum-bound chest he had been carrying, then swept mother and screaming child into his embrace.

"Look at me, Kate!" he commanded and held her tight until at last her clear grey eyes wavered up to meet his. "Before you utter a single word know that I am as certain as we sometime shall stand before God's Throne, that whatever ill has chanced it has been without your will or for your pleasure."

Almost roughly he took the yowling infant from her, gazed raptly upon those tiny, suffused features and inquired gravely, "What do you call her?"

"Your d-daughter's name is H-Henrietta."

Quickly Wyatt placed the baby in her basket then, oblivious to ribald comments from a party of mariners travelling towards the river, he pressed his wife close, very close. At length he released Kate, breathless, radiant and at the same time miserable.

He nodded towards the ancient, crumbling cottage. "Is this where you have bided?"

"Aye, Harry, for above a year. But let us not enter—Polly Foster's children will be awakening. Oh, Harry, Harry, how very strong you have become!"

"—And you more beautiful than I ever dreamed you could."

They settled upon a grassy bank then, with averted eyes and halting speech, Kate told him about her desperate case, described how the Honourable Francis Dexter had made profit from her distress. It was entirely like Harry, she thought, that he spoke no vows of vengeance; all the same about his mouth appeared unfamiliar, cruel lines.

At length he said: "Kate, my own true spouse, pray picture me this fellow's mien and bearing even unto the last detail. I would not willingly kill the wrong man."

"Promise you'll not attack him," she implored in a frenzy of apprehension. "What is done, is done. The Honourable Francis is deadly with the sword and his father, Lord Anthony Dexter, is a favourite at Court. He'd have you murdered in a trice an he suspected your intent."

Wyatt's ruddy features went darker than ever; he spat rather than spoke his next words. "Do not fear. I've learned no longer blindly to thrust my head into a snare. When this dog Dexter dies only he will know that I have sped him to his reward in Hell."

Gradually their unhappiness faded under the warmth of their joy at being reunited. They lingered under the pear tree, he feasting his eyes on his daughter's tiny features.

"Thank Fortune," Kate assured herself, "he knows so little concerning babies that he'll not even notice her twisted foot." The sun sank lower and presently red-and-white cattle commenced to drift along tracks lacing the countryside, the while he described the cruise, the Golden Admiral's guile, charm and original methods of attack. In vivid colours he painted for her his friend Hubert Coffyn and his discovery of Peter among the colonists of Roanoke. He made her see the sack of San Domingo and of Cartagena; the capture of St. Augustine and finally the rescue of those starving wretches on Roanoke Island.

When at length he came to his account of the great gale, Wyatt's sun-darkened features contracted and his voice grew harsh. The words came slowly, awkwardly, when he admitted loss of the *Hope* with all hands—and his hard-come-by fortune.

" 'Twas no fault of yours, my heart, so don't grieve on my account. We will manage, whatever lies in store for us." Kate squeezed his hand and looked steadily up into his dark, wide-set eyes. He kissed her gratefully, almost reverently. "Nonetheless, my sweet darling, this is a vastly different home-coming than I had envisaged. I've no necklace to deck your pretty throat nor yards of silk or brocade to fashion you a new kirtle. Some further time must pass before I can give you these or summon a builder to raise our home."

"Nay, Harry, you have brought home a treasure greater than all in Mexico or Peru," Kate whispered, her mouth close to his ear. "The only truly precious thing in the world for me is your own steadfast self."

They remained silent awhile, watching a big galleass come pulling up the Thames under a cloud of hungry gulls.

"Perhaps, sweet Kate, I overtell misfortune," he smiled. "Indeed we are not quite penniless, and can buy a modest cottage." At her inquiring glance he amplified, "No wonder Sir Francis has ever been beloved of his men."

"And why?"

" 'Twas he who set an example by forgoing his just share of what treasure was won by our armada. I've near twenty-five pounds o' the purest gold in this casket. As I've said, 'twill buy us at least our own roof-tree."

"A home of our own!" Kate's eyes glistened. "Oh, Harry, that would be paradise!" Hurriedly she amended. "Not that Polly Foster has been aught but generous and kind beyond belief."

"The Widow Foster shall be recompensed, first of all, since Nicholas Spencer——" He flushed and was unhappily aware that his gaze had sought the shameful bulge beneath Kate's apron. "You say poor Nick has fallen upon hard times?"

"Aye, Polly says Master Spencer has taken employment as a mere sailmaker in Master Petts' shipyard across the river."

"Has he indeed?" Wyatt's interest quickened. "Then, like as not, he'll speak for me."

Kate glanced up like some warbler startled by an unexpected movement. "Because of me you'll not give up the sea?"

He broke into a quick laugh. "Lord love you, no, Kate; during our expedition I arrived at certain notions concerning the building of ships which must sail on long voyages and fight far from England. I have even listened to our Admiral express opinions anent how a warship should be armed and intended."

"Oh, Harry, Harry! 'Twill be wonderful beyond imagination for a while to see you every day." Her pale hair glistened in the sunset and she pressed close to that lean body of which she had only dreamed for so long. "And let us move across the river. Over in Horsey's Down or Southwark none need ever know that this"—contemptuously she flicked her abdomen—"is a weed, and none of your good seed."

CHAPTER III

IN FOTHERINGAY CASTLE

TO ELIZABETH and her realm of England, the autumn of 1586 brought increasingly ominous clouds upon the horizon. Everywhere on the Continent, saving the Low Countries, there was talk of a great crusade to be launched by Princes of the Counter-Reformation. In Spain, Portugal and the two Sicilys ships of war were being completed, all because Sir Francis Drake's magic mirror for once had failed him and, somehow, he had missed intercepting the *flota* of that year off Cuba while he was doubling back from Matanzas to Cabo Antonio.

Worse still, came indisputable intelligence that Philip of Spain and the Catholic Powers had decreed Elizabeth's death. This was only logical on their part since Anne Boleyn's daughter constituted a principal prop to the Protestant cause and her realm had become a rally-point for hard-pressed Dutch and French Huguenots.

In taverns, especially along the sea coast, even common men muttered darkly that something must be done about Mary of Scotland since certainly she would claim the Crown of England were Catholic power to be restored. Why should this brazen hussy who had had at least two husbands, and God knew how many lovers, continue to enjoy a pleasant confinement at Chartley? After the exposure of Anthony Babington's plot in which it was proved that not only King Philip but the Pope himself had offered rewards for the Queen's assassination public fury broke into a flame.

Despite everything, Elizabeth herself continued ready to ignore her danger and steadfastly had refused even to consider the signature of a death warrant for her incorrigibly intriguing cousin. As was her custom the Queen vacillated between the advice of over-prudent Burghley and Walsingham's exasperated belligerency. Worse still, Elizabeth abruptly stopped the pay of her troops defending the Protestant Cause in the Netherlands.

In vain did her Lord High Admiral, Lord Howard of Effingham, expostulate that this was akin to assuring the loss of her throne. Nor did it feed the public's confidence that Drake had been deemed of too inferior birth to be named Commander-in-Chief over the Queen's Navy—for all that ten thousand men knew of the Golden Admiral's exploits to one who had ever heard of Lord Howard of Effingham. His fame was to come later—but not much later.

Returning sea captains spoke anxiously concerning tremendous activity reported in Lisbon, in Cádiz, Bayona and other Spanish ports. In shipyards yonder, thousands of slaves—Moorish, Turkish and Protestant—were worked until they fell fainting at their toil.

Grim uncertainty ruled the English mind. Why wouldn't Gloriana face up to these dangers? To all but hopeless noddies it was plain as a pikestaff that soon she and England would be forced to fight for their very existence against the well-nigh overwhelming might of Philip. Now that England's friend Anjou was no more, the Duke of Guise was adding, albeit covertly, the wealth and power of France to the forces of the Counter-Reformation.

All along the southern and eastern coasts of England various noblemen, at their own expense, took to building watch-towers, to drilling trained bands and to teaching their heavy-handed farm boys how to use a pike in addition to a manure fork. Once again bows twanged and arrows flew at century-old archery butts while ranges for the use of firelocks appeared on all sides. Granted time, the mere English declared they could stand off the enemy. But would that time be granted? There seemed no doubt but that the *Empresa de Inglaterra* —as the Spaniards termed their projected invasion—must surely be launched by midsummer, before even a half of the Queen's new ships were anywhere near completion.

Optimists, however, found some comfort in the existence of a handful of rakish and handy men-of-war now hoisting in their ordnance. Recently completed in the Royal dockyards lay the great ships *Lion*, *Dreadnought* and *Rainbow*, high charged and equipped with cageworks. Elsewhere four flush-decked galleons, *Roebuck*, *Golden Noble*, *Merchant Royal* and the *Barque Hopewell*, all built by the City of London, were having masts stepped and shrouds rigged.

"They're main fine vessels," Henry Wyatt informed his wife as they travelled the road leading from John Adye's shipyard at Erith. "But they're all too few."

"How fares work on the *Revenge*?"

"Slowly, curs'd slow," Wyatt grunted and, setting a leather-covered arm about Kate's shoulders—her waist had become enormously distended—helped her to breast a gentle slope leading up to their solid, ivy-grown stone cottage near Battle Bridge.

"But why goes the building so lame and halt?" panted Kate and mopped a beading of perspiration from her short upper lip.

"For lack of money. We've not half sufficient shipwrights, master builders or even common carpenters," he explained bitterly. "Still, once the *Revenge* floats, poppet, she'll be a wondrous sight to behold. Nowhere else have I beheld such strength so aptly combined with the promise of speed."

Kate smiled to herself while Wyatt rattled on and on, employing a jargon of nautical terms quite as incomprehensible to her as a Turk's prayer. It didn't matter in the least. Harry was happy. At long last he seemed to have conquered that bitterness engendered by his loss of two commands.

She hoped also he had succeeded in forgetting that this child which would soon be born must be but as a cuckoo in the Wyatt nest. In vain she tried to pray that Francis Dexter's bastard might be born dead or perish in the always critical struggle to enter the world; yet, somehow, she could not. Ironically this baby had grown larger and had proved immensely more active than had Henrietta at a similar stage.

"Is it true," she inquired presently, "that yet another conspiracy against Her Majesty has been unearthed?"

"By the gullet of God, yes! But two days ago an armed assassin was caught behind an arras. Under question he confessed that his master had paid him in Florentine ducats."

"Surely this time, Harry, Her Majesty at last will scotch that pretty French viper she has warmed so long in her bosom?"

"Aye, since the safety of England lies at hazard."

Just before they passed behind a row of ragged privet bushes before their cottage Wyatt could not forbear a final glance over his shoulder towards those distant ways upon which the huge *Ark Raleigh* was taking shape with such distressing deliberation. Upon completion yonder great ship would be the tallest man-of-war thus far built for the new navy.

Beyond her lay silhouetted keels and ribs to show where the *Elizabeth Drake* and the *Elizabeth Jonas* would sometime be shaped. Would they ever be completed in time to attack the Marquis of Santa Cruz's towering carracks? It seemed unlikely, thought the red-haired apprentice shipwright.

On the very same day that Kate Wyatt, in pain and shame, gave birth to a lusty, black-haired infant, a rider spurred out of Whitehall Palace courtyard as if the Devil were in pursuit. Soon his gait became so headlong that his escort commenced to fall behind on a wild ride towards grim and lonely Fotheringay Castle whither that Prisoner of State called Mary of Scotland had been transferred on September the twenty-fifth. There a Royal Commission had tried Mary Tudor and beyond the shadow of doubt had found her guilty of plotting against her regal cousin's life.

The horseman was Secretary Beale and he bloodied his spurs for fear that Her Majesty the Queen might discover last-minute compunctions—as in fact Elizabeth did—and dispatch a galloper to recall the Scottish Queen's death warrant, for all that it had been duly signed and sealed. When well out into the country and pounding across lovely hills and dales of Bedfordshire and Huntingdonshire, Master Beale rode slower, waited for his escort to catch up.

Into the hands of hatchet-faced Sir Amyas Paulet, Mr. Beale, hollow-eyed and at the point of complete exhaustion, delivered that brief strip of parchment which would shape the destinies of Europe and the world, too, for centuries to come.

The Governor of Fotheringay Castle then set about his duties as swiftly as had Mr. Beale. When, next morning, life-loving, frivolous and pathetic Mary, former Queen of France and still Queen of Scotland, bent over the block, it was the executioner who hacked her still pretty, but greying, head from her shoulders. With that blow war with Spain became assured.

Of all these significant matters Kate and Henry Wyatt remained for some time completely unaware, being much too occupied with personal considerations. The wise woman who attended Kate found it passing strange that a young couple could gaze upon a fine and lusty young son with such little satisfaction.

CHAPTER IV

PORTLEDGE MANOR

HUBERT COFFYN lingered before a heavy, nail-studded door leading into what once had been the manor's truly imposing armoury. Beyond it he recognized Peter Hopton's deep tones. He was saying: "You'll never spy another land so fine as this America. Why, man alive, yonder, pearls are to be plucked from every oyster and even the meanest among the Naturals there use chamber-pots of the purest gold and sleep on furs finer than ye'll find on any alderman's cape!"

Hubert hesitated, grinning broadly as the customary chorus of "Ohs" and "Ahs" arose from such yeomen, tenants and independent farmers as had come to take military instruction with Sir Robert Coffyn's trained band and who had lingered eagerly to lap up Peter's fables concerning Virginia.

"And if ye crave warm, submissive and willing wenches," the story-teller winked broadly, "why, me lads, out there you'll have your pick of the savage king's daughters. These lasses are comely enough of feature and well formed, too, which ye can readily tell since they seldom wear so much as a clout about their thighs."

"Coom, man," a voice broke in in broad Devonshire, " 'e wouldn't fun us, would 'e?"

"As God's my judge," thundered Peter, "I'd not lie to ye by so much as a hair's breadth."

An intelligent-appearing fellow with the look of a clerk about him then spoke up. "But where be all these riches ye won, Master Hopton? Ye be but a simple Master Gunner today."

Through the half-opened door Hubert glimpsed Peter's yellow head shaking sadly. "Eh, lad, ye wring my heart wi' such doubts. My loot won at San Domingo and Cartagena as well as the riches I took during the storming of King Chapunka's castle were lost, lost when the *Barque Hope* was overwhelmed in a great sea off the coast of Virginia. With it sank an even greater fortune won by my good friend and cousin, Henry Wyatt."

Peter chanced to glance up, saw Coffyn and grinned impudently. "Squire Coffyn here will bear me out. Was not the *Hope* indeed lost off the Isle of Roanoke?"

Hubert nodded and forbore to mention that Peter had fetched

safely home whatever valuables he might have accumulated—though he still bemoaned his lot for having to part with his Monocan handmaidens.

"'Tis well all you men are here," announced young Coffyn, running level, light brown eyes over the heads and broad reddish faces of the countrymen standing awkwardly about his armoury. At first glance one noted that Portledge Manor's nearly ruinous windows were glassless, as they had been for nigh on a quarter of a century. Daylight beat through the armoury's roof here and there, so poverty-stricken had Sir Robert become.

"I have news fresh arrived brought over from Bideford," he announced in ringing tones. "An expedition is to venture against the Papists in Spain."

"Who's to command—Grenville? Howard? Frobisher?" a chorus of voices asked.

"Nay, who but our fellow Devonshireman—our ever-glorious Sir Francis Drake!"

Even Peter Hopton was astonished at the wild fervour of the shout that followed. The countrymen crowded about Hubert, respectfully begging to learn about Drake's terms of 'listment. What would be the share of a common soldier or a younker? What compensation might be expected for loss of sight or limbs?

"As to that last," Coffyn told them, "you'll not get a farthing by way of compensation; I find it only fair to warn that every seaport in England fairly crawls with armless and legless beggars who once served in the Queen's ships."

"Well enough for mariners," called one gap-toothed young yokel, "but me, I'll go for a soldier. Is not their lot summat better, Yer Honour?"

"That it is not!" Hopton promptly supplied. "And ye'll do a share o' the sailing work to boot."

A signet ring flashed briefly on young Coffyn's hand and the document he held crackled softly when he further unrolled it.

"The Queen's squadron," he announced, "is called to assemble in Plymouth throughout the month of March in this year of our Lord 1587. In its number will be four of our new fighting galleons—the *Golden Lion*, *Dreadnought*, *Rainbow* and some of you have seen and even served in the old *Bonaventure*. The Surveyor of the Ships has honoured her by adding the Queen's name so our old flagship now is known as the *Elizabeth Bonaventure*."

A dense fog, rolling in from the Irish Sea, began clouding the

Devonshire landscape and presently sent tendrils exploring through the ancient armoury's broken windows. The sighing of wind among a grove of tall pines standing beyond Portledge Manor's Norman tower sounded mournfully clear in the silence of intense interest prevailing indoors.

"Apart from these, there'll be four great ships belonging to the City of London and four ships belonging to our Admiral."

Again cheers arose, as indeed cheers were arising throughout all England as her people looked anxiously towards the one man who might keep the Catholic Powers at a respectful distance for, ever since intelligence concerning the execution of Mary of Scotland became known, armies were gathering all over the outraged Continent. Come summer an attempted invasion certainly would be made: everyone was sure of it.

Presently the young Squire looked about, demanded crisply, "How many of you men are for this expedition?"

All save a few older yeomen who could not possibly quit their farms showed hands, whereupon Parson Jeffers was sent for to set down their names and bid the simple fellows to make their mark.

"At sunrise of the day following tomorrow you muster here," young Coffyn informed the recruits. "I will lead you in a march to Bideford and take ship for Plymouth. Now go and attend your affairs."

"And you, Your Honour?" demanded a blacksmith. "Us don't not march lest there be a Coffyn to lead us."

Coffyn's thin features tightened. Recently he had suffered a recurrence, though in milder form, of that fever taken in the Cape Verdes. "I go with you. Just as Sir Robert led your fathers and Sir Geoffrey their fathers before them."

They raised a cheer for their young esquire and, as became free men, each of those horny-fisted fellows stepped forward to look him in the eye and to wring him by the hand.

Leaving Peter Hopton to make an inventory of the few serviceable arms and pieces of armour remaining in Sir Robert's possession, he strode back into the damp confines of the draughty old manor house, oblivious to strident cries of countless rooks and daws circling about its ancient and moss-grown keep.

With the funds he had fetched back from Cartagena considerable progress had been made towards restoring the great hall to something approaching its past glories. He smiled in satisfaction to see its windows show new diamond-shaped panes and strips of lead. New oaken treads appeared here and there along that great staircase which led up to a typically Norman gallery where now glowed a series of tapestries that once had graced the Alcalde of Cartagena's own palace. These, and other decorations such as captured battle flags, ecclesiastical mantles and capes, hung rich and vivid among the threadbare moth and mouse-eaten trophies accumulated by past generations.

He found considerable pleasure to note, glowing on a battered sideboard, two tall, exquisitely chased silver candelabra, a hammered salver and a pitcher of the same metal. Upstairs, new linen sheets and coverlets made of young llamas' fur rendered more comfortable that bed in which old Sir Robert nowadays spent nearly all of his time as a result of a hideous wound taken back in 1580 at the bloody and brutal siege of Smerwick when Lord Grey had routed and exterminated those Papal volunteers who had invaded Ireland under the inept leadership of Doctor Nicholas Sanders.

That the restoration of Portledge Manor had made but a beginning remained painfully obvious for its roof still leaked along the gallery and its stables were just short of ruinous.

Dipping into a wallet laced to his belt, young Coffyn plucked out another missive which had arrived along with the dispatch concerning Drake's impending muster at Plymouth. The writing was delicate, unfamiliar and exhibiting foreign characteristics, but its message was set forth in good, clear English.

This letter apparently had reached Bideford from Spain in astonishing rapid season—only three months. It contained those words Hubert had anticipated reading since week after week had dragged by with no communication from Rosemary Cathcart let alone sight of her. In his private cabinet, a gloomy, dank little room, devoid of that modern comfort, a fireplace, Hubert re-read her missive:

Cadiz, the 18th of December.

Dear my beloved heart. It is only after a long debate in my conscience between my yearning and my duty that I take hand to paper and write that, dearly as I adore you, I cannot leave Father since I am now his only child, his half-Brother and Sister having perished from a pestilence after your fleet had gone. Papa is much broken in spirit and sorely torn betwixt the demands of his Religion and the love of the Country which bore him. You must understand and forgive me, my sweet Hubert, because I cannot come unto you as so sorely I wish to do. Dear Hubert, remember that God's ways are inscrutable and we all must bow to His Will.

Remember only this of me—that I shall never marry, nor shall I ever forget your greatness of Heart and Gentle manners. Believe me ever, thy adoring

Rosemary.

Shivering a little, Hubert rose, crossed to the window, stared out upon the dripping courtyard and the cobbles dully shining there between tufts of long, bright green grass.

"I'll not accept this," he muttered. " 'Fore God, I'll fetch her to Portledge whether or no, e'en though I have to haul along old Cathcart into the bargain." He straightened, made his way into the sick-room to inform Sir Robert of the decision he had taken to serve once more under the Golden Admiral.

Much to Hubert Coffyn's chagrin he was not, as before, posted aboard the *Elizabeth Bonaventure*, but to that same little *Francis* he had last beheld plunging out of Roanoke Inlet. Instead of foundering off the coast of Virginia she had been driven by the great gale so far across the Atlantic that her commander, being critically short of water and stores, had had no choice but to keep on for home, and so became the first of Drake's armada to reach England.

All the same, Hubert found himself accorded that unique respect which was granted a gentleman who had sailed with the Admiral before. He and his followers from the west of Devon were all ordered aboard the *Francis*, Drake's own ship.

This time, the ever-growing port of Plymouth witnessed no such headlong, hurly-burly of preparation such as had preceded the attack on Bayona. The twenty-three ships which Drake led out past Plymouth Hoe were uncommonly well found, armed and manned.

In the seclusion of his gaily redecorated cabin Sir Francis Drake, in profound satisfaction, re-read his commission and instructions prepared by his staunch friend Walsingham and signed by the Queen herself. He passed a hand over thick, yellow blond hair streaked here and there with a strand of silver. He treated Rear-Admiral Robert Flick, a sound and brave soldier commanding the City of London galleons, to that peculiarly winning smile of his.

"Listen to this," he invited over the lazy creaking of yards and the rhythmic *hiss-hiss* caused by waves rushing past the flagship's side. "This is the part of my commission which meets my dearest desire.

"You are to impeach the joining together of the King of Spain's fleet out of their several ports, to keep victuals from them, to follow them in case they should go forward towards England and Ireland, and to cut off as many of them as you may and impeach their landing as also to set upon such as should either come out of the West or East Indies unto Spain, or come out of Spain hither, particularly you are directed to distress the ships within the havens themselves."

"D'you mark that?" Drake smiled in high good humour. " 'Distress the ships within the havens themselves,' " and, playing with an emerald pendant he had elected this day to wear in his left ear, he continued: "Does it not boot much more to crush a whole fleet in harbour rather than to pursue and track it down piecemeal? Aye, friend Flick, I think I shall devote special heed to yon passage of the instructions."

He jumped up suddenly, threw back his head and proclaimed in ringing tones, "I shall so singe the King of Spain's beard that the stench of its burning will reach across the seas and encompass the earth!"

CHAPTER V

THE KINDLED SPARK

DUE to the unusual violence of a gale which struck the English squadron off Cape Finisterre, it was not until the sixteenth of April, 1587, that the last of Drake's ships appeared at a predetermined rendezvous off Cabo Roca, which cape lies somewhat north of the Tagus river's mouth.

Hubert Coffyn wrote in his journal:

As if to atone for their evil ways, ye sea gods, did yield us two stout ships of Middelburgh, fresh out of Cadiz. Their masters on being promised their ships and their lives, did reveal that in ye capacious harbour of Cadiz lay gathered together a great number of big ships and ye supplies therefor, also many galleons and galleasses as ye Spanish King had caused to be built in his possessions and in ye states of Italy. These prisoners further deposed that Cadiz harbour was so choked by shipping that scarce three cables' length of open water remained.

This morning of ye nineteenth signal was made for all Captains to repair aboard ye flagship. As captain over ye *Francis*, I took with me one Peter Hopton, my Chief Gunner.

Ye Council being convened, Sir Francis did set forth his plans, and in them he was greatly opposed by his Vice-Admiral, William Borough. With considerable choler ye Vice-Admiral protested that any attack upon Cadiz would be pure folly, that city being strongly fortified; besides lying in ye harbour where God knew how many enemy ships of war. With a vehemence I have never before marked in his character, Sir Francis Drake over-ruled William Borough crying loudly, 'Your orders are these. You are to follow my flagship and obey my signals.' Methinks there was much in the Vice-Admiral's objections, yet he has served overlong in ye naval service and perchance has grown timid in his old age.

In conclusion, Sir Francis pointed out that, after all, some matters must be left to fortune, and that nothing is sure in a sea fight."

His head aching a little under the hot sun, Hubert Coffyn closed his writing-desk just as his Sailing Master swung up on to the *Francis*' tiny poop.

"Land's in sight, sir. Our reconnaissance has just made signal." A few moments later Hubert himself made out the coast of Spain as a mere yellow brown streak drawn beyond this heaving, dark blue expanse. Fervently he wished for one of those kenning glasses which were gradually coming into use. Through such an instrument distant objects appeared magically near at hand.

Because Drake's own vessel was one of the smallest ships, she sailed far astern of those eight tall galleons and great ships composing the backbone of Drake's power. Between them and the little *Francis* cruised other privately owned vessels—two belonged to the Hawkinses and one to crusty old Martin Frobisher, for all that he hated Drake's bowels and frequently admitted so. There were also private ships out of Hull, Plymouth and the Isle of Wight, mounting only two guns each, but jam-packed with eager, lusty men and boys.

On the *Francis*' deck gunners and soldiers were looking to their equipment while new hands blustered in attempting to dispel any notion that they might be fearful over the fate in store for them.

By four in the afternoon, the English squadron, led by the four galleons of the Queen's Navy and the four London vessels, sailed boldly into the outer harbour's entrance.

Coffyn, his yellow hair bright in the strong sunlight, beckoned a mariner who claimed to have entered the harbour of Cádiz not five years earlier. The new steersman spoke of Las Puercas, two great shoals guarding the harbour mouth, which forced any ships entering the harbour to pass within the range of a powerful fort. Beyond this castle lay the city and below the city was a second or inner harbour; still further up the river lay a secondary town named Port Royal.

While speaking the helmsman threw his weight on the tiller and veered slightly to port to obtain full benefit from a squall racing up from the north-west. This breeze so favoured the *Francis* that she came scampering up on the heels of Vice-Admiral Borough's ship, the *Golden Lion*.

Aboard the English vessels jaws gradually tightened and eyes became narrowed as their ships bowled steadily on towards a powerful battery lying below a landmark called the Column of Hercules. Presently they made out the red roofs of the ancient town of Cádiz shining at the top of its cliff and the weather-beaten castle of Matagorda and a still more formidable series of battlements intended to defend the harbour front.

"God's Life!" suddenly burst out Peter Hopton. "Will you gaze on that!"

The ships of Drake's van were now bearing off to starboard, thus affording their lesser consorts their first unobstructed view of the port. Never had anyone aboard seen anything to approach the dense mass of shipping which lay ahead. Coffyn's crew recognized huge carracks, trim fighting galleons, homely transports, round-bowed Dutch hoys and hulks as well as galleys and galleasses of every imaginable tonnage and design.

As usual when he was deeply excited, Hubert's jaws commenced to work, chewed slowly on nothing at all. Somewhere, in one of those pretty little towns and villages dotting the shores of the bay Rosemary Cathcart must be suffering terrible recollections while watching the approach of yet another English fleet—although at the moment not a single Cross of St. George was to be seen; and none did show until a pair of big Spanish galleys doing duty as guard ships came threshing out to speak the strangers and inquire into their business. Drake allowed the galleys to advance into a long cannon's range before hoisting the Queen's banner and several Crosses of St. George. He then let fly a broadside which sent the amazed Spaniards staggering off towards St. Mary's Port which, with Santa Caterina, lay across the harbour from Cádiz.

Ten minutes later Drake's ships were by the forts and bearing down upon the mass of Spanish vessels, unready and huddled together like sheep in a fold. Many of the craft could not navigate at all since, to discourage desertion, the Spanish Admiral, the Duke of Santa Cruz, had caused their sails to be removed and taken ashore. Others, and they were many, had not yet received their ordnance so that their gun ports gaped blank and black like teeth missing from a man's mouth.

"So opens a reel piped to our pleasure," Peter Hopton exulted from his position among the *Francis*' guns. "See, the *Bonaventure* has opened up on yonder great ship from Ragusa."

As, one after another, they came into range, Drake's vessels poured in a devastating fire upon the massed shipping. Since the English gunners simply could not miss, their every shot wreaked fearful havoc. Broadside after broadside made the harbour water shiver and the uproar caromed from the battlements of Cádiz to rumble off among the surrounding hills. Singly, in pairs and threes, the tall ships of England penetrated Cádiz Harbour, hurled shot from their full cannons and culverins at the hopelessly surprised and panic-stricken shore batteries.

When it came the *Francis*' turn to join in this deadly cannonade, Hubert Coffyn ordered his personal green and gold banner displaying the family coat-of-arms to be raised, donned his morion and, in a ringing voice, bade his Master Gunner to open fire. He ordered his helmsman to make for a middle-sized Dutch cromster which had succeeded in disentangling herself from the furious welter, and was heading for the harbour's mouth.

Nearer and nearer sailed the cromster, her brown mainsail filling uncertainly under a fitful afternoon breeze. The *Francis*' first broadside fell short, though not by much, so, cursing like a fiend, Peter ordered quoins driven further under the breeches of his bright bronze demi-culverins and himself swabbed out the reeking bore of the Number Three piece.

The Dutch ship had now sailed so near that Peter could see the frightened faces peering over her rail. Two of her guns spoke; one of them sent a cannon ball screaming through the *Francis*' rigging while the other tore a ragged hole in her lateen sail. For a second time the little *Francis* quivered, heeled over under a broadside which momentarily obscured the Dutchman behind great billows of rotten-smelling grey smoke. Reloading, the *Francis*' gunners were aware of deafening detonations in all directions and heard the crash of riven timbers and the shrieks of men in mortal pain.

A gust of wind tore aside the smoke and a cheer went up only to be followed by heartfelt oaths. The Dutch cromster had lost her single towering mast and showed such gaping holes along her waterline that it was certain she could not survive to yield her cargo. She must sink in short order. Already members of her crew were leaping into the harbour and striking out for pieces of wreckage on which they could support themselves.

Steadily the infernal din grew louder and the Spanish confusion proportionately greater. Certain enemy ships by now had taken fire and added dense strata of acrid blue fumes to the shifting grey-white patterns of gun-smoke.

"Make for yonder galliot," Coffyn bellowed through cupped hands, then with his sword indicated a long, low vessel which, propelled by sweeps, was seeking safety under the guns of a battery near Santa Caterina. Beyond this craft a number of war galleys were getting under way. These, ten in number, were commanded by Admiral Don Pedro de Acuña.

Once the *Francis* had squared away in pursuit of the galliot Coffyn found opportunity to look about and saw that, obedient to signals from the *Elizabeth Bonaventure*, the four Royal ships, including the *Lion*, *Dreadnought* and *Rainbow*, were swerving to meet the threat presented by Don Pedro's galleys and had left the City of London galleons and private men-of-war to continue mauling that tangle of vessels in the centre of the harbour.

De Acuña elected to advance his galleys in line abreast so that each of his flotilla could use its bow chasers until the moment came for ramming. Everyone aboard the *Francis* could see that the enemy's fore- and after-castles were packed with armoured soldiery—the best and bravest then to be found in Europe.

As Coffyn swiftly foresaw, Drake entertained not the least intention of allowing de Acuña's formidable fighting machines within ramming or boarding distance so, keeping the four Royal galleons in line ahead, he steered directly across the front of the enemy and loosed a series of crushing broadsides. In fact Drake had executed—for the first time in history—that naval manœuvre known as "Crossing the T".

Now that the *Francis* was rapidly overhauling her quarry, Coffyn was allowed only time to watch the lead galley's starboard triple bank of oars shattered by a broadside from the *Dreadnought*. Dozens of blades flew high into the air and, as the galley reeled aside, broken shafts strewed the harbour like withered cat-tails in a pond. Deprived of motive power on her injured side, de Acuña's gaudy blue-and-yellow-painted galley spun madly off course and all but rammed one of her consorts.

Just then the galliot, a Venetian by her flags, was brought into range and began pounding away at the *Francis* with two stubby little sakers whose six-pound projectiles took not the least effect upon Hubert Coffyn's command. By suddenly porting his helm he offered Peter Hopton the opportunity of delivering a devastating broadside into the waist of the enemy which must have slain a great many luckless wretched chained to her oars. The blast also so decimated her fighting men that the Italian screamed an offer of surrender and pulled down his city's gaudy banner—the Golden-Winged Lion of St. Mark on a scarlet field.

CHAPTER VI

THE PRIZE

By nightfall wild exultation had spread through Drake's squadron and ecstatic reports of sinkings, burnings and captures fairly streamed up to that solid little figure pacing the *Elizabeth Bonaventure's* poop deck. Soon it became substantiated that apart from burnt or sunken ships some thirty-three enemy vessels had fallen into English hands! Of these five were towering great-ships hailing from nearly every port in Spain and Portugal.

What proved to be an added satisfaction was the fact that these tall ships were discovered to be deep-laden with all manner of marine supplies, ordnance and gunpowder. All in the space of a few hours the English crews found themselves gloating over vast supplies of biscuits, olive oil, dried fish, salted meat and fruit and, best of all, a wide selection of choice wines—supplies the Spaniards would find hard to replace. The victuals were especially welcome aboard Drake's fleet since the Royal ships had been provisioned for a bare three months, while the City of London ships had been supplied to keep to the sea for a matter of six months.

Hubert Coffyn and his crew slept not at all that night, they being much too occupied with the delightful business of taking on board the Venetian galliot's cargo. Cheers and whoops of joy arose when in the prize's hold were discovered two iron chests so heavy that they scarce could be lifted by four men. No time was lost in using a maul upon the giant padlocks securing them. When the lids crashed back, bag on bag of coins, mostly silver but with some gold, became disclosed to the wide-eyed victors.

Also were found six beautifully ornamented brass demi-cannon and many corselets, morions and helmets, for the most part wonderfully decorated with gold and silver inlays. As further choice booty were many fragile and gloriously beautiful objects of glass, which, no doubt, the *Tres Santos*' owners had gambled on selling wherever a suitable market offered, in addition to bolts of silk so fine that one could read a Bible through it.

Gleefully Hopton patted the treasure chests. "By the smoking tail o' Satan we've won us a real fortune here, sir, and no mistake."

"True enough," grinned young Coffyn. "There'll be plenty for us all even after the Admiral and Her Majesty's accountants have claimed their shares."

Surely the Golden Admiral's famed liberality would be inspired towards the crew of the *Francis*, especially since this fat prize had fallen to his own ship and he would richly benefit thereby.

Towards morning, all prisoners taken during the action were confined aboard one of the captured galleons. These luckless wretches, Drake had foreseen, would go far towards exchanging such Englishmen as might be toiling among Don Pedro de Acuña's galley slaves.

Afire to inform Sir Francis of his privateer's great fortune, Hubert called for his cockboat and through the brightening dawn made for that point where he had last seen the flagship at anchor. To his astonishment she was gone, although *Dreadnought*, *Lion* and *Rainbow* remained as before.

Then Hubert spied the Admiral's ship reanchored off Point Puntal, and in the act of speeding from alongside the *Elizabeth Bonaventure* was a vessel he thought to recognize as the *Merchant Royal*. In her wake sailed and rowed a string of pinnaces suggestive of a brood of ducklings swimming after their mother. Beyond a doubt their destination was that inner harbour in which lay Admiral Santa Cruz's own great galleon. An enormous vessel of above twelve hundred tons and brand-new, she was magnificently decorated. Her lofty top hamper towered above a light harbour mist like a pine crowning a hillock.

By the gathering light, those serving aboard the Queen's ships now beheld one of Drake's most supreme acts of daring. With broadsides thundering at such batteries as dared to open fire upon him, he sailed straight into the great inner harbour and bore down upon the Spanish Admiral's flagship like a young bull charging.

To the breathless and anxious onlookers it became swiftly apparent that either the great galleon's officers were hopelessly inept or that she could not have her regular crew aboard, for only five or six puffs of flame and fire burst from her gilded sides before the *Merchant Royal* ground alongside. Flights of arrows and thudding firelocks then mowed down such of the enemy as attempted a stand and effectively cleared a path for boarders armed with sword and pike. Almost at once the sounds of combat faded away, arguing that the flagship of Marquis Don Alvarez Bacán de Santa Cruz had been added to the tally of Drake's prizes.

Alas that her sails lay ashore, for although it might prove possible to tow this huge prize past Point Puntal and into the outer harbour she could never be fetched past those strengthened batteries guarding the exits and out into the Atlantic. An order accordingly was issued to plunder Santa Cruz's vessel and then consign her to the flames.

Stung to fury by this appalling, unbelievable humiliation of King Philip's ablest and most famous Admiral, the Spanish batteries hurled hundreds of shot which almost invariably fell short of the invading fleet.

All day long continued a transfer of plunder aboard such of the captive vessels as the English decided on taking away. By the ton, stores vital to the "Enterprise of England" went tumbling into the Golden Admiral's holds.

So great was the press of affairs that not until late afternoon did Drake find opportunity to receive and to congratulate his Captains. For all that he could not have closed his eyes in nearly forty-eight hours, Sir Francis strode about as briskly as ever, beaming, slapping this Captain on the back or exchanging a jest with that army officer. In an affable mood despite a recent furious dispute with Borough, his Vice-Admiral, who was of a lather to make sail and get away while the going was good—he bestowed gifts and compliments on all and sundry.

When he heard of how young Coffyn had taken the *Tres Santos* and had scanned an inventory of the plunder, he wrung his hand and indulged in one of his rare oaths. "By God's eyeballs, Hubert Coffyn, you're a true Devon man and if e'er I've met one. Go now and tell your men that I grant you and your crew the half of my share in what has been won by the *Francis*."

Young Coffyn's spirits soared. Now certainly Portledge Manor would become well and truly restored to its ancient splendours! Now old Sir Robert might pass his declining years amid all the comforts that money could buy.

Hubert had descended to the *Elizabeth Bonaventure's* waist in order to return aboard his command when a merchantman was seen to leave the little port of Santa Caterina, situated opposite to Cádiz on the outer harbour. That which commanded immediate interest was the fact that, although of Spanish construction, she was flying a huge white flag from her maintop and a Cross of St. George, apparently hastily devised, at her mizzen. Quite boldly, this enemy barque picked a course among ships and wrecks dotting the waters of Cádiz Harbour. Her master could be seen hailing this vessel and that, until presently she came into the wind a cable's length astern of the *Elizabeth Bonaventure* and dipped her colours in salute.

At once a boat was lowered and an individual wearing a black cloak and doublet descended into her stern sheets. When the small boat drew near, Coffyn could tell that the black-clad stranger was grey-bearded, that his face had been deeply tanned and that he carried himself with surprising erectness for one of his advanced years.

"Ahoy, there," he shouted. "Permission to board the flagship?"

Although the stranger's clothes were typically Spanish and his crew spoke no English, the hail betrayed a definite East Riding inflection. On being received aboard, the stranger strode past the knot of Captains awaiting their boats, thus affording Hubert Coffyn the opportunity of viewing him at close quarters. His, Hubert decided, were the saddest eyes he had ever beheld and his long and sensitive features were set in rigid lines.

Drake, who had descended from his quarters in order to inspect an especially choice chest of plate, acknowledged the old man's profound bow with a gracious wave of the hand then inquired his business.

"I have come, Sir Francis, for a dual purpose. One is to offer my services and that of my vessel, together with the supplies she carries, to our Gracious Queen."

A puzzled quirk lifted one of Drake's sand-coloured eyebrows. "*Our* Queen? Methought you came out from shore just now. Surely there are no true Englishmen left free in all Spain?"

Colour suffused the old man's craggy, parchment-hued features. "I have not been molested, Your Excellency, because I am a Catholic."

Drake's cordial smile vanished. "A Catholic! Then, sirrah, what do you here?"

The stranger's grey head went back. "I came to fight against the most wicked, the most merciless ruler since Herod."

"What mean you? King Philip of Spain?" demanded the Golden Admiral, his hostility fading.

"Aye. Only three days gone by I beheld with these my own eyes an order penned in the Escorial that when England is overrun by his Enterprise, not one single Protestant male above the age of seven shall be spared from execution!"

An angry growl circulated the loot-heaped deck. Sir Francis Drake's mouth curved into a hard slash. "You are certain of this?"

He in black bowed in courtly fashion, said simply: "I should not be here else. Until that moment I believed myself to be a Catholic first and then an Englishman, but since reading that order, noble sir, my opinion is the reverse. I beg only that you allow me, my ship and my household to sail out with you. Pray believe that I'll serve you to the best of my ability, an you'll lend me men enough to sail my *San Marco* yonder. More, I will alter her name to any of your choosing."

Drake narrowly considered his visitor, all the time tugging at his pointed little beard. "Well, sir, I'll think on it. What is your name and station?"

"Until today I have been a merchant of Santa Caterina and Cádiz, dealing under licence with the Spanish possessions in the Carib Sea, more especially with a town"—the stranger's thin lips managed a grim smile—"of which last year you gained a most intimate knowledge."

"Cartagena?"

"No, Your Excellency. I mean San Domingo. 'Twas there your raid clove my wealth in two and cost me the lives of many near and dear to me."

"Indeed so?" Drake's small, bright blue eyes narrowed. "In war someone always suffers. Your name?"

"Richard Cathcart," replied he in the sombre doublet; whereupon the deck seemed to sway under Hubert Coffyn's heels. "I have further intelligence for Your Excellency's privy ear," continued this sad and dignified figure. Hubert started forward, but Drake had already set foot on the poop ladder saying, "And now, my good Master Cathcart, what is this intelligence you would confide in me?"

Not for a long while afterwards would the officers and men of Drake's Squadron learn that only through the goodwill of Richard Cathcart was their capture of the great Portuguese treasure ship, *San Felipe*, made possible. When they sailed her into an English port some two months later her strong-boxes yielded a fortune valued at nearly a million pounds!

In a frenzy of impatience, Hubert strode about the deck, then, trying to learn what was afoot, he hailed the *San Marco* but got no satisfaction. The dark-visaged sailors aboard Cathcart's barque merely stared frightened and round-eyed at these grim English men-of-war lying all about and on useless prizes being scuttled or sent, flaming, to drift ashore near el Diamán and on the reefs called las Puercas.

CHAPTER VII

REUNION

LIGHT from the Marquis of Santa Cruz's burning galleon and sundry other blazing derelicts sent in on a flood tide to damage the secondary port of Santa Maria tinted orange-red the undersides of smokeclouds lingering over Cádiz Harbour.

On the foredeck of that barque formerly called the *San Marco* but which would henceforward be known as the *Rosemary*, English mariners and younkers detailed to her management were drinking, dancing, bellowing out bawdy ballads and otherwise celebrating transfer from cramped and fetid quarters aboard some man-of-war to this roomy and relatively cleanly merchantman.

All through Drake's fleet lights shone for there were still shotholes to be planked over, spars to be fished and rigging to be re-roved. On the dozen or so vessels preserved for England's use, an extra activity was noticeable in that their prize crews were labouring hard to familiarize themselves with the unaccustomed rigging and gear.

On the settle placed in the lee of the barque's lateen mizzen Rosemary Cathcart lay back against a folded sail, her delicate profile tinted alternately pink, yellow and red in the light of the crackling flames. Her fingers, curled inside young Coffyn's brown hand, finally had relaxed. In her rich, rather deep voice she was saying: "Truly, Hubert, it passes all understanding what the lapse of a single week can accomplish. Seven short days ago Papa was bending every energy towards outfitting the Marquis of Santa Cruz' *flota*——" Shc broke off, lifted her lips for yet another caress. "Never will I forget the night Papa returned after reading that infamous order and having heard it lauded by the Archbishop himself."

"Then you were about to sail in any case?" Hubert queried. "Even if our fleet had not attacked?"

"Yes. Papa determined to sail for Holland with supplies for the Duke of Parma's army. We would have departed next week—but, oh, Hubert, neither Father nor I will ever forget the sight of your tall galleons flying the Cross of St. George in the face of Matagorda Castle and all those batteries."

"We took the port by complete surprise?"

Rich lights gleamed in her dark hair as she nodded once more. "Everyone was thunderstruck, and when the dreaded name of *el Draque* was heard, you should have seen the panic which ensued. Why, in Cádiz, the hire of a simple little donkey-cart would fetch a hundred reales, and, as you may have noticed, several ships were run on to the reefs in their masters' terror."

Her figure, slim in a yellow velvet gown devoid of a distorting farthingale, briefly paralleled the outline of his body as he caught her to him. Then she queried him concerning the conclusion of the English armada's cruise of the past year and murmured sympathy over the loss of Harry Wyatt's *Hope*. She even found amusement in hearing the truth about the fabulous and non-existent riches to be picked up in North America.

At length Hubert clasped her lithe and fragrant figure for a final time. "I must be off," he sighed, "and ere I go I would bid farewell to your sire."

Gently, Rosemary shook her head. "No, poor Father will still be kneeling upon his *prie-dieu* telling his rosary and imploring Divine Revelation that he had not done a wicked thing. Dear one, when shall I see you next?"

"In Portsmouth, most likely, or in Plymouth, perhaps. God knows which Sir Francis next intends."

He was right. The *Francis*, together with several other small private men-of-war, was detailed to convoy back to England this prize and the bulkier loot, thus leaving Drake unhampered for a further singeing of Philip II's beard. He would be accompanied by only his strongest fighting ships and swiftest victuallers.

Where would *el Draque* strike next? The Spanish authorities remained in an agony of doubt, so gallopers foundered horses in racing southward to Lisbon, up to Vigo or down towards Málaga. Frantic warnings were also dispatched even as far as Old Cartegena, Valencia and Barcelona; who doubted but that ever-unpredictable *el Draque* would hesitate to invade the Mediterranean? Or was he again making for the West Indies?

Hubert Coffyn was not unique in congratulating himself over his detachment on convoy duty now that he had won a small fortune. All that mattered was the arrival of Drake's prizes in some English port, and the safety of Rosemary Cathcart.

CHAPTER VIII

UNEASY WINTER

HAWKS whistled again in the long-disused mews of Portledge Manor, several sturdy and broad-rumped brood mares and high-crested, rambunctious stallions stamped in the rebuilt stables. Today a rare snowstorm had lent the impression of herring scales having fallen upon new slates protecting Sir Robert Coffyn's manor house. Furniture fashioned in the graceful French or Italian manner had supplanted those clumsy and uncomfortable straight-backed chairs which, for a couple of centuries, had done duty in the family's private living quarters.

Since autumn, crumbling walls had been restored and two new chimneys thrust their outline up into a leaden sky to attest the fact that now the principal guest chamber and Hubert's quarters enjoyed the comforts of a fireplace.

Gallant young horsemen, accompanied by their cloaked and wimpled ladies riding pillion behind them, rode ever more frequently between handsome new stone gate-posts bearing the Coffyn coat of arms—four bezants or, spaced between five crosslets, *sable* upon a field *vert.* The family motto—*Omnia Recte Factis Proemia*—had been engraved there, sharp and clear, for everyone to read.

To Rosemary Coffyn's own vast astonishment, she had proved immediately and immensely popular about the countryside, despite her foreign upbringing and accent and the unusual foods she ordered set upon her table. At the great dance offered to celebrate Hubert's completion of repairs to the great hall, every gentleman of consequence within a radius of twenty miles appeared to admire, if not to envy, his handsome silver table-service, the gorgeous Flemish tapestries, and last, but not least, the raven-haired beauty of Hubert Coffyn's bride. Rosemary's quickness of wit combined with an unaffected familiarity with polite literature, art and music—almost unique in a woman of that day—delighted them, if not their wives.

Old Sir Robert began to mend now that his draughty bedroom had been renovated and his tormented body lay beneath warm, light blankets and heavy velvet curtains cut off draughts from that four-poster which had become his prison. The old officer even rallied sufficiently to permit his being borne downstairs in a chair in order that he might witness the dancing of a pavanne. In fact, it commenced to seem likely that his eldest son now would remain simply Hubert Coffyn, Esquire, for a considerable time to come. Of course the sea captain's younger brothers and sisters followed him about, treating him to adoring glances. His whim was their command.

All this had come about because the specie found in those chests captured aboard the Venetian galliot had been estimated at a value of forty thousand pounds—six thousand of which fell to Hubert's share as captain and because of Sir Francis Drake's munificence.

It was bruited about Devonshire that, by consequence of his capturing the great *San Felipe*, Drake's own share in the venture of 1587 had come to seventeen thousand pounds while that of his eternally capricious Sovereign had amounted to a tidy forty thousand.

Because of a strong north-west wind howling in over chalk cliffs to the northward, the evening was chill and damp when Hubert and his bride ascended to Sir Robert's chamber after having presided dutifully over the evening meal in Portledge's great hall. There, no less than twenty-three servants, from steward to scullery maid, had partaken of a substantial meal of beef, cabbage and onions, washed down with plenty of creamy brown ale.

The old nobleman, his beard neatly trimmed into a short spike, was perusing a despatch received that afternoon from Sir Robert's firm friend of many years, Lord Howard of Effingham. Revealed by a warmly crackling fire, the new, dark green velvet hangings of his bed assumed rich and verdant hues. In a candelabrum burned no less than four tall tallow tapers the thread wicks of which gave off a steady and pure radiance—a vast improvement over that single, malodorous beef-drip candle with its rush wick which heretofore had only emphasized the dreary discomfort surrounding the uncomplaining veteran.

Prettily, Rosemary fanned wide skirts in a low Court curtsey, then went forward to buss the old man's parchment-pale forehead.

"A good evening to you, my pet," Sir Robert exclaimed and rustled the papers. "Sit you down with Hubert by the fire and he'll decant you some wine from Fayal. I find it rare fine stuff," he chuckled, "and if 'twill serve to warm my old blood, God wot, Mistress Rosemary, you'll enjoy a rare fine tumbler ere you retire."

"Sir—then I'll pour Rosemary a full goblet."

Hubert hurried over to the chimney-place for, again, a faint recurrence of the Cape Verde fever, to his bride's consternation, had set him alternately shivering and burning all day long; just now his feet were chilly. Sir Robert's thin, blue-veined fingers plucked up and arranged half a dozen sheets of foolscap, closely written.

"This news, strangely enough," he informed, "touches you, Rosemary. I have here firm assurances from Howard, Lord High Admiral of the Queen's Navy, that he has taken your sire under his protection and has set him to selecting stores for use in the Queen's vessels."

A small, glad cry escaped Rosemary's dark red lips. Far more than anyone suspected, she had lived in anguish for fear that Protestant bigotry, now blazing more fiercely than ever since news of King Philip's infamous order had been circulated, should contrive to ruin Richard Cathcart.

"I shall remember Lord Howard in my prayers every night and morning for a month," she promised. "Indeed, it was wondrous kind of you, Sir Robert, to write my Lord of Effingham on my father's behalf."

The proud, silvery head lifted and his steel-grey eyes transfixed her. "Could I do less for any member of my family?"

It was clear that the long-widowed nobleman had derived deep satisfaction from his daughter-in-law's capable conduct of the household. Rosemary, of course, had been accustomed to commanding dozens of servants all her life, and so never had transgressed that fine line separating understanding from familiarity with the serving people in the manor.

"The news I have for you, Hubert," Sir Robert's still fierce eyes peered out from under shaggy white brows, "is not entirely good. Alas, that Lord Burghley and his Spanish-lovers have, despite everything, cozened Her Majesty into believing that hopes of peace with Spain need not be abandoned."

"God's Blood!" Hubert burst out. "Can the Queen not understand that never in this world can the King of Spain forget or forgive now Drake has shamed him at Bayona, the Indies, Cádiz and at Fort Sagre in the south of Spain?"

"Apparently Her Royal Majesty again has deluded herself." He cocked a quizzical brow at his son. "Do you know, Hubert, that at this very moment your Admiral is *persona non grata* at Court? That the Queen turns a deaf ear to Sir Francis' entreaties and ignores his sworn depositions that Philip is possessed of a burning determination to take revenge? Have you heard that he has taken a solemn oath that he will cause Her Majesty to be burnt as a heretic before her own palace gates?"

Awakened by the old nobleman's vehemence, a greyhound which had lain dozing in a corner came over to rest its head on the diapered black and red silk hose sheathing Hubert's knees.

"Lord Howard deposes that, only last month, Her Majesty refused to accept the Crown of the Netherlands for fear of provoking His Bloodiness of Spain! Even as we speak, the Queen gives ear to those of the Spanish party such as Sir James Croft, Comptroller of the Royal Household, one who accuses our Admiral of defrauding the Queen of her proper share in the treasure of the *San Felipe*. 'Tis even rumoured Sir Francis employs this pilfered gold to seduce from their duties high officers of her Navy. Pah! Doddering Will Borough charges that Drake overstepped his commission in attacking the Spaniards in their own ports."

"But—but, sir, 'tis well known that Sir Francis Walsingham granted our Admiral such an authority, and over the Queen's own signature."

A frail and trembling hand crept up to stroke the old man's lace-fine beard. "Ah, yes. There you have Francis Walsingham again. Methinks I recognize a touch of his usual guile in this matter. It would not be unlike him, he who yearns for war with Spain, to have inserted that instruction, urging an attack which would shame King Philip in his own havens."

"You mean, sir, that Walsingham played the monkey's role in the old fable and caused Sir Francis to undertake the cat's part by pulling the red-hot chestnut of Cádiz out of the fire *against* the Queen's desires?"

"That, in my opinion, is what has chanced. But"—he lifted a reading-glass and passed it unsteadily over the crackling parchment—"you still have not heard the worst. Sir Francis' veterans are to be paid off and his ships placed in ordinary. Further, he is forbidden to dispatch reinforcements to that garrison he left behind to hold Cape St. Vincent. For a fact Drake's whole expedition is to be disallowed and himself deprived of command!"

Sir Robert's voice cracked under his indignation. "Most especially Lord Burghley taxes your Admiral for taunting the Marquis of Santa Cruz off Lisbon, and daring the Don to come out and fight like a man. Further still, Vice-Admiral Borough, who so basely deserted your Admiral in the *Lion* after having seduced her crew to revolt and betray their allegiance, is not to be executed after all. Rather, Timorous Willie is to be reinstated and with fresh honours!"

"But—but, sir, that—that's impossible!" Hubert burst out, thin features scarlet. "Never has been proved a clearer case of mutiny." The young esquire frowned, stared at his wife's fingers skimming above the embroidery on her tambour frame like swallows over a sunset pond. "Indeed, sir, I—I cannot credit such injustice. Why, to lay up the fleet, discredit Sir Francis and to make much of his enemy, Borough, is past belief."

"Little that chances at Whitehall passes belief," grunted the old man. "'Tis a shining wonder, my son, that the Queen's weaknesses long since have not led England to her ruin, as well they may within another year." He leaned forward on his bed and his voice suddenly gathered strength. "Mark you, Hubert, if half of what my Lord Howard's spies report be true, then, come another winter, we lie crushed and conquered by the mightiest army and navy the world has ever seen."

Rosemary spoke for the first time in a long while. "Except that God and *el Draque* fight on *our* side!"

The old man stared, then toasted his approval in a deep draught of Portugal wine from a chalice which once had graced an altar in San Domingo. Said he: "About God I fear me I know too little, but concerning Sir Francis—God above, Hubert! You should have seen him during our attack on Castle Rathlin off the coast of Antrim. 'Twas in Ireland, you know, I took this curs'd crippling wound."

The lord of Portledge Manor spoke but infrequently of that expedition in which the troops he led back in 1575 had been transported by a short, yellow-bearded young Vice-Admiral named Francis Drake. Only of late had Hubert Coffyn ascertained why Sir Robert seldom mentioned the in-taking of Castle Rathlin. This was because the garrison, together with the wives and children of Irish chieftains, sent thither for safety, had been cut down with such savagery that none survived—a deed of infamy which blackened the Protestant cause for generations to come and afforded Catholics grounds on which to refute the cruelties inflicted by the Inquisition.

"So Sir Francis recalls this poor old hulk, eh?" Sir Robert drained the last of his Fayal and banged down the silver goblet. " 'Fore God, I'm pleased he placed my son in command o' the *Francis*."

The three in that pleasantly firelit bedchamber started, turned faces to the door upon which a sharp knock had sounded over the lazy crackling of fragrant, birch-smelling logs.

"Zur Robert, Zur Robert!" panted a country-boy page. "A dispatch bearer ha' rid in 'e courtyard."

"Speak up, ye loon. What tidings does he bring?"

"I do'ent know, Zur Robert."

"Fetch him up, you great noddy, then go order cheer for him in my kitchen."

The messenger tramped in, sparkling flakes of snow sprinkled on his long grey riding-cape. He bowed low, first to Sir Robert and then to Hubert. Rosemary rose, her dark eyes rounded in alarm. Day in and day out she had anticipated the arrival of just such a courier, one who would tear Hubert away from her and back to the wars.

Sir Robert hunched himself higher upon his bolster, fixed the messenger with cavernous eyes. "Well, my good fellow, and what are your tidings?"

"I am come from Sir Francis Drake, Your Honour," replied the courier. "The Admiral and his Lady lie tonight in Bideford. Sir Francis wishes to know whether he and his Lady will be welcome for lodging here tomorrow night.

"Further, the Admiral forwards his fondest greetings to you, sir, and trusts your wound proves not too troublesome these raw days." Obviously this sweaty horseman was reciting something learnt by rote. "Sir Francis sends you also this small token of his affection and respect."

The messenger fumbled in a stained leather wallet until he found a slim gold chain from which was suspended a medallion beautifully rendered in gold and enamelwork depicting St. George riding down a very fierce dragon.

CHAPTER IX

THE FESTIVE BOARD

FULLY an hour before a quarter to six, the usual rising time for the Coffyn household in winter-time, Mistress Rosemary was up and, by the light of many torches flaring smokily in ancient Norman sconces, marshalling her household to resume preparations halted late the night before. Seldom had this ancient manor undergone such a scrubbing and dusting or witnessed such an activity in its kitchen.

At sun-up a fat young heifer was led out behind the byre where she rolled eyes in wonderment until a maul came crashing down upon her forehead to terminate her interest in mundane matters.

By the dozen, chickens, ducks and geese squawked their last, while up from the root cellars were fetched cabbages, turnips and apples galore.

When it grew light, varlets and ostlers were sent into a spinney back of Portledge with orders to cut a goodly supply of fir boughs and holly. Trusses of fresh, dry rushes were then fetched down from a loft and scattered with prodigal profusion over all the floors.

To shelter the expected guests—it having been ascertained that Sir Francis Drake's retinue numbered no less than thirty-seven souls, not including the Lady Elizabeth, her sempstress, and a quartet of tiring maids—sundry house servants were dispossessed and sent temporarily to lodge in nearby farmhouses.

Although Sir Robert's bailiff and steward grew flustered and vented weird Devonshire oaths and serving women hurried, often aimlessly, about, Rosemary, without the customary use of a cane on their backsides, contrived order from chaos, foresaw this need and that, and even found time to descend to the great courtyard and kiss her husband good-bye, ere, at the head of six well-mounted and brawny retainers, he departed for Bideford, some nine miles distant, to escort the distinguished visitor to the manor.

"You're wondrous able," Hubert declared, sweeping her off her feet in a lusty and impulsive embrace. "Yet you've never raised your voice nor beat even the stupidest of our chambermaids. We should, an all goes well, return with the Admiral about noon."

"How dashing he looks in that wine-coloured cloak all embroidered in silver," Rosemary thought when, with supreme ease, young Coffyn swung up into the saddle. Gaily he doffed in her direction a flat velvet cap of brilliant yellow adorned with a curling black ostrich feather. Because the bride herself had supervised their making, she also found pride in those neat, dark green surcoats bearing the family's coat of arms which graced the chests of Hubert's retainers.

A long moment Rosemary lingered on broad stone steps swept clean of snow and watched the little cavalcade splash off down the driveway beneath the naked limbs of tall elm trees which sketched a black filigree pattern against the sky.

A moon-faced serving maid ran up. "Zur Robert prays 'e coom at once." Rosemary heaved a small sigh and returned indoors. Ever since breakfast the old man had been in a turmoil, reminding her of this and that detail which already she had attended to. Probably, he now wished to deliberate upon what doublet he would don for this memorable occasion.

Until this moment, Hubert never before had appreciated how madly popular was the conqueror of Cádiz and the captor of the *San Felipe*, especially here in Devonshire, that county from which Drake had sprung and which he admired to the point of obsession. Not even the Royal Presence in Bideford could have evoked a greater, a more spontaneous or a noisier welcome. Bright, multi-coloured pennants and trade-guild banners fluttered from poles thrust out of windows, merchants even had unbolted yards of precious, richly coloured silks and brocades, permitting them to flutter above the little port's narrow and muddy streets.

During the morning the press became so dense about the Mayor's residence where the great Admiral was lodging that the Mayor was forced to call out the watch to restore some semblance of order.

When Sir Francis Drake appeared to commence his ride to Portledge, women shrieked their excitement and held small children high above their heads that they might some day boast of having laid eyes on him who had made England's name a terror the world around.

Boys and men cheered themselves hoarse and surged forward if only to touch the Golden Admiral's azure-blue saddle housing, or even his stirrup leathers. Pretty young girls advanced diffidently to offer nosegays fashioned of ribbon, there being no flowers in this season.

Far beyond the limits of Bideford a small army of shouting, sweating and wildly excited townsfolk followed the cavalcade and frightened the gentle grey palfrey upon which rode that beautiful lady who had been born Elizabeth Sydenham and whose father was Sir George Sydenham. There could be no doubt that, accustomed though he was to the public's adulation, Sir Francis hugely enjoyed the warmth and spontaneity of this tribute. Drawing upon that uncanny memory of his, he singled out a man here and there he recognized from service on his ships, and called him by name.

When at length even the most tireless of his admirers halted and resorted to waving a farewell, Drake smiled wanly. "Dear God, hardly a wink have either the Lady Elizabeth or I enjoyed since reaching Bideford. I pray, Captain Coffyn, that I'll encounter no similar demonstration at Portledge."

But he did. The whole length of that elm-lined avenue leading from the new gate-posts to the manor house's forecourt was crowded with sturdy, red-faced farmers, their big-bosomed wives and shock-headed children. Their welcome proved no less enthusiastic than that offered by the good citizens of Bideford.

Sir Robert Coffyn had caused himself to be carried downstairs in a chair and placed opposite to Portledge's great front door; it was oaken and designed, long ago, to withstand the effects of a battering-ram. Beneath a warm mantle of crimson woollen cloth edged in miniver, he wore a splendid doublet of flame-coloured satin which effectively concealed that gaping wound, which, year after year, refused to heal, and continued to suppurate despite the best arts of every chirurgeon who treated Sir Robert. The brief winter sun lent false life to the yellow-white of his beard. Across his lap lay a throw of red fox-skins, and about his neck glittered Sir Francis' gift, the handsome Florentine medallion and golden chain which had arrived the night before.

Grouped behind the lord of Portledge stood the manor's principal functionaries—its bailiff and steward. At Sir Robert's left, Rosemary Cathcart Coffyn stood straight, serene and surpassingly lovely in her pale blue camlet gown and a standing lace ruff which made the most of her dark and radiant beauty. A wide farthingale carried her skirts a good foot out to either side of her hips and at the apex of her "widow's peak" shone a lustrous tear-drop pearl dangling between two emeralds. Gracefully, she curtsied, when, in his travelling attire of unrelieved blue, Sir Francis Drake mounted three wide steps leading up to the portal.

"Sir Robert, my ancient comrade in arms!" The Admiral rushed forward, deserting his wife on the top step. Everyone admired the tender fashion in which this famous figure embraced the invalid and with such warmth that tears appeared not only in his own eyes, but in those of Hubert's father.

Sir Francis turned, held out a hand to Lady Drake. "Come, my dear. I would have you greet one of my most valued friends, the bravest of the brave."

Lady Drake curtsied, at the same time bending her proud neck in a graceful arc.

Sir Robert struggled to rise but had to sink back stifling a groan. "My service to you, my lady. Alas, that my legs have turned mutineer. May I present my daughter-in-law who acts as my chatelaine and is become the sweet comfort of my age and disability?"

That night, while awkward farm boys and milking maids, impressed to supplement the overtaxed regular table servants, were fetching in steaming mounds of beef, mutton and fowl, Rosemary Coffyn found opportunity to study that glittering figure she first had beheld almost exactly two years earlier.

So this charming, garrulous and often boastful gentleman was he who by sheer courage, determination and consummate seamanship had girdled the globe. This was the man who, in command of always insignificant forces, had caused Princes, Kings and the Pope himself to tremble; who could inspire the dullest lout in all England to leap, cheering, to his feet. Yonder, daintily conveying a capon's leg to his mouth, sat also he who was responsible for the wrecking of her family's fortune, for the bloody sack of San Domingo, for the violent loss of her virginity and for the deaths of all her family saving only her father and herself.

During the repast a chorus of sweet-voiced lads from the village choir sang such familiar old airs as "The Nut-Brown Maid", "Balow", and "The Bloody Serk". Later, the music of violas de gamba, recorders, nites, lutes and of flutes attempted in vain to penetrate boisterous chatter arising from the well-heaped long table; the most noise came from seats situated below the great salt-cellar of gilded silver brought back by Sir Philippe de Coffyn from the Second Crusade—or so it was believed.

Rosemary found conversation with Lady Drake an easy matter. Only a year or two older than herself, the Admiral's wife appeared radiantly beautiful in a gown of green brocade and a ruff which rose nearly two feet above her marble-white shoulders then vanished to a neckline cut so low that on occasion one could glimpse the upper perimeter of prettily pink nipples.

To watch Sir Francis enjoying this repast no one would have dreamed that, at this very moment, he stood in the deepest disfavour at Whitehall, that a thousand anxieties seethed within that round blond head of his. He had retained most of his teeth and used them, audibly, in gnawing flesh from a saddle of hare. At other times quite elegantly he employed a knife and fork the which he carried at his belt in a little case of blue leather.

It went without saying that Hubert's much younger sisters and brothers for once hardly ate at all, so occupied were they in gazing upon this rare and glittering assemblage.

"Aye, Sir Robert, 'twould seem ye've bred you a true sea falcon in your heir. Hubert betrays the makings of a great sailor. Dear God! You should have seen him at Cádiz Bay. 'Twas not for him to trifle with lesser prey, but to carry one of the richest prizes taken that famous day."

He lifted and absently inspected a delicate silver goblet brought home from Cartagena. "I predict for him high office in the Queen's service and of those who, someday, shall reign after Her Gracious Majesty. God send such a day is far removed."

Later, in the privacy of that same bedchamber in which Drake's messenger announced his projected visit, Sir Robert ascertained the underlying purpose of this expedition from Yarcombe—Drake's sumptuous manor situated not far from Plymouth.

Feet thrust towards the fire, small but powerful brown hands closed tight over lion heads carved on the arms of his chair, Drake kept his eyes on the fire. "In truth, Sir Robert," said he, "the affairs of this realm stand in grave jeopardy. Our pusillanimous friend Burghley has had his way too long.

"By guile and deception," Drake confessed, "I have managed to evade yonder timorous hare's ambition that all the Queen's ships shall be laid up in ordinary at Gillingham Reach."

He lowered his voice, cast a warning glance at Hubert. "At Plymouth, my friend, I have retained thirteen tall ships—all at my own expense—for not a day goes by but that we hear of great numbers of flat-bottomed boats being built by the Spanish i' their Channel ports and in the Low Countries. Come next summer, they will lie ready to ferry the Duke of Parma's veteran halberdiers and arquebusiers across to Harwich."

"Only thirteen vessels!" Sir Robert's weak voice queried from his great green canopied bed. It became obvious that the strain of the day had wearied him greatly.

" 'Tis the sum of the vessels England now holds in commission, saving nine small ships of war under Sir Henry Palmer, lying in the Humber and in the Thames.

"Various gentlemen whom I shall not name," Drake smiled thinly, "and I have conceived it to be our duty privily to enlist ships, ordnance and mariners for duty come spring.

"Thus far I have rallied my friends—who ever trust in me—so at this hour the *Barques Talbot*, *Spark* and *Bonner* are outfitting for sea. Also my *Elizabeth Founes*, *Elizabeth Drake* and John Hawkins' *Barque Hawkins*, which bears his name, are being readied.

"Our party has invited Dom Antonio, that pitiful bastard who pretends the Crown of Portugal, again to attempt capture of his throne."

Captain White, one of Drake's attendants, interjected, "What a sorry rogue is this Antonio; but needs must when the Devil drives."

A puff of raw December wind beat down the flue and dispersed a fine flurry of smoke and ashes over the hearth.

Sir Robert sipped at his cup of mulled wine, surveyed his renowned guest with attention, then cast a shrewd glance at Hubert. "I take it then, Sir Francis, you would have me see what can be done towards advancing your schemes—something like the outfitting of a vessel?"

"Yours was ever a precise perception, friend Robert," Drake chuckled. "From nowhere else in England would I rather welcome a stout, well-found vessel than Bideford in Devonshire." It was to Hubert rather than to his father that Drake posed his next question. "How large a vessel think you you could manage?"

The younger man considered. "I crave your understanding, Sir Francis, but in truth I have been too occupied with restoring our property to speak offhand. But, by the honour of this house, I will undertake to find men and provision for a galleon of"—he hesitated and bit his lip—"say three hundred tons burthen."

"A galleon of three hundred? Do you not overreach your powers?"

Warmed with wine and a full belly, Hubert spoke with unaccustomed celerity. "Nay, Sir Francis. In London I have a friend, one who sailed with us to San Domingo, Cartagena and Virginia. For the past year he has been at Deptford learning the shipwright's art."

Drake's yellow head flashed in the firelight as he glanced up. "Can you mean that big, red-haired Master Mariner named Harry Wyatt?" To Hubert Coffyn it remained a vast wonder that, of all the hundreds, if not thousands, of men the Admiral must have met, that he could so surely place a mental finger on the right name. Briefly, Drake then recapitulated his first encounter with the *Primrose's* Mate.

"An you furnish so fine a vessel," promised the Admiral earnestly, "you'll take your pick of the best ordnance I've collected in Plymouth." He jumped up and went to toast his backside before the fire, spoke succinctly. "I shall expect your galleon there come the first of April."

There it was! With sinking heart Hubert suddenly appreciated the magnitude of this obligation he had so readily assumed. Many an acre of prime woodland would have once more to be sold, and Rosemary must manage with less than a half of the staff now at her disposal.

Drake must have sensed something of the young gentleman's misgivings. "Think not, Hubert, that I accept your offer lightly, nor that I underestimate its cost to you. Never would I dream of soliciting this support were I not aghast that the Queen's present Councillors have left us nigh as helpless as the yolk of a broken egg. It is we of Devon and the rest of England who must save Her Majesty and this realm, come what may."

CHAPTER X

SIR ANDREW OF THURSTON

Now that Her Majesty's *Galleon Centurion* had been launched and floated, a slim, comparatively low-charged vessel awaiting towage over to the rope-walk and mast-basin at Woolwich, Henry Wyatt found a little unaccustomed leisure. Although having deliberately passed over several opportunities of joining the expedition against Cádiz, which had so enriched Hubert Coffyn and his cousin Peter, Wyatt nonetheless had gained invaluable understanding of what went to render a ship crank, slow and unseaworthy, or staunch and swift. Further he had gained friends among the high-born and influential, especially John Hawkins, Treasurer of the Royal Navy, old

Martin Frobisher and, above all, that suave and diplomatic but determined and far-sighted gentleman, Lord Howard of Effingham.

Once more the Queen's weathercock had veered around to favour a further descent upon Spain, as became evident in a proclamation that her good and trusty vassal, Lord Howard, from the twenty-first day of December, 1587, was to be "Our Lieutenant-General, Commander-in-Chief and Governor of our whole Fleet and Army at sea, now fitted forth against the Spaniards and their Allies."

Taverns, sail-lofts, chandlers' warehouses and rope-works buzzed and amplified a rumour that, at long last, Her Gracious Majesty Queen Elizabeth had ordered the taking on of provisions and a hasty completion of such vessels as still stood within their stocks.

Through carefully hoarding his dockyard pay and the practice of stringent economies on Kate's part, Wyatt now became able to contemplate, with his cousin, the purchase of a captured barque with the promise of speed and handiness.

Tonight he decided to seek out his cousin before Peter squandered the whole of his fortune; that blond giant having taken up lodgings in a rowdy tavern recently renamed as the Drake and Anchor. Some pun-minded wag had, on its swingboard, painted an amorous mallard drake comfortably, if unnaturally, perched upon an anchor.

Here, night after night, Peter Hopton would reign over the tap-room freely dispensing liquor and largesse to any broken-down sea-dog who might claim ever having sailed under the nation's darling.

Of course bevies of young and pretty doxies partook of Peter's liberality, but they loved him also for his good nature, amazing strength and endurance. His deeds of prowess in a four-poster were fast becoming legendary the length and breadth of Cold Harbour, that iniquitous slum.

Sometimes it pleased the Master Gunner to pull as many as three giggling trollops into bed at one time and often he kept the whole tavern aroused till cockcrow with his merrymaking. It was understandable, therefore, that shortly before the New Year Peter became afflicted of a bubo on his private parts which put a painful, if temporary, end to his rioting.

When Wyatt found him, the big fellow was seated in what would later be termed the bar parlour, in company with a sallow-faced fellow and a big, bottle-nosed Dutchman. On impulse he lingered in the outer tap-room curious to overhear the conversation within. The two strangers were listening in rapt interest to Peter's richly detailed and graphic account of frolics with his Monocan handmaidens.

The sallow man was setting down his tankard when Wyatt strode in. "And well may you be yearning to return to this America you prate of," said he gravely. " 'Twould be a rare fine place to find yourself come next spring."

"And why?"

"I'll have you know, friend, that at this very hour there lie in Lisbon above four hundred and fifty ships of war!"

The Dutchman stared stupidly. "But is impossible. So many sheeps are not in all Spain."

"Do you give me the lie, sirrah?" snarled the sallow man, starting up.

"Did you count them?" Peter asked.

"Well, not quite," admitted the sallow man. "I gave over when I had reached twice hundred and sixty, but 'tis cert there were as many more, and God alone wots how many more ride in Cádiz Harbour or are on their way out from the Mediterranean."

The Dutchman nodded. "*Ja.* About all this I know nothings, but I haff heard the Duke of Parma gathers twenty-two thousand foot soldiers and soon begins marching them across Flanders."

The sallow man permitted himself to be mollified. "Like enough. I had it yesterday from a rascal i' Capt'n Fenner's ship that in the westward marches of Spain and Portugal are collected forty-nine thousand infantry, twenty-six hundred cavaliers, twelve hundred well-trained gunners and near ten thousand mariners."

That such estimates were exaggerated Wyatt felt quite confident, and yet—and yet, hardly a day went by but some new and frightening report fresh in from the Continent circulated London's waterfront.

A saucy-looking but sweat-smelling wench, distinguished by a mass of frizzed hair dyed orange after the mode set by Her Majesty and her Court, pushed past Wyatt. "—And there's Peter Playful. 'Ow are ye, Ducky?"

"Get ye gone, ye raddled Jezebel!" roared Hopton. "I've no trade for ye and yer like."

The girl laughed and stuck out her tongue but withdrew, patently crestfallen. It was only then that Peter, whose back had been turned, beheld his cousin. He uttered a booming laugh of delight and clumped over to embrace him, then ordered a cold fowl, boiled cabbage and a tankard of the best procurable ale.

"And how fares yer sweet lady?" he presently queried. "And yer offspring?"

Wyatt smiled for Peter was inordinately fond of children. "Well enough, saving only that Henrietta has taken the sniffles again."

"Then hang a slice of raw garlic about her neck—'tis a sure cure of such," Peter informed, puffing hard at a blackened clay pipe and expelling such quantities of smoke that presently the sallow-faced man broke into spasmodic coughing. "By the by, Coz, I spoke to a man from St. Neots. Ye'll recall Joe Alwyn who lived hard by Diddington's windmill?"

As usual when St. Neots was mentioned, Wyatt's expression tightened. "Aye, and what's of note there? Does my estimable father-in-law still maintain his drapery?"

"Aye, but Joe said he's grown sickly and 'tis said he often yearns to buss his favourite daughter again before the churchyard claims him."

"I would gladly take her home," Wyatt answered, "yet I dare not; you well know the reason."

He saw himself once more swinging out of that cell window in Huntingdon Town, running in breathless flight across the countryside to his native village. Curious, how often he completely forgot the fact that, in the eyes of the Law, he and Peter were murderers fleeing the Queen's justice. Again and again he had found cause to rejoice that St. Neots was so tiny a hamlet and that, until he had taken service with Master Foster, he had not travelled beyond Huntingdon Town to the north or to the south at all.

"Fetch your cloak, Peter. I've news of a frigate captured from some Italians that might do us. Let's at least cast an eye over her."

Peter reappeared a moment later wearing a dark blue boat cloak and a conical leather cap, flat-topped and rather resembling a sugar-loaf because of its extremely narrow brim.

Expert examination on Wyatt's part revealed that this French-built frigate promised far better than either the decrepit old *Katrina* or the sturdy but sluggishly sailing *Hope*. Besides, this frigate was bigger, a hundred and eighty tons, her sellers declared, and therefore large enough to cope with that treacherous chop and those cross-currents for which the Narrow Sea was infamous.

The prize master however was undoubtedly misled by Peter's forthright manner and had read on Wyatt's open countenance his profound satisfaction for the price he demanded was astronomical. There followed three full days of haggling, of offers and counter-offers, before Wyatt and the prize master struck hands on the price of nine hundred and eighty-seven pounds.

Of this sum Peter had to assume the lion's share, but he roared and raged like an amorous bull over the suggestion that Wyatt should be entitled to anything less than a half interest in the frigate which they had decided to rename the *Sea Venture.*

For Wyatt now commenced one of the happiest periods of his life. He caused his speedy and low-sided frigate to be sailed over to Lion Quay and there went over her sail by sail, spar by spar and narrowly inspected even the least items of her running gear. Any item of equipment not in the best of condition was instantly sold for what it might fetch.

It was now that his long service in the Royal dockyard stood Wyatt in the best of stead. Unerringly, he ordered the most advantageous positions for his gun-ports—the frigate could, he decided, handle ten broadside guns and as many minions and sakers mounted in swivels along her rail with which to rake an enemy's decks or to repel would-be boarders.

One evening Kate travelled down from their pleasant-appearing, but actually cold and dark, stone cottage at Battle Bridge to view the *Sea Venture.* By osmosis she had grown intimately familiar with all the varying hulls and rigs to be seen sailing up the Thames. Moreover, she could recognize a promise of speed in the lines of a vessel's hull and could estimate whether or no her masts had been properly spaced.

"She is indeed a thing of beauty," Kate murmured delightedly, squeezing her husband's arm, "and like to fight valiantly when the Spaniards come against us. What will you do for a crew?"

A troubled expression crept over Wyatt's broad, copper-tinted features. It was well known that press gangs and intoxicating promises of pay had absorbed almost every able-bodied man in London, Greenwich or in the hamlets dotting the Thames estuary. Moreover, the jails, usually a prime source of raw hands, were being emptied of debtors and felons for service in the Low Countries where the Earl of Leicester was still waging war against the Spanish.

Just now a transport was receiving a long file of chained, hollow-cheeked rogues whose noisome tatters gave off a stench like that of an unclean jakes. Urged on by blows, threats and curses, the luckless recruits were driven below and jammed into the transport's dark and airless holds. That she could not sail until the next day Wyatt soon ascertained from a passing mariner, since she was also to receive a column of prisoners being marched down from such inland counties as Hertford, Buckingham and Surrey.

Wyatt and his wife boarded the frigate, stepped over the little mounds of sawdust, chips and bits and pieces of discarded lumber. On the far side of the deck a tar-kettle still smoked lazily. For Kate it was wonderful to read the enthusiasm, high hope and determination written on Harry's strong, well-beloved countenance, but, for all that, she found it difficult not to visualize the *Sea Venture* exchanging broadsides with the Spanish King's great sea castles—vessels reported to mount as many as sixty or seventy pieces of ordnance. How could the little *Sea Venture* prevail against such, mounting as she did only ten guns? Everywhere in England people were debating similar considerations.

Through slanting rain that sketched brief, pearl-like bubbles across the Pool's muddy waters, Henry Wyatt caused himself to be rowed over to Wapping where the Queen's maritime justice was inflicted.

A light fog, he noticed, was obscuring the hulls of vessels in port, and there was so little wind that the dip and splash of hired wherrys' oars sounded unusually important. Long since he had identified the transport's position, but despite this blinding mist he could guess her whereabouts by those evil odours which came drifting over the water.

Conversation with Peter had advanced the suggestion to purchase perhaps half a dozen likely rogues from among the debtors. Not for any consideration would Wyatt entertain the notion of taking aboard a true felon.

From a stone jetty the Captain of the *Sea Venture* ascended a set of slimy stone steps to find himself confronting a gibbet from which dangled a round dozen of corpses in various stages of decomposition. Some cadavers must have hung there a long time; here and there a sun-dried leg or arm had dropped off from among rags which better had resisted dissolution.

Towards the landward end of the dock a long line of convicts stood in chains awaiting their turn to go aboard. These wretches either stood or sat, heedless of the beating rain, heads bowed, backs bent. A few wept, but many cursed the Queen's law and their luck steadily, monotonously. The greatest number waited their fate in a numbed and humble silence. It was clear that a fair number of these unfortunates would never live to serve their Queen abroad; they coughed incessantly and when they spat, blood streaked their spittle.

To a stunted, black-bearded Sergeant, Wyatt expressed his intention.

"Why, to be sure, sir. Yer free to purchase as many o' these clapperclaws as ye've the purse for. This is a new batch just arrived to the landward end o' this dock. Was I you, sir, I'd look 'em over," he advised, civilly enough. "Ye'll likely discover a few stout farm hands, smiths and drovers among 'em."

Wondering just how far the fifteen pounds—all he and Peter now could scrape together—would go, Wyatt bent his head against the downpour and made his way towards a hut where the name, station and birthplace of each prisoner was being duly recorded. Here receipts for their miserable persons were signed by an officer of the Queen to whom Wyatt explained his need for strong and willing hands.

Wyatt had acquired caution in such dickering. "How many rogues would ten pounds bring me?"

"Four, mayhap five," returned the officer, tilting a helmeted head to rid its visor of a beading of raindrops. "Depends on how choosy ye be."

"To whom do I speak?"

"Why, there's a sheriff in charge o' this last batch," the officer replied. "You'll discover him in yonder tent. Enquire for Sheriff——" He snapped his fingers. "A pox on it! His name escapes me."

Chains clanking dismally and bare feet squelching across mud accumulated on Execution Dock, a new file of convicts, ghost-like amid the fog, shuffled past a small tent. Wyatt perceived that the black-bearded sergeant had been correct; these were once lusty up-county fellows, reared far from the sea.

Glad to escape this dripping downpour, Wyatt ducked his head and entered the tent. Behind a lantern glowing on a narrow table a tall, grey-bearded official sat between an enormously corpulent army officer and a clerk who sniffed continually but failed in ridding himself of a pellucid drop that clung trembling to the tip of a sharp, strawberry-coloured nose.

"William Jonas," intoned the clerk. "Stands condemned in the debt of seven shillings and sixpence—a carpenter by trade."

The army officer made an entry in a book before him then nodded; the prisoner, his chains clinking, stepped back out into the rain.

"I wonder," Wyatt commenced, "whether you gentlemen would entertain an offer to purchase certain debtors?"

"Why, gladly," declared the tall official, turning his silvery head. "Curs'd if I like shipping such luckless fellows off to stop Papist bullets." He stiffened suddenly, but not so much as Wyatt. All in an instant the latter had recognized those lean and hawk-like features. Peering up through this half light were the well-remembered grey eyes of Sir Andrew of Thurston!

"Look who has come to buy fellow convicts! By God's Glory 'tis Henry Wyatt!" the Sheriff of Huntingdon burst out. He jumped up and roared, "Seize this man!"

Everyone in the tent proved too startled by this sudden train of events to obey. Strengthened by desperation Wyatt hurled himself so furiously against the tent wall that a single pole supporting the canvas snapped and collapsed, burying those within beneath folds of sodden sailcloth.

Wyatt wriggled sidewise, groped until he found a bottom edge of the tent's wall. Writhing free, he swayed to his feet, staring incredulously through the driving rain upon the mound of convulsively heaving canvas. Only an instant he lingered because guards were running up, their helmets and pikes' heads gleaming blue-grey amid the gloom.

"A convict attacked the officers," Wyatt was inspired to pant. Then, when the pikemen bent to free those beneath, he turned and forced himself not to run past a file of haggard wretches waiting their turn to pass through the fallen tent. Half-way down Execution Dock Wyatt put on a furious burst of speed and was sickened to hear the hue and cry again rise behind him.

CHAPTER XI

THE EBB TIDE

THE actual chase was shaken off quickly enough. Henry Wyatt found no difficulty in losing his pursuers in the vicinity of a fish-market at Smarts' Key, the which proved well enough attended despite the downpour. But the threat which he could not lose was a ghastly realization. Before long, the whole Port of London would learn that the respected shipwright and Master Mariner they had known was no better than a fugitive felon and a murderer in the eyes of the law.

Bitterly the breathless figure hurrying on through the rain reminded himself that he should have foreseen the inevitable arrival in London Town of someone from Huntingdonshire who would recognize him. Of course he had counted on the protection of its teeming streets along which its nigh on 200,000 human beings dwelt. Why, oh why, had he and Kate not changed at least their surnames?

It went without saying Sheriff Andrew of Thurston would, straight away, hie himself to the Lord Mayor of the City and there lodge a report. Alas, mused Wyatt, that of late he had grown far too well known not to expect detection and arrest—followed in all probability by execution. He overtook and hurried past a funeral plodding dismally along over ankle-deep mire. Shivering, he continued on his way as rapidly as possible towards the Drake and Anchor.

As ill luck would have it, Peter Hopton proved to be out, so the fugitive was forced to waste two precious hours awaiting his return, and when he did Peter was right royally drunk through having attempted to dispel the damp in too many tap-rooms.

"In God's Name, man, ye'd best rally your wits about you," Wyatt implored. Then, in a sudden rage he flung a jar of water full into his cousin's heated red face. "Can't you realize, you sodden fool, that *your* neck's in as much hazard as mine?"

"Full o' play. You shoul'n done that. Wha' say? Wha' neck?"

"*Your* neck. I went recruiting hands over to Wapping this morning and learned what will become of you and me an the watch takes us up."

Only reluctantly would Peter attempt to sober himself with the aid of a bowl of mutton broth and a tall jack of ale. But when at length his befuddlement passed, he levelled anxious, bloodshot blue eyes at his cousin.

"Ye said 'e watch is looking for us?" he demanded thickly.

"Like as not. Sheriff Andrew of Thurston, a pox for ever on him, recognized me, even hailed me by name."

"An' he'll recall me just as well, like as not," grunted Peter. "Well, Coz, what's to be done?"

In the privacy of the still-empty bar, Wyatt passed over a purse containing the convict purchase money. "There's but one thing to do. We must sail incontinent on the ebb."

Peter stared, wiped his still-dripping features. "Are ye gone daft? Why, the *Sea Venture's* scarce half rigged, we've only a half set of sails aboard and the rest won't be finished for a week. Besides, much o' the standing rigging needs to be re-rove."

"No need to remind me," Wyatt broke out impatiently. "Just remember that by tomorrow Andrew of Thurston will have learned of our ownership and lay us by the heels. He's a hard, upright and relentless man, is the High Sheriff of Huntingdonshire, as the presence of so many poor wretches on Execution Dock can tell you." He leaned forward, laid a hand on his cousin's shoulder. "No, Peter, flight is our only chance. Do you fetch whatever you can find by way of a crew—and it won't be much, while I'll get Kate and the children aboard together with whatever I can rescue from our home by the way of food and property. We can supplement our stores at Margate."

"Are you daft?" repeated the yellow-haired Master Gunner. " 'Tis bound to be dark and foggy on the Thames tonight. You ben't seriously proposing standing down river i' the pitch dark?"

"Aye," came the grim response. "I'd rather risk that than finding mercy at the hands of Squire Andrew."

Peter strode over to a wooden piggin and from it spilled more water over his head. "This has struck me all of a heap," he confessed, "but what can you and I and the few hands I can come across accomplish towards navigating a half-rigged ship of near 200 tons burthen?"

"God knows, we will soon find out. Remember 'tis for you, you vast, yellow-pated clown, to bring aboard no less than four good men."

"And where, in God's Name, am I to discover such? Ye must wot well London's been stripped bare of likely hands."

"I know it," Wyatt admitted and as if to cheer himself drained the dregs of Peter's ale. "But needs must when the law snaps at our heels. Remember, all you own, all I own, is risked in the *Sea Venture*." He stood up, fastening the catches of his mire-splashed boat cloak. "You'll have about four hours, Peter Hopton, ere you're to appear at Lion Quay. Remember, we durst not miss the ebb."

Miserably he stalked, cloaked to the ears, over London Bridge and past the shops and houses built upon it.

Kate Wyatt, busily preparing an evening meal, became first perplexed and then anxious over his failure to appear. This certainly was not like Harry. Twice she opened the cottage door and peered down that muddy lane which led across Horsey Downs towards the river. All she saw was a wandering beggar and a stray dog or two.

At last a gentle rapping sounded on a rear window-pane—like most homes of that day the cottage boasted but a single door. Swiftly Kate stooped, picked up a billet of firewood and strained her eyes into the deepening gloom. Once she had recognized him she unlatched the heavy wooden shutters apart. "God's love, Harry! Why come you home like this? You haven't been tossing pots with that worthless cousin of yours?"

In brief sentences he explained that disaster which threatened, informed her that in under two hours their most valued possessions must be packed ready for being trundled down to the water's edge in a hand-barrow. There, fortuitously, a skiff belonging to the *Sea Venture* chanced to lie pulled up on the mud.

It was characteristic of Kate that she neither broke into lamentations nor debated the wisdom of his decision, only kissed him hard then dished up a steaming plate of stew. Later, while he stood peering through a crack in the shutters alert for the first glimpse of approaching watchmen, she piled all the family's clothing on to a blanket, together with her linen, and tied it into a bundle. Their slender stock of tableware was crammed into one chest and every scrap of food she could find into another.

Little Henrietta awoke, peered about and commenced to wail, but the baby—Kate had named him Anthony after the child's grandsire—mercifully slept the sleep of healthy innocence. Even when deposited, swaddling clothes and all, on top of a chest in the barrow the boy slumbered on.

Full darkness had fallen when out into the drizzle stepped Henry Wyatt pushing the creaking barrow before him. Kate carried the little girl and her ungainly bundle of raiment. Uppermost in his mind seethed a crucial question. Would Peter rise to the occasion and fetch on board their incompletely rigged frigate men skilled enough to bend a few essential sails on to the yards?

Even as the skiff trailed at the end of the painter beneath the *Sea Venture*'s newly painted counter the gurgling of the current diminished noticeably, indicating that the period of slack water had come at an end. It proved no mean feat to swing himself aboard by the futtocks of the main shrouds and then to haul up the children at the bight of a bowline. If he had thought previously he could estimate his wife's calm capabilities he had been mistaken. Quite coolly, she remained in that bobbing, swaying skiff to knot a rope's end about the chests and followed his instructions swiftly and with competence.

When at length he hoisted her up over the rail he could not resist a quick and passionate embrace of inexpressible admiration.

"Get the sprats below," he directed. "Down yonder companion. You'll find no bunk ready but they can sleep on your bundle till we get under way." He almost said, "*If* we get under way."

Then followed an agonizing interval of waiting, one in which Wyatt climbed to the fore mast-head and commenced, by sense of touch more than anything else, to bend on a topsail, then he rigged stays, braces and halyards. About the mainsail he could do nothing alone; it being far too heavy to be coped with by even his desperate strength. Snatches of song came floating out from the brothels at the landward end of Lion Wharf Quay. Opposite, the masts of a vessel lacking all her rigging loomed like gigantic spears through the gloom.

An hour dragged by in which Wyatt savagely cursed his irrepressible, irresponsible cousin. Deep-toned clocks in various church towers began debating the exact moment of nine o'clock and as he was balancing precariously on the bowsprit, with weary and torn fingers rigging a spritsail, that headsail without which a ship would sail well nigh unmanageably, a sudden furious bawling at the far end of the wharf drew his attention.

Out of the darkness Kate's quivering voice informed: "Oh, Harry! Men are approaching. God send 'tis not the watch."

If it were indeed the watch, which Wyatt truly did not anticipate, there was nought he could do about it so, hurriedly, he completed his rigging of the spritsail then scrambled back on deck. There arose a raucous ballad and he could hear uncertain feet advancing along the wharf. To his infinite relief the strangers proved to be Peter and four men, two of whom were so hopelessly drunk that they swayed on their feet. The recruits were all stunted, sharp-faced fellows such as infested the evil purlieus of the Cold Harbour district but with whose help, by the Grace of God, *Sea Venture* might grope her way down to the sea.

Ill-spaced and quite inadequate blocks creaked, loudly protested the hoisting of a tattered old mainsail, but presently the frigate was cast off and, under sprit, foresail and mainsail, drifted away from the wharf.

The trip down river was to be a nightmare relieved only by two factors. First, the wind was light and blew from almost dead astern which was fortunate since, under her jury rig, the frigate could not have tacked into the wind.

Another fortunate element lay in the fact that up from the Stygian depths of the forecastle groped a pair of watchmen, still sodden with drink and very dismayed to find the *Sea Venture* under way. Joyfully, Peter cuffed and cursed them into usefulness, which was well since the two waterfront rascals he had dragged aboard had collapsed, snoring, and obdurately refused to rouse despite kicks and buckets of dirty river water dashed into their faces.

Kate, having made her babies as comfortable as possible on the bundle of bedclothing and garments, returned on deck and quietly inquired how she might be of service.

"Your eyes are uncommon quick," said he. "Pray proceed to the port bow and for the love of God sing out the minute you spy anything. 'Tis darker than the inside of a black cat out here."

Now the frigate commenced to slip faster over the waters. A look-out, posted on the starboard bow, leaned far out in the gloom and strained to see, while Kate gripped a forestay and earnestly besought God's help that she might spy an obstacle in time. One of the less drunken mariners stood a few yards down the deck, ready to relay alarms to Peter and through him to Henry Wyatt handling the tiller.

Trembling with anxiety and under the river's raw chill, Kate twice described a diabolically faint pattern of spars against stars showing above the river's mist and called out a warning. On one occasion Wyatt barely put his helm up in time to avoid scraping the side of a vessel he recognized to be the incompleted *Centurion*. Dear God, had he not worked on her for many months?

He was hoping to win clear without mishap when, in avoiding a big howker discerned at the last moment, he crashed into the stern of a pinnace lying low in the water; an example of a fast new class bearing an old name. These little vessels were designed to accompany galleons on their blue-water duties. Following a mighty crash came the noise of falling spars. Volleys of startled oaths rang out of the darkness.

"Ye blundering bastards; ye'll answer for this to the Queen's Surveyor of Ships! Ye've nigh to sunk us."

In a frenzy of despair, Wyatt peered up, glimpsed his main yard tangled among shrouds supporting the pinnace's mast. Peter meanwhile grunted, hacked mightily at a yard of the stranger's which had fouled the spritsail.

"What ship is that?" roared an angry voice out of the blackness. "Damn your soul to hell, answer me!"

"We're the *Petrel* out o' Dover," Peter had the wit to yell back. "Whyn't ye show a light?"

"Anchor alongside, ye clumsy dogs. Come daylight we'll settle this matter."

Praise God the ebb was running strong so, gradually, the *Sea Venture* swung broadside to the current and disentangled her main yard.

"Hold on, curse ye!" roared someone aboard the little man-of-war. "Don't ye dare sneak off i' the dark! Halt! John, you go aboard that craft!"

Obediently the fellow leapt but fell short and into the dark water separating the two vessels. He commenced desperately to cry for a rope to be flung him.

After grinding along the pinnace's length Wyatt's vessel tore free and resumed her sluggish progress downstream. To what extent the *Sea Venture* had suffered Wyatt could only guess. All he now was sure of was that this unchancy collision would preclude any stop at Margate, where he had hoped to improve his improvised rig and charge stores sufficient for coasting.

CHAPTER XII

GALLEON COFFYN

By dint of many leagues sailed up and down the west coast of Cornwall and Devon, Hubert Coffyn finally found in Penzance what he wanted and could afford, a high-charged, old-design galleon of some two hundred tons burthen. As the family had foreseen, silver table service, candlesticks and certain salvers disappeared from Portledge Manor, and several acres of choice timberland again went under lease. Soon the gallery and the great hall lacked that bustle characteristic of the preceding year. But it was only because the Honourable Charles Coffyn, a distant cousin who lived at Ilfracombe, was induced to purchase a quarter interest in the rebuilt man-of-war that the venture was kept within the family.

It had been late April when Rosemary Coffyn, now displaying unmistakable evidence that before long she would produce a grandchild for Sir Robert, bade farewell to her husband. With the coming of spring the old baronet grew querulous and cursed mightily over his inability to sail from Bideford with his son, the Honourable Charles, and many a stout tenant and freeholder of the countryside.

It was greatly to Rosemary's joy, therefore, that, a fortnight after the *Galleon Coffyn* had sailed, a flyboat, one of many which carried dispatches to and from Drake's mighty muster at Plymouth, delivered a message from her lord and master.

In it Hubert begged that she afford shelter and kindness to a Mistress Kate Wyatt and her infants. She recalled immediately, and pleasantly, that sober, red-haired Master Mariner who had been so inseparable from Hubert back in San Domingo. It would be fine, she reckoned, to have another young female about to help her manage the estate, and also to keep some manner of control over Sir Robert's high-spirited younger children.

The two girls met for the first time on an incomparable May afternoon when the air was balmy and delicately fragrant with the scent of apple blossoms and new-mown hay. They could not have been more dissimilar—Rosemary *petite*, slim, raven-haired and dark-eyed with tiny hands and feet, and Kate still shapely despite two pregnancies which had thickened somewhat her magnificently proportioned body. Her grey blue eyes remained as lovely and scintillating as ever while her hair, not reddened in the silly mode of the day, gave off a silver-golden sheen not incomparable with those ducats of which so few remained in the strong-boxes of Portledge.

Rosemary took fondly to small Henrietta whose malformed foot had developed almost, but not quite, straight, but it was on the infant Anthony that Hubert's wife showered her chiefest admiration. Possibly this was because he, too, had dark eyes and hair.

Said she, laughingly, " 'Twould seem a miracle your children, one so light and the other so dark complected, could spring from the same parents." Intent on combing the baby boy's luxuriantly long hair she missed a tortured grimace which momentarily hardened Kate's mouth.

"I am hoping Anthony's hair will turn red," Kate said slowly, "as he grows older. If not, perhaps our third child will more fully favour his father."

"A third——" The eyes of the two girls met. "I—I had not suspected."

"Nor I—'till last week."

"How happy I will be to have you here," Rosemary murmured, replacing Anthony on his pillow. "I—I am, well, somewhat inexperienced in this matter of bearing children."

Later, Kate spoke of the humming shipyards at Plymouth, of the constant arrival of small, privately owned men-of-war such as the *Galleon Coffyn.*

"On Harry's advice," she informed, "your husband has caused six feet of the poop and forecastle to be razed while the galleon's length is to be increased by twice ten feet. This, Harry swears, will render his craft vastly more manageable and permit the mounting of four additional cannon."

While they lingered in Rosemary's airy private chamber stitching embroidery to adorn an altar cloth Kate enlarged upon the spate of activity induced when news was brought that the *Empresa de Inglaterra*, despite Drake's hampering efforts, at last was nearing readiness. It was well known that, under pain of death, all the Spanish ships must be prepared to sail out upon the twenty-fifth of March.

Sir Francis Drake, Kate stated, was begging for an immediate assault to be launched to destroy what the Papists had dubbed "the Invincible Armada", either in their home ports or off the coast of Spain. Alas that the Queen, again in a timorous mood, stubbornly had forbidden so shrewd a blow.

"Rosemary, 'tis a truly noble thing to sail as I have in our pinnace about Plymouth Harbour and to count so many great and noble ships.

Last month there were about thirty collected under our great Admiral." Among others she named the *Elizabeth Bonaventure*, the *Roebuck*, the *Galleon Fenner* and six tall ships belonging to the City of London.

"You amaze me," Rosemary declared. "Your knowledge of vessels and their management scarce could be exceeded in a Master Mariner."

"You forget," Kate replied, needle glinting over the frame, "that for above a year Harry found employ at the Royal Dockyard in Deptford and that from our cottage I could observe each and every vessel passing along the Thames. Then, too, I had cause to learn much concerning various ropes, yards and spars when we finished fitting out the *Sea Venture* in Dover." Kate was tempted to mention the reason for their abrupt departure from London but decided against it, for all that she was certain that, through suffering her own misfortunes, Rosemary would prove an interested and a sympathetic listener. She went on to say, "On the day I sailed for Bideford the *Sea Venture* was hoisting in her ordnance and charging her magazine."

" 'Tis well that Drake and our people are so alert," Rosemary observed thoughtfully.

"And why?"

"In Cádiz Harbour I have seen the kind of warships as will rally to King Philip's standard. Why, the Portuguese own carracks that make the biggest of our Queen's ships appear like mere pinnaces by comparison. You would tremble for what lies ahead had you seen them, as I have, in all their pride and glory. They fairly bristle with cannons. Why, the *Florencia* galleon alone is said to carry fifty-two big guns—you'd dote on the marvellous carvings they show on their bows and particularly their sterns. These sculptures are always of a religious nature and resplendent with gold leaf; aboard the *San Juan* galleon great jewels serve as eyeballs in the images of the Virgin and her Son. What is the most guns carried by one of our Navy?"

"The *Ark*," Kate replied promptly; "she carries only thirty-four, but most of them are long guns."

"And the rest?"

"Not many mount more than twenty."

An anxious "V" appeared between the smooth black brows of Hubert Coffyn's wife. "Why, my dear, the galleons of Guipúzcoa mount forty at the very least and the great carracks of Lisbon up to eighty-eight—so Father says."

"Had you heard," Kate inquired presently, "that their famous Admiral Santa Cruz is dead?"

To her sudden start a bobbin of green silk thread fell from

Rosemary's lap. "So the great victor of Lepanto, may God rest his soul, is dead. But for him the Turks might have overrun all Italy. And yet we may in our prayers also thank God that this is so for he and Pero de Aviles de Menendez were the chiefest hopes of Spain. Tell me," she demanded eagerly, "who has supplanted him?"

"Some say a land General by the name of Alonzo de Leyva."

"I have heard of him as a brave and reckless fighter."

"But others at Plymouth reported that His Majesty of Spain has ordered the Duke of Medina-Sidonia to take command."

"Another General—whom I thought had retired to his properties near Cádiz. Often I have heard Father mention Don Pérez de Guzmán as a very able officer."

Hubert's greyhound, more restless and mournful-eyed than ever since his master's departure, trotted in bearing a mutton-bone discovered among rushes carpeting the great hall, deposited it at Rosemary's feet and then placed his head on her lap.

"But surely we now have more vessels in commission than the thirty we had last winter?" Rosemary queried, absently pushing aside the proffered bone and patting the dog.

"Oh, yes. Harry told me some sixteen sail, under Sir Henry Palmer, patrol the Narrow Sea, ready to drive back the Duke of Parma should a fair wind tempt him to cross over his army in their flat-bottomed boats. Under Lord Howard of Effingham cruise some sixteen more, while eleven small and insignificant men-of-war serve under Vice-Admiral Martin Frobisher."

Kate retrieved a pair of scissors from the end of a ribbon securing them to her girdle and snipped some thread ends. "Harry and many others believe that Lord Howard will sail for Plymouth as Sir Francis has begged and advised, so that England's greatest force will stand ready to assault the enemy when first he nears our coast."

CHAPTER XIII

LORD HOWARD OF EFFINGHAM

PETER HOPTON was in a frenzy of disappointment for despite lashings both from his tongue and a rope's end the rogues signed on as the *Sea Venture's* crew proved inept and surly about the business of getting the frigate under way. In no less anxiety, Captain Henry Wyatt from his poop deck bemoaned the listless and grudging manner in which his men laid out on the yards and how awkwardly they made sail on this lovely twenty-first day of May, 1588. He gnawed his lip in dread that Admiral Drake might note this graceless performance; it lent him but little consolation that several other vessels were presenting a similar lack of smartness.

How galling it was, now that the *Sea Venture* at last was well armed, fully equipped and otherwise ready as could be desired, her crew should be so deplorably bad. He had had to sign on whatever he could by way of hands. So great were the inducements offered by wealthier owners that when he did manage to ship a healthy, able mariner the fellow disappeared overside at night, or deserted when sent ashore on some errand.

The frigate's original crew fetched from London had vanished like mist under the sun and there was none to replace them beyond a succession of half-wits, drunkards and irresponsible rogues who reported aboard only to disappear. Bitter envy stung Wyatt while witnessing the *Galleon Coffyn's* smart performance. Of the men brought in her from Bideford only a very few yielded to the blandishments and promises of other Captains.

It was sheer delight to watch the way her sails blossomed in swift succession as she steered to take her place in a column of vessels sailing three abreast in wake of the *Revenge* which now had become the Golden Admiral's flagship. She was of 500 tons burthen yet she remained handy as a young charger.

As, gradually, the *Sea Venture* gathered speed Wyatt bellowed for more sail and bade his helmsman guide the frigate into her position.

Sir Francis Drake, his Admiral's pennant flying, was sailing out from Plymouth Haven in a pretty gesture of welcome to Lord Howard of Effingham, Lord High Admiral of Her Majesty's Navy. Naturally it had galled Francis Drake no little that even so highborn and gallant a gentleman should have been granted supreme command during this, the most critical hour of Elizabeth's reign. Yet he understood the reason for this preference. He himself belonged to that new nobility which was commencing slowly but surely to dictate the maritime fortunes of England. How could the son of a mere Navy parson, although gently born, hope to hold command over Charles Howard, descended from one of the most ancient, celebrated and noble families in the realm?

The morning was indeed surpassingly beautiful and all the more appreciated because it followed a three-day downpour. With flags snapping and the great Latin Crosses painted on their main courses glowing brilliant scarlet in the spring sunshine, the thirty ships of Drake's command stood out into Plymouth Sound.

Anyone possessing sharp eyes could see a dark collection of townsfolk gathered upon the Hoe to witness the impressive approach of Lord Howard of Effingham's squadron. Sail upon sail, to the number of over sixty, were dotting the crisp blue waters. Experienced onlookers counted eleven great vessels belonging to Her Majesty's Navy, sixteen tall vessels furnished by the City of London, plus seven ships belonging to Lord Howard himself, and some twenty smaller craft from various Channel ports, all trailing small boats astern and each attended by a screen of saucy little pinnaces.

Well ahead of her consorts the *Ark Royal* bowled along. Originally she had been built by Sir Walter Raleigh and named the *Ark Raleigh* but she was sold by that nobleman to the Queen. Everyone recognized the Royal Standard—red, blue and gold—Streaming in glorious colour from her foretop and a Vice-Admiral's pennon flying from the main, while a huge Cross of St. George banner showed at her mizzen.

Her sails trimmed, at long last, to Wyatt's satisfaction the *Sea Venture* fulfilled her promise of speed and rapidly assumed her proper position in the column following Drake's pennon. Probably because many of the Golden Admiral's old Captains and companions were in command, his squadron sailed more smartly than Lord Howard's and kept position better.

They who witnessed the scene never tired of describing how those tall blue, yellow and red ships manœuvred under curving white canvas, how, at that precise moment when the *Revenge* arrived abeam of the *Ark Royal*, Drake's Admiral's pennon was lowered. An instant later Lord Howard's Vice-Admiral's pennant also came fluttering down upon the *Ark Royal's* deck.

Consummate seamanship enabled the squadrons simultaneously to back their wind; Drake, as became a newly subordinate, to leeward, Howard of Effingham to windward. The whole Sound seemed peopled by vessels of every conceivable tonnage. Barges put out from the *Revenge* and from the *Ark Royal* and saluted each other by deftly tossing oars. Aboard the *Revenge*, Howard's former pennant now was bent to the halyards, and Drake's to the *Ark Royal's*. A broadside, and then another, thundered salutes at the appearance of an Admiral's flag at the *Ark Royal's* fore. More salutes boomed, echoed and re-echoed among the hills behind Plymouth when a Vice-Admiral's flag was broken out to float above the *Revenge*.

As Hubert Coffyn wrote his wife, " 'Twas a memorable, dainty and precise ceremony by which was created the powerfullest armada ever to show the Cross of St. George."

Back in port that same afternoon the *Sea Venture's* cockboat could be seen pulling sluggishly over to the *Galleon Coffyn.* In its stern sheets Henry Wyatt wore a look of anxiety born of two grave concerns.

When Hubert Coffyn made Captain Wyatt welcome in his cabin, the latter unburdened himself and bespoke his desperate need for honest, stout mariners. It was a bitter thing, he declared, finally to command a well-found craft only to have her manned by such undependable and ill-trained louts that he durst not trust them to sail across the Sound. Could not his old friend and shipmate spare him just a few dependables from the north of Devon?

"It grieves me sore," replied the galleon's Master and laid a sympathetic hand on Wyatt's shoulder, "to deny you, Harry, for I know your need is great. But I have lost six good men this past week through a pox on board. Next, two more goodly lads from Ilfracombe were grievously hurt in a tavern brawl two days ago. Believe me, Harry, I am really hard put to man this vessel."

"Then in God's Name, Hubert, what am I to do? At best I am but weakly half manned."

"And so are most private-owned vessels. Will you join me in a cup of Malmsey?"

They lingered in a dim coolness created by the *Galleon Coffyn's* cabin, spacious by comparison to the *Sea Venture's* yet devoid of the expensive hangings and those ornate carvings usually to be found aboard a vessel of her class and tonnage. At length Coffyn mentioned Mistress Kate's safe arrival at Portledge Manor and that this spring's planting promised well.

Finally Hubert drew a deep breath. "I have spoken," he announced, "to Sir Francis concerning the matter of Her Majesty's pardon for you and Master Gunner Hopton."

"And what said the Admiral?"

A frown creased Coffyn's brow. "Why, 'twas little enough, he being occupied with plans for greeting my Lord Howard, but I think he took serious consideration of your petitions. It was hard to be certain—I must be honest with you, Harry, about how carefully he listened to my account of the evil and unjust fate which befell your parents."

"Answer me truly. Think you Sir Francis will approach Her Majesty on our behalf? Pray God, Hubert, you'll never know what it means to live in the shadow of the gallows!"

"Were this any other time I'd swear upon my honour that Sir Francis would advance your cause before the Queen." His wide mouth curved into a reassuring smile. "Our Admiral holds you dear; never has he forgotten who it was that brought him news of the treachery of Bilbao and so launched his armada of 1586."

Wyatt took a quick turn about the cabin, clumsy leather boots clacking loud upon the decking. Why had he hoped for something better than this? Drake's loyalty to his following was legendary, but, of course, was it not unfair to expect that he, with all at hazard, should concern himself with the troubles of one of his least Captains? Wyatt broke a tough biscuit and dipped a segment of it into the goblet of Malmsey he carried as he paced restlessly about.

"I wonder, friend Hubert, why thus far no enemy sails have been sighted off the Lizard?"

Greatly relieved to find the conversation directed towards a less difficult theme, young Coffyn described how, off Cape Ortegal, the "Invincible Armada" had become baffled by contrary winds until its commander, General the Duke of Medina-Sidonia, finding water short and supplies spoiling, had put back into Coruña with two thirds of his fleet. The balance, unaware of this action, had sailed on to a rendezvous off the Scilly Islands.

"Thus, again, God has favoured us," young Coffyn concluded. "Otherwise last month we should have had to stand against the Duke with what force we had here in Plymouth."

They spoke awhile further concerning a system of beacons which, in a few hours, should warn all England that invasion was imminent. Then, by no means encouraged, Henry Wyatt returned on deck to find the *Galleon Coffyn's* riding lights haloed by fog.

CHAPTER XIV

HANDS FOR THE *SEA VENTURE*

ALL during the first two weeks of June, Lord Howard of Effingham's Grand Fleet tugged at its moorings and anxiously scanned the horizon for ten store ships promised by the Queen's Surveyor of Victuals. In a series of tiresome false alarms coasters and fishermen reported strange ships off the Scillies. But, as time went by and the wind beat straight into Plymouth Sound making it impossible for the English fleet to seek the sea, crews sickened and supplies ran short for, no matter how Drake's victualling officers bribed, wheedled and threatened, Plymouth and South Devonshire simply could not find more provisions.

Only vessels like the *Galleon Fenner* and *Galleon Coffyn*, whose crews were bound by the deep loyalty of community ties, failed to suffer from a general desertion.

One morning in mid-June, Henry Wyatt was appalled to discover that again he had lost more than a quarter from his scant crew of eighty through sickness or desertion. Not even well-verified accounts of the enemy's overwhelming strength could keep them to their allegiance. Now there was talk aboard the *Ark Royal* of laying up lesser vessels and adding their crews to the rosters of better-found ships.

"Dear God, Peter, what *am* I to do?" Henry Wyatt demanded in the privacy of his cabin. "Were Lord Howard within the hour to signal 'weigh anchor' the *Sea Venture* could scarce make sail."

Deliberately, Peter scratched his yellow pate, then, adapting himself to the frigate's lazy rocking, applied himself to a leather jack of ale.

"Well, Harry," said he, wiping his mouth on his sleeve, "since ye've occupied yerself wi' all the outfitting and have gained us fine guns out o' the Queen's Arsenal, why, 'tis I shall voyage inland and find us some lusty hands, pray God, in time."

Wyatt's shoulders lifted to a discouraged sigh. "Out upon it, Peter! You should know that this coast has been combed time out of mind. We've neither the gold nor the power to find replacements."

Peter yawned prodigiously and stood up, his head brushing the deck beams above. "Ye may deem me an oft-drunken and lustful rogue—which I am," he admitted with an engaging simplicity. "Yet, by the Lord Harry, I warrant that within this week I'll bring aboard hands sufficient to serve our broadside."

"The ale has addled your wits," grunted Wyatt. "Where would you discover fifteen able men?"

"God knows," Peter laughed. "But I promise ye'll have 'em, else I'll freely assign you my share in this craft."

He departed, taking with him one Arnold, the frigate's Boatswain, and two powerful younkers from Cornwall, black-haired and tricky yet, for some reason, consumed with loyalty for Peter. The fifth member of the recruiting party was a merry, blue-eyed Irish giant called Brian O'Brian.

Three days later, one of the Cornishmen came sailing out in a hired wherry accompanied by two big, rawboned farm boys, lashed hand and feet on her bottom and a trio of cutpurses who still cursed the rigours of imprisonment in Liskeard jail. The very next day Brian O'Brian put in an appearance shepherding a party of four, gaunt fellow countrymen who had met with the ill luck of being cast away in that same gale which was keeping Lord Howard's fleet prisoner in the Sound. To these simple bog-trotters Brian had pictured the *Sea Venture* as a vast floating fortress in which they would feast and lie upon soft beds. To this vocal intoxication the Irishman had supplied convincing quantities of strong liquor until, roaring like so many Armagh bulls, they were hoisted over the frigate's rail promptly to be imprisoned in her forehold.

Only then did Wyatt seek Drake's permission—he still took his orders from Sir Francis and would for many months—to shift his anchorage far enough out to render the prospect of swimming ashore an almighty hazardous proposition. When the Irishmen sobered up, they screamed weird Gaelic curses and promised to sink the *Sea Venture* at their first opportunity, which, of course, accomplished nothing towards removing those gratings imprisoning them in the frigate's forehold.

Forty-eight hours later the other Cornishman returned, nursing a knife-slash but conducting a trio of gypsies, furtive, dark-faced fellows, he had captured while they dozed about their campfire.

Five days elapsed but neither Peter nor Arnold reappeared. Wyatt could not know it, but the worst of ill luck had attended their recruiting efforts. Although they had penetrated into the depths of Somersetshire, in the ancient town of Yeovil they failed in persuading a blacksmith to abandon his forge and an apprentice to become a runaway. But at a comfortable nearby farmhouse Peter's vivid tall tales of life in Virginia and of Drake's triumphs and of the wealth won aboard the Venetian galliot in Cádiz Harbour sufficiently fired the imagination of the farmer's second son and a doltish cousin who chanced to be labouring there. At three of the morning they arose and departed with Arnold for service aboard the *Sea Venture.*

Were he to return to Plymouth within the promised time Peter calculated he must commence to retrace his steps. Accordingly he turned his mount—a raw-boned skate appropriated from a lonely field—towards Tiverton and Exeter. Deeply discouraged, Peter came upon a tavern in the pleasant little village of Chudleigh. Here his hopes sank lower than low because press gangs and recruiting parties had swept the country clean as an old bone. The proprietor of a small tavern assured him that hereabouts too many of Drake's men had sung siren songs and promised the easy gaining of great fortunes. Now, only shrewd, sensible and phlegmatic men remained in the countryside.

"But God's love, friend," he confided to the innkeeper, "I must bring back at least three hardy rogues. Are there none such i' this vicinity?"

"Aye," the publican replied, wiping plump hands on a stained leather apron. "An ye follow the road to Newton Abbott half a league ye'll spy Franklin Dawson's farm. His is a main fine holding, worked by himself and three stalwart sons, but ye'll not wheedle them into 'listing aboard your ship or any other, because one o' them has served along o' Martin Frobisher and he wots well a mariner's true lot."

Groaning because of sundry sores, Peter paid his reckoning and set off through the sunset. It remained light, however, when the lights of Franklin Dawson's walled farmhouse gleamed softly on the floor of a rich valley checkered by many small green fields and meadows.

When he rode up to its gate the welcome accorded him proved anything but cordial. Fierce watchdogs ran, snapping and snarling, about Peter's legs and a powerful, black-browed individual nearing thirty who carried a bludgeon set with sharp iron points came striding out to demand the traveller's business.

He was, Peter declared while slapping road dust from his galligaskins, but a poor wayfarer fleeing the misery of service aboard Her Majesty's ships.

The black-haired young fellow stared suspiciously a moment but ended by pushing open the farmyard's ponderous gate. "And be you indeed so? Well, coom in. Methought you one o' those cursed recruiting officers who are for ever besieging this farm and trying to cozen us wi' big talk and fair promises."

Franklin Dawson, apparently, must be a yeoman of more than average industry and ability, for his dwelling appeared neat to admiration, with well-thatched roof and enclosed by a high wall which must have been raised during those days when Saracens and Northmen raided inland even so far as this.

The franklin proved to be a shrewd, sharp-nosed fellow and his wife a gaunt, faded-looking creature. The family had been attacking an enormous supper which included bowls of rich milk, thick slabs of ham and even thicker slices of rye bread smeared with that sweet butter for which Devonshire remains famous, so, perforce, they placed a wooden trench before Peter and bade him fall to.

Peter's cheerful open countenance and hearty manner gradually thawed the stony expressions worn by the farmer's three older sons.

Giles, the black-haired one who had let him in, turned out to be the eldest, then there were Herbert and George his twin. They were about twenty and looked slow and as powerful as young bullocks.

The only other member of the family present to help Mistress Dawson wait on the menfolk was a pretty, vacant-eyed and full-figured daughter known as Peg. It did not require Peter long to sense that Peg could not be quite bright; the family were for ever so watchful.

Apparently Peg heretofore had never encountered anyone even remotely resembling this merry, yellow-haired giant. Nearing her eighteenth year, she enjoyed a mass of chestnut-coloured hair and beautifully regular white teeth which she revealed in an interminable series of high-pitched giggles.

After supper the family and their guest trooped out to sit about and belch beneath a great apple tree flourishing in the midst of their walled courtyard. Once Peter had deduced that Giles had voyaged with Frobisher only to the White Sea, he completely enthralled them with his stock accounts of adventures in America.

"Now you talk sensible-like," observed Franklin Dawson. "When ye speak o' rich earth, tall forests and plenty of good water, yer reasonable. A pox on all this fiddle-faddle about jewels and pearls and Spanish gold."

When Peter commenced, shrewdly enough, to describe farming practices among the Naturals the Dawsons, father and sons, listened in rapt attention. All the while Peter remained conscious of Peg's big, wide-set brown eyes lingering upon him. Icod! The wench's soft red mouth wore a bedside expression. One of her brothers, noticing the girl's rapt expression, muttered something that caused her to wince and then lower her eyes demurely on strong, work-roughened hands. All the while Peter kept groping for an argument which might prove sufficiently telling to lure these powerful young yokels into handling culverins aboard the *Sea Venture*.

"The Naturals," he continued, "space their corn—we called it 'maize' in Virginia."

Thoughtfully old Dawson fingered a scraggly beard. "Did ye closely observe their method?"

"Aye." Peter found trouble in forcing himself to ignore certain luscious curves tightening Peg's coarse wool bodice. "Not only observed, but I e'en planted some rows of maize for my own use, not that it had time to ripen afore we were taken off by Sir Francis Drake."

"Think you this maize would serve to fatten swine?"

"Aye. The deer in America thrive on it."

"And how is it planted?" Giles hunched forward, hands locked about knees and at the same time shot his father a questioning glance. From the tail of his eye Peter watched that sharp-nosed individual incline his head. Presently it came out that, during the past winter, a seafaring fellow had exchanged a small wallet of maize kernels for a night's lodging. Unfortunately, the stranger had known nothing of how this grain should be planted or cultivated.

Would friend Hopton undertake to superintend a planting of those curious seeds? Through the semi-darkness Peter could sense Peg's urgent desire that he linger, and with that moment's realization a scheme sprouted, full-blossomed, into his imagination.

Well, he reckoned he could find time since he could not return to Plymouth until Drake and Howard had put to sea; probably his sea chest would lie safe enough with the proprietor of the Black Bull's Head. Quite casually he let slip the inn's name, but mentioned it a second time ere he smothered a yawn.

"What wi' the spring field to scythe tomorrow, 'tis time we turned in," old Dawson announced presently. "Mayhap, friend Hopton, ye'd do wi' a draught o' my cider?"

"I'll go fetch some." Peg jumped up and hustled off before anyone could hinder her.

In serving the guest she had managed to brush Peter's shoulder a couple of times, and under cover of the darkness he administered a playful pinch to a thigh which felt temptingly firm yet yielding beneath his fingers. He had thought this liberty to have passed unobserved, but apparently it had not. When, late at night, he quite honestly had started a visit to the jakes, George Dawson was nodding in a chair placed squarely before the door to that room in which Peg and her younger sisters slept. The young fellow roused, but nodded pleasantly enough when Peter continued on his errand.

CHAPTER XV

AT THE BLACK BULL'S HEAD

As usual, the Dawson household was up and about its varied occupations long before the sun lifted over the vividly green hills of central Devon. All afire for the great adventure of instruction in the art of planting maize, Dawson and his big strapping sons were bitterly disappointed when Peter announced after a huge breakfast of cold beef, cheese, eggs, watercress and rye bread all washed down by great gulpings of milk, that he must procure at least a dozen unsalted fish. It was ever a Natural's practice to place such a fish in each hillock. There must be twelve carp, trout or some other denizen of fresh water, since the stranger had bestowed an even three dozen brown, yellow or red kernels.

Peter wondered if the donor might not have been some colonist with whom he had shared the rigours and terrors of Roanoke Island, but there was no telling as the traveller had never divulged his name, or so the Dawsons maintained. Eventually Peter learned of a butcher who kept a carp pond on the opposite side of Chudleigh and volunteered to go and make the necessary purchase himself. Old Dawson snuffled in a chill, early morning breeze and agreed readily enough; it would have meant that either he or one of his sons would have to lose time from their scything.

Accordingly Peter was conducted out to the stables where he was amazed to discover a trio of sleek, clean-limbed animals stamping therein, beasts which made his sorry skate look like just what it was. A cluster of the younger Dawson children gathered and remained staring, gaping about while Peter sought a saddle large enough to accommodate his big buttocks.

Presently Peg shyly appeared to shoo her small kinfolk back into the house, then sidled over to where he was securing his girth. After casting a look about, she suddenly threw herself into his arms, her moist and soft red mouth questing fiercely warmly for his. Nothing loath, he bussed the girl very heartily indeed for here, Icod! *was* a warm, tender armful. Right now Peg smelled fresh and sweet—something like a well-tended heifer.

"Oh, Peter! Peter! Take me away!" she panted, round bovine's eyes growing misty. "They keep me all but a prisoner here. I never have any fun. Why, last autumn I never even was took to 'e county fair."

"Why, as to that, Ducky," he chuckled, slipping his hand inside her bodice and cupping its palm over a firm, if rather ample, bosom, "we'll see when I return from Chudleigh. Meantime ye'd best secure your Sunday kirtle and gown, and whatever else that can be carried in a small bundle. But be sly about it. I've no hankering for a bout of fisticuffs wi' yer brothers." He spoke hurriedly for Giles' hulking figure had entered the farmyard. "Which of these is the best horse?"

"Oh, Ben yonder. Pa keeps him to run 'gainst Squire Tipton's White Cloud."

"Good. Now get you gone like a good lass," Peter urged, "and for God's sake don't be for ever mooning at me. Ye'll set yer people on their guard."

Back in Chudleigh, Peter accomplished both of his missions. From the owner of the carp pond he secured a small sackful of six- and eight-inch fishes. Then at the same tavern in which he first had heard of Franklin Dawson the Master Gunner led its proprietor aside, produced his last gold piece, and with it shoved forward a carefully sealed square of paper on which was scrawled the names of Captain Henry Wyatt and the *Sea Venture*. Within, he had painfully written:

Be at Black Bull Tavern without fale at six of this niht. Bring along ate o' our most trustie hands. P. Hopton.

The innkeeper considered the gold piece, bit it and remarked this coin had been both clipped and sweated but, nonetheless, he presently mounted a bony grey gelding and set off down the road to Plymouth.

Back once more at the Dawson farm, Peter, in no great hurry, superintended the digging of a well-spaced double row of corn hills on a well-drained sunny slope. Next he explained that maize kernels should never be planted deeper than six inches and three to a hill, plopped a carp into each little mound and tamped the earth well down, warning that the environs must be kept free of crows, hungry fowls and weeds.

"And now," he announced, "I'll go bid Mistress Dawson farewell, and be on my way."

"I'll go with 'e," volunteered Giles.

"There's no need, friend," Peter smiled broadly. "Ye'll only be leaving yer swath half scythed."

It being broad daylight the franklin and his sons shook hands then returned to their work, leaving Peter to tramp the quarter of a mile over to that neatly thatched farmhouse lying within its ring of walls. He felt confident that no trace of suspicion had manifested itself upon any of the Dawsons' broad, red-brown faces.

Round-eyed Peg must have witnessed his approach for she was already crouched in a dark corner of the stable wearing a hooded cloak and lugging an impossibly large bundle. This he ordered her to halve, and whilst tearfully she obeyed he transferred his saddle to the tall, golden bay called Ben and behind it rigged a pillion used by Mistress Dawson when venturing forth with her husband.

"Can you ride?"

"Only a little," she admitted. "Because like I told 'e, dearie, Father and my brother never will take me anywhere. Oh, me, Master Hopton, I do luv 'e greatly, indeed I do; I'm that grateful I'll make 'e an industrious and a dutiful wife."

Luckily their mount, for all its fine breeding, revealed evidence of unusual strength—which was just as well since Peter was no lightweight and Mistress Peg Dawson must easily tip the beam on eleven stone.

By mischance Mistress Dawson came out to throw scraps to her hens, glanced into the stable door and so beheld Peter in the act of heaving her buxom daughter on to the pillion. She let out such a shriek that Peter judged it must clearly be heard in the next county, and ran, flapping like a stringy hen, to block his escape. Fighting to get the high-spirited beast under control, he was hard put not to ride down the old woman. With Peg hugging his middle like a hungry she-bear, the pillion flapping and still scaring the gelding, he galloped off down the lane. He glimpsed Dawson and his three sons running heavily across a freshly ploughed field shaking their fists and roaring commands to halt.

"Ride faster, Master Hopton!" implored Peg when her abductor's powerful arms slowed their mount to an easy canter. "They'll kill 'e an they catch 'e, and me they'll whip half unto death."

It formed no part of Peter's plan, however, really to outdistance pursuit; he intended to remain just safely out in front. Further, he had decided to avoid the direct route into Plymouth that his messenger might find time to reach the *Sea Venture* and alert Wyatt.

At the top of a long hill, therefore, he reined in, looked back and immediately felt Peg's lips crushed to his.

"La, Master Hopton," she giggled, hugging him harder than ever, "we be so romantical. But, look, look!"

Out from the Dawson farmyard three riders came galloping. One, Peter thought it must be Giles, was mounted on a heavy-footed draught animal, but the twins bestrode beasts which seemed to offer the promise of speed. He lingered just long enough to make certain they had seen him then put his beast into a comfortable canter that raised a lazy trail of reddish dust along the highway and, on topping the next rise, he perceived that his pursuers had closed in considerably. Doubtless the brothers were assuming that the golden bay, through carrying double, would soon tire; actually, that powerful animal was betraying not the least sign of fatigue. Through Carsand Beacon they rode, and High Willings and Tavistock but at Callington they paused because Peg vowed her bladder was nigh to bursting.

In the late afternoon they turned on to that particular highway which stretches between Exeter to Plymouth, and presently Peter pointed out the Hoe looming in the distance. Far out to sea the silvery sails of some supply ships, guarded by two of the City of London galleons, could be seen standing in towards the Mewstone.

Still another glance over Peter's shoulder disclosed their pursuers plodding along, now nearly a mile in his rear. Peter judged that they would enter Plymouth considerably before six o'clock but it was no part of his plan that the avengers should find him unsupported at the Black Bull; he retained a deep respect for fists and sinews of Franklin Dawson's brawny sons. He therefore pulled his mount to a slow jog and half listened while Peg prattled on, describing intimate matters which long had remained locked in her simple mind.

All her troubles had commenced nearly three years earlier, she confessed, when behind the Dawson byre a passing chapman had deprived her of her innocence. Apparently her wide blue eyes, bright lips and eager expression had whetted the lustful appetites of local youths to such a point that her family had kept her in practical imprisonment ever since.

"And will 'e indeed buy me a gown of red silk and a farthingale just as big as Lady Eleanor Meeker's? Will 'e take me to see jugglers and dancing bears?" In the warm afternoon sunlight Peg Dawson looked uncommonly pretty—and impatient.

"Of course," he grinned. "What's more I'll e'en bestow upon ye a pearl I fetched back from Sir Walter Raleigh's own colony in America."

George and Herbert, the twins, had closed in almost to hailing distance when the big golden bay's hooves began to clip-clop over cobbles on the outskirts of Plymouth Town. Giles, however, being astride the draught animal, had lagged far behind. Peter clattered straight into town at last losing his pursuers in hopes that they might be delayed in ascertaining where the Black Bull was situated. Soon he dismounted in the tavern's stable yard, lifted Peg, vastly excited, down from her pillion, at the same time tipping broad winks at a group of ostlers and grooms lounging there. They grinned back, knowing him for a whole-hearted wencher.

While dickering with the publican for a room he deduced, to his alarm, that Henry Wyatt had not yet put in an appearance, for all that the church clock's rusty hands showed a quarter past six.

"You cry a private room!" the landlord railed. "Ye must ha' lost yer wits. Wi' my Lord Howard's fleet i' our haven this town is fair bursting its seams."

In his mounting anxiety Peter commenced to sweat. He drew the publican aside, while keeping a weather eye on the door and an ear cocked for the clattering of hooves. "Peace, friend Jarvis. I require a chamber only long enough to tumble this pretty country wench. Besides, I'll pay ye well."

On the promise of silver shillings, the publican saw matters in a different light and, keys jangling softly, led the dust-splashed couple into his own quarters, out of which he herded his fat wife despite shrill objections that could be distinguished half-way the length of the street.

What in God's name could be keeping Harry? That rascally inn-keeper from Chudleigh undoubtedly must have turned into the first convenient lane to drowse there until it was time to make a pretence of returning from Plymouth.

When loud voices suddenly sounded in the stable yard Peg squeaked like a trapped mouse. "Oh, dear God save me! 'Tis me brothers!"

Peter could hear them plainly enough; they were blaspheming and demanding breathlessly whither the fugitives had betaken themselves. The landlord swore manfully down that no couple such as they described was lodged beneath his roof, but a half-drunken patron spoiled the lie, describing Mistress Peg in such detail that Giles' horny red hand closed over the publican's collar.

Peg uttered terrified whimpers and clung limpet-like to her abductor. Should he make off through the back door or risk standing a siege in hopes the *Sea Venture's* men would appear? Deciding that discretion was the better part of valour, he had started for the rear when, through a small leaded window giving out on to the street, he saw Arnold, the frigate's Boatswain, striding up, followed by Wyatt and four burly younkers.

"Save me! They'll murder me!" Peg was screaming and clung pitifully to his arm.

"Be still, 'e noisy heifer, and let go my arm," he snapped. When she only held on the harder, he sent her reeling across the bedroom. She fell across the four-poster and lay there screeching out her terror.

Grinning with the joy of impending battle, Peter unbarred the bedroom door and called out, "Come in, my fine lads, and witness our frolics."

Once the three Dawsons, still scarlet-faced and sweat-bathed from hard riding, beheld their quarry framed in the doorway, they hurled furious curses and charged. Shouting, "Here, Harry! Here!" Peter retreated, picked up a stout chair and braced himself for the onslaught.

The fracas lasted longer than it should have because the Dawson brothers in their outrage proved to be powerful beyond imagination. The landlord and his spouse howled for the watch as their furniture was smashed, windows were shattered and any object useful as a missile flew about. Peg, all the while, kept up a shrill screaming that was dreadful to hear.

When, belatedly, the watch arrived it was to find the three Dawsons trussed up hand and foot; all were bleeding, and gigantic, black-bearded Giles completely insensible. With his shirt torn to ribbons, Peter mopped a bloody nose while Brian O'Brian sucked at a split lip and Arnold fingered an egg-sized lump on his bald scalp.

Silver pieces promptly pressed by Wyatt upon the watchmen persuaded those worthies to lose all interest in the affair. After all, were not such activities on the part of press gangs the order of the day?

CHAPTER XVI

RED CROSSES OFF THE LIZARD

ASSIGNED to service under Vice-Admiral Sir Francis Drake, the black-and-red-painted *Galleon Coffyn* lay at anchor on the seaward fringe of Lord Howard's Grand Fleet, not far from the *Mayflower*, a small, privately owned vessel, which, years later, was to become one of the best known ships in history. On the poop deck Hubert Coffyn, Esquire, conversed in undertones with his distant cousin, the Honourable Charles Coffyn of Ilfracombe.

" 'Tis cert an' we sail not tomorrow, this fleet must rewater and revictual," gloomily observed the Honourable Charles. Perhaps a year younger than his cousin, he reflected the dark complexion of a Cornish mother.

"A pox on this infernal dillydally," Hubert broke out. "Twice we have started for Spain, and twice the curs'd wind has risen as contrary as it blows today. I wonder——" He broke off because the anchor watch suddenly had roused, had peered over the rail and then had cupped a hand to his ear. Two or three idle grommets—ship's boys—ran across the deck to join him.

Hubert lost interest. Probably some clumsy oaf had fallen overboard from a nearby ship or an insubordinate fellow was being ducked from the yardarm, but then he saw someone pointing out to sea. The *Pinnace Golden Hind*, watchboat, was bowling into Plymouth Sound before that same strong south breeze which had held Howard's armada prisoner. Her Captain, one Thomas Fleming, put up his helm under the *Revenge*'s blue-and-gold stern and, through a leather speaking-tube, bellowed something up to her Officer of the Deck. On receiving a reply, he came about and steered a zigzagging course between the more important men-of-war. While scudding by, Fleming pointed his trumpet straight at the *Galleon Coffyn*'s poop and shouted in a voice rendered hoarse through over-use: "Spaniards, by the—hundreds—off Lizard—— Standing this way!"

The *Golden Hind* rushed by, heading for the great scarlet-and-gold-painted *Ark Royal*.

Aboard the *Revenge*, a gunnery officer caused an alarm shot to be fired, an example successively copied by her consorts: accordingly it proved difficult for Henry Wyatt to understand what was afoot when the watchboat drove past the *Sea Venture*. Club in hand, he had been driving the sullen and openly mutinous crew through still another gun drill.

Peter Hopton finally grasped the news shouted across from the *Bear*. He turned to his gun crews. "Listen well, ye nameless sons of gutter-sows. The Dons are come at last! Soon we'll all be fighting for our dirty necks."

Giles Dawson's heavy features lost their perpetual scowl. "What? Do 'e Papists truly be upon us?"

" 'Tis been so reported." Wyatt seized this opportunity to make a brief address and although he had ever been clumsy with words, the *Sea Venture*'s Master made so moving an appeal that all saving the three Dawsons broke into a deep cheer and agreed to sign the frigate's muster roll—thus entitling them to share in any profit won from the Spanish King's ships. It was George Dawson who finally persuaded his brothers to make their marks by pointing out that since they would soon be forced to hazard their lives they might just as well stand to profit by that risk.

"All the same," Giles growled at Peter Hopton, "I'll kill 'e first fair chance."

"Yer welcome to try, Cully," Peter grinned. Then, almost apologetically, he added, "I'll have ye know, Giles, that I made not so much as a dent i' poor Peg's virtue, and even have made her the compliment o' a pearl ere that tavern keeper from Chudleigh fetched her home."

Meanwhile, so many ships were firing recall signals their cannonading sounded as if a moderate engagement were being fought. All over Plymouth Sound pinnaces, cockboats and little row galleys commenced to skitter about like frightened water-beetles and vessels charging water and provisions hurried to cast off, their supplies abandoned or tumbled helter-skelter about their decks.

At long last the great Spanish fleet, *la Empresa de Inglaterra*, the Invincible Armada, had appeared!

Coffyn, busy mustering his crew, watched the Golden Admiral's barge thresh by, stout ash oars bending to the mighty rhythm of her rowers. Drake, it was later reported, had been ashore when the fateful news arrived, engaged in a game of bowls with certain of his Captains. He had indulged in a characteristic bit of showmanship by insisting on finishing his game—so expert a seaman would have known that many hours must pass before the first hostile sails might glimmer on the horizon. And the wind was contrary.

Now he stood in the barge's stern and hailing those six tall London galleons which constituted the best and most powerful units in his division. In addition to these, his command included *Edward Bonaventure*, *Roebuck*, *Galleon Coffyn*, *Hopewell*, *Galleon Fenner* and the old *Merchant Royal*. Offering considerably less fire-power was his second line, although it included such heavily gunned vessels as *Elizabeth Drake* and the *Barques Hawkins*, *Talbot*, *Bond* and *Bonner*. Other good, privately owned ships had come creeping down the south coast of England and he had five hulks in which to carry surplus supplies, of which, alas, there were now almost none.

Up on the Hoe a slender pillar of smoke commenced to spiral lazily up into the bright azure June sky. By the time it had thickened into a dense, grey-white column another beacon took fire ten miles inland; then a further one. Within the space of a few hours all England would know that the Spaniards had appeared off the coast and that invasion —so long dreaded—was imminent.

Further inshore, furious activity was visible aboard Howard's own squadron, which composed the main battle. Everyone could see his long pennant streaming from the *Ark Royal's* lofty fore-topmast. Near by lay the *Golden Lion*, *Dreadnought*, *Foresight* and the *Mary Rose*.

Aboard the *Galleon Coffyn*, her Sailing Master's expression was grim. "Sailing up from the Lizard as they are," quoth Lynwood Clough, "the Dons cannot fail to hold the weather gauge of us. God alone knows how we can be expected to beat out past the Mewstone."

"Dear Lord, why don't our Admiral make signal to up-anchor?" the Honourable Charles Coffyn grumbled after nearly an hour had dragged by.

"Why, Charles," Hubert explained, " 'tis certainly because of the tide which, at this hour, sets strongly to the westward. Were the wind to fail, we must be swept further into the Spaniards' lee than we already lie, thus leaving the Dons free to sail in behind us and make good a landing before we could so much as turn about. The Lizard, as you wot well, lies but a scant forty-five miles to the south-west of our anchorage."

Although the sun lowered and finally disappeared, the English fleet remained in Plymouth Sound for the good and sufficient reason that the wind had commenced to fail, while the tide continued to run strongly from west to east. To render matters still more discouraging, a drizzle set in, accompanied by a veiling mist. Not until slack water could there be any hope of warping out to sea the Queen's great-ships and the City of London's galleons.

The enforced delay proved not without profit, however, and permitted a general rally of all able-bodied men. Now that the enemy was off the coast many who had been hiding came out to volunteer, and soldiers set ashore to recruit their health were returned to duty. Indeed, so many lanterns and torches in addition to the alarm beacon flared over the water that Plymouth Haven appeared to have become a lake of fire.

Towards sundown another spy-boat came scudding up to the *Revenge* and the *Ark Royal* with some reassuring intelligence the Duke of Medina-Sidonia had hove-to his vast armada four miles offshore, opposite to the Cliffs of Dodman and somewhat to the west of Fowey. Later, one of the spy-boat's crew, attracted by lavish offers of strong drink, clambered over the *Sea Venture's* rail. Every soul aboard clustered about while the fisherman, a small, sunburnt and one-eyed fellow, swore that already about two hundred sail had been counted, but more were constantly appearing out of the broad Atlantic.

"They be main easy to recognize," said he, throwing back his head and gulping ale without swallowing.

"How so?" demanded George Dawson.

"Each and every Spanisher shows a great red cross painted on his main, and a lot o' saints and angels and such Papist rot on his tops'ls and gallants."

"Be their red crosses like ours?"

"Nay—theirs look like this——" In dew beading the rail the fisherman drew, "✠ or this ☩, whilst ours are more simple and honest, like this ✝. I tell 'e, mates," his one eye rolled fearfully, "ye've no notion of how vasty be their vessels, how guns do bristle from their sides like quills upon a porpentine. They've with 'em great towering carracks out o' the Levant, galleys and galleasses from Genoa and other Italian States what can move independent o' the wind."

"Have we none such?" demanded a little grommet's high voice.

A chorus of "Nays" answered him.

Henry Wyatt inquired, "In what ship does the enemy Admiral show his pennant?"

"Heard tell 'tis the *St. Martin*, but I've no certainty of that." Over his jack of ale the visitor gloomily considered the strained and anxious faces crowding about under the torches. "We'll be hard put to keep these curs'd Papists off our shores. God preserve us if them Spanishers get into Portland Sound or behind the Isle o' Wight."

After what seemed like a fatal delay, word was passed for the great ships and large galleons to kedge themselves out of Plymouth Sound. This was accomplished by rowing out an anchor in a small boat, then, by use of a windlass, to draw up on that anchor. Meanwhile a second anchor was in turn being advanced.

For the smaller men-of-war, such as the privately-owned galleons, frigates and barques, the problem was simple—they were merely towed out by their pinnaces until their sails lifted under a faint breeze commencing, praise God, *to blow out of the north-west*!

Seldom did Hubert Coffyn, Henry Wyatt or any of Drake's Captains remove their eyes from a great stern lantern glowing, yellow-white, above the *Revenge's* elaborate stern gallery and slowly but surely heading out to sea. Not to lose sight of it proved difficult work because of a slanting rain and whirling mists.

Daybreak found Drake's division abreast of Eddystone Rock and safely out from under the coast. Next in order behind Drake sailed Lord Howard of Effingham's main battle, then, dangerously close to shore, those divisions destined to fight under John Hawkins and Frobisher. Of these last, Drake's men could see nothing when, shortly before dawn, the flagship made signal for all to furl sail.

Full daylight revealed the English strength as some fifty-four vessels of varying tonnage.

Still no vessel bearing a red Maltese or Jerusalem Cross on her mainsail had yet been sighted.

The day of Saturday, July the twentieth, 1588, proved to be all but windless, so the two offshore squadrons rolled heavily in the trough of glassy billows rolling in from the Atlantic. Noon came but the western horizon remained unspeckled by sails other than those of terror-stricken coasters or fishermen running for shelter. Nor was there any sign of the divisions commanded by John Hawkins, now in the *Victory*, and Martin Frobisher.

Nerves grew ragged as the long day dragged into dark and still no foreign red crosses appeared to offer battle.

Drake and his senior officers were of the opinion that the Spaniards must be advancing very slowly, parallel to the Cornish coast. No doubt they must be waiting for some laggard element of the *Empresa* to catch up and take position in Medina-Sidonia's great crescent-shaped formation. Again and yet again gunners were ordered to their posts to repeat loading and swabbing exercises until they cursed sulphurously and refused to practise further.

Could it be that the Dons had turned back? A number of Captains thought this a possibility, for so slow had been the Armada's progress up from Coruña that they must be running dangerously short of victuals and water, especially in sea-going castles unmercifully crowded with land troops.

Only when the westing sun had sunk very low could English look-outs atop the tallest masts discern a faint black streak marking the horizon far to the westward and, by hurried calculation, some twelve miles off the coast of Cornwall. Yonder lay the enemy! It was the ominous length and density of that dark line which aroused misgivings and sufficient trepidation to quiet even the noisiest boasters and give pause to the most optimistic.

Experienced seamen, however, found considerable satisfaction in the situation. Medina-Sidonia apparently was still ignorant that Drake and Howard, during the night, had sailed right across their bows and now lay upwind behind them, in possession of the weather gauge and thus able to fall with the ferocity of sea wolves upon their rear.

When day broke with a favourable wind coming out of the north-west, the *Galleon Coffyn*, probably because she was small and extremely swift—due to Wyatt's redesigning—was dispatched to learn the enemy's course. Hubert Coffyn's heart surged when Clough, his Sailing Master, ordered all canvas made. So with his green-and-gold personal gonfalon streaming from the foretop, he bore down upon that distant mass of Spanish vessels.

By ascending to the main yard Hubert presently perceived that the Medina-Sidonia, being a land General, had disposed his ships just as if he were marching an army into battle. In general, the Spanish formation now resembled a vast horseshoe, along the outer rim of which sailed the main battle with the breath-takingly huge carracks of Spain and Portugal occupying its centre. At either heel of the shoe cruised more big men-of-war.

Out in front of the Armada cruised two huge galleasses; Hubert could distinguish the dip and flash of their oars in the distance. Contained within this protective horseshoe was an amazing collection of transports, victuallers, supply and hospital ships. To count the exact number of vessels dotting the deep blue waters off Eddystone proved to be utterly impossible, so, pursuant to orders, the *Galleon Coffyn* sailed only near enough to make certain that the enemy were forging slowly inshore, as if to strike at Plymouth.

Once the *Galleon Coffyn's* pinnace had delivered this intelligence aboard the *Revenge* and Drake, in turn, had gone aboard the *Ark Royal*, signals were made to bear away in pursuit.

Lord Howard now occupied the van while Drake was in the rear, also maintaining the extreme seaward position he favoured since it allowed him plenty of room for those swift manœuvres for which he was famous. Still nothing was to be seen of Hawkins' and Frobisher's inshore divisions. Where in God's name could they have gone?

CHAPTER XVII

FIRST BLOOD

THE *Sea Venture* for the moment found herself sailing as almost the last of Drake's line because the Vice-Admiral had decided to commit his heaviest men-of-war first, leaving, he hoped, crippled or disabled vessels as prey for his lesser craft. The engagement commenced around nine of the morning when Lord Howard came sweeping in from the Atlantic and firing into the Armada's relatively defenceless rear. From a few scattered ranging shots the cannon grumbled louder and louder until it seemed as if a continuous thunderstorm were raging beneath that pall of gun-smoke which gradually veiled ship after ship.

" 'Fore God," roared Peter, bright blue eyes agleam with excitement, " 'twould appear a whole city floats ahead o' us!"

Because dun-coloured battle-smoke lingered low over the sea the *Sea Venture's* people could see clumps of topmasts bearing red Jerusalem Crosses. Presently, while the frigate neared the conflict, they made out several of the Queen's ships hammering hard at two enormous carracks—later, he would learn that these were the *San Juan* and the Portuguese flagship the *Gran-Grin*, a huge vessel of eleven hundred tons and biggest of the Biscayan squadron, displaying the flag of Don Martinez de Recaldo, second-in-command for the Enterprise of England. Both were bearing up manfully to deadly and rapid gunnery from the English galleons.

Ship after ship of Howard's and Drake's divisions, in line ahead, sailed by these monsters and at long range pouring in broadsides which knocked great gaping holes in their bulwarks and sent spars spinning crazily skyward. Also their thirty- and forty-pound balls hammered into bloody pulp armoured Spaniards crowding their castles. These clamoured for an opportunity to board the heretics. In vain Master Mariners pointed out to cursing colonels and generals that the enemy vessels were too nimble, especially since they held the weather gauge. The military might command all they cared, but it remained impossible to sail their cumbersome sea castles alongside.

A small Spanish galleon on rearguard duty appeared suddenly out of a bank of gun-smoke and steered straight at the *Sea Venture*.

"Have at her!" Wyatt shouted over slamming reports all about. For all that the enemy must be twice his size he made for her. Subconsciously, he noted a segment of broken mast drifting by, its sails tattered and resembling white sea-weed. To it clung half a dozen dark-faced men who yammered in vain for rescue.

Peter strode among the five guns composing the frigate's starboard battery, spoke a good word here and there, and then rested a reassuring hand on the shoulder of a debtor who had commenced to sob.

"Be not affrighted," Peter urged. "We'll smash yon galleon."

The fellow turned, features working. "I be not afeared," he choked indignantly, "only excited."

"Then blow your match, my lad, and await my word." With anxious eyes Peter waited until the Spaniard loomed less than a hundred yards distant. From her side spurted a series of vivid flashes and four cannon balls screamed overhead but did no damage beyond punching a hole through the *Sea Venture's* main-topsail.

"Fire! For God's sake, fire!" Wyatt was shouting for now it seemed that the *Sea Venture* must collide with the enemy. Giles Dawson, waiting by the breech of the saker he served, obtained a view of a row of heads protected by gleaming morions. Far above him on the galleon's poop stood officers in gold-decorated cuirasses and tassets. He could even see their varicoloured plumes wave in the wind.

"Ready?" Like a trumpet Peter Hopton's great voice rang out. "Fire!"

Giles Dawson pressed the end of a glowing match into his saker's touchhole and leaped sideways out of the path of its recoil. One after another the gun carriages, mounted on clumsy wooden wheels, lurched back against breeching ropes. Under their recoil the frigate rolled to port.

"Run in!" bellowed the Master Gunner and picked up an eighteen-pound ball for one of his culverins—the heaviest cannon aboard. Dripping swabs meanwhile were thrust down the throats of the starboard battery. Amid the choking, rotten-smelling smoke could be heard crashing noises as if some giant were engaged in splitting kindling. Fearful screams and shouts in several foreign languages alone could pierce this opaque veil of powder-smoke.

The frigate's gun crews were tamping home fresh charges when Wyatt's ringing accents penetrated the tumult. "Quartermaster! Starboard your helm!"

"Christ above! Ben't we to finish her off?" bellowed one of the Cornishmen. "Two more broadsides she'll strike and we'll all get rich."

"No! Look, look yonder!" One of the gypsies levelled a skinny brown finger at a gap which had opened in the wall of battle-smoke. Through it one of the great Genoese galleasses could be seen rowing up to effect a rescue. There was no doubt that were her Captain so minded she could overtake, board and overwhelm the *Sea Venture*. There was just time to loose a broadside at long range before the *Sea Venture* came about and at her best speed sped for safety among her consorts.

Bitter and loud sounded the disappointed curses of Wyatt's crew as she drew away. They watched the little galleon's lateen mast totter like a drunken dancer, fall over her port rail.

That Peter Hopton's gunnery must have caused fearful casualties among land troops packed almost solidly into the galleon's waist was inescapable; rivulets of blood could be seen dripping through shot-holes in her yellow-painted sides and somewhere she must have taken fire. All the same the enemy limped on into the galleass's protection.

Thankful that the Genoese failed to pursue him, Wyatt directed the *Sea Venture* back into Drake's formation now readying itself for an assault upon that vast mass of enemy ships heading at snail's pace of two knots an hour in the general direction of Prawle Point.

Despite a series of imploring signals raised above the *Revenge* Lord Howard kept on without further attacking the Spanish formation. To the Lord High Admiral it was a matter of importance that he be reinforced since he had not yet assembled even a half of his strength whereas the Duke of Medina-Sidonia held a very dangerous advantage in ships and guns. Later, it was reported that the Golden Admiral had raged like a madman on being thus forced to abandon two rich prizes in so dire straits as the *Santa Ana* and the *Gran-Grin.* Nevertheless, Plymouth and the ships remaining there for lack of crews were safe.

The afternoon was well advanced when the English fleet ceased its shoreward progress and became united with the squadrons of John Hawkins and Martin Frobisher. Soon the English crews beheld evidences of the success of Drake's tactics; that of cutting off a few of the enemy vessels and then concentrating all the broadsides at his disposal upon them. The evidence came in the form of dozens of dead bodies, some hideously mangled, others seemingly whole, that drifted by among horse carcasses and a number of stoved-in pinnaces. Apparently their gunners had wrought far greater havoc than the disappointed English had suspected.

The *Sea Venture's* company had to endure taunts from the little *Elizabeth Drake* as, slowly, she overhauled that sixty-ton vessel in compliance to a signal to advance her position.

"So ye found that Spanish chestnut were too hot, eh?" mocked Thomas Cely, her Master, as if to rub salt into the frigate's disappointment. "Why didn't 'e grapple wi' her, Wyatt? Be 'e fear'd o' a dousing with Papist Holy Water?" So long as the two vessels remained in earshot the jeers persisted, then the *Virgin God Save Her*, a big barque, moved up until she sailed so close that the shadows of her mastheads fell across the frigate's big mainsail.

"Ha'e you any corn powder to spare?" her Master shouted through cupped hands. "We had to sail with but little."

This plea was repeated by the *Nonpareil*, commanded by Thomas Fenner—the same who had been Drake's Flag-Captain during the expedition against San Domingo and Cartagena. Such calls for ammunition would recur in ever-increasing frequency throughout the long-drawn-out running struggle which had commenced.

The Armada's slow speed undoubtedly had its disadvantages yet that very sluggishness made it difficult for the English to attack because, miraculously, the Spaniards were able to preserve their horseshoe formation. Further, the Duke of Medina-Sidonia found means to reinforce his rearguard with tall carracks out of Lisbon with gallibrazos—small handy galleons designed by Menéndez to convoy treasure fleets home from America. Vessels of this class were known as "the Indian Guard" and provided by far the most effective opposition to the still speedier and lower-sided products of Sir John Hawkins' imagination.

The *Sea Venture's* crew was consuming a hastily contrived meal and gulping pots of bitter ale when, towards the rear of that vast cluster of white sails and red crosses, sounded an explosion so prodigious it made the frigate's sails shiver. Everyone ran to the rail in time to watch a huge, mushroom-shaped pillar of smoke rise above a galleon thought to be the *San Salvador.*

Like wolves scenting blood of a wounded elk, the nearest English men-of-war altered their courses and started in her direction, for indeed the big yellow-and-green-painted *San Salvador* must have suffered critical damage since the two top decks of her towering stern could be seen floating in her wake and flames were soaring into the evening sky.

Unfortunately, the wind proved so fickle that *Revenge*, *Edward Bonaventure* and two London galleons, followed closely by *Galleon Coffyn,* could not converge upon the stricken vessel before those accursed Neapolitan galleasses could come to her rescue. Medina-Sidonia's flagship, the huge thousand-ton *San Martin,* chanced to be near and lumbered over to offer immediate assistance.

Again Drake and his hard-bitten veteran Captains fumed to see a recall signal climb to the *Ark Royal's* signal yard so there was nothing for it but to haul off and watch the *San Salvador's* crew put out the fire and start repairs. Taken under tow, the *San Salvador,* being quite unmanageable through the wrecking of all her steering gear, presently became absorbed amid the dark mass of her consorts.

A second misfortune befell King Philip's Armada when, in the early hours of the night, his *Nuestra Señora de la Rosa* somehow collided with two galleons of the Biscayan squadron and so entangled her rigging with theirs that, before they could be separated, Don Pedro del Valdéz, one of Medina-Sidonia's three Rear-Admirals, had lost his foreyards and then his bowsprit. The hurt vessel had barely commenced to repair this damage than sundry English lookouts shouted down that *Rosa's* foremast had gone crashing overside. Only a stump of it remained visible above her bulwarks.

When he heard this Sir Francis Drake licked sun-cracked lips. "By the Glory of God," he growled, "this one I *will* have and none shall say me nay." He made his vow barely loud enough for Jonas Bodenham, his Flag-Captain, and his Boatswain to overhear.

Reluctantly, the Queen's ships once more returned to the English fleet now sailing in four lines ahead, a formation which to Lord Howard seemed to offer the greatest adaptability and ease of concentration.

Hubert Coffyn and his cousin, jaws tightened by disappointment, peered through the gathering dark and watched a towline passed to the crippled *Rosa* but their expressions brightened when, almost at once, the towline parted and that great galleon slowly fell astern of the Spanish fleet. When she commenced firing guns to emphasize her distress signal flags climbed, sank and rose again aboard the *San Martin*, so, presently, the two galleons, *San Francisco* and *San Cristóbal*, together with their pinnaces, dropped back to protect the crippled one until those indispensable Italian galleasses could take her in tow.

A breeze sprang up out of the west-south-west and soon wind and waves were making up so shrewdly that, mindful of the dangers lying off Start Point, the English squadrons kept on until finally Lord Howard ordered them hove to between Prawle Point and Salcombe.

A straggler, a converted merchantman belonging to the Levant Company of London, in the dark blundered upon the helpless *Rosa*. To the utter delighted amazement of John Fisher, her Master—for the *Margaret and John* was only of two hundred and fifty tons burthen —the galleass incontinently threw off her towline and the protecting galleons and pinnaces deserted the wallowing *Rosa* and disappeared into the dark. Too weak by himself to attack the *Rosa*, John Fisher then sped inshore where, as far as the eye could see, the flames of alarm beacons leapt and danced on every headland.

Near midnight an assortment of varicoloured lanterns displayed aboard the *Ark Royal* ordered the English squadrons to make sail and resume their stations. The word was circulating that since Lord Howard suspected the Spaniards were on their way to seize the Isle of Wight for a base he had decided to attack King Philip's Armada before it could approach The Needles. Also that he had written to the authorities ashore saying:

For the love of God and our country, let us have with some great shot sent us of all bigness, for this service will continue long, and some powder with it.

Nature smiled on the defenders by parting the rain-clouds and permitting the moon to shine and so allow them to get under way with a minimum of disorder. Once again the various squadrons bore away after the great stern lanterns of their flagships.

On this occasion the *Sea Venture* followed close behind the *Revenge* as long as she could but soon that galleon's great spread of canvas and excellent design sent her rushing through the night far faster than her consorts. Gradually the great lantern on the flagship diminished in brilliance and though the other vessels crowded on every rag they could carry the *Revenge* rushed on out to sea all silvered by the moonlight—a stately and unforgettable vision.

Again banks of clouds obscured the moon, then, to the dismay of Drake's division, the *Revenge's* stern light winked out and she became lost amid the wind-filled darkness.

"God's blood! What now are we to do?" Wyatt demanded in an agony of uncertainty. By their lights he could tell that some ships were continuing on the course they fancied Drake to be sailing; others had hove-to. Still others became involved with vessels from the other division who were equally nonplussed by the *Revenge's* abrupt and inexplicable disappearance.

Aware of the Vice-Admiral's character, Hubert Coffyn was among those who stood out to sea fervently praying that dawn would reveal Sir Francis' topsails. Also, by standing out to sea, he reasoned he stood less chance of being rammed and so lose that investment which meant so much.

CHAPTER XVIII

OFF PORTLAND BILL

So GREATLY scattered had various elements of the English fleet become, it was not until late in the afternoon of Monday, July the twenty-second, that Lord Howard of Effingham's force was able to resume its order. Now it numbered over a hundred sail by the addition of many small converted merchantmen which came tumbling out of almost every little port along the south coast.

Of Sir Francis Drake there still came no sign; it began to appear that the sea had swallowed him and his *Revenge* in a single mighty gulp. Acrimonious to a degree were charges hurled at the missing

Vice-Admiral by Frobisher, ever his enemy, Sir William Winter and even his relative and benefactor, John Hawkins.

Why had he extinguished his great light without a word of explanation and seemingly had deserted his van of the fleet at an all-important moment? Martin Frobisher in particular raged; it was all of a piece, he reminded his fellow admirals, of Drake's mad dash into the inner harbour of Cádiz to seize Admiral Santa Cruz's own galleon.

To all the complainants Lord Howard gave ear, listened with a patience which afforded no hint of his own reactions. He looked almighty relieved, though, when at sunset the *Revenge* lifted her topsails above the horizon. After a space the missing Vice-Admiral appeared aboard the *Ark Royal* as cocky as ever and in company with a tall, brown-faced individual who bore himself with disdainful if not arrogant composure.

Those who happened to be aboard never forgot the jaunty flourish with which Drake tossed a bundle of brilliant banners on the deck at Howard's feet, then with bright blue eyes sparkling, swept off his cap and bowed to his tight-lipped commander.

"My lord," said he briskly, "I have the honour to present His Honour Don Pedro de Valdéz, Rear-Admiral of the enemy."

The Spaniard bowed deeply and in rapid French deplored the fact that he had not been able to make a better defence of his great-ship. But who could hope to prevail against the terrible *el Draque*?

It turned out that just as Frobisher had predicted, Drake had dashed off alone, confident of finding the disabled *Rosa*, of carrying her and so of winning her treasures for himself. Sir Francis, however, was not to be caught without a plausible explanation. He declared that, while leading the fleet from its anchorage the night before, he had spied a group of big ships sailing west.

"I deduced," he declared in that voice which always seemed too big for his small frame, "that this must be a detachment of the enemy's seeking to get the weather of us. I pursued, thinking that my squadron would follow."

"Follow? By the gullet of God! How could they?" thundered John Hawkins, red-faced with indignation. "Why did you put out your light?"

"I thought," Drake smiled—he appeared more chunky than ever in his gold-encrusted breastplate and tassets—"the *Revenge* could easily be distinguished in the moonlight and that my lantern would only serve to warn the enemy of my approach."

There was a considerable exchange of incredulous glances among those present and Lord Howard of Effingham looked his subordinate squarely in the eye.

"And what, Sir Francis, were those vessels you departed to chase?"

"Only some miserable neutrals, my lord, Germans on their way to Ireland."

So a Rear-Admiral of King Philip's Armada had been taken prisoner and his flag tossed on to Lord Howard's deck by Drake's own hand? Gradually scowls vanished from all but a few of those drawn, bearded and weatherbeaten faces congregated upon the *Ark Royal's* lofty poop deck—like all Hawkins' designed craft the flagship was built very high in the stern and low in the bows, she boasted hardly any forecastle worthy of the name while her foremast had been stepped with a slightly forward rake to promote handiness. At length even Lord Howard commenced to smile when he learned that the *Nuestra Señora de la Rosa* had been captured with twenty-six battery guns and, more precious by far, a most generous supply of ammunition.

When the council of war broke up and Drake departed, politely shepherding his distinguished prisoner, Frobisher spat over the side and, features gone scarlet amid his frosty hair and beard, snarled, "If yonder reformed pirate thinks to cozen me o' my share, I'll make him spend the best blood i' his belly!"

A north-east wind treacherously sprang up on the morning of July the twenty-third, making the Duke of Medina-Sidonia a handsome present of the treasured weather gauge and forcing Lord Howard's fleet on a long board to the north-west. Medina-Sidonia followed, the Neapolitan galleasses well out ahead of his great fleet which now had become strung out over several miles.

Through mischance, the bulk of the English vessels held on to their board longer than Hawkins in the *Victory* and about a dozen other vessels had anticipated. Accordingly he found himself with the Armada's rearguard bearing down upon him in overwhelming numbers. Since the English would not be able to weather them, the enemy at long last anticipated an opportunity to employ those tactics at which they excelled—grappling, boarding and sweeping the enemy decks with their veteran infantry.

The *Galleon Coffyn* found herself in the first line, and appeared small indeed when, with painted sails bellying and great scarlet Maltese Crosses glaring on their main courses, the Marquis of Oquendo's sixteen ships from the Squadron of Guipúzcoa came bearing down. This time the cannonading became truly deafening as, successively, more and more ships became involved.

Again rapid and deadly fire from English guns caused the Spaniards' gaudily painted sides to splinter and smoke and to run with gore. Coughing amid swirls of gun-smoke, Hubert Coffyn suddenly found himself peering up at the quarter-deck of some unknown galleon. He shouldered his petronel and by good luck dropped a fat Spanish officer who was shouting something to the enemy's helmsman. The Don's helmet came off and commenced rolling about to the galleon's heavy motion.

Closer and closer together sailed the two ships with the Englishman still attempting to weather his enemy.

"*María y el Rey!*" screamed the enemy and exultantly brandished their weapons. A pair of Spanish grapnels came flying through the air and lodged themselves in the *Galleon Coffyn's* fore shrouds. But just as a swarm of shouting Spanish soldiers in black-painted armour prepared to leap down upon the *Galleon Coffyn's* deck the Honourable Charles himself hacked through the grapnel lines. Meanwhile Sailing Master Clough dexterously put over his tiller and bore away, barely in time to avert boarding.

The rumbling of gun-carriages being trundled forward now increased because the smoke-grimed men from Devonshire were striving to pour in every possible shot at close range.

Thanks to a brisk wind, visibility on this occasion was far better than it had been during that action off the Cliffs of Dodman and soon the *Galleon Coffyn* sailed out of the battle-smoke with only two holes in her bulwarks and three men wounded while her late adversary wallowed in the trough of the sea smoking ominously. In all directions, it seemed, knots of ships were hammering and banging away at each other. Now the roar of the guns could be heard for miles, since Frobisher had been attacked off Portland Bill by Medina-Sidonia himself and the four Neapolitan galleasses.

Martin Frobisher stood in grave danger since, with the exception of his *Triumph*, he had no regular men-of-war, only converted merchant ships for consorts. Nevertheless, that stout old veteran made no effort to flee and ranged his *Merchant Royal*, *Golden Lion*, *Centurion*, *Mary Rose* and the *Margaret and John* in a tight line ahead and prepared to fight it out with the much heavier galleasses and the Duke's towering *San Martín*.

The *Sea Venture*, hulled twice, was fighting for her life with a caravel from the Squadron of Andalusia. Built not so high-charged as the bulk of her consorts, the Andalusian was therefore able to depress his guns sufficiently to bear and a single shot blew the crew of Wyatt's Number Two starboard gun into bloody rags. Among them died

Herbert, one of the Dawson twins, naked to the waist and so smeared with powder that his body resembled that of a Negro.

"Haul off for God's sake!" shouted Peter Hopton. "We cannot match their weight of metal!"

There was nothing for it but to put over the *Sea Venture's* helm. She fell away sluggishly and barely in time, because her spritsail had split from being pierced too many times. She limped off showing jagged holes in her bulwarks, severed stays and halyards a-dangle, yielding her place in line to another converted merchantman. When the wind, always tricky at that time of year, failed once more a dense cloud of smoke smothered the sea, creating a pall through which ships groped like ghosts of themselves.

Henry Wyatt, ears still throbbing from the incessant roar and nerves jangled by the narrowness of his escape, tried to forget the agonized cries of his wounded collected by the base of the mainmast where they survived or died unattended save for the awkward ministrations of a pair of grommets. He remained necessarily uncertain of what lay ahead, especially now the wind was hauling—the all-important, fickle and victory-giving wind. Within twenty minutes it shifted from south-west to south-south-west.

Hammering by the frigate's carpenters hard-driven by Arnold, the Boatswain, partially disguised splashes caused by the bodies and parts of bodies being unceremoniously heaved through splintery breaks in the bulwarks. Giles Dawson and George, the surviving twin, however, did bend their heads and mumble a prayer when the sanguinary remains of their brother were tumbled overside. Grimly, they then returned to their stations at the Number One demi-culverin.

One of the gypsies, bleeding slightly from a splinter wound in his side, came running aft to find Peter Hopton. His thin, dark face was anxious as he shouted, "Only two chests o' corn-powder remain!"

The big, yellow-haired Master Gunner glowered, incredulous. "Go below, ye great loon, and look again. There *must* be plenty more." But there wasn't. So it was with the rest of Drake's hard-fighting division.

The *Sea Venture*, favoured by this new slant of wind, came running down upon a big isolated galleon flying a Vice-Admiral's pennant. That huge, blue-and-scarlet hulk was wallowing heavily among blue-white crested rollers but Wyatt steered the *Sea Venture* right up under the stern of the man-of-war, so close that he could see how the whole lower half of a gilded wooden angel had been shot away, and some small shot had smashed through a golden effigy of John the Baptist.

This huge carrack was none other than the lofty *San Juan*, flagship of Vice-Admiral Martínez de Recaldo.

There remained only powder enough to permit a half-dozen broadsides.

"Aim at the Papist waterline!" roared Peter. "That's where she'll feel it most." But ere the guns could be discharged Drake signalled his command to bear away and attack a group of caravels dispatched by Medina-Sidonia to succour his hard-pressed Vice-Admiral. By so doing, the Spanish Commander-in-Chief deprived himself of support and the *San Martín* was left alone to protect a swarm of helpless victuallers, transports and supply ships.

Lord Howard, perceiving this golden opportunity, promptly bore up until he found the breeze streaming over his starboard quarter and the *San Martín* directly downwind.

Quixotically, the Duke ordered his huge red-and-gold-painted carrack into the wind to display also the Pope's sacred banner and show the Royal colours of Spain from his mastheads. Howard's men could now glimpse their quarry only intermittently because billows of smoke, driving downwind from a dozen minor fights, continually obscured her. Indeed this engagement off the Bill of Portland was no single battle but a number of semi-independent fights, each presenting its own problems.

First the *Ark Royal* sailed across the *San Martín's* bow and managed to pour in no less than three broadsides; Peter Hopton was estimating correctly enough that the English fired three times to the Spaniards' once. The damage dealt the enemy flagship must have been prodigious yet she kept up a furious cannonade even when the *Ark Royal* came about and repeated her devastating manœuvre.

Howard's tall ships *Rainbow*, *Vanguard*, *White Bear* and others then sailed up and joined in pummelling the Don. A great triumphant yell arose when the Pope's sacred white-and-gold banner had its halyards severed by a volley and so fell into the débris-littered water.

Watching from afar, Hubert Coffyn waited for the Spanish Royal colours to be struck, but gradually the English fire faltered and died out and the *San Martín* was permitted to stagger on after her charges, riddled and limping but still afloat.

"Why in God's name forbear now?" panted the Honourable Charles after running aft from his forecastle. "They had her at their mercy."

"No more powder," came Hubert's laconic explanation.

The very fact that not one ship of either fleet was sunk through gunfire that momentous Tuesday gave that master shipbuilder, John Hawkins, and his ordnance officers food for considerable thought. Why? They themselves had suffered no slight damage aloft and yet not an English vessel was in serious trouble. The Spaniards had been hard hit indeed but not a single enemy ship had gone down.

Could it be that the cannon balls on neither side were heavy enough to penetrate that heavy hull fabric of a typical galleon? On the other hand, various master gunners swore that had the powder not run out just when it did, then surely the Duke of Medina-Sidonia and Iago Flores de Valdéz—a distant cousin of he who had surrendered to Sir Francis Drake—would have been sent plunging down to greet squid, conger eels and halibut foraging about the entrance to West Bay.

Resentful of their empty powder-chests, the English drew off towards the coast and leaving King Philip's Invincible Armada to limp on, battered, but minus only two ships—the *Rosa* and the *San Salvador*—whose magazine had blown up.

The Enterprise of England had been hurt, but all the same it continued to remain as deadly a peril to England as it had been when first sighted off the Lizard.

CHAPTER XIX

POWDER!

NEVER in the history of Weymouth, a tiny fishing port on the south coast, had it witnessed a fraction of the sea traffic such as came crowding into its wharf and two quays. Since the day before trained bands, summoned by the alarm beacons, had come marching down to the coast ready to slaughter any foreigner who dared set a hostile foot ashore. Experienced old knights, war-wise veterans of many a foray along the Scottish border or of campaigns in Ireland, spoke quietly, deploring the presence of so many zealous young bloods overloud in their Queen's defence. They were burning to prove their valour on Spanish bodies.

On the outskirts of Weymouth camped hundreds of phlegmatic archers, descended from the bowmen of Crécy and Agincourt. Most local warehouses had already been emptied of supplies lest they fall into Papist hands. Food was well nigh unobtainable.

The little port's chief interest, though, centred about two small hoys freshly arrived from Dartmouth. It was thither that Henry Wyatt had plodded at the head of a band of well-armed mariners out of the *Sea Venture*. In his fist he had held clenched a requisition for powder bearing the Golden Admiral's own crabbed signature which, in these parts, bore a lot more weight than did Howard of Effingham's.

Long since, that astute individual, Drake, had ordered the powder captured by him aboard the *Nuestra Señora de la Rosa* shipped into Weymouth by coaster from Dartmouth, a scant fifty miles to the westward. Because of this, Wyatt held a vast advantage over powder hunters from other divisions. Soon chest after chest of gunpowder came to rest upon the *Sea Venture's* crudely repaired bulwarks.

After nearly fifty-six sleepless hours Wyatt felt so tired he swayed on his feet and spoke in hoarse undertones; he might have fainted had not a kindly housewife pressed a jug of milk, a loaf and a lump of cheese into his hands with a fervent, if teary, "God bless 'e, sir, pray keep 'e murdering Papists from our shores."

More small boats from the Grand Fleet kept arriving low in the water under cargoes of sick and disabled men. Their places readily were filled by volunteers from among the land levies and fishermen.

Wyatt slumped on to a hogshead, chewed mechanically on his bread and cheese and wondered how long this new supply of corn-powder would satisfy the seemingly insatiable demands of Drake's gunners.

A roar of blasphemous indignation arose from an officer dispatched by Martin Frobisher when he learned that nearly half of the supply available in Weymouth had already gone aboard the *Sea Venture*.

John Hawkins' Powder Master also spouted oaths and dire threats ere he raised his pinnace's sail for Lyme Regis where a considerable store of the precious stuff was rumoured to exist.

Other late-comers departed empty-handed and sought to satisfy their needs at Poole and Bournemouth off which King Philip's *Empresa* was now crawling along at its customary two knots.

Few women were in evidence about Weymouth; as elsewhere, the vast majority of them together with their children had been sent inland.

To Wyatt's dismay, Drake was downright furious that he had allowed even a small portion of the *Rosa's* powder to fall into hands other than his own. Clearly, the Golden Admiral was burning to render an attack on Medina-Sidonia possible only to his division and so blazon his name across yet another page of English history.

On the dimly lit poop deck of the *Revenge* the Golden Admiral actually stamped his foot as he glowered upon the *Sea Venture's* unhappy, hollow-eyed Captain. "Get ye hence, you dismal dog; follow the coast and steal, beg or borrow a full shipload of powder. Meet me off Brighton, an ye fail, by St. Peter's beard, I'll have you dismissed the Queen's service!"

Tears actually started from Wyatt's weary eyes and coursed down his weather-darkened cheeks. Well as he knew his commander, the injustice and meanness of Sir Francis' present attitude was something with which he had been utterly unprepared to cope. That his idol should thus, in pure ambitious selfishness, deny the balance of Lord Howard's fleet its share of ammunition was difficult to digest. He returned aboard the *Sea Venture*, pummelled Peter Hopton into consciousness and brokenly described what had happened.

" 'Tis plain our Admiral is overwrought," Hopton explained simply. "Now get ye some rest, Harry, whilst I shape us a course to Bournemouth."

"No, Peter, not Bournemouth," Wyatt objected in the act of collapsing upon a tattered sail; "too many others have started there already. Try rather Gosport or Southampton." He fell asleep long before Peter's footsteps had died away upon the poop companionway.

The wisdom of Henry Wyatt's decision to seek ammunition in ports further ahead of the enemy's position proved sound. Powder-hungry expeditions from other divisions were despoiling, often at the pike's point, all the nearest ports of whatever powder had not already gone to sea aboard local vessels which, crammed with fire-breathing young bloods and old salts, had departed to serve Lord Howard.

In gaining Brighton the *Sea Venture* was forced to sail very close inshore for the floating castles of the Armada lay plainly visible off her starboard bow, so, for the first time, her crew was afforded a leisurely opportunity of viewing the extraordinary assortment of craft composing the Armada's supply division. Yonder sailed such outlandish vessels as Mediterranean zabias, feluccas and dhows, also flutes, pataches, neffs and countless caravels and caunters. They sighted round-bowed Dutch hulks and hoys by the dozen, their red-cross-marked sails filling only fitfully for, still again, the wind was failing.

Fortunately, a land breeze drove the *Sea Venture* along rapidly enough to discourage any attempt at pursuit even by some swift Catalonian galleys acting as a screen for the enemy fleet. Quite clearly the frigate's bone-weary crew could hear the sounds of hammering and saw the enemy busily repairing battle damage. Increasing numbers of horse carcasses came drifting in on flood tide along with the corpses of such wounded as had died during the night. Over these great clouds of grey-and-white gulls screamed, circled, and finally settled to feed upon this grisly manna from Spain.

At Brighton they found the conditions typical of those prevalent along the south coast. Here beacons still smoked on hilltops and columns of cavalry were visible marching parallel to the slow-moving enemy. Behind these, foot levies fresh from field and forge toiled along, pitiably convinced in their simple fashion of their ability to annihilate any and all Spaniards who dared set foot upon English earth.

It was just as well, Henry thought, but did not say, that thus far they had not been called upon to stand against Medina-Sidonia's veterans who certainly would have cut these clumsy masses of militia into cat food.

The greatest of these troop concentrations were sighted near Portsmouth because the Generals ashore felt positive that the Dons would drive in behind Spithead, capture the Isle of Wight and then establish a base there. After all, the Duke then would lie a little less than a hundred miles from London and what could be more reasonable than for the Duke of Parma and his excellent Netherlands-trained regulars to select that moment for crossing over to Dover? To prevent this disaster there now lay in the Narrow Sea only Lord Henry Seymour's weak Thames fleet—eighteen vessels in all. No one seemed to know how much naval strength Parma could muster.

Once the *Sea Venture* had tied up to a dock in Brighton harbour a swarm of volunteers appeared. These were fine, strong countrymen from counties lying inland; many of them were well equipped, even offered bribes to be permitted to fight aboard the frigate.

It was then that Wyatt suffered the surprise of his life for when he mustered his hang-dog crew on deck, told them that they were free to go ashore if they listed, not a man moved towards the gang-plank. Giles Dawson thereupon was promoted to Gunner's Mate, replacing him who had suffered a broken arm during the battle off the Bill of Portland, and George to Boatswain's Mate.

The *Sea Venture's* Captain then concluded his visit by permitting a dozen sturdy farmers and nearly as many eager young gentlemen to enlist in his company. One of these gay young blades went below and innocently stowed his gear in Wyatt's own cabin; presently he returned on deck scarlet-faced and still seeking a place for his possessions. When another dainty fellow emphatically refused to lend a hand at hoisting in some supplies, Wyatt ordered him incontinently ashore and addressed the remaining volunteers.

"Aboard the *Sea Venture*, as on any ship under Sir Francis Drake's command, all gentlemen," he thereupon employed the Golden Admiral's own phraseology, "must hale and draw with the mariners."

For the benefit of well nigh desperate powder hunters the Governor over those crumbling castles defending the port generously halved his own powder supply and thereby alleviated Lord Howard's mordant anxiety.

Already great news of Drake's single-handed capture of the *Greatship Nuestra Señora de la Rosa* had travelled the length of the coast and lost nothing in the telling. Much, too, was made of that terrible hammering the Spaniards had endured on their way towards the Channel. Less comforting rumours circulated that the Spaniards were about to make a landing.

By the night of Wednesday, July the twenty-fourth, the Armada, as vast and ominous appearing as ever, sailed abreast of the Isle of Wight then started shorewards.

On Wednesday night, too, the *Sea Venture's* hold discharged into the *Revenge's* magazines sufficient powder to satisfy even the Golden Admiral's insatiable demands.

CHAPTER XX

TIDINGS FROM THE FLEET

ONE warm July afternoon a dust-stained horseman trotted up to that stately avenue of elms leading to Portledge Manor. From her window Kate Wyatt noticed first that he rode stiffly because he carried one arm in a sling and next that he was peering about like a complete stranger. A messenger! Hastily she finished swaddling little Tony then, speeding downstairs, arrived in time to find a groom helping the stranger to dismount.

"I bear letters for Sir Robert Coffyn and his lady," the man said, wincing as he resettled his injured arm in a leather belt looped over one shoulder. "I served aboard the *Galleon Coffyn* till a cursed splinter broke me arm."

"They are here. Have—have you heard aught of a frigate called the *Sea Venture*?" Kate burst out. "Is she safe?"

"Aye," replied the tall man, wiping dust from a big spade beard. "She took a summat o' a beating off Portland Bill, but I spied her not a week back sailing out of Brighton conveying powder for Drake's ships."

"Come in! Come in!" Kate cried, pointed features shining. "Betty! Fly up to Mistress Coffyn's quarters and tell her this good man has brought letters for her."

Had its tocsin sounded, the old manor could not have stirred to greater excitement. Sir Robert roared for varlets to fetch pillows and his reading-glass while, shaking with joy, Rosemary fled to the privacy of her own chamber, there to peruse the missive she had crushed spasmodically to her breast. This was almost as exciting as having Hubert come home, for always he wrote with clarity and exactitude.

My Heart's delight would that I could encompass myself within these pages. How fare you with our child? Are you much taken ill of ye morning? Pray present my most distinguished compliments to Mistress Wyatt and inform her that our entire squadron rings to ye praises of her husband. Twice has he valiantly assailed ships near thrice his size, but thus far has been unable to seize and hold them.

As for ye *Galleon Coffyn*, we were roundly raked once by ye *San Martin*, ye enemy Admiral's *Capitana* or flagship, and so lost some lusty Devonshire men. You must know that, off ye Isle of Wight, another great battle was fought on Thursday last. Two of ye Spanish King's biggest vessels, one a galleon called ye *Santa Ana* and ye other a Portuguese carrack named ye *San Luis*, became becalmed astern of ye enemy's main force, whereupon Rear-Admiral Hawkins ordered out his pinnaces and small boats and caused them to tow him into range of ye enemy. This he accomplished together with perhaps a dozen of his strongest vessels. Next my Lord Howard entered ye dispute with his own *Ark Royal*, and ye *Golden Lion* belonging to Lord Thomas Howard, his cousin. Ye Don then ordered up those plagued Neapolitan galleasses which, throughout this business, have ever been as thorns in our side.

Rosemary glanced up, overheard Sir Robert cursing in excitement over his own letter. She deliberated calling Kate but heard that young woman eagerly interrogating the *Galleon Coffyn's* former Gunner's Mate.

These delivered some excellent broadsides and so damaged ye *Santa Ana* that she could be used no more in ye fighting and when ye dawn broke she was nowhere to be seen. Ye Spaniards aquitted themselves as ye brave—if mistaken —men that they are. One of ye galleasses lost her prow and another her mainyard. Had not a wind sprung up from ye south and so enabled ye enemy's vanguard to reinforce his rear, nothing could have prevented our destruction of these terrible fighting machines.

To thwart these newcomers honest Martin Frobisher's squadron sailed up and hammered upon ye Spanish line like so many smiths on their anvils. Indeed, my Heart's Comfort, ye Spaniards are becoming crafty fighters for, swiftly, they fell upon ye *Triumph* with their *Gran-Grin* and ye *San Juan de Sicilia.* Together with ye squadron of Hawkins we meanwhile worked around their weather ships and fell in concert upon ye *San Mateo.* A *decisive* victory lay within our grasp when yet again we failed for want of corn powder alone. Dear my sweet, it was dreadful to witness how Sir Francis raged having long pled in vain for greater reserve stores.

After nigh on a week of skirmish and battle we still do not know how this contest will end and we are weary as old soldiers following a long march. To our dismay ye Papist Armada remains, still near as strong as ever, although much punished. Surely their victuals and water must be running short? It now seems certain that ye enemy Admiral will strike at Dover. Ill tidings have just been received that ye Duke of Parma lies ready to join with Medina-Sidonia. Ye Good God alone knows whether we can prevent their juncture.

Beloved Rosemary, I can say only that thus far we in ye *Galleon Coffyn* have borne our part as best we could and lost but four mariners killed. Fourteen have suffered wounds, among them our Assistant Gunner, Edward Sexton, who will hand you this letter together with my undying love and service. Should I not return remember always that you dwell ever first and last in my thoughts. So, my sweet Rosemary, remember me in your prayers and believe me your ever true and devoted husband.

All evening long Edward Sexton regaled those who came pressing into the great hall of Portledge with accounts, highly embellished of course, of the *Galleon Coffyn's* valiant part in the long struggle.

"But she has made no prizes?" Sir Robert demanded querulously, tapping his chair-arms with long pallid fingers. "Not even a hoy? Damn it, but how are we to pay our creditors?"

"Alas, no, Sir Robert," Sexton admitted. "But neither has any other vessel saving only the *Revenge* when their *Rosa* fell to our victorious Admiral." The narrator suddenly grinned. "But be of good cheer, friends, 'tis sure that, with each passing day, our enemy becomes more fatigued and his corn-powder in ever shorter supply. Rest you easy. The day surely will come when we'll be up and over their bulwarks. Then there'll be plenty of treasure and captives to be ransomed."

That night Kate Wyatt lay in her bed sobbing softly, drearily into the dampness of her bolster, weary from prayers she and Rosemary, on their knees for over an hour, had offered in the old manor house's forbidding Norman chapel.

"Protect him," she whispered earnestly. "Protect my husband, O most Merciful God, for without him I have no wish to live."

CHAPTER XXI

GRAVELINES

PAST the bold, grass-crowned headlands of Dungeness and towards Dover the two fleets struggled on. The English, inshore, enjoyed a great advantage. Continually small, hastily armed merchantmen arrived to replace similar strength from the battered and exhausted vessels ready to return to port. Westward, the antagonists skirmished towards the Straits of Dover where, as usual, the alarm beacons and a scattering of trained bands could be seen manœuvring along the famous chalk cliffs.

Although the English could have overtaken King Philip's ships at any time, Lord Howard shortened sail and contented himself by harrying the Armada at her own speed. Jubilation reigned aboard the *Revenge* and the other squadron flagships when it became apparent that the Duke of Medina-Sidonia apparently would not attempt a landing at Hastings—where another invasion had succeeded all too well. Instead, the Spaniard, skilfully keeping his formation and unbroken, made for Calais, a fact which brought a fierce, anticipatory grin to the lips of Sir Francis Drake.

"An the wind but hold as it now blows," he predicted to several of his Captains brought aboard for a conference during this fightless day, "why then we have them surely on the hip."

The others grinned, too, Lancaster, Whidden, Marchant, Adam Seager and the rest. Not a man present but realized that Calais offered no haven worthy of the name. By consequence that vast array which was the Armada would be forced to lie in an open roadstead where the tides ran swiftly, and one over which the prevailing winds came from the west!

Aboard the *Galleon Coffyn* there was no less appreciation of this extraordinary risk assumed by King Philip's General-Admiral, and that red-and-black galleon's grindstone hummed all day long lending keen new edges to pikes, bills and swords.

On gazing forward, Hubert Coffyn found no small satisfaction. True, his men had grown haggard during the long week past, their hair and beards were unkempt and their clothes in ruins, yet they remained alert and eager to reap a golden harvest which at last seemed to be ripe.

Shotholes in the Devon galleon's sails had been neatly patched and two fine new bronze demi-culverins replaced a pair which had seemed about to split—as indeed many had in the English array. All save a few replacements taken aboard at Eastbourne were from home and talked in familiar broad accents while viewing the gradual deployment of the English fleet off Calais.

By nightfall the enemy, with the exception of watchboats, had struck sail and anchored, an example soon followed by Lord Howard's command.

Aboard the *Sea Venture* they watched the arrival of a welcome reinforcement in the guise of Lord Henry Seymour's Channel squadron, fresh from its long tour of guard duty off Dover. These numbered twenty-five in all and belonged to the Queen. They all, with the exceptions of the *Antelope* and the *Achates*, were small. To Wyatt, sunburnt and hollow-cheeked from lack of sleep, the sight was an inspiring one, but he ordered the frigate's anchor let go with a sigh of relief. Thank God, the Armada now lay where even a blind man could have foreseen what was very likely to occur.

A dispatch boat passing from the new arrivals to the *Ark Royal* shouted over that the Spaniards would soon taste a sample of those fires awaiting them in the Next World.

In other words, Sir William Winter had foreseen the fact that once the enemy entered the Channel fireships should prove invaluable in an area where the wind ordinarily blew west to east and had managed to collect some nineteen aged hulks and worn-out hoys in and about Dover. These he had laden to the gunwales with all manner of combustibles. Unfortunately these fireships, at the moment, lay near Dover and not less than twenty-four hours would be required to fetch them over to Calais and launch them on their brief if brilliant adventure.

All day long the English fleet pitched and tossed to their anchors, alert for any possible odd chance that the Spaniards might catch a favouring southward or rare west breeze and so would be able to claw up the Dutch coast, past the perilous sands of Wardelear, Sandettie and the shallow waters off Zeeland.

During the day considerable activity took place among the English. Drake was busier than ever. There would be an attack of fireships launched that very night. For it Sir Francis sacrificed his vessel *Thomas*, a far from inconsiderable ship of two hundred tons. The *Bear Yonge* of one hundred and forty was also doomed. Because the prepared ships would not arrive possibly until too late, eight fireships were selected from the hundred and forty sail now more or less subservient to Lord Howard of Effingham's commands.

From the *Sea Venture* was sent a barrel of tar, from others broken spars or bits and pieces of smashed bulwark or shattered small boats —anything that would burn and burn well. A call for volunteers sent black-bearded Giles Dawson over to help man the *Bear Yonge*. Ever since the death of Herbert, he and George had transferred their hate from Hopton to the enemy, and two more willing and capable hands were not to be found anywhere.

Those of English crews who had not sunk into the sleep of utter exhaustion witnessed the departure, in the dead of night, of the eight fireships, all with loaded guns run out of their ports and towing a longboat behind. By starlight they set sail and like embodied ghosts steered towards that huge, huddled dark mass of shipping anchored off Calais.

The Honourable Charles Coffyn on watch aboard the *Galleon Coffyn* beheld them sail by without a sound beyond the gurgle of the water along their sides. These were not just hulks cast aimlessly adrift and abandoned to the fierce currents prevalent in these waters; although doomed, they were still live ships, guided by human intelligence.

Sir Francis Drake ascended to the *Revenge's* forecastle to watch his own ship *Thomas* sail by, her canvas palely a-glimmer. Soon she would become a complete loss to his personal treasury.

Straight towards the heart of that dark tangle caused by the enemy's vessels cruised the fireships. They were less than a quarter mile distant from the Armada's outer fringe before a watchboat spied them and fired an alarm gun, whereupon cymbals and drums clashed and rattled and dozens of Spanish trumpets brayed. More alarm guns boomed when, aboard the *Thomas*, a flame suddenly sprang into being —the first light to be shown by these shadowy attackers.

Fireships the enemy had seen before, but never ones manned and sailing true on a determined course. Surely *el Draque* must be at his magic mirror again and had summoned up the Seven Devils— Apollyon, Belial, Lucifer, Beelzebub, Asmodius, Mephistopheles and Satan, to captain and steer his hellish squadron.

Weary unto death after five long weeks at sea, tormented by sickness and wounds, the sight of these flame-spouting craft bearing straight down upon them proved too much for Spanish nerves. A wild, ungovernable panic, understandable enough in men in their condition, swept King Philip's fleet. They never even noticed the real crews of the fireships tumbling helter-skelter into their longboats and rowing back towards Lord Howard's jubilant fleet.

Inevitably the sacrificed vessels crashed into the scrambling, cursing and terrified enemy. When their sails and well-tarred rigging took fire the resultant flames soared hundreds of yards into the air and revealed Calais in a throbbing pinkish glare.

When guns left loaded aboard the fireships commenced to be fired by the heat and hurled broadsides at random into the struggling welter of ships, the last bit of self-control deserted King Philip's Captains. Some ordered their anchor lines hacked through and so rendered themselves helpless to anchor again until they visited a dockyard. Others collided and, their rigging becoming hopelessly entangled, lost masts and yards by the dozen as the powerful currents turned and twisted the drifting vessels.

Some Captains, terrified in the belief that these fireships actually were manned by Drake's demonic familiars, ordered broadsides fired and so sank not a few of their own supply ships. Still others drove themselves ashore, stove in their bottoms and drowned helpless soldiers by the hundreds. Many of Medina-Sidonia's best galleons had taken fire and went drifting off on the fierce Channel tide to spread the incendiary contagion to such vessels as were luckless enough to lie in their way.

Awe-stricken, the *Sea Venture's* company, on that memorable Sunday night, watched huge banderoles of orange and scarlet flame ending in shimmering pillars of sparks soar into the heavens. Wyatt kept his men at their stations, yearning, aching for daylight, because now those of the enemy who had been able to disentangle themselves from the holocaust had set rags and patches of canvas and were groping off to the north. Soon occasional English broadsides thundered, smashing at some Portuguese or Spanish vessel that chanced to pass within range.

"Is't not a bonny fire we've kindled to toast Pope Sixtus' toes?" exulted Drake, his pointed yellow beard glowing in the firelight. "God send their bloodthirsty priests sample something of the fiery tortures they have inflicted on so many of our friends."

The dawn of Monday, July the twenty-ninth, disclosed a fearsome vista. The whole east coast of the Narrow Sea below those forts defending Calais was dotted with smouldering, burnt or stranded ships and charred corpses by the hundred bobbed on oily swells rolling in from the distant Atlantic. Here and there the topmasts of a sunken vessel remained above water and supported a few survivors.

Surrendering to personal ambition—much as had Drake in the matter of the *Rosa*—Lord Howard of Effingham abandoned his fleet to lead an inshore sweep with his strongest galleons to make a prize of the huge *San Lorenzo*, flagship of the Neapolitan galleasses. She who accomplished so much in thwarting Lord Howard's tactics had become stranded under the guns of Calais.

After a bitter hand-to-hand fight she was driven so far up on the beach that most of her hull rose clear of the water. Those of her crew able to do so leapt over the side and waded ashore, thus cheating the victors of many a fine ransom for scarcely any family of wealth or renown in Spain or Portugal was unrepresented on the Enterprise of England.

With Howard busy playing truant Drake joyfully headed a pursuit. His vessels and those of Hawkins in the *Victory* found plenty of candidates for captives—fat Flemish merchantmen, rakish Levantine feluccas, Dutch supply ships, caravels and lesser galleons.

Henry Wyatt, cruising in the flagship's wake, called down to gunners mournfully eyeing nearly empty powder chests.

"Now, by the Grace of God we shall take us a fat ship!"

His crew cheered him to the echo when he selected a small galleon gorgeously decorated and painted brilliant blue and red. Smoke curling from her forecastle attested the fact that she must have brushed a fireship during the night. They changed their tune when they noticed a small barque from Lord Henry Seymour's squadron also standing in to attack. The barque, being nearer, fell upon the victim first and ground alongside.

The frigate's company watched their compatriots swarm up and over the galleon's rail. Then on her deck hard-swung blades created windmills of fire under the morning sun, and pike and halberd points dipped and flashed, but the Spaniards were tough and with the coming of daylight restored to sanity. Wyatt was about to shift his course in the pursuit of a galleon which seemed down by the head and sailing sluggishly.

"Hold hard, Harry!" Peter yelled. "Look! Our fellows are being driven off." It was so. The *San Pablo's* soldiers, at last fighting the kind of fight they liked, were beating the English back over the rail and would indeed have followed them aboard that foolhardy little barque had not she cut herself loose barely in time.

Like a hot flood-tide excitement surged into Wyatt's being. Yonder lay *San Pablo*, wallowing in the trough of the sea. She had not been carrying topsails and apparently her mainsheets had been cut during the fight so that that invaluable sail flapped loose as washing on a housewife's line. He himself took the tiller while Hopton leaped down in time to restrain his over-anxious Gun Captains. On this occasion the *Sea Venture's* guns must fire lengths of trace chain—no balls remained aboard.

When the frigate's starboard battery finally did let fly it was with an effectiveness that shook the confidence of Spaniards who had only just rid themselves of one enemy to find another bearing down upon them. The frigate had time to get in another broadside, so adept had Peter Hopton's gunners become, then, with a grinding, resounding crash, the *Sea Venture* drove alongside this galleon called *San Pablo*. The frigate's powder-blackened gunners promptly abandoned rammers and handspikes for axes, pikes and bludgeons.

Screaming "Death to the Papists!", they scrambled up those shot-riddled blue-and-red sides, swayed an instant on the Spaniard's rail, then jumped down upon her deck to enter the fight of their lives.

CHAPTER XXII

THE *SAN PABLO*

ALTHOUGH the *San Pablo* was undoubtedly one of King Philip's lesser galleons there was nothing small about the courage of her defenders. Officers, their armour painted black for the most part, soldiers in morions and breastplates, and hairy, unarmoured mariners alike, rallied on the *San Pablo's* lofty fore- and stern-castles and rained bullets, darts and crossbow quarrels upon the boarders.

That this galleon, which was still afire forward, must have endured a terrific hammering Henry Wyatt perceived the instant his foot landed on her rail, for several of her perriers lay dismounted among the mangled corpses of their crews. Wide streaks of blood turned dark red-brown streaked her decks and had collected in puddles beneath a tangle of fallen spars and tackle to soak such bits of singed canvas as had fallen.

His head whirled amid the uproar of shouts, shots and the ringing clang of steel. Wood and powder smoke eddied about to sting the eyes and rasp at his throat as he stood trying to appraise the situation while clutching the enemy's main shroud. The unlucky attackers from

Seymour's squadron lay dead or were squirming like hurt animals in their efforts to reach some point of comparative safety.

He heard himself yelling—he never afterwards could be quite sure what it was—but very likely it had been something like, "Up for St. George and our Queen! Up, *Sea Venture*!"

And then the *Achates*, Seymour's defeated barque, returned to the attack and ground alongside.

Several brilliantly attired young gentlemen, with a certain Amyas Dexter at their head, dropped onto the blood-spattered deck. A few paused to fire dags and wheel-locks at a mass of the enemy yelling on the forecastle.

"Come on, Harry! We be waiting long enough." Peter Hopton sprang down onto the *San Pablo's* deck; with both hands he gripped his favourite hand-to-hand weapon—a double-bitted axe such as was favoured by woodcutters in the forests around St. Neots. His resonant bellow of, "On them! Slay the accursed Papists!" dominated a sudden braying of trumpets.

The Spaniards, headed by a knot of glittering, armoured officers, came charging down from the poop. Very few shots now rang out—there was no opportunity to reload. Only shouts, curses and the rasping scrape of steel on steel and the thud of hard-struck blows filled the air. Time and again boarders and defenders alike reeled off balance when the *San Pablo* rolled in the oily sea.

"Slay 'e torturers!" Arnold, Brian O'Brian, Giles Dawson and his brother, armed with pikes, led a charge to meet a swarm of Dons from the sterncastle while young Dexter and his fellows held off a similar rush from the forecastle and made their sword-points flicker like summer lightning across an evening sky. "*San Pablo! San Pablo! Viva el Rey!*" howled the defenders.

Wyatt, panting and sweat-bathed, took on a hulking, red-haired officer probably from the north of Spain. The Don aimed a whistling cut which Wyatt barely managed to avoid by ducking low.

Then, putting his shoulder behind the point of a bilbo taken at San Domingo, he aimed it at the reddish tangle of his enemy's spade beard. He saw, rather than heard, the other scream when the point caught him square in the mouth and snapped his head back. The officer's helmet clattered onto the deck as he reeled back, beard and breastplate drenched by a furious scarlet spray. Then an arquebus was fired not two feet from Wyatt's ear and all but deafened him.

A sickening realization struck Wyatt that the Spaniards were relentlessly driving him and his companions back against the bulwarks.

Gasping for breath, he tried to find a target amid this wild *mêlée*, but it seemed that whenever he aimed a blow his enemy had disappeared. His arm ached and his legs wavered, and twice he missed his footing, what with the galleon's rolling and the trickles of gore all about.

"Here's for ye, ye cruel devils!" he heard Peter Hopton scream as, gripping his axe with both hands, the giant charged straight at the Spanish ranks—if indeed that tangled formation of fighting men could be so dignified.

Once again Wyatt found himself facing a black-haired officer whose left arm, shattered by some firelock's ball, swayed uselessly below the elbow. He retained strength enough, however, to deliver a blow that beat down Wyatt's guard, and surely would have split him, crown to chine, but for that same heavy morion he had selected from among the spoils of Cartagena and had chanced to wear ashore on Roanoke Island. As it was, he slipped onto both knees, half recovered and raised his guard but, off balance, he knew the effort to be futile. Helpless, he watched the black-haired officer's sword whirl up.

The appalling certainty that Death at last was upon him did not prevent Wyatt from lurching sidewise. The whole world spun about his head and a sour, acid taste surged into his mouth. What? The black-haired fellow had disappeared. Even as he tried to raise the bilbo, another auburn-haired Spaniard—there were many such as testimony of the Vandals' passage through Hispania nearly a millennium earlier—took his place.

This new enemy swung, but just then the *San Pablo* pitched and his slash missed. He recovered and had whirled up his blade for a *quietus* when his legs appeared to slip from under him. In one of those amazing flashes of clarity which sometimes come in the midst of turmoil, Wyatt realized that an Englishman from the *Achates* who must have fallen during that barque's first unlucky attack had jerked his enemy's ankle. The effort must have required the last of the stranger's strength, for he collapsed again, to lie sprawled in his blood-stained armour worn over a gay red-and-yellow doublet. He was peering helplessly up at the struggle being waged above his inert form.

"*Hola! Para la Virgen y el Rey!*" The Spaniards panted defiance, levelled their pikes and, fighting expertly, would have driven the boarders overboard had not Peter Hopton, bleeding from a terrible wound in his shoulder, first flung his axe into the Spanish array and then, lurching forward, gathered a double armful of spear points. By hugging them to his chest he opened a gap through which his shipmates hurled themselves.

As in a nightmare Wyatt beheld two reddened pike-heads burst through the worn leather jerkin covering his cousin's broad back, then Peter collapsed, breaking the shafts of several pikes as he fell. Pierced by at least ten points, he died, and his spirit departed for that eternal reward which an understanding Father reserves for those who give their lives in the defence of freedom.

Quite suddenly the fight ended. The enemy, their formation riven, flung down their arms and, dropping on their knees, raised supplicating joined hands and pleaded for that mercy which they would never have accorded any captive of theirs.

Here and there some battle-heated Englishmen continued to strike at their enemies because certain officers, disdaining surrender, in full armour leapt over the rail calling upon God and the Virgin to witness that they had perished in defence of their Faith.

Lazily, the *San Pablo's* great red Jerusalem Cross billowed and idle blocks rattled above partially disabled men from the *Sea Venture* who came clambering aboard to help in securing the prize. Their eyes grew round at that scene of carnage and destruction which was the *San Pablo's* deck. Spanish officers came struggling to surrender their arms to Wyatt and his volunteer gentlemen as the only persons fit to accept a capitulation. The red-haired Master of the *Sea Venture* was scarcely aware of accepting the Senior Lieutenant's handsome sword.

"Your name?" he demanded thickly.

"Diego Suárez, Señor Capitano," the other choked while tears of bitter chagrin coursed down his pointed features. "To you, señor, I surrender myself at discretion, and to you my family will pay the ransom."

His head still swimming and with nausea almost upon him, Wyatt then shuffled over to his cousin's body lying half concealed beneath a pile of Spanish pikemen. Peter's dirty yellow hair was stained with the enemy's blood and his bright blue eyes were fixed and glazed, but a satisfied grin curved his lips.

That Peter actually was dead Wyatt could not bring himself to believe. That bloodied corpse could not be that same Peter with whom he had played about St. Neots? He who had helped capture the outlaws and had fought beside him that horrible day in Huntingdon Town? How readily he had tried to share his Monocan maids, Jane and Jill, with him—generous in this as in everything. Yonder lay Peter who always had made so much of little Tony and Henrietta, who forever spoke of marrying and settling down—and who never had.

Jerking a mantle of green velvet from the shoulders of a prisoner, Wyatt, stony-eyed, placed it over his cousin's big, encrimsoned body. By a supreme effort he collected himself. After all, there were other Spanish ships in the vicinity. When his head cleared he realized that, beyond prizes, no enemy vessels lay within a mile of him although in the further distance groups of ships were blazing away at each other or were locked in a death grapple.

Steadying himself against the *San Pablo's* rolling, Wyatt started for the poop deck but, at the foot of its ladder, sight of a yellow-and-red doublet attracted his attention and prodded his memory. He went over to that gentleman from the *Achates* who had undoubtedly saved him from destruction, dropped onto one knee and gazed down into a darkly handsome young face upon which the sweat of death was beginning to collect.

"Good sir," he commenced, "I scarce can thank you for saving——" He broke off as suddenly he seemed to hear Kate's voice saying in forlorn, lifeless tones, "You will recognize Francis Dexter easily because of the small cross-shaped wound he bears on his left cheek, and the fact that his right brow grows near a half-inch higher than its fellow."

His hand closed over the grip of his poignard thus far unused. "You are Francis Dexter."

"Only for a little longer," the crumpled figure wheezed. "Should never have attempted—too few men . . . Water," he choked. "As you hope for Heaven, kind sir, water!"

So this was he who had threatened helpless little Kate and then callously had seduced her. "I'll see you in hell first," he snarled, but beckoned forward the nearest of the *Achates'* men. "This fellow," he almost spat the word, "craves water."

" 'Fore God! 'Tis Francis!"

"You know him?" Wyatt demanded stupidly.

"Aye, I'm Amyas Dexter, his cousin." He pillowed the Honourable Francis' head on his lap. "God above, he's near sped. Is there no water?"

No one paid any attention. They were too busy securing prisoners, heaving the dead overboard and re-rigging essential sheets, halyards and other tackle. The sooner the *San Pablo* could be started on her way back to England, the better.

" 'Tis no matter," gasped the dying man. "Bide with me, Amyas. I—I—not keep you long."

Try as he would, Wyatt could not tear his eyes from those pallid, patrician features. He felt strangely compelled to witness the passing of the man who, blithely, had done him the most grievous of wrongs—and who also had saved his life.

"Ship—safe in English hands?" gasped the heir to Dexter Hall.

"Aye, Francis. We had a pretty bicker, though. This gentleman and his men from the *Sea Venture* saved the day."

"Would I could have borne—better part in it." Young Dexter's eyes rolled up at the faces bending above him. "Amyas, attend—well—I to—tell you. Somewhere—in this fleet—amongst Drake's people—sails, I'm told, a certain Captain—Wyatt."

Amyas's eyes flew wide open and he glanced up at that scowling, red-haired figure standing over the pair of them. Wyatt's head shook slowly as he, too, bent over the figure in red and yellow.

"Find him"—the Honourable Francis' voice was steadily losing strength. "I would—not go to God—bearing so great a sin——"

In perplexity, Amyas' gaze sought Wyatt's grim, powder-streaked features. The dying man's eyelids commenced to quiver, slowly to lower themselves.

"He was away—Drake—his wife—Kate her name, came to—music—I—I forced her—become my leman."

"—Against her will!" Wyatt prompted.

"Aye. Grievously against her will." A trace of scarlet froth appeared at the speaker's mouth-corners, formed a vivid contrast to the pale lavender of his lips. "I rode—to join—Leicester—she was carrying my bastard—sought later—find her—no avail." The stricken gentleman drew a slow, bubbling breath then his dark eyes opened wide once more. "Find him—I charge you, Amyas—upon your—honour—see that Kate Wyatt's child—my child"—several eternal instants dragged by before he continued—"inherits—my estate."

"I will," Amyas promised in bewildered fashion. "You have my sacred word."

"Beg Kate—not to remember—me—too harshly. Tell her—that I—I . . ." he faltered. "If a girl——"

" 'Tis no girl, but a boy," Wyatt was surprised to hear his own voice saying, "and he is named Anthony, after his grandsire."

"Anthony, my son . . ." A quivering smile curved the blood-stained lips of the Honourable Francis Dexter and he died even as the Cross of St. George was broken out from the *San Pablo's* maintop.

CHAPTER XXIII

SHEERNESS

TAKING only time to select a prize crew, under Giles Dawson and Arnold the Boatswain, to sail the *San Pablo*, Captain Henry Wyatt set sail in pursuit of Drake's topsails, now barely visible on the northern horizon. When the *Sea Venture* came up she, and the rest of a steadily diminishing English fleet, continued to harry King Philip's battered ships and to cut off stragglers one at a time.

Meanwhile, to his bitter disappointment, Lord Henry Seymour was ordered back once more to guard Dover and the Channel ports against any *démarche* on the part of Parma. That sagacious soldier, however, disbanded the invasion fleet so painfully collected at Dunkirk and, at the head of his army, retired to Bruges.

On the third of August, off Scarborough, a gale from the west grew so violent that the English were forced to make for harbour wherever possible. With their rigging decayed, sails tattered and spars cracked and fished the Spaniards were lashed out into the cold and choppy wastes of the North Sea.

Now it became quite impossible for Philip's Armada to come about and once more bear down upon the coast of England—especially since prisoners had reported disease to be running riot aboard vessels which had been nearly seven weeks at sea! Many of their strongest carracks and galleons, declared the captives, had been riddled through, time and again, while the loss of human life had been enormous—afterwards the Spaniards admitted losing about five thousand men. Corresponding loss to the English was less than one hundred men killed.

Accordingly, Lord Howard of Effingham and his subordinate admirals, in council assembled, determined to make for the North Foreland, confident that Medina-Sidonia's losses had been so great that he would never find stomach to return. Indeed, the Spaniards themselves admitted the loss of sixty-three ships.

One by one the victorious squadrons sailed into the Thames estuary; some bound for the Pool of London, some for Margate, but the bulk of them were for Sheerness. This particularly delighted Wyatt for it was hither he had directed the *San Pablo* to be taken. Naturally, he was burning with impatience to learn the value of his prize. He recognized her soon enough, red and black in the mid-August sunlight and sharply delineated against the vivid green shore.

In the town, joy bells began clanging when the *Revenge* and the *Ark Royal* dropped their anchors and the last powder remaining to the shore batteries was expended in salutes while all the ships in harbour hoisted gay pennants and banners.

Perhaps two cable-lengths away lay the *Galleon Coffyn* which, during the fight off Gravelines, had evidently suffered serious hurts for her mizzenmast was new and her carpenters still occupied in patching shot-holes in her upper works. On thinking back, Wyatt last recalled Coffyn's galleon standing north, hard on the heels of the Biscayan squadron. Certainly he had never seen her since. Accordingly he ordered his gig and directed her coxswain to make for the Devonshire vessel. Happily, she was anchored very close to the *San Pablo*.

At the sight of his prize, which at this distance appeared sound and undamaged, Wyatt's heart lifted. At last! At last his losses in the *Katerina* and *Hope* should be amply compensated whilst a lifelong security for Kate and their children lay within his grasp.

For many a night while running back down the coast from the North Foreland he had debated within himself the question of claiming little Anthony's inheritance. One fact remained unblinkingly apparent; thus far no one, saving Kate and young Amyas Dexter, was aware that little Anthony was not the child of his loins. To claim the baby's inheritance would undoubtedly render the lad independently wealthy, yet it would also condemn him forever to show a bend sinister across whatever coat of arms he might claim. Of course, bastards on occasion *had* risen high in England's affairs, an example set by William the Conqueror.

The *Galleon Coffyn's* side was looming above Wyatt before he was aware of it, and a few minutes later he was ushered into the Captain's cabin where he found Hubert alone and penning a letter to Portledge Manor. His expression kindled as he jumped up.

"You fought excellently well in the matter of the *San Pablo*," he cried. "I'm so glad for you, Harry. She will make you rich."

Wyatt's coppery features contracted. "As to that, friend Hubert, I have yet to learn."

"Aye. Your prize Captain has reported to the Queen's Treasury officers that her pay chest alone contains 100,000 ducats and her cannon and furnishings should fetch as much again. Lord's mercy, Harry, can't you smile over that?"

Gravely Wyatt then described the manner of Peter Hopton's finish. It was not unexpected that Coffyn's eyes should fill and overflow; sentiments were not so jealously guarded in those days.

"May the Merciful God rest his bones," he mumbled. "There died a true friend and a most valiant servant of our Queen."

Presently Wyatt glanced up and, half hesitantly, inquired: "But you, friend Hubert, did you take no prize? If you've not you'll be well nigh ruined."

Coffyn clapped hands for a steward to fetch a pitcher of Málaga. "Save your pity. Indeed I had thought to be bankrupted for, even on the last day, I could not close with an enemy. But," he tilted back his chair, sent a cloud of tobacco smoke whirling upwards, "just as we started in pursuit, we passed a tangle of wreckage. Lying half-drowned on some broken crosstrees was a fellow who hailed us in English and begged in God's mercy for rescue.

"Although sore tempted to continue after the enemy, I thought this castaway be one of ours, so wasted time enough to bring the fellow aboard. 'Twas well that I exerted the quality of mercy because——"

He commenced to laugh louder and louder until the whole cabin rang to his merriment. "God's Blood, Harry, I'll never forget how sorry he looked when fished up out of the sea. To my amaze he proved a Spaniard, and can you guess his first question when he had puked up enough salt water to talk?"

"Nay, Hubert, let's have it."

" 'Are any among you gentlemen of coat armour?' Charles and I both spoke up, but I chanced to speak first. Our prisoner—he is tall and lean as any hop pole—thereupon bowed low to the deck and addressed himself in my direction. 'Señor, I regret to have lost my sword, so I cannot seemingly surrender my person. I—I am the General Conde Narciso de López y Echegaray.' 'A long name for a long man,' laughed Clough, our Sailing Master, whilst my crew stood about and snickered. 'Silence, you lowborn dog!' roared this Don who could speak the most excellent of English.

"I learned afterwards," Hubert continued, "that my prisoner has served as aide to Bernardino de Mendoza, once the Spanish King's Ambassador to Whitehall. Echegaray turned to me once more, eyes flashing and head thrust back. 'And what ransom do you require of me, Señor Coffyn? Be pleased to remember that I am a grandee of Spain.' "

Hubert chuckled. "I talked a bit with my cousin Charles and so we decided to hold him in the amount of 50,000 ducats." Hubert commenced to laugh again. "Harry, had I named his mother a whore he could not have acted more insulted. The General folded his arms and glared down his long brown nose at us. 'How unkind thus to insult an unhappy prisoner'."

" 'Insult?' I cried. 'Now how is that?'

" 'Do you deem a grandee of Spain worth so niggardly a sum? Nay, señor, I will remain in England forever an you do not demand a ransom of 100,000 Portuguese escudos! Otherwise, I can never hold up my head in the Escorial.'

"Well, Harry, I told the Don that were his pride truly at hazard, then Charles and I would not really be satisfied with anything less than 150,000 escudos. And for this he thanked us, Icod, better than he had for fishing him out of the sea! So you see we are not so badly off aboard the *Galleon Coffyn* after all. Believe me or no, the very day we made port, Don Narciso went ashore on parole and dispatched a pinnace to Portugal bearing orders for his ransom money to be raised with all speed." Hubert wiped tears from his eyes. "And so you see, my friend, the age of miracles is not passed, and we shall return to Portledge and Bideford with full coffers after all."

All those good things Hubert Coffyn had predicted indeed came true for, apart from not inconsiderable ransoms offered by certain gentlemen taken aboard the *San Pablo*, her cargo turned out to consist mostly of very valuable brass fieldpieces and a whole magazine full of splendid small arms. All this was in addition to the 100,000 ducats contained in the galleon's pay chest. The mass of golden specie it disgorged was enough to brighten even the most avaricious of eyes.

Also found aboard the prize were certain less pleasing items which, when displayed on the quayside, drew frowns and curses from crowds collected to view those ships which had spared them from these very shackles, gyves, chains, branding-irons and even a portable rack.

"Aye, Bert," chortled a gap-toothed bumpkin, "I warrant ye're sore grieved the Dons didn't come. They'd uv straightened yer back for ye." When he patted a hunchbacked companion the crowd shouted with laughter.

All in all, Wyatt calculated the *Sea Venture's* crew stood to divide nearly 130,000 ducats, a sum which drew broad grins even to the dour faces of Black Giles Dawson and his surviving brother.

Judging by the sound of music and a display of knightly banners, the Queen's flag and Drake's ensign, a ceremony of some sort would soon be taking place aboard the *Revenge*. Wyatt dismissed the matter with the conjecture that Sir Francis Drake was about to return the Lord High Admiral's hospitality of the day before.

Soon small boats began putting out from the principal men-of-war and making for the flagship. The *Sea Venture's* Captain had composed himself to the enjoyment of a well-earned cat-nap when he was roused by a brisk pounding on his cabin door. Brian O'Brian, as Officer of the Deck, reported that Sir Francis Drake required his immediate attendance aboard the *Revenge* and would he please to dress as elegantly as possible?

Filled with wonderment that the Golden Admiral should condescend to summon aboard the Captain of so unimportant a vessel as the *Sea Venture*, Wyatt pulled on hose of heavy blue-and-red-striped silk, then buttoned on his doublet—a gorgeous affair of grey and vermilion velvet found aboard the prize—which fitted him passably well.

In the shade of an awning rigged over the flagship's poop deck was gathered as brilliant a group of famous figures as one could imagine. Among them Wyatt recognized Lord Henry Seymour, Sir William Winter, Sir John Hawkins and nearly all the leaders of the various victorious squadrons saving only Martin Frobisher who, in his curmudgeon's wrath, had sworn never to shake hands with Francis Drake nor to board his ship, saving in line of duty.

For the first time Henry Wyatt met Lord Howard of Effingham face to face and was struck with the innate digity of that great nobleman's weather-beaten countenance. At his right hand stood Sir Francis wearing an enormous cartwheel ruff and a doublet of his favourite blue and silver. About his neck, from his ears and on every finger flashed great jewels.

"This is the man, Your Lordship," Drake announced. "Captain Henry Wyatt, of the *Frigate Sea Venture*."

"At your service, my lord." Wyatt managed a bow which was not overly successful from the point of view of elegance. When he straightened he became aghast at the severity of Lord Howard's expression.

"So you, then, are the rogue, the felon who has dared to intrude himself upon the company of honourable gentlemen?"

Wyatt's throat closed spasmodically once the breath had rushed from his lungs. Scarlet of face, he turned beseechingly to Drake. Surely he must have learned the truth about the tragedy at St. Neots? But Sir Francis remained for once expressionless, and in the background Hubert Coffyn gnawed his lip.

"Do you deny, sirrah, that you are indeed a fugitive from justice and a convicted felon?" Howard's voice was harsh as the cry of a peacock.

Still deprived of breath by shock, the red-haired figure in vermilion and grey could only nod in speechless misery.

"Shall I tell you what else you are?" Lord Howard's voice rang out so that even the mariners working in the waist could hear. "You are as true, as capable and as valiant a man as has served in this my fleet. Sir Francis here has oft related of your constancy in adversity, of your uncomplaining obedience and of your rare ability as a navigator.

"Therefore, by virtue of the authority vested in me by Her Most Gracious Majesty the Queen, I do now pronounce you, Henry Wyatt, pardoned now and for evermore of any and all crimes of which you may stand accused."

The deck seemed to sway under Wyatt's feet as if the *Revenge* were struggling in a tempest, but he managed a deep breath and recovered his voice.

"Her Majesty and Your Lordship have made me the—the happiest man in all England."

He had turned to go when Drake stepped forward and flung an arm about his red-haired Captain's shoulder. He had to reach up to do so, so great was the difference in their heights.

"Before you depart there is one more matter to be attended to, Captain Wyatt."

Drake unsheathed a jewel-encrusted rapier, then offered it, hilt foremost, to the Lord High Admiral.

"Kneel," Drake directed and almost pushed his subordinate into the required position.

Profoundly confused, Wyatt heard Lord Howard's rich voice saying: "Know you all that the Queen's Majesty has accorded me the high honour of bestowing the order of knighthood upon such gentlemen as I find deserving. While such a knighthood is not hereditary it yet bespeaks Her Majesty's appreciation of services rendered."

Lightly the rapier's blade tapped Wyatt's shoulders, then, as from an immense distance, he heard Lord Howard's kindly accents direct: "Arise, Sir Henry Wyatt. May you ever serve our Queen in the future as you have in the past."

The first to grip the new knight's hand was that of Vice-Admiral Sir Francis Drake.

L'ENVOI

No one living in Bideford ever forgot that glorious October day upon which the *Galleon Coffyn* came bowling into port before a stiff southwest breeze. She was their ship—Bideford's specific contribution towards that victory which forever had banished the sombre threat of slavery.

A fishing smack, homeward bound, had sighted the beloved galleon cruising grandly up the coast with all her flags flung to the breeze and a red Latin Cross ablaze on her mainsail. Her sides, however, displayed many new planks nailed over holes caused by Spanish cannon balls.

As they had not since Sir Francis Drake's memorable visit, Bideford's citizens and people from round about flocked to the waterside to view the victorious galleon.

Wives, sisters and sweethearts and even younger brothers hugged and kissed those broad-faced fellows who came tumbling over the galleon's rail. There were those, too, who turned aside and wept—those who had seen their men depart but not return. There were those, too, who sobbed while watching the pallid sick and wounded being helped ashore.

The Honourable Charles' entire family came riding down from Ilfracombe to greet him, even an ancient great-grandfather who in his youth had served as the King's Marshal, and had attended Henry VIII upon the Field of the Cloth of Gold. They clustered about Hubert's cousin, the men clapping him on the shoulder and the ladies pressing warm kisses upon him.

The first passenger to disembark from the *Galleon Coffyn* was an elderly, straight-backed gentleman wearing a flat cap and rich garments of severe black. His only adornment, the crowd noted, was a splendid collar of gold filigree set with quite the largest emeralds and diamonds anyone had ever beheld. He gazed curiously about at the homely roofs and chimneys of Bideford and at the busy warehouses lining its harbour. Under his breath he muttered, "Here, after all, is where the heart lies."

Again Portledge Manor bestirred itself, and loud sounded the wails of Rosemary Coffyn and Kate Wyatt that their pregnancies were much too advanced to admit of their riding into town. So they had wiped their eyes and joined in a quiet celebration with Sir Robert, long since apprised by courier concerning the great fortune won to his son and heir.

Hardly less had the veteran rejoiced over the extraordinary honour bestowed upon red-haired Henry Wyatt. He had even teased Kate, offered to teach her how the wife of a nobleman should conduct herself, and had catechized her on various forms of courtly address. She had endured his gentle rallying with delight—that Henry was but a simple knight whose son would not inherit the title troubled her not at all.

" 'Tis ill," she had smiled, "for a lad to loll in the shadow of his family tree."

A cloud of dust, climbing into a bright azure sky, warned those waiting in Portledge Manor that a considerable party must be drawing near. So once more the drive of Portledge again became lined by neighbours and tenants come to cheer a young lord of the manor come home in victory.

As befitted their condition, the ladies of Portledge awaited their husbands in their particular chambers. Hubert raced upstairs, gathered Rosemary in his arms, showered her with caresses which lovingly, eagerly, she returned.

Suddenly he broke away. "A pox upon me!" he laughed. "I've forgotten that you have a visitor!"

"A visitor? I'll see him later, dear my heart. This moment is for us alone."

"Nay, I think you had best not keep the gentleman waiting. You see, he also claims some demand upon your affections."

He stepped back and threw open the door. Rosemary uttered a joyous little gasp when her father strode in, black cloak flying to his stride.

"*Caríssima niña!*" Involuntarily, Richard Cathcart employed the language of Rosemary's childhood.

"*Mi padre!*"

They were still clinging to each other when Hubert reclosed the door and sought his own sire.

In another apartment Kate finally escaped her husband's embrace and attempted a curtsey rendered awkward by her misshapen figure. "I, myself, must salute the noble knight," she laughed. "Oh, Harry, Harry! Hear 'tis a great and precious treasure you've brought back."

"Nay, my sweet Kate," he corrected gently, "the greatest treasure has been here all the time."